SHADOWS OF THE EMPRESS

SHADOWS OF THE EMPRESS

Tales from M'Diro

R. F. DEANGELIS

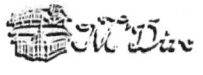

R. F. DeAngelis

Copyright © 2022 by R. F. DeAngelis

All rights reserved. No part of this book may be reproduced in any manner whatsoever without written permission except in the case of brief quotations embodied in critical articles and reviews.

First Printing, 2022

This book is dedicated to my daughter Raven.

In 2013 I was challenged to write some of the stories I told around the table. I had been DMing since I was 16 and had ran for my groups pretty much every since. I dedicate this book to them, my players. I also dedicate this specifically to my Husband, and my two subs. You guys put up with a lot to help me make this a reality. Also to Jasen Jacobs who was the first ever Holy Champion of Ca'talls hailing from the township of Bax'el, I still think you should have gone Blackgaurd on them.

CONTENTS

Dedication	v
M'Diro's Calendar	xi
Author's Notes 1	1
The Mouse who Roared	8
Author's Note 2	11
Awakenings	13
Author's Notes 3	24
The Final Day	25
Author's Note 4	32
Mouse	33
Author's Notes 5	39
Tulock	40
The Gates at Dawn	46
Author's Note 6	52
Throne of Bone	53

VIII - CONTENTS

Author's Note 7	70
1 Early Days & Life's Lessons	71
2 Hanna	81
3 Of Dwarves and Metal	86
4 Men and Magic	96
5 Missing	100
6 Sister of the Night	107
7 Hopscotch	116
8 Raided	130
9 Dreams	135
10 The Day After	148
11 To Trip a Trick	153
12 Jax	161
13 The Death of Reason	167
Author's Note 8	172
Piper 1	173
Author's notes 9	223
00 The Fool 1	225
01 The Magician	233
02 The High Priestess	239
03 The Empress	244

04 The Emperor	263
05 The Hierophant	272
06 Lovers	279
07 The Chariot	285
08 Strength	296
09 The Hermit	304
10 Wheel of Fortune	311
11 Justice	317
12 The Hanged Man	323
Author's Notes 10	333
Bitter Sweet	334
Author's Notes 11	344
The Eve of War	345
Peoples of M'Diro	363
About The Author	367

M'DIRO'S CALENDAR

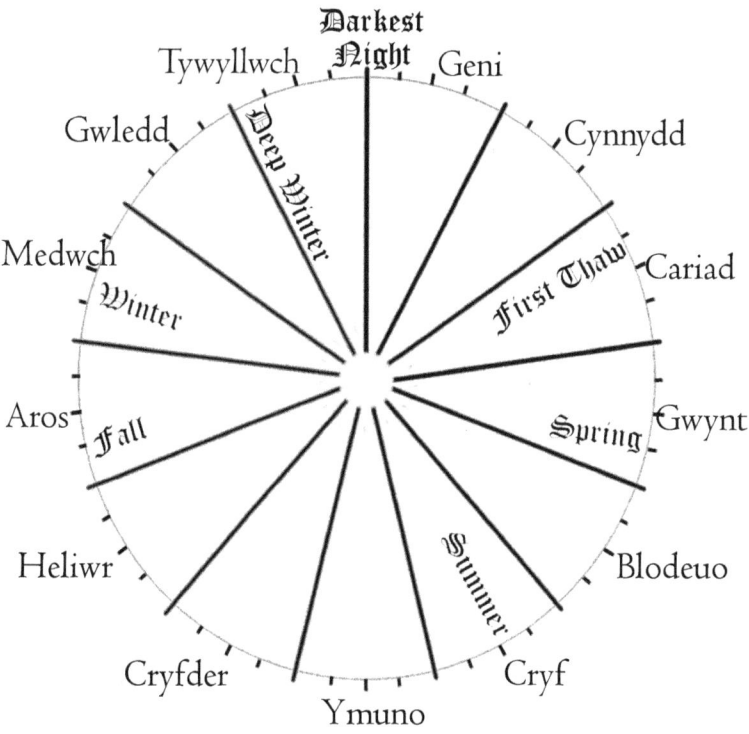

Author's Notes 1

Welcome, to M'Diro, those three words launched this mad scheme back in 2013. M'Diro the world is much older, first glimpsed by my players way back in 2001 as a home brewed world for D&D's shiny new third edition. The Children of Am'met, the cult of Nuktela, and the weird world that included places like Bax'el and Hurst, along with the gods Ca'talls and Ba'teece, first made their appearance around a table with a bunch of friends, too much pizza, and lots of Mountain Dew. Ok, so there is no such thing as too much pizza.

Fast forward a few years and thanks to a bit of disappointment with 4th ed, I and a few people decided to write our own version of an RPG. One that ultimately fell through due to problems with permissions. The less said the better.

So, there I was, sitting with a ton of written rules, none of which made the cut by the way, and nothing to do with them. Then I got an idea. I started compiling my own game with no outside help. It was just going to be an add on to 3rd ed, a 3.75 if you will. Pathfinder of course debuted a few weeks after I got started.

Now something you must understand about me, I love the story, and I think differently. I'm Dyslexic and probably Autistic, so with 75 pages of rules I could no longer use, I just started writing my own rule set.

Now, there is something I must tell you about myself, I do tend to think and do things differently than most people, see problems differently and so on. I tell this story often to illustrate it, the story of the time I faced a six-foot wide tarantula.

Many years ago, I was lying in bed with my husband. Things were tight then and we slept on a mattress on the floor. We loved each other and we loved our orange cat Gabriel.

So, anyway. I sleep nude and usually out from under the covers, we have a fan going and the sliding glass door open, so anything can get in.

So, in my sleep, I feel something fuzzy on my back. Then touching my ankle. Finally, something fuzzy and sharp rubs across my ass.

Now mind you, I am sound asleep. My brain has calmly relayed these three facts to me. I queue for more information, specifically about the 'sharp' part of the equation. What I get is this. Soft, but firm, round, fuzzy, sharp point.

My mind then at astonishing speeds spits out two options and ask me what to do...

1. the cat, for whatever reason has decided to actively pet my ass in the middle of the night.
2. a six-foot tarantula is in the bed with me, its pedipalps are by my ass and its fangs are close enough for me to feel.

Ok... one, I live in GA. The biggest hairy spider I have to deal with is a wolf spider. They are not 6 feet. Now I can hear you say, tarantulas are not 6 foot either, and while that is a fair point, and one I made to myself at that time, still asleep mind you, I felt hairs on my ankle and some on my back. If one foot was by my ankle and its mouth was by my ass, true six foot may be a little big, more like 5 foot 6 inches... but sure let's get hung up on half a foot.

In all fairness, you may be thinking, those are all... well kind of fucked up points if I am honest.

The alternative is, a cat, was petting me. On the ass. In my sleep.

Let me stress this again, a cat was petting me in my sleep.

Ok you may say to yourself, no brainer, strange as it is, a cat petting a human is far more believable than a six-foot spider.

You good sir, madam, or other, would of course be correct.

You would also not be me.

See if the cat was petting me, and I did nothing I would be fine.

If the cat was petting me and I freaked, I would be fine.

If the spider's mouth was that close to my ass and I did nothing, it could decide since it was larger than I was, that I would make good food. Seeing as I don't see myself as sacred, I am well aware I am on the menu and bear no ill will to whatever winds up eating me.

If it was the spider and I reacted and got out of its way, I maybe could scare it off.

Also note, that given how I was laying, it was standing over my husband.

I needed to act fast.

So, with a blood curdling yell, that is nothing like a battle cry and more along the cry of a Krayt dragon slowly being strangled by a Sarlacc I go from dead asleep to standing, flailing and screaming.

"Turn on the light, there is a six-foot tarantula in the bed, there is a six-foot tarantula in the bed, there is a six-foot tarantula in the bed."

My husband gets the bed side light on and looks at me, rightfully I may add, as if I had lost my mind. Still mostly asleep he asks me "Wuht?"

The cat of course was now hiding under some boxes in the corner vowing to never again pet a sleeping human.

So, here's the thing. 1) I will never come to a snap decision, it's not how my mind works. 2) That doesn't always mean I come up with the correct or even sane decision. 3) I don't care how silly I look, how wrong I am, if I think I am protecting people I will act. 4) I have zero problems admitting when I was wrong.

So here I am hacking away at a new system, ground up, taking apart the mechanics of it, the maths involved, doing research on everything I can get my hands on and taking my time. I had decided on my homebrewed world for the setting, and I was in full creative mode. Maps, coins and currency, political intrigue, blood lines, cultures and more. Cultures were one thing I was huge on, I didn't want seven different elf stats, I wanted one set of elf stats and seven or more different cultures.

During this time, I was helping to run a salon LARP. One of the things as a ST for this game I needed to do was write what were called meanwhiles. Meanwhiles were basically short stories meant to flesh out the world and make it feel more real for the players. Since they were things that the players would have no way of knowing in game, I thought of them just as ways for the other ST's to flex their writing chops, writing chops I didn't have as I was dyslexic. I had in all honesty tried writing novels in high school and well into my 20s to be honest.

When you're five pages in and you can't read page one due to it 'cooling', and you're not remembering what you had written due to what some would call bad spelling, but what I called crimes against written English, it puts a dampener on you being able to do what you have wanted since Arthur C. Clark helped you learn to read with Cradle.

So, I avoided meanwhiles until the head ST told me to do one.

I wrote a short story from the point of view of a fetch off to cheer practice, and the poor things life being tragically cut short. The story was the tragic ending of a 10-year-old's life by professional hit, where she passes away in the ambulance on her way to the hospital, dissolving into a collection of old broken vinyl's, hand me down clothing, and other things found in attics. Such is the life of a fetch.

Need to see if I still have a copy of that one.

I turned it in and frankly didn't think much of it. It was a first draft, what to me was a, more or less, half-ass attempt, and 'phoned in' kind of thing. I was playing in someone else's world, playing by their rules. I thought if someone was able to read it, they might enjoy the dark tone, but not much else.

I was wrong.

One of my players, a woman I had a lot of respect for, cornered me and asked me why I wasn't a writer. I patiently explained the problem, thanked her for her compliments (she thought the story was amazing and chilling) and that I had tried to be one, but it never worked out. I even had a few blurbs I had made for my world, but they weren't much. They were meant to be things like flavor text. I knew I was good at starting a story, but never seemed to get it done, what's more is reading it afterwards was useless.

"You know spell check has gotten a lot better since 2005, right?"

Needless to say, I lost the argument. I agreed to try just a short story, see if I could make one full short. It took a couple of weeks, but I eventually hit upon something rather simple. The problem I was having, outside of being terrible at spelling, is nothing I wrote held up. I invented a character whose sole purpose was to start out normal and be introduced to the strange.

I named her Chloe.

35,000 words in I knew I had a problem; this wasn't a short story anymore.

Originally thanks to a popular tv show of the time, I had the story happen and flash backs come up when relevant. It didn't take me long before I had a complete novel, Chloe's Collar. Sadly, the back and forth didn't work like I wanted them too, so I untangled the work and put everything back in order. When I was done, I was left with 12 of the flash backs that just didn't fit in the novel. So, I cleaned them up, and added one, and they became the 13 short stories known as Blackthorn: Once a Thief.

Now that the novel is out in paperback, henceforth referred to as dead tree format, I wanted to collect those stories and have them printed too. Sadly, at only 36k words it really wasn't worth it. So? What was I to do?

Simple, I gathered up everything I had written that happens before the end of the first novel and have compiled them into this one collection. I hope you enjoy.

The format from here on out will be simple. An Authors note, then a story or group of stories in chronological order, not of writing, but of when in the timeline they happen. I will clean up the older stuff as best I can, Tulock as an example needs serious help, but other than fixing lore changes they will be presented as close to the original as possible.

Welcome To M'Diro.

But first, I give you a tale, the tale told to young children throughout the Empire of the Five. A simple morality tale. Trust me, it matters.

The Mouse who Roared

Once, there lived a Mouse.

She was small, and very poor.

Stronger animals like cats and dogs often used her as they saw fit, hurting her in the process.

But the mouse endured, what else could she do?

Soon Mouse didn't think much of herself at all.

One day she noticed, the ruler was hiring new servants.

Her life was suffering and survival, one day to the next.

Perhaps, there at least there would be so many that no one would notice something as small as a mouse.

She snuck in with the other hopefuls, all with clothing that had no holes even if they were poor.

With hers more rag than cloth she again hopped that no one would notice her.

Perhaps the kitchens need a scullery maid?

Soon she and the others were led into the ruler's hall.

There, pacing and waiting, was the little mouse's doom, a Hawk!

The Ruler of this land was a hawk and there was no way a hawk would not see a mouse, no matter how small or how still.

She trembled as the Hawk paces, speaking to everyone at the same time. Back and forth the Hawk walked.

Mouse's heart speed up. Cats would bat her around for fun, dogs would step on her, but a hawk would eat her in one gulp.

Then, the most remarkable thing happened.

With nothing left to lose, fear slipped away from her.

She spoke up.

"If you're going to eat me, go ahead. I am not scared of you."

The hawk turned and looked at this little mouse and watches as its whiskers quivered.

"Oh, really now?" Said the Hawk. "And why not?"

"I am a little mouse; I have lived, and I have lived hard. I am not strong, but I am not a bully. My whole life I have been afraid of you, of cats, of dogs, and anything better than me. But I realized standing here. None of you are better, just bigger."

The hawk walked over to the little mouse and looked her in the eyes. "Go on little mouse, you think you dig your grave. Do you yet find it deep enough?"

The mouse swallowed. Then yelled! "We are not beneath you. We are equals, not in rank but in life. Just as I am hawk food, you are eagle food. Each of us are our own. What matters is not who eats who, but how you treat the ones smaller than you."

The Hawk nodded. "You have said your peace, now reserve your reward for such words." The Hawk drew forth a mighty sword and, looking at the mouse said, "Kneel."

The Mouse did. What else could it do? In front of her betters, no not betters biggers, she had done the unthinkable. She questioned how things were.

So, she knelt.

As the sword fell, the hawk spoke. "I dub you The Mouse Who Roars. I task you to sit at my right hand and always tell me when I am being unjust. To remind me of those of whom I will forget, and to speak for those that have had terror steal their voice. Rise, Mouse Who Roars. You were the only one brave enough to stand up to me, brave enough to stand up for yourself, and brave enough to point out others who are not here need protecting too. Today you have become strong, and today you have protected the weak. Now your job is to do so again and help others who are weak become strong. Rise, my Mouse, we have much work to do."

And so, the Mouse and the Hawk became friends. And the Mouse reminded the Hawk daily that it is always important to look after everyone, not just those you think have worth, for worth comes in the most surprising of packaging.

Author's Note 2

The world of M'Diro has a few key events that play a part in the novels that happened a long time before the events of Chloe's Collar, one of them is the Awakening of the LeatherWing Empress. The Empress is one of their gods and is responsible for their way of life. Gods to LeatherWing aren't a nebulous 'other' that floats on a cloud playing a lyre but were at one point living breathing people who did great things. Each god's essence still exists and can be inhabited by a modern person, this is called "Taking the Mantel" and is considered a great honor. The Empress is slightly different, not that she doesn't have a mantle a mortal can take, she does, but the fact is, she seems to be immortal herself. In order to give her people the freedom to make mistakes and grow, she 'goes to sleep' and has to be awoken by a special ritual.

LeatherWing do not do this ritual lightly. The Empress is not a warm and cuddly kind of person. She is deadly, bloody, and bloody minded. In any other story she would make a perfect villain. According to their own lore at one point she was indeed just such a monster.

We open with the current priestess who is responsible for the Empress' care, on the day they are deciding to break glass in case of emergency.

Awakenings

Four years before the fall of Unstoma, BFU 4

The sound of my split heels was a cold comfort as I moved down the hall to the balcony that I knew 'she' was at. Cold dread filled my mind with each step. The ritual had awakened her just as it was supposed to, but it did not make me feel any better. For the last eight hundred years despite ups, downs, and even horrors happening within our own empire, no one had dared to do such a black deed.

The Empress was once again among the living, may the god of all have mercy upon the world.

My mind turned to the shoes I wore as I walked. The shoes I had worn since I was eight, or at least the same style shoes. I had worn shoes like this for over thirty years. It's funny how things like this play out in your mind. When I first received them, I was told to meditate upon them and their meaning. Black leather to go against my white skin. Twin spikes of polished wood sprouted from either side of my heel, they curled like the horns of a dragon, only to come down into dagger points where they met the ground. To be fair there was a support that ran under my foot that placed the load of my weight on those two spurs. They hugged my feet and calves in a vise of highly polished leather. My dew claw hung out the back of them, the twin heels were almost seven inches high now. This new height forced me up and onto the balls of my clawed feet. Their black leather laces and straps held them securely, if not comfortably to my feet.

I had always assumed they were meant to hobble us, to prevent us from running on all fours comfortably. A way of making us stand tall, to show we had no need to run. We were after all in service to the Empress herself. I received my first pair at the temple when I was accepted, they had started out a much more modest two inches so that I could learn to move and fight in them. They grew longer as we aged, longer spikes that I, and others, were expected to walk on at all times when we took our place at the Citadel.

That fantasy of mine about standing tall because we were 'hers' was shattered when the high slaves, the ones meant to look after her personal affects during her sleep, got out her clothing.

I should introduce myself, as well as my position. I am Salien, a LeatherWing priestess. I am a born white, and I have the task of seeing to and looking after the needs of the Empress in all things. It is one of the highest ranks I, or anyone, can hold. It's a position I wanted and earned, only her personal Slave outranks me. Until last month both the Slave positions and that of Handmaiden, my position, were seen as important, but largely ceremonial.

Veka, leader of the Slaves and a human, would do the tasks seeing to the needs of a woman we knew would never wake. She and I have become great friends over the years. She earned the title of Mouse that Roars just last year. The duties even when she is 'asleep' may be strict but are open for a lot of interpretation. When your champion and master is 'dead' and in her tomb you don't really have to do the day-to-day stuff. Mostly we cleaned, took care of things, and advised. We had access to the library and both of us were well versed in history, laws, and the like. Mostly we listened at conical meeting, me being the voice of reason, Veka kicking doors in and demanding the 'least' always be remembered and treated, not just well, but as the revered people they should be.

For our society, how we treat those at the very bottom of the pile, the worker, the slave, the poor, says far more about a civilization than the lavishness of the rich. When even the poorest had money, food, and comfort, a kingdom runs well.

My partner made one hell of a Mouse who Roared.

Normally I would also help the Great Mother; the highest-ranking priestess for the Imperial LeatherWing, make her day-to-day judgments. Now I would have to see to The Empress's bath, her food, make sure she ate. If stories were to be believed that last one would be important as she was supposedly notorious for not eating unless made to. My first duty was helping her acclimate after her long slumber.

As to why I now found myself at the beck and call of this woman? I think I should explain further. This woman was the Empress, I had watched the flesh grow back over her bones, but in the end, she was just a woman. We revere hero gods, people, who despite the flaws we all have, lived lives dedicated to causes. We don't worship them, but their ideals, their philosophies of life. The worship of them is to live up to those ideals, not them as a person. The Empress was as much a flawed flesh and blood creature as the rest of us.

As to her being alive? A trick of the gifts her God gave her made her virtually immortal. She uses this to usher us through dark times. Only when needed, otherwise wisely she leaves us and the world alone. Hard to learn and grow if you don't risk failure, and who wants to risk pissing off a god who is standing right there?

What ideals do you practice if you follow her? Freedom, accountability, helping everyone who is in need, and killing those who threaten the freedom of others. She was born in the age of entitlement, or what she calls the "me" generation. She tried to help, well, she did after she broke herself of being one of the evilest most vile of the humans at the time. The dark one showed her a better way; the way of helping people and boy did she run with it. She added on to his ideas and tried teaching others. Then as she fought under his banner, she fell. Killed by the corrupt.

However, for her dark deeds, the true gods sent her back to this plane as the first of us, the first LeatherWing. The fall finally happened, as it was meant to, the cycle must continue after all. Out of the ashes of that fallen world she carved a bloody domain, our domain. The start of the Empire. When it was built, she gave it to us.

Well, us and the others. Together we are known as The Five Races: Humans and all their kin, LeatherWing, GrassLord, SkyLord, and the Heard.

Once things were stable, she went to her tomb, laid down, and went to sleep. She promised us she wasn't dead and left us the ritual needed to awaken her. In all of our history it is used only in the most trying of times. For if she wakes, the world bleeds.

Now she walks the world once more. Gods pity the world, and god forgive us.

The primary thing I had to bring her at the moment was the elixir we all need first thing in the morn. Its blackness cut by cream and its bitter taste soothed with fire powder. Coffee, I drank it every dawn myself.

See? A perfectly normal, mortal woman.

Now if I can just get myself to believe that.

The deck of the balcony was much brighter than the hallway; it took me a moment to adjust my eyes. The white marble of the floor polished to a shine from centuries of care and use didn't help. This balcony overlooked the city itself. Our city, the capital of our lands, is often just called The Citadel after the building where all of our governance took place, but it was so much more than that. Rings of walls blossomed beyond, each larger and in a different style as the city outgrew each set in turn.

All of the five races complete with the full rainbow of humanity lived sheltered in the wings of the Citadel. The Elven district is beautiful, but I have to say it's the Dwarven district that I enjoy the most. Trade town with its gnomes always has the best stuff; exotic goods from the tropics like coffee and fire powder, neither of which would grow in our frozen land, as well as spices and peppers. They were the beating heart of trade for the city.

The temple that was the Citadel proper was cut into a mountain, the building was the product of the Architect. A mad man whose gifts with stone, design, music, and all things mathematical drove him to obsession. The Temple proper was a hollow statue of a LeatherWing from the waist up. Her outstretched arms gave bounds to the courtyard and the outstretched wings the bounds of old town. The city had grown quite a bit since it's temples construction.

I had always thought that the face of the woman was that of the Empress herself. Now, looking at her I knew that wasn't the case. I wonder who was immortalized in that white stone, an old lover of hers perhaps?

I found her leaning on the railing overlooking the city, her city. What must it have been like then, in those first days, or even the last time she was awake? Her thoughts seemed to be far and away from here. The look on her face was serene with a dreamy quality to it. Her nine horns had almost no wrinkles around them, her skin was the color of soft lavender, it too was without trace of time. Her violet hair had not yet been cut; as such it hung down to the floor and snaked out a few feet behind her.

Her clothing, fittingly I suppose, was from another time. The top was an odd thing, very out of style; the leather of it only covered to her ribs but stretched all the way up her throat and down to her hands to form fingerless gloves, her claws could be used at a moment's notice. The back piece went down between her wings, and I could only guess how it was tied, her hair was in the way. With her stomach bare the rings of steel that sat at the hip to hold her flowing loin cloth were a stark black on her skin.

It was her boots that let me know that my thoughts on why we wear split heels were wrong. These black leather boots went up well past her knees, almost to mid hip. They encased her legs like armor, they too had the same split heels I wore. I was in a pale imitation of her own foot ware.

It hit me then, I was imperial!

Why run when it was your duty to lay your enemies still bleeding hearts at their own feet.

Her magic belt was the only thing she was not wearing. It was a belt with three silver life-sized half skulls, top teeth to crown of head. They would lay flush against her bare skin, one for each hip, and one over her mons, The Belt of Lightning. It was her weapon of war. While she wore it, all injury, even death itself would not touch her. She would heal any wound. What's more her hands could become lightning. It is said that with her belt she could flow like water, moving from one place to the next in a flash of light and heat. I looked into the eyes of a woman I knew to be a cold-blooded killer, and she smiled at me.

"Hello, I'm sorry, your name I don't know yet." Her voice was the sweet voice of a young adult, not yet into their second decade. That voice, like her skin, was ageless.

With both hands, head slightly bowed, I held up to her the clay mug, hot from its aromatic contents.

"Salien, ma'am, I am your Handmaiden."

She took the cup lightly from my fingers, and slowly brought it up to her nose, her hands still shaking slightly due to her long 'nap'. Inhaling its aroma and enjoying it with closed eyes, a benevolent smile crossed her face. When her mouth parted and her lips touched the hot liquid, a sound came from her, the same type of sound heard in most morning breakfast halls. If it was too hot her features didn't show it.

"Yes, Salien, you were there... forgive me my mind is always a little foggy when I first wake. Veka speaks very highly of you." She turned back to the sun and let its warmth and light embrace her. "It is good to be awake and of the world again. What year be it?"

I winced. "The one hundred eighty seventh year after the reclaiming." She turned towards me slowly, one eyebrow raised slightly. That look was obviously a question. "The Imperial city fell into madness when a new male priestess decided to "codify" a few new laws."

I cast my eyes down awaiting her displeasure. It may have been my job to tell her, that didn't mean I had to like it, or wasn't terrified of what would happen.

"Really?" she sounded almost amused. "How many new 'Laws' did he decide the world needed?"

Understand, the Empress felt breaking the law should be punished with death, to that end, she only made five laws. Everything else is merely a guideline and subject to change as a culture grows.

"Before we rebelled? I think over six hundred, my Empress."

Have you ever watched someone choke on, then spit out of their nose what they were drinking? Imagine it is hot coffee, and imagine it is someone you just woke up to kill a bunch of people. Courage did not keep me rooted there, fear did.

After she got done coughing, choking, spurting, and wiping the droplets from her face, she wheeled on me.

"What in the hells took you so long?"

I took a deep breath, stood my ground, reminded myself that I wasn't born yet, and it was not in fact my fault.

"This was done over about six months, and he started this madness in winter. It was nearly a year before we managed to breach the walls. He burned a lot of the texts before we got to the citadel, and we were scared he was going to harm you. We or rather my ancestors found him weeping over your body saying that the city needed him..." I stopped not sure how the next part would be taken, "to continue the cycle so the city could be reborn. He was apologizing to you for those who died and begging your forgiveness."

"What became of him?" Her words were quiet, soft, haunting. She was facing away from me, arms and wings tucked arounder herself.

"His skull is by your throne, all nine of his horns removed, Empress." I bowed low.

She merely nodded.

Then she turned to address me, "One, don't do that. You are my Handmaid, I may have to put up with that from the others, but I won't put up with it from you. I need people who can look me in the eye, if they are to guide me in this new age. That brings me to two. If you are going to be close to me, call me Jess, or my lady if you insist."

I blinked, stunned. Formality is one of the things I had always been taught was important when addressing her, that her slightest mood shift might mean your death. Formality was supposed to be the armor that protected you from her wrath.

"Jess?" it was more a breath than a word, an exhalation of my confusion. Certainly not a question I was asking her. She answered anyway.

"Jess, Jessica, my name. My name before all of this began. Didn't anyone teach you that my court here was meant to keep me grounded, to keep me here instead of my head being in the clouds. Meant to keep me a servant, the lowest of servants, answering to everyone? You are here to make my job easier, to serve me as I serve all. That is what a ruler is after all. The lowest of servants. I don't deserve gold; I need gold to make roads, to build walls to keep people safe. I don't make laws to enforce my whim, my morality, or my vanity. I do so to guide and to draw a line in the sand that says, 'No More.' I don't need slaves to tickle my lusts; I have slaves to make my job easier."

She looked back out unto the city, her city. "I built this, so you, my children, all races of men and beast could know peace. I sleep soundly when I know you are safe. I wake to protect and stop those that would take from you, what was taken from others when I was a girl. I watched one ruler after another take away responsibility from the people in the name of security, then take away freedom in the name of safety."

She was looking up into the sky now, tears starting to color her violet eyes. "Do not pick up a sword and defend yourself, call a guard." She shook her head. "What I gave you, it is not perfect, it is meant to grow and change, to become more with each generation." Her last word trailed off, sorrow, I think, creeping into her voice.

I had been taught to expect a flawed person, a normal person, but the legend of what she did colored my perceptions of her.

Now here she was, as she had probably been the day she woke from her first death changed, a scared confused uncompromising dreamer. Someone that believed in people, not lords, ladies, or priests. Those, by her own words, were only there to help guide people along, not tell them what to do.

With hope replacing the fear that had gripped me since I had watched the horrors of her awaking, I began to realize we had not called forth some battle god, a god of destruction, but a person like any of us.

With a tremble in my voice, I called to her. "Jessica, the council awaits your pleasure." Lords help us, the council. What had been a forgone conclusion to me moments before, was now my job. I had to help the council convince a dreamer, a woman who built a kingdom on high ideals to go to war.

Damn that priest, how much more did he destroy if we had gotten it so wrong? How much knowledge was lost in his madness? Would something in there help us convince her of the need? Or would she go back to sleep?

Author's Notes 3

Conflicts are not one sided, there are at least two, but often many more sides to a struggle. The heroes to one side are the villains to the other. While the Citadel and its Priestesses found out the hard way their blood god was anything but, a lot of the people of Unstoma would certainly not agree.

Below is a letter written by one such man, a historian and loyal servant of the God King of Unstoma, in order to preserve what little could be of those last days. This originally was meant to be part of the RPG books.

I give you The Last Folio of the Great Alexis Cain of Hampshire.

The Final Day

AFU 0

This is the final folio of The Great Alexis Cain of Hampshire, Historian of Unstoma. It is the year 987 of SF, the era commonly observed by the civilized world. It is also the last year I am afraid. It is my sad duty to, to put it bluntly, ecord the obituary of history itself.

Over a thousand years ago, a simple man named Aluguston, Son of Falrichter, heard a tale in the ancient city of New Caledonia. It was a bar tale, a fable, told by all the locals, one well known in those parts. A tale as to why one of the oldest cities in the world has 'New' in its name. In short, Caledonia was a thriving civilization in a faraway Land known as Dogger. There a man of great stature and Lord in his own right made a deal with a dragon, a dragon that wanted to protect the world.

The dragon failed, and with that failure the dread goddess of destruction Elie was born. With her birth, the old world of man was wiped away. To redeem himself the lord and his family set his kingdom down upon the shores of her birth. To this day the dragon protects Elie's birthing chamber and its horrors from the prying eyes of men. According to local legend New Caledonia is named after their lord turned king's original homeland.

This is one of the few places with a history, albeit an oral one, that says humans, not elves with their hedonist ways, were the original people of the world. Elie's birth had all but wiped us out allowing the lesser races to take over. Bear with me, I know that to a contemporary reader this is common knowledge, but I write not for you, but for those poor sods yet to come, so that the true history may not be lost.

As Aluguston adventured, he collected lore from all the people and races he encountered, not just humans, but the lesser races of demi-humans as well.

Although these poor beings didn't understand it, they too had pieces of the puzzle. When he finally managed to speak to the eldest of Elven sages, they themselves admitted that yes, Humans, not Elves, were the oldest race.

In their propagandized rewrite of the true history, they claimed to believe that all true humans had been wiped out. You see, Elves aren't elves. They are a degenerative race of humans; they took magics that gave them their unnaturally long lives. They sought ease of life and to avoid death altogether. This hubris twisted them into the form of women for their arrogance. A fitting punishment if you ask me. This long and unnatural life they admit allowed them to weather Elie's birth far better than real humans. They had turned their back on humans, and humanity itself.

They let us die.

Yet we remain. We, the true humans, are stronger than that.

This is the reason for their acts of 'kindness', their 'good deeds' of shepherding us. It is to make up for the death of the first men. It also kept from us our power, our birthright. They do not see us as true humans, but we know better. We know who we are, all thanks to Aluguston. He went to the great hill, he found the oldest records lost to time and he built a Republic, named it Unstoma, and declared all men free.

For 300 years that kingdom grew, and its light brought the religions of the world together based on their common roots. This is the Pantheon of the Sacred Light, and may those Gods never abandon us. Soon we became the center of all reason, of all learning both scholarly and mystical. Our goal was to reform the world with enlightenment. We succeeded, and humans are once again the dominant species and masters of all in this land. We call the land itself M'Diro, it's from the old tongue, but the word simply means 'my land', and it very much is... or was.

We had become so beloved by the Gods that one of them came down and graced us with his child upon the world. He grew strong and led us to even greater Glory. He was Aminter the First, God Emperor of Mankind, Protector of the Realm and Arbiter of the Devine. He is the one that stopped the holy wars and truly brought peace, law, and stability to us.

We had always had some push back from the lesser races, despite how much we gave them. Just as we have always had some push back from the lesser sex, as well as the deviants that pop up from time to time. Such is the way of children when faced with their betters. We had long found ways to work with them, integrate them, educate them. Ungrateful children never understand the rigors of obedience, loyalty, and discipline.

Outside our borders of course, the Elves, Dwarves, and such do still make sacrifices of their own, as well as eating the flesh of their own kind and the flesh of any they can catch. Even babies are not safe from these savage practices. That, of course, is the case for the other so call 'civilized races.'

The savages known as Orcs have always acted as the locus they are. Yet of the twisted beings known collectively as Goblynoids, they alone have proven to be tamable. Goblyns and the more dreaded Hobs are a blight upon the world. Extermination is the only recourse, sadly now that will never happen.

Of the non-humans, only the Liberi have never given us trouble, but then, they also ignore us tending to live alone, isolated. When we come to their towns they would rather pick up and move. Such an odd people, still they have never given us cause to defend ourselves against them. While they are a bit lazy and shiftless, they cause no trouble.

Within the borders of the Empire of course, such peoples live much better lives. As one example, Liberi settlements are not attacked. For another, when given proper framework and reference, Elven music and art are a wonder. As such they are the most sought-after artisans by the nobility. Dwarven Craftsmanship can hardly be surpassed, and the mining ability of any given clan is superb. No clan has ever failed to meet quota.

Still such mixing of peoples does have its unfortunate drawback. The poor bastard children of an elf and human have their problems. Of course, this has led to laws, and taboos, about cross mating. Not that it seems to matter much, more of them were born every year. Deviants know no propriety. Such an unnatural paring always leaves those poor children listless and wandering for all their days. A pity really. We did find that breeding Orcs with human criminals who otherwise would have died has given us some stunning gladiators for the arenas. Human females are best for this, as human males tend to not survive mating with Orcs. Some of the women do die in childbirth but that is the hazard of being a woman. We can afford to waste them, whereas male convicts have better uses elsewhere.

You would think the paring of human and elf would produce something wonderous, but it is the paring of those deviants and the Orc stock that has given us something useful. Why this is, and how they flourish is beyond me.

In the last 600 years of our Empire, we have enjoyed peace, prosperity and harmony with the world around us, we have even mastered the elements. We stretched north to the tropical lands were winter lasts only a few moons and summers can bake a man if he is not prepared for it. Fire powder comes from there. Despite its name, I find it quite nice to put in my teas, and what it does for breads is, in my opinion, better than dull honey.

We of course sit in the west with the rising sun, and we stretch all the way to the frontier with its boundless river rightly called the Mistress of the Land, as it is the widest, and possibly the longest river in the world. Stretching all the way from the great freshwater sea that is our southern border, to the great bay that is home to New Caledonia. This behemoth of a river is, at its widest, a full mile mark across.

Beyond the river is a grass land that stretches out to the horizon and beyond. With its grassy wastes are great beasts, one of which I am told is a bovine like creature whose temperament has earned it the name the Murder Cow. This I am told is the favored prey of the beast men and other savagery that call the place home. With no running water that way for weeks, the dull brown grasses are unsuitable for civilization. Yet life there finds a way I am told. It is overrun with those who have nothing but disdain for civilization and the proper way of things. Barbarian humans, Goblyns in all their hideous forms, the afore mentioned beast men, all live freely out that way, and as such taming the east is a useless endeavor. Nothing of value out there anyway, they can keep it.

We had thought nothing could live in the frozen wastes to the south, beyond the strip of land that separates the Freshwater Sea from the vastness of the western ocean... we were wrong.

Had any of the malcontents, or the lesser men, managed an uprising, we might have stood a chance. None of them, no matter how loathsome, would willingly make deals with the Devil.

Perhaps we had been too kind with the deviants, too lenient with the lesser races, or maybe we had just become too decadent and wasteful. Either way, when the beasts came, they brought their Dark Goddess Lunavner with them at their vanguard. For whatever reason, the gods took their protective hand from us. Not even Ca'talls answered our prayers.

What took a millennium to build, they destroyed in less years than it takes to ween a babe.

Arnital The Wise fell yesterday, The God Emperor is dead. His heir fell in battle with the forces of evil, and their deviant allies, at the main gate of the palace earlier in the day. There are none left to continue his divine line.

I personally witnessed the tragedy with my own two eyes. He stood in combat with the Devil herself. It was as if lightning came from the sky and was given hellish form. She was a great beast of twisted and sparking snarled light, a never-ending bolt on earth with its own diabolical thunder that deafened all who dared approach. Fingers of the fell beast's power reached out and touched those who dared come near, and everyone this demonic blasphemy touched convulsed and danced until dead. The smell of cooked flesh spread through the air. This beast was a perversion of light and fire, it offered no warmth, its light too blinding to behold.

The God Emperor of Mankind met her mere feet from his thrown and wreathed himself in the holy black flames of heaven. He uttered words in the divine language and condemned her as he struck, but his strength was not enough.

As the two clashed her hellish army of demons fought brave and honorable men. Their flesh was the color of base flame and blood. They offered no quarter and took no surrender, slaughtering men who fell to their knees and begged for mercy, such was their blood lust. These devils took great pleasure in those screams and suffering, babbling in some barbaric tongue and screaming with all the terrors of hell itself.

When the God Emperor fell, the men ran, and I am sorry to say, I too took flight from such horrors. The last sight I beheld on that battlefield, the sight which broke my nerve and will forever be etched into my mind, was the fiend giving up its mockery of light to reveal its true form. A wisteria hued version of her red and orange kind, her beauty took me for a moment. She was an exquisite form, beautiful and terrible to behold. I was awe struck. Until she tore into the divine chest of the God Emperor with her clawed hand, ripped out his heart, and ate it.

Upon seeing that, my courage broke and I fled.

The God Emperor is dead... Civilization itself has fallen.

Alexis Cain of Hampshire, Historian of Unstoma. Year 0 After the Fall of Unstoma, AFU.

Scribe's note.

I, Bishop Mikle Rex, Bishop of the Temple of the god Ca'talls, here in the year 390 AFU do here by state, that I have copied this as closely as possible from what is, as far as the church has been able to identify an original account of Alexis Cain. It appears to be an account made mere days after the fall of the last Empire of Man. This is translated from Unstoma to the best of my ability.

It has been nearly 500 years since the events of Alexis' time, and we have learned a thing or two. The name of the creatures he mentions, the ones he calls demons, are the LeatherWing. That is the translation from their tongue. I am afraid I can't replicate the sounds they do into common lettering, or I would put down what it sounds like. It has a lot of Rs and Gs and I think a K or two. I can write it in their script, but their script is, let us call it illegible and confusing.

That being said, the fact of the matter is they did declare war upon the Empire, though few know why. Perhaps it was a slight between two gods, their Empress, and our God Emperor. Despite all the norms of war, they came quickly, striking swiftly, and with little warning. (I will address the warning they did give, please be patient.) Yet as quickly as they came from the frozen south, they returned to it. They didn't loot or pillage, and while I would never dare call them civilized, they do seem to have some kind of honor. Perhaps it is something they have learned since. To the best of our ability to tell, they challenged every town and garrison they came across. If a town surrendered, the tide of the creatures washed over them without harm. They even traded and bought goods fairly. To each town that stood and said no, or offered resistance? It is said they killed every man, woman, and child. Or so the legend goes.

I find it odd that this document, which has probably been in the archives for most of its life, was found only now during a cleaning. It has been given to me to translate and update. It seems to be genuine, written on the correct paper, with the correct vernacular, and it does match the writing style of the scribe who is reported to have written it. I have no reason to doubt its authenticity, none but the timing.

It is odd because, while the people of the Empire of the Five, did indeed leave all those years ago, a few of their more elusive races have been seen out and about in the world again. Yes, we have Grass Lords on our border and have lived with them and their 'pranks' for as long as Five Rivers has been a free city. Yes, Sky Lords do call our city home. Now the elusive LeatherWing themselves are on the move once more, and they are the beating heart of the Empire of the Five.

No, I do not yet know why their Empire is named thus.

These new sightings of LeatherWing do not seem to be on the kind of rampage history shows they are capable of. They do not attack random people, instead they seem almost curious about us. One of their kind, an orange man (the color of common flame), named Tulock has spent time with me. Yes, he is a man, holy items do not harm him in the least. He has been with us for weeks and he seeks knowledge and questions everything, the way I wish my own students would.

They do indeed look like the devils of legend, legends that predates their appearance five centuries ago. So that cannot be the origin of our assumptions of what demons look like. The devil's form predates our knowledge of the LeatherWing's existence.

I have trouble squaring the knowledge of this text, and the numerous other such accounts that collaborate it, with the man I have come to know. He oaths to me, something they are deadly serious about, that he is not unique among his people. From his words his people see oaths much the same way as certain clans of elves. To them, 'broken words' are reasons to kill.

He seems to earnestly believe all of his people are of the same temperament as he is. He confirms that the accounts are mostly true, even if a bit embellished. He claims that by tradition the children were spared... for whatever that's worth.

I sincerely hope that the reader of this document and its accounts are not finding it in the burned out remains of my little temple. I want to believe Tulock, I really do.

Author's Note 4

Our next story came about as nothing more than a bit of lore building. It was meant just to be a private thing, a quick note as to what "Jess" got up to after...

The year for this is purposely ambiguous and it needs to be. This is an intimate moment between Jessica and the Mouse Who Roars.

Mouse

Torch lights shone and reflected their glow off the walls, illuminating *her*, as she hung from chains before me. Twenty-nine months, for twenty-nine months I had been anticipating this day. I would wait no longer.

I stalked towards her, smelling her fear coming off in waves. Her eyes widened as I deliberately dragged my claws across the stone. She was tied, hung from chains, dangling helplessly with just her toes on the floor. Just so much prey before my might. She quivered as I came closer. Small sounds escaped her. Not the begging or screaming she would soon be doing, no. Just the whimpers of a mouse before a hawk. That thought made me chuckle.

This was going to be good.

I reached out and grabbed her face in my hands and squeezed as I forced her to look at me. The white leather of the gag and my lavender skin were both in contrast to her dark flesh. A defiant look shown in her eyes, her breath quickened. So did my pulse.

"I don't want you gagged; I want your screams." The knife from the sheath on my bare hip flashed out and cut the leather that held the muzzle in place. A thin bead of blood came to her cheek. My tongue darted out, caught, and licked those beads away. I stayed close savoring her flavor, everything about her intoxicated me. This night, I would drink so much more than just a few drops of blood.

She stayed stubbornly silent.

My smile grew, she was defiant.

"Good, fight me. It will make this go on so much longer and I have so much," a shiver of anticipation went through my body, even causing my wings to flex. "Frustration to take out on you." I reached down and cut her loin cloth from her, then unclasped my belt of skulls. Both of us were now naked from the waist down, and I was going to violate her thoroughly on top of the many tortures I had planned for her. The bruising would show up on her skin so nicely.

She twisted in her bonds, then let out a shriek as her left leg came up off the ground.

"Shit, RED. I am so sorry, red."

With a flick of my magic, I reached forward and broke the chains that were holding her up. Severing their links, I took hold of her so she wouldn't fall, and helped her to the ground. As I got her down it became obvious the leg wouldn't hold her weight, so I scooped her up. I used my wing to clear the candles off the altar, the hot wax and flames striking the fragile membranes and searing my flesh, but I didn't care.

I laid her out on the stone. "What is it, what's wrong?"

"It's, nothing, just a cramp."

I laid her down and went for her leg.

Just a cramp? Not likely.

My Mouse was one hell of a masochist.

I ran my hand down her thigh to her calf and found it. The knot was the size of my fist, hells I would have screamed over it.

"Veka, why didn't you say something?" I began working gently on the muscle.

She gave me a look. "You've been gone for over two years."

"I could have waited one more night, or just the few moments it would have taken to get this out."

She gave me a dismissive snort, then a look of pain. Through gritted teeth she said, "Wasn't that bad when the priestess put me up. We thought I would be fine. Besides, you're not the only one who was anticipating tonight."

I stopped working on the cramp. "Are you telling me they haven't been taking care of you?"

That earned me an eye roll. "They've been trying. None of them have your touch." She gave me a smile. "Or your creative streak." Then she shook her head. "They're all too gentle, at least for the most part. One of the guards, he was good. At least until he messed up and hit me in the face."

My vision went red, hitting her in the face was a hard limit for her. The slight cut I gave her on the face was an accident, what's more it was pushing it. It's why I slowed down after I saw what I had done, and it was why I switched gears to soft and gentle. It gave her a second or two to adjust, to decide to call it off without me being the one to break scene.

Veka put a hand on my arm. "Jess, it was an accident. Soon as he did it, he backed off. Hell, he spent the next few days groveling before me every time I saw him." She leaned back as I, now calmer, started back on the cramp. "After I manage to get him to realize I wasn't upset, he refused to come near me." A sigh escaped her. Whether it was exasperation or relief from my work I wasn't sure. I was getting the leg muscle to let go, so that was something.

She continued, "Being the Empress's private toy has its advantages, but it's got its drawbacks too."

I looked up and into her eyes. "Veka, you are so much more than a toy, mine or otherwise."

The smile she gave me reminded me of why she was my Mouse.

"No, really? Here I thought I was just another wet slit for you to fuck."

"Ha ha." Her calf jumped in my hand as it tried to knot back up. "How did you get this anyway?" I turned her leg over in my hand and saw the remnant of a bruise, one hidden from me due to the lights in here. Looking her in the eye I arched my eyebrow.

"Staff work. I got my mastery in knives while you were gone. Staves work better for me than swords."

"Someone should have been rubbing you down." My voice held an edge.

She sat up and took my face in her hands tenderly, "Jessica, they have been."

I nodded and let it go. I'm overprotective and I know it. Its why I take the hands-off approach with my people, the reason I 'go to sleep'.

As I worked the sun finally made its way into the room from the back windows, it lit her body up. Each curve, from her breasts, to her thighs, to her belly, was perfect to my eyes. Her dark skin was what would have been called black in my youth, back when such things mattered to people who gave more meaning to it than it deserved. Even back then I thought it was odd. Now in my new world, in my lands? Such things didn't matter.

I had thought those things long past. At least until recently.

"So, what were you doing?"

Her words shook me from my thoughts. "Excuse me?"

"My Empress, you've been gone for two years. What in the hells were you doing?"

My thoughts turned dark, turned to Ra'agan. "You know, the normal, seducing a mortal, getting pregnant, having a kid... dying in childbirth."

"For real?"

I gave a shrug as I kept working the muscle, giving it little jolts and shocks to help with the healing. "It's part of the plan."

Her groan echoed off the walls. "The plan, oh gods no, not 'the plan'." This time I knew it wasn't my hard work.

"Yes, the plan. Unstoma..." I paused. "It should never have happened."

"It was just an empire; they didn't even stand for a millennium. Yeah, they were bad, bad enough to wake you up from your eternal slumber." She made an off-hand gesture. "But you dealt with them."

I thought about them, the iconography, the rhetoric, the way they acted, their policies. She just did not understand. None of them did. Umberto Eco wasn't a name they were familiar with.

"They weren't just an Empire." Sexism, racism, prejudice, hate. They never went away. My people did what they could to fight such things, but even they fell victim to them.

But Unstoma?

"When I was young, still human, that's the last time I saw things like that on that scale. Saw such evils that baked into how everything was done so even the most decent, good, well-meaning, and hardworking people did such cruelty and evils casually." I turned from her and hugged myself, pulling my wings in tight.

She was the only one I would let see me like this. She was my Mouse. I could never hide from Mouse, not in any lifetime. They always knew me. I turned to her and smiled.

"I won't let that type of bigotry rise again unchallenged."

Author's Notes 5

The Orange mentioned in the third story is a LeatherWing Warden named Tulock. Tulock's story was probably the very first thing I ever wrote in M'Diro. I wanted to explore the world through his eyes. The problem of course being they are alien eyes seeing a mundane world. Sounds nice, but it didn't give my readers anything to hold on to. These next two stories are Tulock as he first sees Five Rivers, and the Gate Guards of Five River seeing Tulock.

I am cleaning these up for spelling, grammar, and readability, as well as lore fixes for things that have changed. I am also keeping them as close to what they were when I wrote them as I can.

Tulock

AFU 490

Tulock looked over the city before him, awed by the sheer size of it. At its founding it would have been nothing more than a few buildings on the banks of the river known as the Joyful Greetings, the western river of the four that fed the behemoth known as The Mistress of the Land. Most who lived on her simply called her ol' Miss. Since its start the city has filled the banks and islands, and now with its bridges and towers of gleaming white stone it dominated all five of the rivers, the four that fed into it, and the Mistress herself. Five Rivers was, simply put, massive.

That explained why he had been passing farms and small 'orbit' towns for the last few days. The Citadel was the only other city he'd heard of that needed that much food, and it was dwarfed by this, this megalopolis.

If any commerce wanted to go down river they would have to unload on the city's southern docks and reload on the northern ones and her larger ships meant for a river like the Mistress. The City of Five Rivers really was the strongest, and richest, city of man in this modern age.

The LeatherWing warden looked north to the wonder that was The Mistress and fully grasped why it was named after the

Strongest of the Gods of the Five Races, the Empress herself. She was Mistress to them all, and this river, this gargantuan of water, lived up to that moniker.

Past the city whose bridges and walls had cut off the four smaller tributaries she was wide enough to be mistaken for an inland sea. The best of swimmers could not cross it safely, and even flying over it would take almost half a candle mark. Tulock could do it mind you, but even a strong young man like himself preferred land to be under him in case his wings cramped.

A SkyLord could make it with no problems of course; they were SkyLords after all. Smaller, lighter, and far more agile than even the most practiced of LeatherWing, such a flight would be no problem for the birds of prey. It was said that they could take wing in the morning and not have to come down till the moon was high in the sky.

Of the Five Races, Man was by far the most versatile, the most creative, the most ingenious, and hands down the stupidest. This city was proof of their power, prowess, and mastery of the world around them. A crescent shaped city that had started on a riverbank and now bridged the other four rivers with sections of the city built on each V where two of the rivers met. Almost unsiegeable, with plenty of water and fish to see them through hard times and optimal defenses; it could last for years under attack with few discomforts felt by its inhabitance. With ballista and catapults pointed towards the sky and ground, as well as a small navy to handle encroachment up the Miss herself. Be it by accident or design they had almost built the perfect city.

Their stupidity was the insistence of dividing themselves into different "Races" based on looks, lifespan, height, and in some cases skin color.

One group were called Elves, and much to their detriment, they at some point in their past had discovered how to become immortal. These humans were always fair and slender and were so beautiful even the males had the breasts and hips of a woman. Their immortality brought with it something the elves called the Wee, a wasting disease of the mind and sanity. It drove them to hedonistic heights until they sought the final embrace of death herself.

Another group of Men are called Dwarves. These humans were stout and strong, so strong even their women had beards. Their simple lives had granted them longer life spans, but they still knew the joy of death. They had further divided themselves based on culture and religious beliefs into Astrue Dwarves and Celtuce Dwarves; one agrarian by belief, and one who were raiders. Both were strong warriors, and the young Orange didn't see why they need to separate themselves.

The Men of the Swamps were often called Gnomes, and at least were smart enough to call themselves 'cousins' of the Dwarves. They could, and often would, eat any plant no matter the taste or poison. They were also known for building great machines that should not work, but often did. With little fear of starvation, and a keen sense of taste for what others could eat and would like, they were hardy traders. Their trade caravans were always a welcome sight back home.

The Liberi or "Free" were just Men of short stature, most no bigger than a child of 3 to 4 winters. They did tend to live simple lives, and as far as Tulock was concerned, that just showed their wisdom.

Then of course you have Hu-mans, the race of Men that saw itself, and only itself, as pure. Some of these hu's went so far as to say that those born with skin tones that were too dark were somehow less than those born with skin the color of cream. Purity was something that hu-mans seem to care far too much about.

Tulock shook his head.

The races of Man, it seemed, always wanted to feel as if they were better than someone else. Some used metrics like reason and longevity, some used hard work, some religion and the gods themselves, sex, age, haleness, and worst of all usefulness. It had gotten so bad during the Unstoman Empire that they had actually force bred their own women with the peoples known as Orcs just to produce "something useful".

Now you had Half Orcs and True Orcs, or as they were sometimes called "dear gods what is that?" Anything too different was viewed as bad or wrong.

Tulock sighed to himself and looked around once more. To his knowledge no LeatherWing had set foot on this bank since the end of the War of the Empires. His ancestors had been there that day, she and the man who would be her mate had joined their clans together to fight the evil of Unstoma. Their arm of the Empress's great campaign had led them east towards the setting sun, and finally to the small garrison that had once been here. They arrived to find that the women and men of the town that housed that garrison had already turned on it. They had not only destroyed the imperial legion but had cleansed the land of the blood of the tainted families who ran it. Five Rivers threw open their gates when the LeatherWing army approached, welcomed them not as conquers but as liberators.

The young orange spoke to his companion, his voice cracking with its first use of the day. "My mother told me that they were surprised when we didn't demand tribute, nor their food or land. She said that, according to her mother, and her mother before her, they simply did not understand us not wanting them or their blood; spoils of war they called it." Tulock spoke gently to the hawk that followed him willingly. In a lot of ways, the two were inseparable. The Orange had never had a truer friend. He knew the animal didn't understand him, but still he continued. "The elders say the men of the south are not ready for our return. That they are not yet ready to learn the ways of peace and war, the true way of civilization."

He turned and looked at the circle of stones, the rocks of the first law. One in the middle with five evenly spaced around it, each big enough to be seats. Where they were, the five laws were there.

"The Shadows, it would seem, disagree my friend." He made the reflexive sign of gratitude to the creature who placed the rocks here. All of his kind did when speaking of these mythic beings. No one had ever seen a shadow or even knew what manner of beings they were. No LeatherWing would risk incurring their wrath knowingly.

He bent down and examined the soil around the nearest stone. The dirt slid from between his orange fingers. Grass grew right up next to the rocks; the land was long healed. Trees grew in a protective circle around the place of judgment, and their age, while young, was not that of a sapling. A judgment circle, within a few hours walk of a city of men.

"These sacred stones have been here at least a generation, if not longer." He looked out to the city again. The Grass Lords had been traveling this far south for as long as anyone could remember. The Heard traveled wherever they wished, and the Sky Lords had been hunting this Land for several generations.

"We are the last my friend... and we are late." And with that, the first LeatherWing to be seen by the city of Five Rivers in nearly 500 years headed towards its gates.

The Gates at Dawn

<u>AFU 490</u>

The Dawn Gate, named for the fact the morning sun came into the city through this gate first thing every morn. As the most westerly gate, every morning saw priests of a few of the smaller faiths up there on the top of the wall doing everything from joyously greeting the new dawn, to praying in solemn reverence. The Acolytes of the Risen One, saw every morning as a triumphant resurrection of their most holy god. The Brothers of the Songs of Nature came to bask in the dawns light and the song of the 'Tide of Light' as it washed over the land. Both groups of course pissed off the other to no end.

The few that did neither just tried to ignore the first two.

For the first few moments of dawn twice a year, the sun shone directly through the crack between the doors. These two days were the equinoxes and as such the people in the Dawn District use that as an excuse to throw a district wide party.

As Falion reported to his guard post that morning he was heartily glad it was not one of those two days. No, for today was Bored Day.

Bored day came once in a week, officially it was known as fourth day. Every culture that lived in the city had a different name for it, and for Falion, that name was Bored Day. Bored Day meant no travelers coming through, not through Dawn Gate at any rate. There was no market today, well at least not the big ones of the weekend, no grain shipments either. Fifth and sixth day saw the big grain and produce shipments, thus, seventh day saw the biggest markets. First day was sacred in most religious teachings, so first days were always busy; so busy in fact every gate was open with the Gate Guard only waving people through and looking for problems instead of checking everyone. Second day saw the merchants coming through to deliver goods to shops, and third day seems to just peter on forever.

Bored Day only saw two types of people, missionaries from the various faiths, or adventurers.

Falion liked Bored Day for that very reason, even if he had just about seen it all in his years as guard. Yes, you were probably going to be bored out of your mind most of the day, but adventurers were always worth at least a few moments of excitement. At least that's how it was for his first and second year on the job. By his third year he realized he had seen just about every song and dance these people had to offer and knew their stories on sight for most of them.

The True Heroes were always the same, bright shiny and always out to do 'good,' usually with no understanding of the mess they left for others to clean up. Oh, visually they were always appealing and almost always audacious in their dress and mannerisms. A large sword or other implement of death, check. Armor that told you all you needed to know about them, check. Often some type of banner or some such, with a minstrel or Bard tagging along if they had actually done something to be proud of. They blew in, and then back out, of people's lives like fluff on the wind. These people were always about as deep as puddles.

The Mercenaries were at least tolerable. Little more than swords for hire they often came in with the caravans. They were usually a good sort at least until payday, and then the guard would have a few behind the clink. A rough and tumble lot they were, get strong drink in them and they were going to start a fight somewhere, usually with True Heroes.

Falion shook his head and hid a smile as he looked out at the nearly empty west road. Most of the time *he* didn't have to deal with them in that respect, which was a good thing, because there were quite a few of the regulars he liked.

Then you had The Wackos, and you could always see them coming. Those were still somewhat fun, but always meant trouble. Wizards and Mages were always strange, but some of them seem to delight in going overboard. These were wackos of course, but others could be as well. Hells Falion had even at one point seen a warrior who counted as a wacko. The man was a walking piece of work, with his black armor, skull helm, and severed human heads tied to his horse's bridle.

Poor animal wasn't happy about it.

The frightening thing was that, that dumb son of a bitch could not understand why the city guard had a problem with letting him pass. He got really upset when we let a few Orcs in passed him. That really set him off and had him demanding to know why they were stopping a normal 'real person' from going in but letting beasts in with just a nod. That guy was proof trash could take human form.

"Cuz Baz and 'is group never 'urt anyone in 'is life! 'E just got the misfortune of being ugly outside." Falion had yelled at the man.

Being a good guardsman meant you quickly got over most of your race based biased, at least in Falion's opinion. If you didn't, the Lord Marshal would have words for you sooner or later. Ol' man Thunderhammer didn't like you overlooking a problem just because it was wrapped in pretty skin and didn't like you making trouble for ugly skin that weren't doin' no harm.

Unfortunately, wackos were few and far between, and it had been far too long since Dawn Gate had a Wacko. East Wood gate had one a few days ago. Two Grass Lords had decided to come into town. Normally this wouldn't be a problem. Five Rivers had gotten used to the cats a long ways back. According to the gossip these two were about eleven, maybe twelve summers old, which for a human puts them nearly into their twenties. Problem was the two girls had with them one of their "slaves".

Now a few things you got to understand, Cat women have four breasts, and while they are covered in a light down of fur, it's still easy to see them and know they are boobs. These two girls hadn't a stitch of cloth nor strip of leather above the waist. The cats are nomads and don't have the same concept about bodies that people do. The second thing is that slavery is illegal in the city. Oh, it used to be very legal back when the Empire ran things. It had been made illegal just days before the destructive hoard known as the LeatherWing showed up.

LeatherWings were a demonic looking race of barbarians that lived to the frozen south, and centuries ago they declared war on the greatest empire of all times... and won. It seems that in some weird way slavery breaks one of their laws.

For that sin of slavery, they burned an empire to the ground, and then just up and left. They didn't take land, nor gold, nor slaves. They just slew, and killed, and slaughtered, with absolute abandon, and all of it done because they had a problem with slavery. Only it turns out they were indeed slavers themselves... just not in any way that made sense. They didn't buy them, or sell them, and after a while they just let them go. While they have them, they treated them better than they treated members of their own family. Grass Lords are a part of LeatherWing society, so they treat their "slaves" the way that LeatherWings did, more as indentured diplomats that just happen to also be servants. Live in Five Rivers long enough and you are going to run into the cats and their weird ways.

The brand-new gate guard didn't know any of that, not only had he been with the guard less than a moon, but he had also just moved to the city from somewhere back west.

Running it through his mind to amuse himself, Falion shook his head at the interplay that must have happened.

Two, nearly naked four breasted cat women, walking up leading a probably equally naked human on a leather leash must have been a shock for the new guy. Kid sees it and decides to get all holy roller and gets righteous with the cats. As he thought about it, he thinks he remembers the new kid being one of Lut'har's bunch. That would fit with the scuttlebutt about him proceeding to get high and mighty on their vulgarity and the evils of slavery. How dare Beastmen enslave a human.

Falion really wished he had been on duty at that gate just to witness the hell those two would have rained down on the lad. Cats think the concept of anyone being better than anyone else is one of the evilest thoughts a person can have.

Then again... the cats also tend to shed blood over insult quite quickly, maybe it was better that he wasn't there.

Gav grunted a "Hay Fal," bringing the seasoned veteran of the boredom of a slow day back to the here and now. Gav was the guard on the opposite side of the gate from him, "lookie what we got here."

Yanked from his thoughts of the rumors of days past, and gates not his, Falion looked down the road to what his Dwarf guard mate was seeing.

Coming towards them, and obviously headed to their gate, was a figure in leathers. Over his head was a hawk lazily flying around, the bird was not too far out of reach. The sword by his left side, the wild animal circling him, a gait that said he spent more time walking were there were no roads at all, yes everything about him said "Warden". The odd thing wasn't a Warden out of the wood, though that was somewhat abnormal in and of itself, it was the orange tint to his skin, and the large, folded wings on his back.

An honest to gods LeatherWing was coming their way. Maybe today was looking up after all.

Author's Note 6

M'Diro had started out as just another fantasy world, but at some point, it had grown into so much more. The first novel was finished, the second was in progress, and I loved the discussions that were cropping up amongst my beta readers.

When I was in 9th grade, I read the Lady or the Tiger and loved it, I loved the idea, the choice of it, the discussions it would create, all of it. Throne of Bone is my love letter to that short story from so long ago.

Some will ask me what "the" right answer to the question the story asks is, what happened, what did the Thief decide. For almost every single story I have made, there is a "what happens after the final page", every story but this one.

Enjoy.

Throne of Bone

<u>Between AFU 490 and AFU 494</u>

The thing about being a thief, some jobs pay poorly, and some pay well. When I was offered this job, as far as I was concerned this pay day was as big as you could get, my life.

Now? As I looked over the mausoleum, I wasn't sure I had been paid enough.

I had spent weeks going further and further south looking for this damnable place. Each and every day, with every step I walked, every breath I took, every meal I ate, the words of his holiness echoed in my head.

"Go to the LeatherWing city, there you will find a tomb, the tomb of their so-called Empress, that demonic bitch. Bring me back a bone from her corpse. I will know if it is hers or not."

Thankfully I didn't have a time limit, as that son of a motherless frog didn't give me a lot of information to go on.

Never get caught robbing a church and definitely never get caught robbing the house of a Bishop.

I screwed my eyes shut. "Go to the tomb, bring me a bone." Over and over again, it never stopped. Those words endlessly poured through my head as if the thought was my own, it was always quiet, just under my hearing, but always there. The old fart had called the spell a Dilyn Trefn, and it wouldn't end until I gave the damn bastard what he wanted.

I guess my sanity could also be part of the payment.

The worse part was I had agreed to it, it was this or the headsman. It seemed like a sweet deal at the time. How was I to know I would never have a moments peace, or worse what the creatures known as LeatherWing were actually like.

Now?

Not so much. With each passing day the deal seemed worse and worse. The Dilyn Trefn was annoying, but the area, the people, the...things? This was nothing like what I had expected.

LeatherWing are a race of half demons who live in the frozen south, which trust me isn't a desolate wasteland. The forest, the mountains, all of it was quite breathtaking. I had figured going into these barbarian lands would be about like walking into an area with too many goblyns, with everything torn up, burned down, or worse.

Looking back, I honestly had no idea what the hell I thought this place would be like. I had just conjured up images in my head of where the creatures that once destroyed the world would live, figuring that maybe that kind of mindless destruction was just what they did.

Back in the old days when men were men and the world was right, they had poured out of the south like angry wasps, slaughtering every town they came across, eventually even killing the God King himself. Then they just left. I mean these were the people that destroyed the old empire, plunged us back into barbarism and in fighting, and for what? They didn't so much as take a coin, an ounce of gold, or any land. At least that's what the old stories said.

Personally, I always thought that part was a lie. I mean they had to take gold didn't they. Everyone took gold. It was the only true religion and the only thing that could be counted on. If you took gold out, then the only thing that made any sense to me about them was that they came for the slaves. The people brave enough, or foolish enough to trade with them said LeatherWing were slavers.

Granted most towns and cities had slaves. It was just life. Very few places had outlawed the practice and the ones that had, often used prisoners for that kind of labor.

That was another reason I agreed to this job, a life in chains didn't interest me much.

That, as they say, was then.

Now?

Now part of me wished I had taken the date with the axe.

It took weeks of traveling, hitting taverns, gossiping at every camp I came across, and plying minstrels with enough beer to float a ship before I found out that the 'tomb' I was looking for was on top of some mountain or other. Even longer still to learn that at the base of that mountain was a city. Only a few nights ago did I learn that that city was the capital of the LeatherWing Empire.

Yesterday I saw for myself that it was far worse than I could have possibly imagined. That city was enormous, well defended, and bustling. Yes, looking back, I should have realized this was where the tomb would be, of course it was, but I was expecting barbarians, nomads, settlements that were, well primitive. If I were smart, I would have turned tail right there. Sadly, my intellectual prowess had nothing to do with the decision.

"Bring me a bone from the Empress."

The sound reached my ears, it was no longer something just in my head but a whisper from someone right on top of me.

I jumped, first in terror that someone had gotten that close without me realizing it, only to freeze in horror as I understood that I had said it out loud. That I had spoken those words, those cursed words, unbidden. My heart was pounding in my chest.

The city of Chal'trus, or more simply known as 'The Citadel', was massive. The town got its name from the royal palace, a huge statue of a female LeatherWing, but only from the waist up. Her arms circled in front of her to form the walls to the palace proper and the wings stretched out to encompass the town. It was literally carved out of the mountain. When the sun rose out of the west, it would grace the face of the woman who was probably the great grandmother of the person who's grave I came to defile.

The Citadel itself was huge, by far the largest palace I had ever seen; a building complex that could hold a town all on its own. Now understand, the city proper dwarfed it. From where I was, I couldn't make out a lot of details, but buildings were tall, many of them had spires, and there were towers and donjons everywhere. There was no way, I, a human, was going to sneak through that much city unseen. A westerly approach was never going to work.

The eastern face was much better. That side of the mountain was left to the wilds all the way to the top, all the way to where the Empress's tomb stood. No walls, no guards I could see. That was my way in.

I hadn't slept in a bed in days, the closer I got to this place the more I avoided staying in towns longer than it took to supply and move on. I was here to steal something that was undoubtably seen as holy by these people. The new guy would be the first suspect and I would stand out. I didn't trust any human that lived in these lands. After all, the locals all talked about the demons as if they were admirable in some way. I had almost started to believe it too, till I came across a battle.

A noise had woken me that morning, the sounds of trumpets, and this weird wailing scream that curdled my blood, add to that a drumming that was in tune with the beating of a heart. That sound introduced me to an emotion I had only thought I had made an acquaintance with before, terror. In that moment I knew I was quite wrong.

Following the sound to its source was no task, and what I saw shook me.

Two groups of the creatures, naked, all arms and teeth and talons, were tearing into each other. Women on the front lines, wings outstretched, tails flashing, each side fighting, biting and clawing at each other. Their hisses and growls, the blood, the blood, gods it was everywhere, they bathed in the blood of their battle. It was an orgy of death.

That battle, that sight, more than anything else, made up my mind that the locals were mad. There was nothing honorable or civilized about these demons.

Starting just after dawn, I had snuck up the back of the mountain until I reached the top. Only woods, a large herd of deer, and some simple tree houses greeted me. I had at least expected some kind of patrol or some such, a guard post, anything.

None of that was to be seen. Had I wanted I could have strolled up the deer trails in a matter of hours, but I needed not to be seen, so I snuck the whole way.

That took me all day and it was well and truly dark by the time I reached the summit of the small mountain. There stood a stone house, a thing of columns and marble. It was beautiful in its form, but small. It overlooked a balcony that seemed completely out of place with its carved spires rising to the sky and supporting nothing, that is until I remembered the crown on the head of the colossus.

That balcony with its simple table and chairs, three in all, would overlook the entire city, and it was large enough to set a ship down upon. The scale of everything here was *WRONG*. The size, the grandeur of the vista, it all clashed with the simplicity of the house, the mausoleum, the tomb, whatever it was... that's what it had to be right? This was where it was supposed to be... right?

No, this was something a merchant could afford. Granted a good one, but it was modest. Modest in everything but its placement. Madness was taking me, nothing made sense. I was starting to talk to myself due to that damn spell and now the tomb of the Empress was this humble little thing.

Shaking my head, I realized it made about as much sense as everything else about these people.

Something else that stood out about the place, something that chilled me further than even my own loss of sanity, there really were no guards. Not on the backside of the mountain, not on the approach, and not around the tomb.

That could only mean one thing, and it sent shivers down my spine.

Curses.

Traps I could find, but a curse? That was the bane of any good break. Many a rook has withered to the curse of some mage. I myself, right now, was in the grip of one laid upon me by a priest. Curses and magic were always bad news for those like me.

Thankfully that priest had given me a few things to help. One was a chicken's foot that would twitch if I came across magic meant to harm. Another was a flask of water that he swore would burn any and all of evil intent, doubly those with the blood of the devils in their veins. I had had to use a bit of the water to convince an ogre I wasn't worth the trouble. Finally, he had given me a lantern that would only illuminate words written for eyes other than those of men.

Between these and my own abilities, I hoped to see morning, a morning well away from the inconsistencies of this place.

I loosen the latch on the lantern to let out its odd, purple, glowing light, and made my way across open ground, looking for the glyphs that would mean a spell anchor. I made it to the wall of the little house itself before I spotted the first one. An odd rune that glowed golden in the strange, cursed, light of the lamp. I held the foot close to the symbol, but nothing happened. I wasn't sure if I was relieved or not. Just because the spell, or curse, or magic, wasn't meant to harm, didn't mean it wouldn't send the people who were supposed to be guarding a place like this running.

Using this thing was unnerving. A circle of the writing was illuminated as if I were holding a focused lantern to it, but no real light was coming out of the thing, just that strange purple like glow. Suppressing a shudder, I looked around, it seemed as if the writing was just on the walls, not the ground, nothing for me to trip. If I kept my hand off the stone, I should be fine.

Once I got to the highly polished marble walkway, I checked for more of the writing, but I didn't find any.

Writing on the walls, but not the approach, not the table or the chairs either.

I snuck a quick glance out over the city.

It was a marvel. I could see several city walls that this place had simply grown beyond. No less than six outer walls could be seen. Six times defensive walls had been built and six times the city had just grown beyond them. This city was far older than three hundred years. Unstoma had lasted for almost a millennium, I could easily see this place being that old. That meant the woman who was the colossus was probably more like the great-great-great etc. grandmother.

"Bring me a bone, the tomb is right there." Again, I spoke the words out loud, this time louder than a whisper.

I felt myself cringe. I swear the damn spell had a mind of its own. Or more to the point, the mind of its master, my master now as well, it would seem.

I turned my attention back to the house, the tomb proper. It really did look more like a house. It was far too large for a single body, but frankly far too small for the body of a ruler. This entire job was beyond senseless. Three hundred years ago this woman had led an army that wiped out legions of trained soldiers. Why was a Bishop from a no-where town like South Point interested in a bone from this bitch?

The lantern showed the lettering going up to the door, and on the doors themselves, but nothing that opening either of those doors would disturb. The foot was still, not so much as a twitch out of it. I looked at the dried-up thing in my hand and hoped it was working.

I used my dagger to check the seals of the place, something I had done hundreds of times before, only to my surprise there were none. Of course, there wasn't, whoever heard of security for the body of your ruler? There was one surprise for me, the slight pressure of my blade in testing for those seals sent the left door moving inward.

The inside of the place was well lit with floating balls of glowing warm light. No, not floating, they hung from chains that the shadows made difficult to see at first. The room itself had sitting couches and the walls were packed with the dreams of some thieves, books, folios, maps, this was less a tomb and more a library. Only two things let me know I was indeed in the right place. Whatever this place was lit with, it was certainly better than a torch.

One was a stone sarcophagus, sealed with its lid on tight, the other, at the back of the room was something that could only be called a throne.

Looking upon it, I felt the blood run from my face. These... people... got worse the more I saw of them.

The stone coffin was as plain as the throne was frightening, simple white marble to contrast the blue walls, it was polished and gleaming with rounded edges and even little handles to make moving the lid easier.

That throne was the nightmare cliché from every time you imagine a devil worshipers lair; a literal chair made from the bone of Humans, Dwarves, Liberi (gods above let those be Liberi skulls) and even LeatherWing. It sat silently, ominously, at the back of the room, each of its empty eyes following my movements, each horrific face grinning menacingly at me. Skulls for hand rests, ribs for backing, leg bones, vertebra, more skulls to round it out, on a dais of even more skulls artfully arranged into steps, and all of them old but well cared for, well maintained. It was huge, the actual seat of it would hold someone human size, but you needed to walk up a set of stairs made from the fallen to get to where you could sit upon the cursed thing. The cut of it left no imagination to the fact that the intended occupant was winged, and the back rose another few feet making it truly imposing just to see even in disuse.

If I had any mind of my own at this point, I would have run. I had yet to set foot inside this accursed place with its nightmare fuel. I would never sleep soundly again, just knowing a thing like that existed. I would always be imagining how the beast that sat upon that abomination had acquired the material to craft such a horror.

"BRING ME ONE OF HER BONES!" The words filled my head, my mind, they were all I heard, and they brought pain with them.

I felt a chuckle escape my mouth, and with it a little drool. "Which one would you like?"

The Dilyn Trefn would not be denied. Even my joke, the thought of grabbing one of those bones instead of one of the ones from her body, was enough to set it off. It wracked me with pain. When the thing screamed at me just moments ago it was a sudden headache, this was a crippling blinding thing that turned my stomach against me and made the darkness outside seem as bright as daylight. The inside it made look appealing, peaceful, a promise that if I merely obeyed all would be well. Dying would be better than this. Dying was clean, but if I kept disobeying, what the Dilyn Trefn would do to me wouldn't end until my body died of starvation.

I stepped across the threshold, what choice did I have.

With the end to this madness in sight, I made my way over to the centerpiece of the room. The floor was open, and empty, and it was the quick work of just a few steps to get to the sarcophagus. Ignoring the thing that dominated the back wall with all my might, I pretended this was just any other job.

Stepping up to the ossuary I examined it and found a few things strange. One, the lid was on hinges and counterbalanced for ease of lifting, it was designed to swing open. Two, it had no latches only hinges. Three, a braided wire of something that looked close to electrum but with iron in it was cleverly concealed and ran from one corner of the thing along a groove in the floor, and up the wall to the outside, presumably to the roof.

What I didn't find were any traps, no magic writing, and the stupid chicken's foot had yet to so much as twitch.

With no sign of danger, I lifted the lid of this stone reliquary.

After a quick glance inside I closed the lid, peaked again, then leaned on it and gibbered. This, could not be, happening.

Screwing my eyes shut, I slowly rose to my feet and lifted the lid once more, it didn't resist, didn't creak, and moved as easily as before.

Inside I found dust, a few scraps of cloth that were lost to age, and a silver belt. The belt was skulls cast in silver joined by links, rings really, with a basic latch. A simple thing, not cheap but well made. I had seen such belts on women who walked the night looking for coin, just none with such a gruesome esthetic.

A woman's voice, in Trade Speak, brought me out of my frustrated search. "She's not in there."

I hadn't heard anyone come in, gods above and below that spell made me stupid. I jerked my body to face her and the hoard of guard that undoubtably would be escorting her to check on the noise I had been making. As I readied myself for a fight, my hand slipped on the lid, and it came rushing down. Ok so readying myself for a fight looks a lot like jumping in fright. I may or may not have made some strange noises as well. The lid was swinging down and would have landed on me, I had to roll to get out of its way and not be trapped inside the stone box. I wound up on my ass looking up at my new 'friend'.

My mouth went dry, before me was a LeatherWing, her skin was white as the marble of the cist. Her ghost white hair was in a tight braid that trailed down between her wings, and she was dressed in a loin cloth and a top. It was tied behind her neck to cover her breasts while letting you know they were very much there.

She wore sandals on her clawed feet, feet meant to grab and tear, but she couldn't do that with those shoes on. The backs of them had long protruding heels, two of them that left a toe hanging out the back. Walking in them must have been a kind of torture. Her legs were shaped like a dogs or other beasts, but she was mostly human otherwise, if you ignored the wings or the tiny horns above her eyebrows and down the center of her forehead. Her eyes were green, and she looked far more amused to find me there than shocked.

Finally, I managed, "What do you mean?"

She walked over to one of the bookshelves and put something back, I hadn't even realized she was holding anything. I'd never been this close to one before, I didn't realize they could be so beautiful.

She nodded back to the empty reliquary. "She didn't lay down again after the last war. It took us two generations to find that out." She turned and looked at me. "That's why you came right? To see if she was really dead?"

I found my mouth answering before my brain caught up. "A bone, I was to bring back a bone."

She shook her head, "Sorry to disappoint, but I will tell you the same thing I told the last two. As soon as you set foot through those doors the laws freed you of the compulsion." She smiled at me. "You're free."

Confusion filled me. "Two others?" Then what she said hit me, "What do you mean I'm free, the laws freed me." The LAW has never freed me in my life.

She gave me a sad smile and turned to face me. "Around here we are very big on free will. Here in this place such a curse can't hold. You, like they, can simply leave and live your life."

I looked at her as if she had lost her mind.

"Sadly, they chose to attack me and died." She looked disappointed at that thought, then intrigued. "Will you?"

I looked over at the abomination, such a central position, so important, then back over to this... woman. I concentrated for a moment, that feeling, that pull, the voice, it had been there so long. I still felt it, I could feel the words.

But...

But...

I wasn't being forced anymore. My mind reeled, as I concentrated on the sound of that bastard's words, they were fading.

"Feels good to be free, no?" I jumped when she spoke again. She had kept her distance, hands lose and out by her sides, wings folded in tight. Even the way she held her head was non-threatening.

She was treating me like a spooked dog.

To be honest, that was not far from the truth.

Only one question had burned itself into my mind.

"Why? Why free me from that? Why not just kill me?" Ok so more than one, give me a break. This job might still cost me my life instead of paying me in it.

She looked at me, cocked her head as if listening to some far-off sound, then she looked back at that thing. "It disturbs you doesn't it" she asked and gestured towards it, "her throne bothers you?"

I screwed my eyes shut. If she wanted me dead, I would be dead. She was too far away for me to make a break for her or the door before their guard came. That abomination was their glorious leader's throne. A leader I was supposed to bring back proof of her death, proof that didn't exist because she wasn't dead. The Beast that sat upon that pile of bone was very much still alive.

Her tone was completely dismissive, "Always, they misunderstand. What an odd and backward culture you must come from."

That got my blood boiling.

I mean, yeah, I was a thief. I had taken a few hearts as well as jewels, even took one of my lover's family jewels because they thought fucking me meant they owned me. I had known a life, and a hard one at that, I was selfish to the same degree everyone else was. After all who else was going to look after me?

"Backwards?" Having your culture questioned, to be called backward, by creatures who used bone as a chief decoration? "You", I gestured at the thing behind me, "that is monstrous, an abomination." How many skulls had I seen at that glance, how many dead for her to sit upon?

"Yes, backwards. You see horror, and so do I, but I bet the horror we each see, are two very different things." She looked me up and down, "What's more I bet you a good meal, a hot bath and a warm bed that after I tell you the horror I see, yours will pale."

I shook my head, nothing she could say would be worse than what I was thinking, so it was a fool's bet, but I couldn't pay up. "Sorry, I don't make bets I can't pay, and when I win, I've got nothing."

Her chin went up, "If you win, I will give you a hundred Small Crown, a horse and an escort to anywhere you wish, including far away from the task masters that sent you here. If I win, I feed you, bathe you, and look after you. Simple as that. I will even let you go first."

A hundred gold and a horse? I could lose the escort simple enough. When you have a hand full of aces and The Wheel, it doesn't matter what you bet, not here anyway, I had nothing to lose.

I looked back at it and steeled myself, I still thought my chances of leaving here alive so small as to not matter. Creatures like this often did things on whim and I was about to insult her whole way of life.

Taking a deep breath, I spoke what well could be my last words. Well, last words if you didn't count, gods no gods no.

"I see madness. Murder and death, she surrounds herself with it. Her seat of power is the dead." I swallowed hard. Doing my best to keep an eye on her while still looking at that dreadful chair. "She rules by fear, every person who stands in her presence has to look at those empty sockets and wonder what that person did to earn such a dubious honor." See, I worked for a guy once, a guild leader who had much the same taste in decor. I knew the type. "She won't hesitate to kill, to maim, just to get her point across, hells maybe even just for jollies. It's a way for people like her to gloat."

I looked back at her. The ball was now in her court, and she had to convince me I was wrong with one argument. Else wise she wouldn't win the bet. I was sitting pretty, either I was dead soon or a hundred gold richer, and since no twisted truth she said could justify that thing I knew I had won.

Yet... she didn't look shaken or upset.

She smiled and shook her head.

"My turn." With a deep breath she began. "My Empress sits on a throne of her failures. Each bone is a life she herself ended. A life that will exist no more. Rather than just bury her past, pretend she didn't fail at peace, she sits on bone. Every death was someone she had to kill or execute, every single one of them is blood on her hands. They remind her daily how she should have tried harder to find a path to peace. That is the horror we see."

I shook my head. I had won. One hundred gold and a horse, if she kept the bargain that is. "Sorry, your little 'she sits upon her failure' doesn't change the fact that she's a monster."

She raised both eyebrows and looked at me? "Really? Pick a king, a lord, any ruler, how many do they order dead every day, how many do they send to death in war, and how many clothe themselves and their victories in gold, pretending blood doesn't drip from their exalted roosts? How many great leaders of yours sit on thrones of gold, genuflect to your gods of mercy, and hang men for stealing bread for their families? You think the horror of my tale was that my ruler sits upon her dead? No human, it's that your rulers do not."

With that she turned and walked out, and I followed behind, to settle our bet.

Author's Note 7

Blackthorn: Once a Thief, isn't required reading for the novels. I believe each of my novels should be able to stand on their own as their own works. I did Chloe's Collar that way, Chloe's Fathers and the Collection that is Chloe's Wars should feel the same. Having said that, there are things that happen here that matter, clues spread throughout. While each work can stand on their own as a self-contained story, I have also dropped threads of M'Diro and its plots throughout all of my works. These next 13 stories are the reason I've made this collection and I hope you enjoy.

1 Early Days & Life's Lessons

Medwch 17th 386 AFU

Every story starts somewhere, even mine. If I am to tell the truth, it started the day I decided not to be a beggar and petty thief anymore. The day I talked my best friend into a life where we made the calls, not someone else.

Our town, South Point, isn't small, but it isn't one of the huge places I keep hearing the merchants talk about, like Cliffport. Most of the houses are on the outskirts beyond the wall that guards the city proper. They are nice places, made of wood with sod covering the walls and roof. Grass grows on the sod, and it is kind of pretty.

Others, closer to the walls and city proper, are stone buildings or old wooden cabins with thatched roofs and stone fireplaces and chimneys. The fireplace's function is double; they are used to take care of heating, but also for the day-to-day cooking. Those wooden buildings are rough but not drafty, and while the stone ones are a sign of having more wealth, being outside the city they are still uneven and not polished.

The town's walls are carved stone and high, crenelated at the top and easy to defend. In its history this place, my hometown, had been an Unstoman outpost, trade depot and hub; thus, a garrison. This is why a town like ours, small though it is, has such good walls.

Inside those walls you have three distinct districts: the rich, the merchants, and the schlubs working for them. Out by the docks you have most of the town proper. Warehouse upon warehouse, some in good repair, some not. Now that the new docks have been built out into a deeper part of the river, the older ones are almost completely run down - though still useable. When the old docks were constructed, that area had the deepest waters, best for merchant ships carrying high priced rare goods, but so many years of use has built up the bottom making it too shallow for any but the barges that carry simple things. The old docks and areas around them have become the cheapest land and have tenements and slums galore. The new docks have them as well but being closer to the work means you get charged higher rent no matter the condition of your housing.

The merchant district is all polished brick buildings with clay shingles. It is the heart of the town. You can get anything in the South Point markets. Granted, you still have to go to the bad parts for some of the more interesting items, but if you work at it and ask around you can find it. There are about a score of houses here, all in good repair, used by the merchants and their families.

The town's center has both the Mayor's house, and houses of the local Lords. All small time, no royalty, but a few minor nobles. The Count keeps his Estate outside and to the north of town across the river. All the town's day to day business is run by a Mayor that the Count appointed.

In town there are about five exceptionally fine houses, one of them has even got three whole stories... not counting attics, of course. If counted like that, then all the finer homes stand three stories tall.

Also, in the center of town are two churches. The smaller of the buildings houses the Church of Pentagla. It's a small church with maybe two hundred adherents in town, most of whom are farmers and trappers that live outside the walls. One of the noble families is their patron, but the church itself is modest, unlike its neighbor.

The Church of Ca'talls stands as a genuinely magnificent edifice of the rich and powerful. Gold and gems are to be seen as soon as you walk through its wide oak doors. In its courtyard you can purchase clothing, toys, and such things to help support the local orphanage that the church owns and operates. Of course, to make such purchases you need to buy the coin of the church, as money - the root of all evil - is not allowed onto church grounds. You must have their chits to buy anything at their little 'Angel Made' market. Donations, however? I'm sure you can guess how that goes.

The orphanage sits outside of town by about a mile on its own small farm. I am more than familiar with it. It is where all the Angel Made items come from. The church does all manner of charitable work throughout the city and countryside. At least, that is what people believe. I decided to steal from that church. Convincing my partner to join in on it, however? That will be the issue.

"You gotta be kiddin' me, Chloe! A church? Of Ca'talls no less? We be smited 'fore we even make it to th' alter!" The gruff voice of the orc girl got others to take notice. They looked at the two of us and quickly turned away. Even at our age an orc is not to be trifled with.

Piper was not happy with my latest idea. She had found me on the streets, taught me how to live as a beggar and kept me safe. Since that time, we had been moving up in the world. Now, we had a break. She may not like some of my ideas but both of us had long grown tired of the hungry bellies that came from asking "them" for scraps.

I drank down the last of my watered beer and looked at her. "There are no gods to smite us, and even if there were, this is the same people I grew up in the care of, why you found me on the streets. Trust me. There is no god there."

With everything going on there in that place, it was as far from godly as you could get. Oh, on the surface everything looked alright. They do the dance of being pious better than most, but behind closed doors all they are, is just another bunch of rich leeches using legal slavery to make more money.

Piper made the sign used by her faith to invoke forgiveness and looked up toward the heavens for even thinking of such a thing. How had I managed to get saddled with a best friend that couldn't get that gods were fake? Beyond me, but I loved the girl and trusted her with my life. So what if she was superstitious? She was also smart. She would get it sooner or later.

"Chlo-Chlo girl, you gonna get us caught and roasted 'stead of just caught. I gots no intention of takin' a trip to the coals for a few gold."

I smiled and looked up at her. Piper was over six feet tall, and whip cord thin. She had board straight black hair that cascaded down her shoulders and skin the color of spring olives. As for her teeth, well, for an orc they were straight. Hells, they were straighter than some humans.

Unlike hers, my frame is small, and I have stringy and uncontrollable red curls that I keep short as best I can, because brushing that mess is pure unavoidable pain. With my pale skin that shows every smudge, and my blue-grey eyes, we made quite the odd-looking pair of girls, one human and one orc.

"Pip, I ain't talkin' about a few coins. I'm talking about all the candle holders, all the braziers and all the other things that were acquired after the new priest turned the orphanage into slave labor," I let my hands flop onto the table, hissing quietly through my teeth at her, "I am talking about twenty pounds of gold, or more!"

Piper and I had been partners for over a year, and friends since she took me in when I was about seven. We usually stole from those who were able to afford it or had it coming, never from the neighborhood, never from the poor. I, myself, would never dream of hitting a church, if that church was doing right by people. This one wasn't. I knew it and so did she, despite going there every Firstday.

She let out a sigh and shook her head, hair obscuring her face for a moment before she looked back at me, "Ain't no way we can move that stuff. No one take it, and it's gonna be far too hot soon as dawn come. Prob'ly 'fore then!"

Her jaw was set, but not in the 'we are not going to do this' way, more in the 'make it worth it' way. Piper was well aware of what was going on in that hell that was once an orphanage. The guard, of course, would not do anything. So, I hit her with the rest of it.

"Covered Pip." I grinned quite proud of myself, "Jax is a waitin'. All we got to do is get it out, and we get our cut. He be needin' us cuz kids walkin' in is no big. We got at least one, if not two more winters 'fore people take us as adults. And I, for one, am gettin' tired of bein' hungry and of just gettin' the scraps the nobles give out for the street kids." I waved my hand, "This'll keep us going for weeks, and maybe even get us a place without us worrying about being rousted."

Piper was not reassured. "Jax is a t'ief. He's only into himself and no others. Why he wants us in on this?"

She had a point. She and I were lifters and sometimes pick pockets. But Jax was big time, a Guild crony who had made good. He ran one of the crookedest money houses in the city. Nobles came to him when they didn't want their money noticed. He always had at least a few willing to fight the guard for him, but on the back end he was a fence.

I rolled my eyes, "Duh. We are young enough to slip in, and old enough to carry it. But you are right, he'll just get someone else to do it. I hear Tommy is getting desperate."

Tommy was a pinch purse that had the hands of an ox. He got caught more often than not, but since he had the face of an angel, he usually just got put on scrub gangs to wash the windows and streets for a week or two. The guard would make him on sight, him and his tears. It often fooled his marks, but it never worked on the guard. If they caught him at something like this, he would wind up short one of those clumsy meat hooks, and I knew Piper knew it.

Piper lowered her head, looking at me from underneath her thick brow, "Low Chlo, real low. But you right. Jax don't care who do it, long as it gets done." She stopped and thought for a moment. "He didn't ask for us, did he?"

I smiled to myself, "No, but I took it before someone else could."

***

Hours later and dead at night, well after last watch had started, we found ourselves outside the church. Piper had done the run around, and I had checked the doors. She got to go in to take up the time of the priest; go into her dumb orc song and dance. When it got hot, she would get super religious.

I got the snatch. It was a simple enough plan with a lot that could go wrong. If I make a sound while they are in the confessional, the priest will look out and the jig would be up.

It was biting cold, and that made for numb fingers. Despite the temperature I slipped off my shoes so the noise would be less, then tightened my shirt around me with a rope belt. Normally I keep it loose, it made me look more downtrodden when I did. Finally, I grabbed the number one possession of all waifs: a simple grain sack. Normally anything you owned tended to be kept in such a bag.

Yes, guards always wanted to have you turn them out, all supposedly to see what mischief a child was getting up to. At this time of night, with the possibility of the old priest kicking up a storm, I would be less noticeable if I looked a little suspicious. It would help me look more like part of the background.

I watched as Piper walked in, roused the priest from his prayers and got him to take her confession. If I knew her, she would have him bored but obligated inside of a minute. I counted to thirty while I sucked my fingers to keep them warm.

I slipped in when the moon passed behind a cloud. Sliding carefully along the stone floor not on tip toe, but on the balls of my feet. I danced from one place to another. I took what was new, and all of that was gold. My money, my work paid for some of this. I wasn't stealing so much as reclaiming what belonged to me. 'Angel Made' indeed.

Most of the lights had been put out for the night and the place was quiet. I could hear Piper going on about her gluttony and envy as she expounded on her sin. Blaming herself for her feelings as she watched a good, God-fearing family feast as she stared in their window. She really knew how to milk the guy's attention. In less than ten minutes I had danced back out into the shadows of the night.

I made my way to the alley where I would stash the stuff to wait on Piper. Her acting needed to be good, but I had faith in her. Then I felt something. Not much, but it made me stop for a second. I shook it off and moved on.

The pain of that mistake was immediate.

First, I could not understand why my head was suddenly moving forward faster than the rest of me. Then, I became aware of a sharp, almost tearing sensation, just at the back of my head where the hair stops, and the neck starts. Finally, a dull thud rang in my ears as I felt a crushing sensation.

When people tell me they remember getting hurt, I never believe them. I have yet to recognize pain for what it is when it first comes to call. Instead, I see it as a slowly opening flower of understanding that something has gone horribly wrong.

All these sensations dawned on me like a newly discovered secret as I watched the street rush up to greet me. My only thought being, how nice of it to do so, as suddenly all I wanted was sleep.

I came too with Jax standing over me. Looking up at him, I was confused. We weren't supposed to meet yet. I tried to speak but between my mouth and my words existed a chasm of pain and the realization that someone had hit me. Faintly, I heard my mouth open, and a sound escaped it, but whatever it was, it wasn't what I had wanted to say.

The dark-haired scoundrel loomed over me, chin thick with stubble as he smirked, yet somehow, he still sounded polite as he stated, "Change of plans love. No offense, but now I know I am going to get my merchandise. Not to worry, you'll still get your cut."

With that he tossed a bag down on my prone form. I grabbed it and looked back up at him. My mind still rang with the confusion and pain. Like the stupid child I was, I didn't recognize the double cross.

"Piper. Pip helped." I was still trying to deal with this man that had just had me assaulted.

He paused, "Oh, your little friend? Yes, I suppose fair is fair." With that, he tossed another bag on my chest. He and his bully boy walked off, leaving me there to my fate.

An hour later when Piper found me, I was still mostly senseless and bleeding, though not badly. I had not moved much and was clutching the bags tightly against my chest; fifteen shillings each, thirty total, a pittance of the worth of the score.

The worth of the lesson, however? Incalculable.

Piper, for her part, never made me feel bad for it, and we got just over a moon's wages for a grown man. We ate well, and we managed for a while to get a small space where we could keep warm. In some ways, it was still a win. At least we thought so. It took us time to trust Jax again or, as he put it, not trust him. It wasn't much, but it was a start, and we certainly never had to beg again.

From that start we built a working relationship with Jax. We also began to legally pay the rent to lease a warehouse. It was a nice beginning to our own little empire, and a good place to help others that had been turned out on the streets.

2 Hanna

Blodeuo 10th 389 AFU

All it takes is money.

We finally had some and knew exactly what we were going to do with it; set up a group home of our own. A place for kids to be out of the cold and rain. There was only one problem with it. Hanna.

Our pad is the last one in a line of old warehouses, and Hanna Vel'din was the poor unfortunate Guard who'd been tasked with the onerous duty of keeping squatters out. Hanna was a middle-aged woman, somewhere in her third decade, and had gray peeking through her blond hair. She had been a guard for so long that her leathers had faded from bright rust red to a muddier brown kind of color. For her to be assigned here, to our little home, meant she was severely out of favor.

It's an old place, and too far from both the new docks and the road to turn a decent coin. Our silver was all the owner had seen out of the place since someone bought all the land down river and made better docks. He couldn't sell the place because no one wanted it, which meant he was stuck with the taxes for it. If we paid the taxes and a little extra, he didn't care what we did there.

We spent the first few weeks just ducking her. We would get the kids we were taking in into the place and back out of it while she was off duty... right up until she started showing up when she was off shift.

So, we started making false trails and hiding places. We found hidden ways in and out, made sure there were distractions, and found other ways to hide the comings and goings of our tenants.

She worked through them all systematically, finding each and every one.

At the end of our rope, we looked into who this woman was. It turned out our new nemesis had once been an up-and-coming Guard Sergeant that had made it to that rank on nothing but her own merit. Not an easy feat in a profession with mostly men, a lot of whom were bullies.

Something happened, and, as politics were not her game, she got the worst duty they could give her. We had to do something, so we waited for her on her rounds and invited her to our office.

Piper and I were legally renting the place. Hanna found this hard to believe to start with, but when the drunkard of a landlord came down and explained us to be the actual proper tenants then, believing or not, she had to take him at his word.

"You've got to be kidding me. They're barely more than girls!" I stifled a giggle as her voice cracked.

The response she got to start with was a belch, that had an odor with it almost thick enough to see. We watched Hanna take a step back away from Wilfred, the owner of our little castle.

"Be that as is. They got the coin; they signed the proper documentation." Old Will had once been a well to do merchant, back when his father had been alive to run the place. He probably would have been fine had the new docks not been built. "There is no law against children owning or renting property to my knowledge."

She leaned back into the old drunk, "That's for the children of Lords, so they can learn. What are these two going to do with a warehouse?"

He met her gaze with one of his own. Will still had some steel not yet worn away by the rotgut he drank, "I don't care. If they pay on time, they can do anything they like with the place." He chuckled. "Ya can take 'em in, make a fuss, might even get them stripped of it. But as sure as you do that, one Lord will use it on the brat of another, and then where would we be?"

"There is a law against child labor. Where are they getting the money?"

"Not my care. Now be a good girl and take it up with them. Until they miss a payment, this place is theirs." With that he, his rotting finery, and stringy blond hair, got up and left the office of our little enterprise.

After watching him leave Hanna turned her glare on us. "Alright, then I will simply investigate you and make your lives miserable until you give this up."

I smiled at her, "How about we make it easy on you instead? Pip, would you be so kind as to show the good lady what exactly it is that we are doing here." Both Piper and I had worked hard to learn to speak 'properly' for just such occasions as this.

Piper stood; her own grin as fit to burst as mine. She took Hanna around and let her look in the small crates, the large ones, and so on. Showed her the pallets and the meager possessions of our tenets, none of whom were here for this. She showed her the working latrine we had rigged up to take the waste out, and the shower we had set up by tapping into the water barrels we had on the roof to collect the rain.

After an hour of poking around, they both came back to where I was still seated on top of the old desk someone had left from the last time this place had seen use.

Hanna got the first shot in, "So, you're some kind of slum lord?"

I watched Piper tense up for a moment before I shot back, "Far from it. Pip and I are from the streets. We go to the temple to learn readin' and writin', and we are looking to talk more proper." I chided myself for the slang that had crept in and doubled my efforts to keep it out, "And we rent our own rooms, but most kids ain't got a place. We begged and saved, then we opened this place, and we charge a farthing a night for anyone that wants floor space and a toilet. Shower's two farthing, but most don't take it."

She pursed her lips, "How many you got staying here most nights?"

"About a hundred."

She nodded, "I suppose it keeps them out of trouble, and out of the other warehouses, but I don't like it."

In this town there is in fact a law against sleeping in warehouses, and we all knew it.

"Look, I'll make you a deal." She pursed her lips again, and made a sour face, "You ain't gonna make much money like this, but I will tell you what. You keep them out of the other properties and keep whatever you're really doing low profile. Keep these kids off the street, throw in a shilling a month, and I will not only keep my mouth shut about what goes on down here, I will do my best to keep the other guard off your backs as well."

I could hear Piper's jaw pop as she tensed.

Everything we'd heard about this woman had said she was honest, and here she was shaking us down. We would see maybe three or four billonbuck in a month from our tenants, but as bribes went this one was small, too small. A shilling might be a lot of money to us, but she could earn that in a day by picking up extra work on the docks.

I held my hand out to stave off Piper's anger, "Why? That's more than we will make from our tenants in three months right now, true, but if you're going for a bribe, that's rather pitiful."

"It's not about the money. The money is so I can say to some people that I am being paid off. It means those people get to think they won." Her expression was grim, "I am no fool, and I know for a couple of pick pockets like you a single silver isn't much to come up with." Her words made Piper squirm, but I knew there was no way she didn't know what we were. "However, I don't care about that. I'm not on duty at the markets, so that's not my problem. What I do care about is that you can keep some of the street kids safe and keep them out of my hair down here. If you are doing that, I might be able to get what I need."

She was using us. Playing a game where she needed time. Whatever she was doing wasn't my problem. We would help each other out.

I stood and offered my hand, "Done."

With that handshake, two street kids bought themselves an honest guard.

3 Of Dwarves and Metal

Medwch 4th 390 AFU

"He's late."

I rolled my eyes. That was all Varian ever said when the contact didn't arrive when we did, even if we deliberately arrived early to scout the place. I stared up at the moons to give myself time to decide whether to respond to his whining or not.

Alhar had her round, silver face half covered by the night, while Pan's red form crossed and darkened even more of her brightness. The small red moon circled the larger one, so for part of each night Alhar was alone in the sky.

Varian is a good guy. Well, he is at least not a double crosser or snitch. Sometimes expectations for what qualifies as good are low in this line of work. I decided not to bother with his impatience, as it wasn't worth the fight. He's about a foot taller than me, and already starting into his beard growth, with black hair that hangs down to his swiftly broadening shoulders. His dark green eyes and fisher's tan help him blend into the night far better than my moon glow sheen does.

Piper and I worked with him anytime the score was big enough to permit a third. We'd been pulling a complicated lift and lay for the last year. It was meant to be a long game, but it didn't count as a con.

Piper, myself, and Varian were still young enough to slide into places unnoticed. We'd been using it to nick smalls; little things that wouldn't be noticed. Silverware, junk, old jewelry, odds and ends, but nothing that would be missed for at least several hours. It was low risk, which also meant low return. That is, until Piper came up with the idea of hording the stuff until we had enough to sell for some real money.

One silver fork doesn't get you much, but a whole set? A whole set, sold complete, was worth a lot more than a piece or two sold for scrap. The only problem was that you were running a higher risk the longer you had the goods on you. Sooner or later, you would be found out by the guards. We had an advantage most runts didn't, we had a pad, and we had Hanna.

So tonight, on the moonlit docks we sat waiting on our contact, all to unload all our junk and not so junk metal. We had it sorted into six piles; gold, mostly gold, looks like gold, silver, silver-plated, and iron. All of it was in neat little crates that we'd stacked on an old wagon.

We'd taken all the stones out of settings in the rings and stuff. Most of the rocks were nearly worthless, but we could sell them in bulk to one of the jewel-smiths at their own back door.

Our metal dealer was an old dwarf who was tired of the rip-off prices the nobles' made dwarves, or any race other than humans, pay. The forged documents were ready for him. We'd done this twice before and it worked both times. I learned Dwarven to deal with the guy, out of respect.

Oh, he understood perfect Trade and when he dealt with the local guilds, he used it. He said we were young enough to learn instead of treating him like he was lesser, and I agreed with him. It fit in with me and Piper both working to lose our street accents and needing to be seen as educated. The more we learned, and the more languages we picked up, the more we could deal with other peoples. More importantly, we could understand what was being said about us behind our backs.

We had no torches or lanterns to light the space near us, but we didn't need them as we were used to this area. The city sure wasn't going to put any out this way. It would have been a waste of money, time, and energy to keep them lit, not to mention taken care of, and replaced when they were inevitably stolen.

Varian started fidgeting, "You sure they comin'?"

"It's 'coming' and yes, he is." I frowned, "We got here early Var. Always get there a little early if you can. It helps prevent surprises."

"Or helps get ya caught. An' why ya keep work'n to talk like you better'n me?" He looked down his nose at me, "You an da orc both."

I sighed, "Varian, I want you to listen closely to me. When you act nervous, run, or talk like a street kid, the Guard take a bigger interest in you and harass you. Right now, if the Guard showed up, they'd want to know what we are doing. What would you say?"

He crossed his arms, "I'd tell 'em I ain't doin' nothin'."

I shook my head, "And they would then harass you." Giving any attitude to the guard meant you were hiding something even if you weren't, "You got to relax."

He snorted, "As if you a big timer. You as much of a runt as me."

He was right, we were both runts; the bottom rung on the Guild's ladder. "Yea, but you? You've been at this for what? Two years? Before that you were what?" Even through the shadows of night I could see him shift uncomfortably, "I'll tell you what you were. For as far back as you, your dad, or his dad could count you were fishers. You'd still be one if they hadn't locked your dad up."

His voice came out gruff, "So?"

"So, you are damned proud not to be one of the highfalutin, and that is fine, but it lets everyone peg you for what you are and where you come from soon as you open your trap." I took a deep breath, "Var, when you got nothing to hide and the guard search you, no harm. If you are up to no good, you want to appear to be as much someone the Guard don't want to stop as possible."

"Look like a badass. Got it, Chlo."

No, he didn't. "No, dumbass. Take us, right here. The Guard came out and started bugging us. What do we do to make sure we walk away clean?"

"Don' know, what?" He crossed his arms back over his chest and sulked at me.

I caught a flash of his eyes in the moonlight as he turned, and I grinned at him, "We're down here necking, or we were getting ready to, but I'm too nervous."

His reaction was an immediate, "Ewwww."

"Exactly. It makes them uncomfortable, we act uncomfortable, and everyone is a little put off."

"That works?" he asks, incredulous.

I smiled, "We become innocent by being caught doing something we shouldn't be, but which isn't the guards business. They caught us; we are embarrassed. It covers our guilt because they expect us to feel guilty about meeting out here to kiss and stuff."

"What happen if they ask 'bout da wagon?"

"What wagon? Oh, this thing?" My smile got bigger, predatory even. "We needed somewhere out of the way," I shuffled my feet and glanced over at the wagon as if for the first time, "It was here when we got here."

"An if they open it?"

"Then they open it. It is not our problem." I shrugged, "Hell, at that point we want to know what's in there too, and when was the last time you saw a guard turn something out or open something and everyone around not try to get a quick peek in?"

He thought about it for a moment, "True nuf."

"The only people that don't want to know what's in there are the people who already know what it is."

"Yea, but they'll take it if they open it," he whined.

"Yes, they will. And better they take that than they take us."

"But we'd lose months' worth o' work!" His whine hurt my ears, or maybe it was something deeper inside of me that felt that pain.

"Months of work, or your life? Your call, but for fuck's sake, grow some balls," I growled, "We are supposed to be professionals. Sometimes, you lose."

He's a great kid. If I kept telling myself that I might keep the patience needed not to ditch him. Piper was out moving the stones. I needed back up here, and despite everything, Varian was in on this and did his share of the work.

Note to self, we need a new partner.

"How we gonna signal 'em again?"

At that point, my patience ended. "Good gods, Var. Do you work for the Guard? Are you trying to get us caught? What signal? Should we light a lamp so that anyone looking this way can see it, and us?" I took a deep breath. I'd pray for sanity, but that would be insane. I don't talk to imaginary people. "We sit here, they see us, they load the crates. We get paid, we split the take. I get two you get one. One of my two goes to Pip." I spun and looked at him, hissing out through my teeth, "There it is, all out in the open. The Guard can come get me now and you can get your reward."

In a sullen voice he slurred at me, "I ain't no pigeon." His tone was dull, flat and dangerous.

I knew he wasn't. If I thought he was, I never would have said anything. I would have done everything I could to wave our contacts off. "No, you're not. Damn it, Var. You're nervous and that is just about as damned bad."

He crossed his arms, "They're late."

I heard something in the water. Turning towards the town center I saw a fresh light had been lit on the bell tower, like they did every mark, "No, they are right on time." I turned to greet our contact.

Dwarves live underground, so their eyes are sensitive to light. It makes them squint a lot during the day. Humans, tend not to trust them because of this. If all you are used to reading is humans, the squinting makes it look like they are hiding something. Don't get me wrong, they are almost always farmers and herders. They build terrace farms up into the mountainside and are as surefooted as the goats they keep. When they are deep in the mines, however, they see with heat. To them, any heat source shows light. They swear they can see perfectly well by the light given off by people, forges, even banked coals.

The shallow barge came from upriver and glided quietly up to the dock. We stood aside as they tied up the shallow bottomed craft and began disembarking. The first few off ignored us completely and went straight to the wagon with the crates. Varian started to move, but I touched his shoulder and brought him up short. When the last dwarf's feet hit the dock, the first of the crates went onto the boat.

That last dwarf walked up, and we traded pouch for papers. Now if they were boarded, they would have papers saying they were transporting twenty crates of iron. Only some of those crates, the ones at the back and bottom weren't iron.

After getting the bag Varian and I got off the dock quickly and quietly, ducking over to the shadows of the alley to hide. I reached in and pulled out one of three identical smaller pouches, passing it to him. He opened it and looked inside. "You sure it's all here? You didn' even offer to weigh it."

"It's either there, or it isn't. If it isn't, then we don't work with them again, and they get a bad reputation." You always hear about how there is no honor amongst thieves, but that isn't true. We just have a different code than most.

One, if you double cross someone, and that person is alive to talk, it will destroy you. Two, when on a job you trust your partner to do their part. If you are working a job and worried that your teammate is off doing something else, you are distracted.

If you are distracted, you are not doing your job. It really is as simple as that.

It was why Varian sometimes got on my nerves so bad. He always worried about what everyone else was up to. So far it hadn't cost us, but if he pulled much more of this crap, I would replace him.

He rubbed his hands on his sides as if trying to get oil off them, "Glad that's done. Dwarves give me the creeps."

I stopped, turned, and looked at him. I felt one of my eyebrows straining as it reached for my hair line while the other tried to drive my eye closed, "Huh?" It came out more grunt than word, and I hoped it conveyed my confusion, as well as the same warning the crunchy tinging sound of a booted foot hitting thin ice did.

"They're just so creepy. Walkin' round in the dark, grubbin' in the dirt, livin' in holes, and they smell."

Though Dwarves had a distinctive odor, I couldn't believe what I was hearing, "Excuse me?"

Dismissing me and them, he continued, "Don' worry 'bout it. Not like we got a lot of choice in things like this. Dwarven greed'll at least keep us in money, so long as they don' shave the coins they give us."

"Um, this is the third time I've dealt with these men. They have never been less than honest in our dealings." At this point I was still trying to reason with him.

"Yet. And who knows? They may be a good lot. Kind of like how you found an orc who isn't stupid. You seem to have knack for it, findin' honest dwarves an' a non-lazy, smart, orc. 'Course

Piper still sounds like a dum..." His words turned into a gagging sound at that point.

That was because my fist had just connected with his throat. "I think your mouth had better stay closed. Any sounds coming out that aren't an apology to Anthol and Pip, I might break your jaw for." Anthol had been nothing but honest with me. As for Piper? While True Orcs often were less than bright, thinking of them as dumb was a good way to find out how smart they could be. Half breeds like Piper often had brains that work as well as any humans.

Varian had doubled over from the shot to his windpipe but was quickly getting his breath back. "Fuck, Chloe, it's not like it ain't true. Damn, you think they were real people way you're actin'. It's not like they got souls or anything."

If you ever have the chance to fight fair, don't. He was still doubled over, so I pretended his head was a leather bladder stuffed with cork like the kind used for games. Funny thing was it made a similar sound.

I hoped I hadn't killed him, so my next shot was to his crotch. He curled up when I connected, so I knew I hadn't hurt anything he'd need.

"You can go find another crew. I won't tell Jax that you look down on some of your fellow guildies, and you don't mention a girl kicking your ass. I see you again, the deals off." My voice was cold, and that was when I realized how much he had gotten to me. Piper was the only person I had counted on in my whole life who hadn't abandoned me.

I don't like bigots. Jax doesn't stand for them either. Says it's damned unprofessional. To quote him, "Anyone can be a good thief, and anyone can be a good fence. Leave bigotry to the nobles, the merchants, and the good honest townsfolk."

A little pain might teach Varian not to judge, or maybe he would come after me. I didn't know, and I don't care. He wanted to make something of this, I would. If he left it, he would have his cut and a bit of a reputation that was still intact. His call, not mine.

As far as the actual job, when it was all said and done it went off without a hitch. Anthol took me and Piper down to the bar to celebrate a good deal. It may have been a seedy hole in the wall, but no one there asked questions. He spent the rest of the night teaching me more of the Dwarven language and culture.

Did you know drinking after you conclude a good deal is a Dwarven promise to continue trading fairly with you? Apparently, the nobility around here didn't.

That night Anthol told me of his wife and the fact that he had two daughters and six sons. Dwarves apparently believe in having big families.

I have to say I liked his culture. His gods were as weird as any other peoples, but they at least didn't interfere with how someone lived, nor condemn people for being people. The night had proven fruitful, and it was better to get Varian out now than later. As the Dwarven saying goes, 'All metal may look sound, but if you put a twist on it then strike, you find out its real worth.'

4 Men and Magic

Cryf 16th 391 AFU

"I know of something that will make you believe in the gods."
Oh, for the love of sanity, here we go again.
We sat in Black Boar Inn's common room drinking watered ale. Usually, we watched the out-of-towners that always seemed to be here and listened to their stories. The barbarians of the south and those of the east were always fun to listen to. Once in a while you got a Beast Man. Great Cats people with four breasts and animal skins for clothing. Sadly, nothing that exciting here tonight.
So, when we had no people to watch we discussed what ever came up, and about once a month Piper came up with a new argument. She was always good natured about it and always swore one of these days she would do it.
I shook my head. "All right Pip, go for it." The least I could do was humor her. Besides one day she might realize she had been lied to, to keep her where the high born and the priest thought she belonged.
"Member Olin Gord?" Olin was a guy we both seen around, he was a bit of a break boy. Big but not as dumb as he looked

or pretended. Olin, however, was dead. He had died when the Guard were on him and his partner.

"Yes. What he sent word from beyond that Meth'adilis is the one true heir to the throne of the All Father?" Ghosts were somewhat common, but they were all insane.

Piper grinned. "Something like that. The head priest brought him back."

"Back from the dead?" I shuddered.

It was ghoulish. The dead were dead. That a few mages and priest didn't leave them dead always made my skin crawl. "Is he ok?"

She punched me in the arm. "No, he was dead. They brought him back because apparently, he had been in the Lordships papers. They wanted to know who his accomplice was."

"No, I mean is it still," I paused for a moment and leaned in and whispered, "him?"

"Yes, from what I understand. They let him go this morning."

"They let him go? He died at the hands of the guard while committing a crime."

"No, his partner killed him. Cuzz of that Olin told 'em all they wanted'. And since he had already died for his crimes, the head Priest said let him go."

That seemed mighty decent of them. "Why's Olin doing papers and stuff to begin with?"

"Said someone paid him and sent him with his help. He was supposed to be muscle, probably one of the Lords spying on another. Now granted Olin's hair's all white now, and his eyes gone black. But he is alive."

"Pip, mages can do that too."

"Necromancers, and they got the power from ol' split tail. Devil can do stuff too, only it's twisted."

"I've never heard of anything a priest can do, that a mage can't, a mage or a swindler."

"We got a miracle right here, and you think nothing of it. You got to look for the beauty of life."

"I got a miracle a mage can do. And any how any mage will tell you that anyone can do what they do if you understand the way the world actually works. Stuff like the strings that hum at the smallest part of you, of everything. If that's true and you ask me, you want a true religion, you should worship a bard. Mages swear everything is made of these vibrations."

"Someone had to strike the first cord."

I snorted. "More likely something exploded elsewhere, and we are just the vibrations in a puddle of water."

"Well then, worship that."

"What? An accident? Then I would be worshiping my own life. It's one big accident." I decided to have some fun with her. "I like that actually. Chloe Blackthorn, Goddess of Accidents. I'd have a lot of followers if nothing else so they could placate me and ward off my bad luck."

She looked at me, face fallen. "S'not funny Clo. Better to have no god than a false one."

"How do you think these gods got started? Someone thought they would be a good idea and made them up." OK so I generally thought the motivation a little more sinister than that, but Piper was a good girl and my best friend. At least some of them had to be started out of someone's misguided notion of lying to people being good. After all, we tell small children a jolly man delivers toys to them while it was their parents all along.

To my surprise she smiled at me. "You're a smart person Chlo. Sooner or later, you will see their hand in the world around you."

"Aye my friend, and sooner or later I hope either your faith is rewarded, or you realize that they are just like us, thieves and liars.

5 Missing

Heliwr 26th 391 AFU

Nighttime for a street kid is one of the best times for begging. Good, upstanding stores are closing up and things like food that didn't sell are being tossed away, just like us. Every vendor recognizes that as soon as the day ends, the street kids will come around and scavenge. Most of them realize we will go through the rubbish for a bite. They can't stop us, and the guard won't stop us because the collectors get paid by the pound for the trash they haul off. So, at the end of every day there is a free market for us kids. We buy old and bruised picked over fruits, vegetables, sausage ends, and such for farthings and pennies. No one else wants the stuff.

Bakeries are the best. Fresh baked goods sell for quite a bit more than we can afford, day old is cheaper of course, and second day is still sellable for things like toast and for oldsters to give to the squirrels and birds. I know more than a few old timers that buy it just to resell as bird feed for the nobles. Come the third day it is far too hard to sell, and then we get our crack at it. The cheaper taverns will also by third day bread, but they usually prefer to buy fails, breads that didn't rise right or were a bit burnt.

Piper and I each had full sacks when we walked back into the warehouse that night. We had even managed to get a two-pound slab of butter that had sat out too long and yellowed. Tonight's toast wouldn't just be edible, it would actually taste good. We had started picking up the bread ourselves after a few of our kids got pinched by the guard for stealing it. It wasn't true of course, but the guard needed someone to wash windows and kids were easy game. We started handing out the bread while we watched everyone else divvy up what other little bits they were adding to the pile. Piper kept looking around like she was waiting for something.

Arm deep in the sack to get the last of the loaves I looked over at her, "What? Seeing if anyone got meat scraps to cook?"

Without looking back my way, "Lowll's not here."

That stopped me. Lowll was a kid with six winters under his belt. He might be late, but he should have been here as he was paid up for the week. Kid had a knack for getting big bowls, beggar bowls that filled up with coins fast, even if they were small coins. It'd gotten him into trouble more than a few times with people who felt they deserved his money more than he did. That's why we partnered him up.

I raised my voice and bellowed over the den, "Anyone seen Mal'nak?"

A gnome kid with wiry copper hair came running up. "S'up Chlo?" His small form only came up to about mid-thigh on me. Other than his size he looked like the rest of us, waifs that the world would rather forget.

I turned towards him and asked, "Where is Lowll, Mal?"

A simple roll of a shoulder was his first answer, annoying me, but his second answer pissed me off. "How's I suppose to keep track of him? Little leg pisser keeps running off."

I wanted to slap him, to shake him. If we didn't look after each other who the hell would? Our little enterprise had been going for years now and we even ran a kind of beggars' camp where we taught you how to get more sympathy and less kicks. As such, I got to know a lot of our tenants rather well. Unfortunately, we also had enough that though we identified them on sight we didn't really know everyone. I picked Mal'nak because I thought he could do the job. My fault, my bad.

Piper stepped forward and looked at him, "Where did you last see him?"

The little gnome looked at the floor and scraped his foot against the grimy floorboards, "Over by Second Square, down next to the garment districts."

My tongue didn't bother asking my brain if it was ok to speak, which I guess is a good thing because I was not so sure I would have been as nice if I had time to think about it, "You left him down by whore alley?"

The kid cringed as I reach back behind me for something to hit him with. Piper grabbed my arm, stopping me, "Not gonna help." She turned to the gnome, "Mal, we got to look out for each other. Go eat. I'll calm Chloe down, and we'll go find Lowll."

The little gnome nodded, head hanging low and looking like we'd come back with dread news of Lowll's death already. I hoped for Mal's sake Lowll was ok because if he wasn't I might kick his scrawny gnomish ass all over this place.

Back out in the night air Piper dragged me along behind her, making sure I couldn't go back and give the little shit a piece of my mind. "Chloe, how often have we left someone to their own devices?"

"Not the point," I snapped. The look she gave me took some of the fire out of me. "Things were simpler then. You are just as aware as I am that someone is grabbing kids off the street. Lowll's got a pretty face, I would hate for one of them to get ahold of him."

None of the whore houses dealt in kids, though most of them had more than a few hanging around. The prostitutes tended to look after their children, house girls did at any rate. Lately, the Guard had started picking up more and more kids off the street and sending them off to the orphanage. Still not a lot of them mind you, but more than normal and enough for the townspeople to notice. It took us a while to find out why. Someone was stealing kids right off the street, and the good churchgoers assumed that the orphanage would mean they were at least safe, with a side effect of them being out of sight and out of mind.

So, the Guard, as usual, were doing just enough to say they were doing something. There was a chance they had picked Lowll up, or that these snatchers had. Granted, I hadn't heard of anyone going missing that hadn't been just picked up by the Guard, but I wasn't quite ready to think the child snatching story was a complete lie. Not yet.

"Too much can happen to a boy like Lowll out here. Some drunk could mistake him for a woman, someone might have robbed him again, the guard are just as likely to have caught him and shipped him out to the Bishop's little slave labor camp. Anything really."

Piper looked at me, "Do you really think a drunk would mistake a six-year-old boy for a grown woman?"

I shook my head, "No, but I think that is exactly what they would tell the guard." That was one of the reasons I was so mad at Mal and myself, nobody cared about us and that was what made our little group so unusual. We were trying to change that.

She was about to argue, but I saw that argument die a grim death on her face as she realized I was right. "Come on, maybe he just got robbed again."

I hoped so.

***

We got down to Second Square just as the Alley Girls were doing a brisk trade. Most of the street girls had a place to take their fellas, Alley Girls couldn't afford that. We moved from alley to alley, shadow to shadow, trying not to be noticed. The girls didn't care what we saw, but some of their 'admirers' cared a little too much.

As we went, we whispered Lowll's name and tried to find the brat. I hoped he was down one of these back alleys since it meant I wasn't having to put up with the smell for nothing.

After seeing one too many girls bent over, or propped up on convenient crates, undoubtedly put there for support hours earlier, I caught the little bastard peeking out from some barrels watching a rutting. I snuck up behind him.

"It's so weird, isn't it?" Lowll barely moved as he spoke quietly, not wanting to interrupt the show. "We starve, are beaten, forgotten about, and ignored, and yet adults still fuck. Don't they get that's where us unwanted kids come from?"

I felt myself beam with pride, he had heard me coming. I put my hand on his shoulder. "Come on squirt." I led him away from the adults and their pursuits.

After whistling to let Piper in on me finding him, I tried to answer his question to the best of my ability. "I wish I knew what to tell you little man. I've seen people do that pretty much in every alley and dark space throughout the city. If they had kids every time they did it, it wouldn't be a few hundred of us, we'd be in the thousands."

He looked up at me. "Then why do it?"

I felt myself sighing, "The same reason they get so drunk they can't stand, or smoke so much green weed they sit in their own piss."

Grumpily he looked down, "The devil makes them do it."

"Oh kid, you have no idea how much a part of me wishes it was that simple. There are no devils, no gods. People do that so that for a few moments they can forget how much life sucks. They aren't bad people, they aren't weak." I shrugged, "They tried being strong for too long and broke. A person buying a bit of tail from a whore, a bottle from a tavern, or growing weed be it brown or green, when done in moderation keeps you sane. It's when you start drinking more than not, or screwing more than not, that you got a problem." I smiled at him and ruffled his hair. "And watch the language. Cursing is meant to shock people. If they hear you use it all the time, it loses its effectiveness."

Piper slid in beside us as we walked home, "And it makes you look crass."

I smiled and added "That too."

6 Sister of the Night

Tywyllwch 13th 392 AFU

When Sister Beth of the Ladies of Light sat down across from me, it took me a few moments to realize who she was. A Sister in this bar would be highly out of place, but seeing her in plain clothing shook me, almost as if she was naked somehow. It made me more uncomfortable than if she had come in wearing her full kit.

"I know it's you Chloe, you have your father's eyes," she whispered. As she smiled her deep brown skin crinkled around her almond-colored eyes. Her ebony hair was laced up in braids tight against her head. I guess it would have to be, her curls were far worse than mine. I always respected the woman, well, I did when I was younger. Now the things she stood for turned my stomach.

Sister Beth had tried to protect me when we were both at the orphanage. Unfortunately, she got sent out to a convent a few weeks before the new Bishop took over the place.

I looked straight at her staring her down, "My father felt church and god were worth more than me and mom. When he died his 'church' stole everything from us; gold, status, all of it. Like anyone of the faith, I figured it was right. Then mom died and I went to the orphanage, and that was right too. Then I, and others, were made into fools. I'm done with it. Ca'talls can rot." Anger stirred within me, giving my smile and my words a sarcastic tone, "If he's even real."

The woman before me didn't deserve my venom, as her only mistake was to believe in a lie that she'd been told her whole life. That made her kind of dumb, but she genuinely believed in helping others. Now, while she was as sweet as could be, she was also a painful reminder of something I had left behind me years before.

She swallowed hard and looked around to see if anyone was watching us, "Father forgive you, me, and everyone else. Your life is your own. I won't ask you to go back to the orphanage, but I do need your help."

I raised an eyebrow at her, waiting for her to continue. Despite what I wanted, I still could not stop myself from being mad with this woman. Her next words began to change my mind and make me like her better again.

"Chloe, I quit the Order," she leaned in and confessed, "The Bishop got stricter and stricter on the Tenets. It got to be so bad that simply disagreeing with him called for a striping. Then," she paused, disgusted, "Then I discovered he had taken to bedding some of the Sisters. Unwilling Sisters."

I leaned back, unimpressed. The Fathers and the Sisters bedding each other was nothing new to me. Chastity was supposed to be the rule, but I had long ago seen how well that went over. As for unwilling? While I was still at the orphanage, one of the Fathers took a special liking to one of the boys. Later, when he left, sent off to a different church or monastery or some such, the boy remained. That boy had a fear of people touching him for years and as far as I was aware, he still avoids it. As I got older, I came to understand what had happened, understand and resent that Priest for still being alive. Just another thing I hated the Church for, them and their lies of gods. I leaned back in my chair and stared at her, unmoved.

She sighed, "I know you have no love for the Order, the church or even the gods themselves." She smiled then, "People talk, and you have been preaching against the gods down here when you are drunk enough."

True enough, I suppose, though I wouldn't call it preaching. I guess when all you know is the hammer, all problems are nails.

The former sister leaned into me. "I am also aware that you spend a great deal of your ill-gotten gains helping others who have been turned out into the streets."

That froze me for a moment, and I leaned in closer to her, silently urging her to be quieter. If it got out what Piper and I were doing, there would be trouble. Other gangs would try to move in and exploit our little base of operations, as well as the rats we took in so they wouldn't starve. We had been at this for years now, and some of the littlest ones were as young as their fourth winter. Children turned out, outcasts, we took anyone... as long as they told no one. To some, little kids that young were keys into some very wealthy places. To others, they would get the same treatment that made me sick with the Church.

"Not here," I hissed through gritted teeth, still leaning in close, "Follow my lead and meet me down by the old wharf, last dock."

I jerked back away from her and stood up in one fluid, angry motion, knocking my chair over as I did. "You WHORE! Take your seed dripping ass and shove it back on the rod of that bald wank." I threw my drink at her and made damn sure it got her face, hair, and blouse. It confirmed the fact that she and I were not friends and that she and her company were not desirable to me. Also, it just felt good.

Petty? That was certain, but this woman and what she had stood for had ruined not only my life, but the lives of countless others. It had been going on for as long as they had been selling their false gods. How many had been slaughtered, starved, beaten, and all for faith? That drink was my divorce from who she used to be and helped me deal with the woman I would be helping.

***

When she arrived, she still had the same meek way of moving as any other Lady of Light; head bowed, hands clasped before her, eyes downcast.

"Beth dear, you have got to stop walking like that."

As I spoke, she spun around to face my direction. She had one hand clasped to her mouth while the other produced a strand of prayer beads from somewhere and clutched them to her chest, over her heart. A sound akin to that of a wren in the hands of a cruel child escaped her parted lips. She backed up and nearly tripped over her own feet to escape. The realization it was me might have been the only thing that kept her from outright bolting down the cobbled path, screaming about her virtue being in danger.

"Light and darkness! Lunavner take you child." She hissed out the curse from between thin pressed lips. She looked somewhere between the edge of tears and as if the measuring stick and my bottom would be having one of their long talks. "Tis not nice to sneak up on a folk. My heart nearly jumped to the demons to get away from you."

She cussed. Ok, definitely not the Sister I remembered. She never made it to Mother, and now she never would. I liked her better for it.

Suddenly, it clicked where her accent came from. She hailed from much further south, one of the human settlements on the coast looking out at the Narrow Sea. The Narrow Sea was a strait that separated the island that the old Empire started on from the rest of the mainland. She had grown up a crabber. It was hard work, and it created a hard people. If you startled one, the demon heart thing was a favorite saying of theirs, but it could also be considered complete blasphemy.

"Now now, sister. Language like that, and your Father won't protect you. Holding your prayer beads to your chest won't do a blasted thing." I chuckled and unfolded myself from the crate I rested on. This woman was a decade older than me at the least, yet here and now? I was the adult and wiser in the way of things.

Shaking my head, I tossed her a dagger still in its new leather sheath. It hadn't cost me much, but still it was a decent blade. "That'll do you more good than a few wooden beads."

She nodded and slipped the dagger into her sleeve. If she ever got that trick with the beads transferred over to the dagger, she might be dangerous to more than herself. "All right, this is close to my place. No one else's territory. So, talk." I sat to listen, but still I suspected that I was wasting my time with her.

She spoke, and my world turned upside down, "Someone is trying to become a Whore Master in town. They are squeezing every house, room and back-alley girl and guy in town. It's all been quiet and no; the Guard don't care. They might be in on it." Her eyes were once again down cast, "So we need help."

I was shaken to my core. She just said 'we'.

This sister really had fallen from the teachings. She smiled at me with the look of someone that knew my perch had just been shaken and my footing was not as sure as it had been even a moment ago. Unfortunately, it was obvious she still had no street smarts. That meant she could only be a house girl, she had to be one to claim 'we'.

"After I left, well let's just say I got sent to the Order because I hungered." She glanced at me from under hooded eyes, a red flush crept up her cheeks. "It is what the people where I am from call a woman or girl who wants to dominate men in the bedding. It's not a rod of rulership, it's a handle," she explained, "You can turn a man any way you want with their stick. My father sent me to the convent to straighten me up. For a while I became happy. I believed in them."

I could feel the confusion starting to show on my face, "I thought you needed my help because that fat, wet fart of a man is bedding Sisters." I narrowed my eyes suspiciously, hoping she hadn't noticed the confusion. Real feelings were bad for business if they crawled across your face.

"No, that's why I quit the Order. I came to you because I've got several Walkers that no longer have a home to go back to.

We hope you can get us an 'in' to talk to the Thieves Guild's Master."

I felt my eyes widen, "I thought the works had a council of people who oversaw things."

She shook her head. "Taken out, all of them are in jail."

I took a pace toward her and waved my hand at the city in general, "Walkers, house tarts, even back alley is legal if it is after light fall. What are they in jail for?" The church didn't like it but one of the Lord's grandmothers had started out a whore. She had been an alley girl, if stories could be believed. She talked her husband into legalizing it after the marriage.

She turned to look straight at me again with a sick smile, "All of them for child running. They've also been accused of taking children off the streets."

My mouth hung open in horror. More than a few of the kids Piper and I took off the street had had that horror forced upon them. That the so-called Lords and Ladies of the Whore had done this made me hate them. From the look in her eyes everything must have shown on my face. Need to remember to stop doing that.

"They didn't do it Chloe." She shook her head and sighed. "Sure, some of them were smuggling kids out of town. Some of them keep kids for housework, but none of them ever let the idea that kids were for 'use' happen." Her gaze urged me to believe her as she continued in a beseeching tone, "They were so against it they helped stop it themselves whenever they found it."

Confusion clouded my mind. Some of those people were Lords and Ladies within the city. Minor nobility, and they were almost always looked down upon, about like the merchant lords were. "Then how could this happen?"

"Through lies, manipulation, planted documents, and faked evidence. Despite the potential scandal it's all being kept quiet." She looked directly into my eyes, "All the proof the Guard needs is a lot of kids in one place."

My blood ran cold. My place fit that bill, and at least one Guard knew it. "Are they going after everyone like that?"

"Well, yes." She looked confused for a minute. "That's one of the reasons I came to you, to warn you. I also thought it might go well, and it would help convince you to talk to the Guild Master for us."

I nodded, "I will get you in to see him. Meet me here again in three nights. Be prepared to grovel," I said with a sigh, "He'll like that."

Jax would help them. It would just be good business, but he would make Beth squirm first. "How is it you came to talk for them? The workers I mean."

"I may have been only working as one of them for a little over a year, but I've been helping them with healing for a very long time." She smiled sweetly, "I never thought of what they were doing as wrong."

With that, she walked off. As much as I hated it, Piper and I were about to turn a bunch of kids back out onto the street. If you got convicted of running kids as whores, it was the same penalty as if you raped one. You were burned at the stake. Nobody's worth me smelling my own flesh cooking.

Piper and I had to turn the kids away, but only for about a month. We finally came up with a way to have them and to survive a raid. Digging a tunnel down to the old docks made for a quick escape route.

Beth wouldn't be the last Sister to find me. The next time they came, they pulled my heartstrings.

7 Hopscotch

Gwynt 17Th 393 AFU

This inn is a complete dump, reeking of beer long since gone bad and sweat curdled on bodies that had worked on the docks through the heat of the day. What little light there is crawls forth from rancid fish oil lamps in desperate need of cleaning, and yet here I sit and wait for one of the Ladies of Light.

The old wenches working the floor were too slow to escape the hands of men who were either too desperate or too drunk to care that they were not beautiful. These women had never been beauties in their bloom of youth, and now were coated in the years of grime and exhaustion their lives brought them. I swear men will grab anything that does not move fast enough, but maybe they like the scrape of gums. I suppose it is better to get it from the old than the young.

Each time one of the women walked by me I lifted my arms as I had been forced to do at the orphanage. The old habit served me well, showing them I wasn't taking things and so keeping their attention off me. Granted, my shirt's tucks could have held every coin within reach, but the meager scraps this place offered were not worth the trouble. While I knew they were only doing as the Innkeeper demanded, it made me want to steal something just to spite them and I felt a little guilty for that. So, instead of the coins the wenches held I'd just nick a bottle from behind the bar. Why get the women in trouble when it wasn't their fault?

The Sister had taken my advice, her clothing was shabby and old. Not dirty, but not clean, instead colored with that dinge that all cloth gets with wear. Her hair flowed down to her waist, hanging loose. A sacrilege for her order, but one she believed necessary to help the children. Her feet were bare, and she'd walked through dust and ash to make them more like all the others here.

Despite all her work she was still the best-looking woman in this place, but we had taken that into account as well. She had dyed her lips with berry juice and used kohl on her eyelids. Tonight, the Sister masqueraded as the whore, and my whore at that. Even in this den, two women were something to be ignored if they were lovers, especially if one was not yet fully a woman and was buying a bit of skirt to play with. It made them all too uncomfortable to look at us, which was exactly what we wanted.

She played her part well, and she'd better as this wasn't a safe place for either of us. I'm old enough to be used by these drunks, and if I was, then Bretta certainly qualified. I at least belonged around here, and it was early enough that the danger wasn't as bad as it could have been. Even so, it was better to be safe than sorry. With us off the table as sport, the beer, and the maids that brought it, were of much more importance to these men.

Sadly, for what we were doing this den happened to be the safest place to meet. After all, if we were caught a bit of sport might be fun, at least compared to the hangman's noose or the stake. Stealing children from the Church was a crime that would make you taller for your last few uncomfortable moments of life... unless they thought you were using them for other things. For that, they burned you.

The Ladies of The Sacred Light believed all of this was worth the risk to get these children out of a place that used them for what amounted to slave labor, complete with daily beatings to maintain discipline. That's where I came in. I found them someplace to go, someplace not here. With children not being allowed to work there were plenty on the streets, but nearly two hundred new faces would be noticed.

A former Sister had approached me months before, driven out because of 'differences' with the new Bishop. I set her and her friends up with Jax. Now I found myself working with a different one on a heist. While it was dangerous for the two of us to be here, if the rest of the Sisters were thought to be in on the conspiracy, they would all feel that sudden drop too. So, for children, a Sister let someone she considered still a child pretend to touch the place where men would pay to lay their seed. For those same children, I pretended I liked what I found there.

I actually rested my hand against the underside of her leg with my wrist bent back at an almost painful angle, touching nothing that would make either of us more uncomfortable than we already were. What we seemed to be doing, from most angles, turned these drunks' guts. Not enough to throw us out, but enough so they looked anywhere but at us.

I leaned in for a lover's kiss upon her neck and whispered the words she yearned to hear. "My contact can get them all out at once. It is a risk, but in a moon they will be with the Dwarves. All of them starting new lives among the mountain Clans."

Anthol was a great man in my eyes, and very honorable. When I talked to him about this he didn't hesitate. For him and his Clan taking in these poor children was just a matter of course, like breathing... or drinking.

She leaned in to nibble my ear with the sweet caress of her teeth and tongue. Her words blew into my ear softly, "Good. God forgive me, I don't know how much more of this I can do. I pray every night for forgiveness, but the Bishop is wrong. If I must damn my soul to the hells to save those children, so be it."

Still in her ear softly, gently, I spoke, "Any god that would damn you for saving the abused is no god to worship, Sister." My words caused her to draw back, so I flipped my hand around and squeezed her thigh painfully. Her intake of breath seasoned with her fear and panic at being overheard made it sound a lover's utterance. The movement was noticed and for a moment we had eyes on us.

I may have misjudged. They may not have been drunk enough yet. Too drunk and they would join us whether we liked it or not. Too sober and they would throw us out, probably after a beating. Months of work about to be blown because I misread the crowd. I can be so stupid sometimes. Thankfully their interest faded as they felt shame for the excitement of watching us. Too drunk to throw us out, not yet brave enough to take us by force.

I reached up and pulled her back in, mouth slightly opened as if to kiss. I breathed my next words instead of speaking them. "Tonight. Make sure the South Gate is forgotten. The gatekeeper there is old. Take him wine before sundown. He'll be asleep before the bell."

I was terrified out of my mind, my guts cramped with fear. I needed to get this explained and quick. I didn't wish this woman any harm. "Then you and the others go to your bath meant to clean up the blood of womanhood." I paused and looked at her. "I know this is done once a week and not due for another two days yet. Make a stink about it, accuse one of your sisters of being of the fish," I smiled at her, "Say that you and the others insisted on being clean for the gods early rather than reek like you came from the docks." I put my forehead to hers and moved as if something far more private began out of sight. "For once the silliness men accuse women of will work in our favor. Your 'joy' at this task will cover our escape."

"How?" she whispered back to me, as much an exhaling of breath as a word.

"A strong wagon and vapors to make the kids sleep. We will move quickly and steal them all away." With that I shuddered and giggled. I made it sound as if it came from the throat of a much younger girl. The shuddering of the men nearest me let me know that we had our audience.

My actions, particularly that giggle, labeled me as 'touched'. Touched children tended to do things like drag a blade across your flesh because red is a much better color on you. It made them sorry for my whore, especially when I grabbed her and pulled her to her feet. "C'mon silly, let's go play outside. It is much too stinky in here." With that, our escape was made. A little discomfort avoided a great deal of pain. Screw my reputation, this might work even better for me and get me left alone if men like this thought me mad.

***

That night, I was still shuddering inside. We had done that three times now, and thankfully would never have to do it again. Each time did not get easier, as I had wrongly hoped. I knew it hadn't been easy on her either. She bore no unnatural love for children, and I had yet to have any interest in men... or women for that matter. I don't get the big deal and I'm not sure I want to.

The wagon stopped, letting me know we were here. Since I left, the local farms had grown up and around the place. As long as they paid taxes to the Church and the town the Bishop didn't care. The orphanage itself was big enough to hide its sins from prying eyes.

Like I said, this was not the best plan. We could only build one wagon, and two hundred children would not fit in it all at once, despite its size. Any kid we left here tonight would not be able to get out, so instead we were playing hopscotch. No idea where the term comes from, but it's used anytime you have to move a lot of contraband quickly.

Hopscotch is simple, but it requires a lot of people. For the first part of this we needed to move the kids out of the orphanage in a way that wouldn't be seen, and by not seen I mean in a way people might see and wouldn't care. To do that we managed to get a wagon that we made up to look like one of the drunk wagons the guard use. They are covered and a sight people see all the time but ignore. This wagon was a little different, however. Its 'drunk box' was detachable.

On the underside of the box were wheels so the box could be slid off the back while still loaded with the goods, or in this case kids, while a second empty box was placed back on the bare wagon frame. This type of set up can be used any time you have too much to move to fit on just one wagon, and two hundred kids definitely qualified. We picked an old, abandoned farm to make that switch. It was close enough to the orphanage to give us a fast turnaround, which meant we could do this as quickly as possible.

Getting the kids to the barn was only the set up for the game. Once the kids were at the farm, the sleeping children would be loaded into wheelbarrows, each with a person to wheel them along. A second set of wheelbarrows with people dressed the exact same way would also be there, but that one would have barley in it. The two similar sets of people would then go into the city carrying the goods to their ship, but the ones with the children would stop along the way and a new person with a wheelbarrow set up full of something else normal would go off. The goods, children in this case, are referred to as the pebble. The second set of non-illegal goods is called the skip. Each time the pebble lands in a spot a new skip leaves the spot when the pebble does.

By the time all was said and done, we would have four skips for every pebble making the chances of the guard catching the right group fairly slim. Skips could be anything that wouldn't get the guards attention when searched. The carriers of the skips would deliberately act out in small ways to call attention to themselves, all while the pebble merrily goes on their way as if carrying on a boring but normal menial task. Since all of this looks like what everyone expects, and the skip people are acting out in small ways; whistling, way too happy, going too fast, going too slow or whatever, this means the chance of the pebble being discovered is reduced even more. It works well with normal contraband or stolen goods; I had my doubts about it working well with children.

We had the farm lined up for that outside the city, a couple of warehouses ready inside of it, and now we had the players as well. We had built the wagon over the week before this last meetup, got a Guard uniform for Piper, and finalized the plans with Anthol. Piper was big enough to pass for a grown man in this light as long as she kept the hood up.

As for the rest of the players, we had an entire ship of Dwarves to help us. Fifty in all to carry both pebbles and skips. It might not have been comfortable, but small children will fit in barley sacks and those will stack quite nicely in wheelbarrows. I got to be the tosser, the one that started the whole game.

Walking up to the gate as if I belonged, and with the robes I wore I looked like I did, made it easy to go unnoticed. A skin of oil from inside the robes was quickly poured into the hinges to make sure things stayed quiet. Once past the door, which was mercifully unbarred, I hurried down the short hall to the back of the orphans' privy. The hallway started as a kindness from years gone by to make fetching water for the baths easier. The privy opened onto a room that should have held a mere fifty children.

In light of some of the recent arrests the church had no choice but to take even more children in. Everything happening on the other side of this door was perfectly legal. Hells, most people thought what the church did here was wonderful. They had no idea what was really happening just outside their city. The problem being most of them didn't want to know any more than they already did. As long as the children weren't underfoot, it could only be good for everyone.

The vapor I had was an alchemical concoction. It was meant for surgeries, or so I'd been told. Problem was it held dangers big enough that most healers wouldn't use it. Something about it being like drink, something a man could wind up seeking out, but for tonight it would work well enough. All I had to do was open the door, open the container, and slide it into the room. I would then shut the door and wait the fifteen minutes for it to do its work. Again, not the best plan, but it was all we had. I cracked the door open and got ready.

There is an old story about a kind of twisted saint named Murphy. He lived long ago and is said to have been a great hero. He became the patron saint for crap like this. Nothing in Murphy's plans ever went right, and yet he always came out on top. Tonight, he apparently decided to be with me.

A girl in a ragged shift stood waiting impatiently on the other side of the door. With the voice of a mouse, she spoke. "What took you so long? I been standing here since last bell. Are you here to save us or not?"

I blinked. No one should have known. If the kids had overheard, then the Clergy may have. This is what I get for working with amateurs. "Where did you hear that?"

"The girl told us. She said that a hero was coming to save the Priest by saving us."

"Saving the priests?" Now that confused me. The people doing this were in no danger that I knew of.

"She said, that if the hero didn't come soon that this place would run with blood, someone needed to put the world right again, that it starts with us."

One of the Sisters had a serious delusion. "Uh-huh, and which of the Sisters told you this?"

She stomped her foot defiantly, and yet somehow there was barely a sound as she squeaked, "No, silly, not one of the Sisters, a girl!" Under normal circumstances the insistent glare, the foot stomp, and the pout would have been cute... OK, even here it was cute, but I really didn't have time for this. Before I could say anything, she continued, "Only we can see her because she is a kid like us. The adults don't bother to look at her, even if she doesn't live here."

Right. No telling who the woman was then. I would have to find out, but not right now. Right now, I had to get back on schedule, "Ok love, whatever. You got to go to sleep now."

"NO!" She insisted, still quiet, "We are all awake and waiting. The lady said you were coming. We are ready to go."

Great! I couldn't afford a fight with the kid, the kids really, as more were awake and looking at me. Do that and risk causing enough noise to wake the House Guard or change plans. "All right, but you got to leave everything here and do exactly what you're told. No questions, no sounds." I hoped my new idea would work. She nodded and ran off telling the other kids. A few of them were obviously not believers like this little mouse, though all of them were as quiet as only abused children could be.

This might work out better than my plan. If, that is, the kids did what they were supposed to do. Dead weight, even as little of it as these kids were, is difficult to carry. The problem with this much live cargo is that it also has a mind and its own fear. For now, at least, I was the only inside man. A Dwarf would join me, but only after the kids fell asleep and that would no longer be happening.

What I witnessed next hurt me in ways I can never describe, and yet it made me proud of these kids. I knew I had made the right call. Two hundred kids all got together and left every last stitch of clothing not being worn, girls left their ragged dolls behind, and boys abandoned what few things they had too. Pallets and beds were stuffed with anything that made them child shaped. There was not a whimper, not a word, no sound from them but the faintest whisper of bare feet on cold stone.

With a dance that had the look of practice, two hundred kids moved like the ghosts that a hard life, rather than death, had made them. I did notice two other children helping all the others. One was the girl I now thought of as The Mouse, the other appeared to be a young woman closer to my own age. She obviously could have gotten out anytime but had stayed to take care of the kids. Given what was happening to these children, she must have suffered greatly, but each child trusted and obeyed her simple orders.

Right on time I emerged from the gate. Piper knew instantly that there had been a change of plans, asking quietly, "What's up?"

"They were ready for us."

"What? The guards?" The panic in her voice was almost funny.

"No, the children." With that, the first one came out of the gate. "Change of plan, we're going with a Snipe Hunt. Have the skip guys run the barley as planned. Each of the pebble guys will lead the kids down to the boats by the same route as before. The difference is, they are all street kids that are bugging them, which of course they should look a little put out by. When the Guard comes to intervene, they should brush it off with something like 'got little's at home, no big deal, they aren't doing no harm,' that kind of thing. Once they and the kids get down to the docks, we can run them in the tunnels and get them the rest of the way to the river. It might be higher stakes, but it will go faster this way. Tell them to stroll, and we don't want them taking direct routes or moving too quickly."

Piper nodded and grinned at this new plan; she hadn't liked the old one any more than I had.

A Snipe hunt is a big game of misdirection. The kind of thing to have people chasing their own tails going after things that don't exist. In this case we were going to turn the orphans into beggars. I turned towards the kids, "We want you to do something that will be very hard for you now. You must forget the pain and play. When we assign you a Dwarf to go with, I want you to sing songs, dance, and ask for food as if you are asking it of a Great Lord. You must be tiny little jesters hamming it up for the adults you are begging from, in this case the Dwarves."

I took a deep breath. I was relying on the good will, hope and humor of children who hadn't seen these things in so long I didn't know if they still knew them. The only thing going for us is the fact that kids tend to be invisible. If they even acted halfway decent this would work, just because the Guard didn't want to deal with them.

I looked them each in the eye, this was their chance for freedom, and I wasn't going to screw it up for them by being either overly complicated or too vague. "This is the style of begging most often used by those as small as you. Adults are much more likely to give money to you if you're funny. If you're seen as pathetic, you're more likely to get out of trouble when the Guard catch you. The adults will ignore you if you're pathetic and the Guard will run you in if you're happy. Got it?" The rules for a group like this were simple, and sadly heart wrenching.

One of the littlest piped up with, "Why they run you in if you happy?"

"Because if a poor kid is happy, it means they are up to something. What's more, if you're happy when the Guard stop you, it means to them that you don't respect them enough to be scared of them. So, even if you aren't doing anything wrong, they want to put the fear of the gods into you."

"That's not right," she pouted.

"Welcome to the world, kid." I reached over and rubbed her head gently. How she still had faith in a right and just world I couldn't understand. If this worked and we lived to see tomorrow she would learn. Then again, maybe not. This was supposed to get them a better life after all.

"What happened to you in there wasn't right. Now come on," I turned and nodded to my partner, "Pip, run the wagon by and let the House Guard see that someone is getting into trouble."

She smiled and got the wagon moving.

***

That night two hundred new homeless kids bugged a group of Dwarves that were in town to trade. The Guard logged it, but other than that no one noticed anything odd going on. Dawn saw the ship already on the waters and headed out. Good thing too.

An alarm bell split the morning air.

It seems some villain had stolen all the children out of the orphanage in the dead of night. By the end of it no one made the connection to us. If the dwarves had stolen kids why not take the homeless children that were bugging them? The Guard said that all the regular kids were on their corners being just as annoying as ever. Why go to all the trouble of stealing kids from a mile out of town when so many of the rats ran the streets?

The Sisters all got lashes for losing the children, as they were the ones blamed for the disappearance. This despite the House Guard confirming that all the Sisters were where they were supposed to be and that they had done their jobs.

Nobody ever talked about the two women alone in a seedy tavern enjoying each other. Nobody even thought to think that one of them was me.

It wasn't the perfect crime, it involved too much luck for that. If anyone ever figured out I had a hand in it, I may wind up paying for it. Yet if I had to do it all over again I would. I may not believe in the gods, or the hells, but if I went to the gallows tomorrow for this, I would go with my head held high.

I didn't need to believe in a hell, this world was hell enough. It was up to me, and others, to stop things like this whenever possible. It also meant that I had yet another excuse to never deal with any of those Sisters again.

A win-win in my book.

8 Raided

Blodeuo 3rd 393 AFU

As Piper came in, I gave her the look she deserved. I mean, how could she? I stood on the far side of the room with a shirt clutched in my hand. It was something to keep my hands busy.

She stopped, worry etched on her face as she looked at me, "What?"

She seemed genuinely confused, but I knew it was an act, it had to be. I mean how could she not know? Fine, I'd play along. I asked her oh so sweetly. "How was church?"

"It was church," she shrugged, giving me a puzzled frown, "What's going on?"

I stepped away from her, wrapping my arms tightly around my chest. We had both worked so long and so hard to get this. We'd come so close. The sting of betrayal ran deep inside me. Her faith, and the guilt they taught her to have, obviously meant more to her than all we had worked on.

I moved around the shabby little room we rented at the boarding house, fidgeting with the clothing I'd been folding. It's a good place to hang your hat if you don't have somewhere else to call your own, and the more central location made it easier to get things done. Things like making deals or setting up a job, not to mention arranging to sell goods, all without exposing the kids to harm or letting people know where our stuff was. We worked hard to keep the warehouse a secret, even sleeping here most of the time. We kept this place because we needed to, not because we wanted to. This way no one could even begin to accuse us of forcing the kids to stay at the warehouse. It wasn't the best of situations, but it wasn't the worst. It worked, and this place made for a good hub.

Now it's all we have left, and all because Piper couldn't keep her damn mouth shut. She'd been compelled, trained, to share every dirty deed, every trick, every emotion the church disagreed with, or the fires of damnation awaited her. Fires that were as much a lie as her imaginary gods.

"Damn it Chloe, what?" she demanded, worry sounding thick in her voice.

I turned my back to her, keeping my voice as calm and neutral as possible, "It's gone. The warehouse." The lump in my throat kept me from going on with what I had been about to say, so I changed strategies. Let's see if she could put two and two together for herself and get an answer that hadn't been spoon fed to her by her Priest. "The Bishop came today, walked right in and took everything."

"Gods, no. The kids?" she squeaked.

I relaxed a bit. The concern in her voice was genuine, so at least one of her priorities was right. That was today's only real good news. "Out in time, I got warning of the raid." I felt anger overwhelm the calm that thinking of the kids had momentarily brought up in me. The rapid transition of emotions got the better of me. "Fuck, Pip! How do you suppose he found out?

Every trinket, every ounce of goods, nearly a year and a half of work. All 'donated' to the church, your church."

She took a step back, "You don't think I told them, do you?"

"You go into that box and pour out your heart. Your priest told him." OK, so my voice definitely went higher with the last of my words. Yelling? I'm not sure I would call it yelling, but I was definitely angry.

Piper stood her ground. "Michael would never do that, never. He hates what the old goat is doing to the church." I noticed she didn't deny spilling all our secrets to him, though.

"It's gone, Pip. All our work!" I threw the shirt I'd been twisting in my hands at her, the one that I'd been trying to fold when she came in. Folding the clothing was to give me something to do to calm down.

That didn't work out particularly well, so I walked out instead.

***

She found me at the bar. We had little money left, but I had enough to buy a bottle of rotgut. Well, most of one. Despite the taste, most of the noxious liquid already found my guts to its liking. The smoke in the place wasn't bad. We always found ourselves at this bar... it's probably how she found me so quickly. I had hoped to be good and plowed by the time she showed up. Maybe then I could forgive her and move on. Then again, maybe not.

She sat down next to me and let out a long sigh. "Wasn't me. Remember that brat Valail? He works for the Bishop." She took the bottle from me and took a long pull before handing it back. "Took me a little while to find out what happened. Not that hard, really. Rather than wait on evidence, something you swear by, you thought Michael sold us out."

She was still defending the Priest and the fact that she was telling him everything. I mean how could she? I felt tears well up in my eyes, but then her words hit me, and my anger popped like a soap bubble in a breeze. Valail, one of the many kids we took in. Gods I hated that kid. Always preaching, always telling everyone that were going to burn. It got so bad I had to throw the little bastard out.

I felt low. No, not just low. A groan escaped me as I slumped forward to the table, I had gotten mad with Piper over this, and didn't even think of the little zealot shit stain.

Piper continued twisting the screw, "I asked our Hanna. Valail had never seen her, so that's good. She is in trouble with her Captain for this being on her route." Through sheer familiarity with Piper, I knew she had leaned back and was shrugging. She'd made her point; she wouldn't rub it in further. "Neither of us thinks this is as bad as it could have been, and she still wants to help us." I picked my head up off the table to look at her; to make sure I was right.

I saw her pick up the bottle again and make a face after she swallowed, "And they didn't get everything. They didn't know about the stacks. Our 'Lord Shamus' is still on the books, so we didn't lose it all. It's only a setback." She leaned forward and put her arm around me. The stacks were tomes and books we had saved from various places we hit. Most were worth at least some money, and some were worth a lot. They were damned hard to move, as books are too rare and too noticeable. Jax was helping, for thirty percent, but it still took weeks to move even one book. We weren't dead in the water, not yet.

I learned that day there were at least two sides to any story. Never assume.

9 Dreams

Cryfder 21st 394 AFU

The world of dreams is a funny place. There are hundreds of different things that can happen there.

Tonight, I was standing on an unfamiliar battlement, in armor both fine and gleaming, the steel reflecting the light of a setting sun. Beside me was a woman, plain and unassuming, and she was stretching her hand out as if to say all of this was mine. She was my 'mother,' but I knew that she wasn't, as my mother had been like me, her head a mass of copper curls. As soon as I thought that, this woman's hair was as well.

"War, it is inevitable." This not-my-mother looked at me, "You are my knight."

I looked at her. Her features shifted as I watched. "I'm dreaming." Dreams, I have always believed, are your own mind making a play in your head. They don't tell you anything you don't already know, but they do tell you things you don't want to know. See, I am at war. Every day of my life is a battle, for food, enough money for me, and enough to do some good in the world, enough to feed a few more hungry mouths than just mine. "What does this mean?" I already knew, it was my past, and my present.

Not-my-mother turned towards me, as I knew she would. Time to see what I wanted.

"The enemy is here." That's not helpful. "Never let it be said."

Did I mention I hate my dreams? They are always like this, someone telling me something, or I'm running from some unseen thing, sometimes I can even fly. After a repeated dream about a job, however, I started actually trying to listen to them. You see, Piper and I had planned out a hit on one of the larger homes, and I kept dreaming about it in the days leading up to the job. In the dream we got caught by the Guard.

On the night of the heist, I held back a bit and had everyone watch. Turned out a guard that I had seen while scoping out the place was actually the one on patrol. Tonight, he was being extra vigilant. I had obviously noticed the guy before, and my mind had worked it out. We went with the second entrance we had planned out. Since then, I always paid attention to any dream I have more than once. No, it isn't a power. It's just the way the mind works. Unless, of course, the guard would have eaten my entire crew with a mouth wide enough to swallow the river.

Dreams can be useful, but mostly they are crap like this. That doesn't mean there isn't something here. Sure, most are nonsense, but I had had this woman show up before.

Hanna smiled at me - great now she's Hanna – and stated, "Two noodles one pot, and more cookware than you know."

This was getting nowhere. I had made myself a promise that if I put this woman back in my dreams. I would find out why.

The scent of burning wood hung in the air.

"Why are you here, what am I missing?" The world shifted. I was standing in woods, no I don't know where, it was just me in the trees. No, not just me. Piper was standing there with a crusader's shield and a sword strapped to her hip, and we were with others. We were adventurers! Piper and I had talked of this, getting a group together and striking out. Mercenary work was good work, and if you made it big it came with titles. Suddenly, the shining armor and the parapets and war and the knight thing made sense. I relaxed, this was about the plan.

Not-my-mother turned to me both faraway and close at hand as she stood in the wood, "Get out!"

Not a bad idea, all things considered. We took a hit, a bad one, when the Bishop raided the warehouse. So bad that now either me or Piper always stayed there at night. It was my turn tonight. We needed to watch our stuff, make sure the kids got out, save anything we could; just in case something happened again.

The sun blazed hot upon me, high overhead, and I could smell the campfire.

"Pip and I are going to leave as soon as we can. We've got to find a few more people first, get some equipment, stuff like that." I could feel myself shrug even though I stood stark still.

One of the others in our little band, one with no face, screamed and ran.

"Passion burns, will you be passion?" Her hair went back to the flame of my mothers, only it was a literal fire now.

I did/didn't shrug again. "I do what I can, feed who I can. I help. I'm not a monster."

"I am!" Wreathed in flame and flowering vines not-my-mother erupted into a demon. The screams of the damned echoed off the walls in the office, the screams of children. "Fear not, soon you will suffer." The room shook, the burning got louder, and the smell engulfed me. "You will die, but it is only the beginning."

***

I jolted awake. I hate my upbringing. The echo, screams, and the smell followed me into the waking world. I could make out someone screaming my name. My mind reeled from the images of damnation fed to me as a child. I hate that that fear was still so much a part of my dreamscape, it meant I wasn't yet free of the lie of the gods.

***

As my mind cleared, I realized that someone really was screaming my name. I blinked, trying to free myself of the haze of the dream. My vision didn't clear, and the heat of the sun was still on my skin. I couldn't understand what was going on ... until I started coughing.

The room was awash in reds and oranges, the light was dulled by gray and black smoke, and the screams of the damned were real, they were the screams of the children, trapped like me, inside of an inferno!

"Chloe", she shook me harder, screaming at me as my mind started to understand what was going on. "Everything is burning! All the doors are blocked!" The girl beside me had come to me, and saved my life, all because I was the only adult. Her voice was high, screaming both to be heard over the roaring of the flames, and the panic of her impending death.

Fear does a lot of things to a person, paralyzing you as you try to think what to do is one of them. Yet this girl had fought that panic.

I pushed the chair I had been sitting in backward as I stood. It clattered to the floor and illustrated my mistake. The smoke was everywhere. Choking on the fumes, blinded by the light, and feeling my own panic, the heat told the story of how bad it was. I hit my knees, taking the girl with me.

I plan. It's what I do. "The water barrels, go to the water barrels." She didn't argue, she simply fled. Keeping low, trying to escape the smoke, I made my own way out of the little office and glanced around to see how bad it really was, and get my bearing.

Smoke was pouring up from the walls, but the fire hadn't eaten its way down, as of yet. Light was coming from the places in the roof that had caught and were burning through; places that were thin and had let rain in before. Now they let the fire in to rain little embers down upon us. In the center of it all was huddled a crush of human lambs – over a hundred street children, all of them staring at the fire licking its way through the cracks in the wall, the cracks in the doors, the cracks all around us. Full circle, we were engulfed in flame.

The girl I sent to the water barrels was screaming at me. "I'm here, now what?"

I shook myself. We would not die here, not like this, not now. My paranoia was about to pay out. The tunnels Piper and I had dug so the children could run in case of a raid, they were our way out.

"Listen to me, all of you!" I bellowed to be heard over the flames. "You will die if you stand. Take your shirts off and dunk them in the water, do it now!" Not a one of them moved. "Move, you bastards!" All of them jumped, but they got moving.

While they did as I had told them, I ran over and opened the largest of the tunnels... only to have smoke billow up from it. That let me know, more than anything else, this was deliberate. Someone wanted to cook us all.

I screamed and went for another tunnel. The same thing greeted me.

On to the next, then the next. All of them did the same.

I felt the tears run down my face, it wasn't from the smoke.

It left me with only one way out, just one. Piper and I always considered that if a raid came, we might be inside. As such, we had a tunnel dug for us from the office to the outside. We had tried to dig it ourselves, but it kept flooding. While all the other tunnels might have been damp, about halfway down to the river this one just filled up with water. We had to get the dwarves to finish it for us, something Anthol was more than happy to do.

It should be safe; no smoke, no flames, I could get out. I could swim.

Most of these kids couldn't.

I felt my face screw up. Looking around, I saw all the kids had broken out of it and did as I instructed. All of them looked at me for what to do next.

Screw it.

With the flames from the tunnels starting to show up as an orange light coming out of the openings, I smiled at them all. "Alright, everyone. We are all going to go into my office," I looked back over my shoulder to see that the far wall of said office was showing the burden of the flames as they forced their way inside. "And we are going to go out my special escape tunnel. It's safe because the last of it has got water in it. The fire can't get through the water, now, can it?"

I watched, cringing inside as all of them shook their heads. One of them spoke up. "I can't swim."

I smiled at him sweetly. "That's ok hun. It lets out in the river, but its right up next to the shore. You won't have to swim. The tunnel is small, so all you have to do is hold your breath and push yourself along on the sides. Got it? It'll be easy," and it would be. There wasn't enough room to swim the tunnel, that wasn't what I was worried about. The fifty feet of water was, as well as the panic that would hit when their lungs started burning for air.

"Everyone grab a small, we are going now." With that, I led them into the office, having them keep low as I turned my desk over. I pulled up the hidden trap door and was mercifully greeted with cool air. "Alright two by twos, go down until you get to the water, breathe deep until you feel your lungs fill up and start to get a little lightheaded, go in, and pull yourself along the floor and the walls."

"Where's it come out?" a small voice asked.

"Under the docks, now go." I practically pushed the first kid down into the hole. The ladder wasn't that high, only about seven feet. Only.

I stood there, well, squatted there as I listened to the cracking of the timbers and the growing roar of the fire, watching as the smoke filled the room. I waited for the kids to go before me.

To their credit the line never slowed down, so none of them balked at the water's edge. I briefly thought about just staying in the tunnel, but it wouldn't work. Piper and I may have been able to fit, but not all these kids. With the last of them down I fled, pulling the door closed behind me. The last sound was the crumbling of all our years of work.

The tunnel was pitch black, the only light down here was what we were fleeing from. As I moved on my belly, I could hear ahead of me the rapid breathing of the few children still in the space with me. I felt the wall on either side of me brushing my shoulders. I knew this place was big enough to handle Piper crawling through it, but somehow it seemed as if I banged the sides and top with every shuffle I made along the way. The breathing and coughing of children ahead of me was the only sound that echoed through the space. The cold gripped me. I imagined I could make out the sound of each child sliding into the cold water. I knew I could hear it lapping against the stone of this place.

My world narrowed down to just these few feet, and my final worry kept working its claws into my brain. If any of the children didn't make it through, if they passed out, they would block the tunnel and the rest of us would die down here. The tomblike feel of the place hit me hard. Moments ago, I would have given anything to be cooled down, now I would do almost anything to be warm again... anything but turn around.

My hands started to feel the damp on the stone before I reached the water's edge. By the time I got to it, I knew I was alone. Blind panic or courage had kept them moving, and all of them were in the water. The dwarves had insisted on small air shafts down here, now I was glad for it. I had argued so hard that it was unnecessary seeing as the tunnel was so short, and less than a dozen body lengths back, was the opening to my office. I gave in out of respect, now I was glad I did. The cool night air held a hint of the heat of the fire in it but, much more important, it meant that the smoke wasn't sucking all the good air out of here. If the children were anything like me, they had greedily sucked in the fresh air on the crawl through. Hopefully it gave them the breath needed to finish the trip.

I sucked my lungs so full they hurt and plunged into the water. The cold tore at me as I pulled myself deeper and deeper into the tube. I felt myself panic as I pulled my bulk along the bottom and felt my back scrape the upper stones. There was no one in front of me. Had they all been so quick?

I made it halfway before my mind registered what had happened. I was being pulled along. The closer I got to the other end, the faster the water around me pulled me along its course. Just as my lungs started to truly burn, I found I was no longer able to keep up as the water pulled me out and into the river proper.

I broke surface to the sounds of the nearby fire, as well as the sounds of children crying. I saw all of them clinging to the support struts of the docks. I tried to swim over to them, only to have my hands encounter the sand of the bottom. The current that had grabbed us kept the sand from filling up the hole of our escape route, good old Dwarven ingenuity, but it had swept some of the small children off their feet. I watched as the older, taller kids helped the younger and smaller ones out of the water.

I let the water move me to my feet and stood up to help. All of us were shivering from the cold of the water combined with the early spring breeze. "Go, run, find a place to hide. Don't go back to the fire. Be thankful you're alive, hide, and don't tell anyone you were in there when the fire started." My voice was horse, but I gave the message to every kid I saw.

I promptly refused to follow my own advice.

Hiding in shadows, I worked my way back towards the inferno. I watched as the Guard, and any local that could, heft bucket upon bucket of water onto what had once been my seat of power. A fire in a town made primarily of wood, especially these old docks and warehouses, was a nightmare no one wanted. I watched people try to contain the blaze from spreading to the next building, all of them dangerously dry. Ours wasn't the only building on fire, not by a long shot, but people were doing their best. For once it didn't matter – rich or poor, human or not - everyone was working to keep this from spreading.

As I looked around, I noticed someone besides me who wasn't working to stop the blaze. I knew why I wasn't, but why weren't they?

I snuck around behind them, staying to the darkness. As I got close, the roof of my home collapsed fanning the flames momentarily higher and illuminating his face, a face I knew!

Varian stood, a bucket beside him, with the tang of fish oil still wafting from him. That scent was so strong, that this close, it momentarily overpowered the scent of smoke. No one would think twice about the stink of fish oil, not this close to the docks. The grin painted across his face showed him caught up in the mad joy of his handiwork.

Rage gripped me completely, and I grabbed a discarded board.

He never saw me coming; never saw me swing.

I like to think that to him it was just a bolt of pain, as if the wrath of the gods themselves suddenly overtook him. With that first blow he crumbled to the ground, "Deal's off you sack of shit!" I wish I could say I spoke with all the white-hot rage I felt, but instead, those words were uttered with the same icy cold I felt in my core. I lifted the board again, getting a better handhold on it as I raised it over my head to finish this.

I would never, never know if all of them made it out. I would never know if any of them washed away never to be seen again, to either drown or to wash up in the wilderness downstream. I would never know how many died tonight, or if any did. And now? Neither would he. He wouldn't live to see his handiwork, to see his payday.

I swung down with all the force I could muster. My swing went wide as the ground beneath my feet suddenly fell away. Something around my waist was lifting me off the ground and screwing up the justice due to this murderer. I screamed my frustrated rage. To be so close and be denied!

A voice, one I knew, cut through the red that had become my world. "Not like this girl. Not like this." Hanna spun me around in her arms, taking up the last of the momentum of that fatal swing. "You're no killer." The board fell from my grasp as she pulled me in and hugged me close.

She petted my head and rocked me as I tried to explain who he was, and what he did, and why he needed to die. None of it would come out of my mouth right, but she got it anyway. "Calm, girl. I got him. You got him. Red handed. He's got fish oil all over him. He's got buckets of the stuff. Let me handle it. Did ya get everyone out?"

"I think so," I could feel the tears pour down my face. "They're better at minding Pip than me. I yelled" I sobbed into her, "some of them hide from me when I yell." Her arms crushed me against the hard exterior of her armor. She rocked me and made noises. "All the tunnels were burning too. Varian was out before the tunnels, he didn't know about them."

She put me at arm's length and looked at me, "How did he find out about them?"

"The same way we got hit before. All the kids know about the tunnels." I took a deep breath, composing myself. "He knew about the tunnels. He hired this animal."

A sigh escaped her, "Now Chloe you don't know that. You got no proof."

Only I did. "The kids know about all the tunnels but one, mine and Pip's. That's how we got out. My tunnel. No one knew about it but us, and it wasn't hit, or guarded. It's him, it has to be."

I watched as Hanna's face paled in the light of the fire. "Then you got to get proof."

***

Varian stood trial. Through the whole thing he kept talking about how no one could touch him. He kept saying someone would stop what was going on, right up until his legs danced a jig several feet above the ground.

Two days later the Bishop announced that a cousin of the local Duke had left him a large section of land. Between the squatters and the fire this Lord felt the land would be better off in the hands of the Church; that he, the Lord, believed he would find greener pastures in another town. That Lord's name was Shamus. He had the paperwork, the deeds and titles, everything.

Some of the holdings turned over to the church included lands and farms I had never heard of. I don't remember ever owning a farm, nor do I remember turning everything over to the Church.

The message was clear, he won ...

... for now.

10 The Day After

Gwynt 18th 396 AFU

I woke with a start and stifled a cry. My heart was pounding in my chest, but I didn't know where I was and didn't dare risk giving myself away. It was dark and I wasn't sure where I was. The last thing I remembered was Piper pushing me out of the way. I saw her fall, the Guard crawling on top of her, then one of them threw something at me, and then... nothing.

We'd been inside a house, the Bishop's place, but I seemed to just know every room, and where every door would open. The place was so familiar that I got distracted. The Watch showed up and cornered us.

I got distracted. I let myself become distracted on a job. What had I done?

We broke for the side door and made it to the courtyard. Piper pushed me out of the way as Guardsmen sprang out and on her. They would've been on me, should've been on me. I ran, looking back as I got to the wall and climbed to the top. Just as I got my feet under me to run, one of the Guard turned and threw something in my direction.

Whatever it was, it made my feet lose their grip on the wall and I fell.

As I sat up, the pain nearly overwhelmed me. Examining myself I found a small set of stitches right below my collar bone. The wound was small, not nearly enough for the amount of pain I was in, nor the stiffness in my shoulder. It took me a moment to take stock of my surroundings. I discovered I was in a simple, hard bed in a small, sparse room. A cell, but like at a church, not like a jail cell as there were no bars.

My movement must have alerted someone, because the door opened and flooded the room with light. In the door was Michael, a Priest from the Bishop's church. Pip's church, Pip's priest. I'd been caught after all.

"Don't make a sound and don't move. No one knows I brought you here after you fell from the wall. I was going to warn you and Piper that someone tipped them off. The Bishop's got a spy in your ranks."

I kept quiet, since it was much more likely he'd tipped them off. But? But I'd had such thoughts before. If he was the one who told, then why bring me here? Why hide me and stitch me up? I let go of my suspicions for the moment. "Got any idea who it is?"

"No," he shook his head, "but it has got to be someone who knew you were hitting his Holiness today. Did you find the papers?"

Piper had insisted that if we were going to be robbing the Bishop anyway, we should find his ledgers as well. Now I understood why. "No, the Guard were on us shortly after we got in. I guess the old bastard didn't want us getting caught with anything from that house."

"Probably not, but at least they aren't going to execute Piper." He sighed, "Not that the Bishop didn't try."

"How long have I been out?" I asked as panic seized me.

He grimaced, "Only two days, but they rushed the trial. Piper's been caught before." His voice turned cold as he quietly continued, rubbing his right wrist, "So the sentencing was pretty standard."

A lump I couldn't swallow formed in my throat. Piper had been caught before, but with this high profile a target there could only be one punishment. "Can you help?"

His frown deepened, "No, I am not allowed, nor is anyone else in the Church. You will have to go to the other temple, and even then, they won't take it as a charity case. Not this." He stood suddenly, "Damn. With those papers we would've proven his Lordship was behind all of it; broken the back of his blackmail." He looked at me again, "I am so sorry. I wish I could do more. It's my fault you were there."

I looked at him for a moment. "Yeah, you're right. I had a few houses picked out, but she said she wanted the Bishop. I agreed because I hate the motherless son of a festering boil, I just wasn't going to push for his place because of all my own baggage." The Bishop was scum, but he was hardly the only one. A figure simply called "His Holiness" was at least as bad.

He flinched, whether from me and my venom or from the cussing I didn't know, nor did I care. If he was looking for false sympathy, he wouldn't find it here. The words 'it's not your fault' weren't going to be leaving my lips. It was his fault as much as it was mine. My hatred, his cause, between us both, we cost Piper her hand.

As the burden wasn't his alone, I gave him what I could, "Look, I am as much to blame here as you are. I will take care of her, I vow it. For as long as she lets me." I'd do it anyway, but if Piper was right about him, he was already suffering as much as I was. I wasn't going to add to it.

"I'll do what I can as well. I may not be able to heal her myself, but I will see if I can find someone who can."

***

It took hours more of waiting before we could get me out of the very Church that wanted my head, but we did it. I left that place dressed as a Church page being let go to return home. So, what if I am a little old to be doing the job; hide my hair and suddenly I was a young boy, my size helped me look the part.

Two days after I woke up, Piper was released. When I picked her up, she was still mostly delirious with pain. Her right hand was gone. They know thieves will be collected by their families, their friends, maybe even by partners. They don't check to see. They want us well aware of what happens if you get caught too many times.

It's a warning, meant to deter further unlawfulness - some former Lord's idea of the best way to make sure thieves recognize that once the hand is off the crown will no longer foot your bill. Prisons are expensive, after all. Some people think it is a kindness to let the thief go back to their family to be taken care of rather than letting them rot away in a cell. Others think it's better to keep them locked up and out of the way of good and decent people. Neither group really gets that most people that lose their hands, are stealing bread to feed hungry bellies. It doesn't matter to the Guard if it's a hand in a purse or a hand in the bread stall.

Most real thieves don't get caught unless they are unlucky or betrayed like me and Piper.

I took her home, to all we had left after the fire. I thought about all of it on the way. This score we hadn't been stealing for riches, but for food and apparently evidence against the Bishop. All our supplies, as well as our stash, went up with the blaze at the warehouse. At least all the kids had gotten out. That was good, or so I kept telling myself.

In the end, Piper got caught so we would be able to pay the rent that is due here in a few days. This place charged far too much for the hovel it was, but here we were left in peace; our comings and goings weren't watched, and we could do our own cooking rather than relying on an Inn's kitchen.

I had to; I didn't have a choice. I would have to flip a trick to get the money we needed. It took time to plan a job, time we didn't have, so - rent first, then job.

I would start the planning now, do the flip and pay our rent, then do the job. Flipping might be a little gross, but I had no other option. Besides, the act itself is perfectly normal.

As long as the rent was paid, we'd be fine.

Sure.

We'd be fine.

11 To Trip a Trick

Gwynt 20th 396 AFU

As I left his room, my opinion on working girls both went way up, and way down. How could they do this, day after day? Didn't they like themselves? I hurt, tears stained my cheeks, and all the bastard had had to say on the fact was that it was nice to see me cry. Hell, he even gave me an extra silver for it. The son of a bitch paid me extra for crying during it.

Still, I had the rent taken care of and enough extra to get some red willow for Piper. Last night she woke screaming from a nightmare, something about the city surrounded by water and the Bishop killing me with a pike. Demons were with me as we tried to kill the Bishop, while Knights of the Order stood protecting us all. It says something that in Piper's mind this man is so evil that Holy Knights would fight side by side with demons to save me from him.

I made it almost home before I couldn't stand it anymore. I had to wash. I had to wash now.

I ducked into an alley, and me and a rain barrel started what promised to be a long talk. I could feel the tears streak my face once more as I washed.

I could do this, it wasn't that bad.

I scrubbed.

I scrubbed it again.

Gods help me, it was still coming out.

A hand grabbed my wrist. Someone had gotten that close, and I hadn't heard them. I was dead.

It was obviously not a breaker, a Guard, a thief, or a bully-boy. No real thief would keep that accent and, as I was still breathing and not being yelled at or dragged off to jail, it wasn't one of the others.

"Yer a little wild one ain'cha?" A woman whose hair was like flames escaping a hearth was looking at me with a warm smile on her face. One of her hands was vice like on my wrist, pulling it firmly away from myself, in her other hand was a basket of vegetables fresh from market.

She looked at me, and then looked down, then up into my eyes. "First time huh? And by the looks of it the bastard was none too gentle." She sighed and somehow looked both amused and reassuring, "Well, that ain't gonna do it, luv. Come on in, ye be splashin' the contents of me barrel, and while I don't be minding too much ye ain't gonna accomplish crap doin' it like that."

With that, I let her lead me inside her home. She was firm but gentle in her guidance of me, as if she were afraid I would bolt or hurt myself. She made sounds like you would make to a drunk on a wall's edge as she led me over and sat me down in an actual chair.

The kitchen I found myself in was large for a house this size, yet still small. It wasn't cramped, it was just... cozy.

This woman was one of the uppers, despite her Outland accent. These were the people you tend to leave alone. They were low enough to know that you have to fight to keep what's yours, but high enough for the Guard to believe what they said. They were not nobles, not merchants, so probably tradesmen. I looked around nervously. Things could still go bad for me in a place like this.

She smiled at me. "O' relax yer head, child. I was once yer age, and no, I didn't make it to me weddin' bed 'fore my skirt first hit me back. I ain't gonna lecture ye on how it's sacred. If it was sacred every time would result in a crotch-droppin'. I'm a woman, luv, not a Priest." She looked me over more thoroughly, "Be ye even a woman yet?"

All I could do was nod. My voice seemed to have wondered off all on its lonesome. It took me a few tries to find it. "A-a few winters ago."

She raised an eyebrow at me. "Really now, whole winters?" She patted my arm as I cringed. "Now don't be like that girl, I only made it two moons 'fore some boy talked mine up. Nice enough bloke, I guess. Almost in his twenties."

I made a face, and she snorted as she turned to get something from a chest, "Don't you be like that, neither. T'wernt nothing wrong with him and he was a damn site nicer than my husband's first turn at it, I'll tell ye that."

She turned back to me with a wine skin in her hands, "Now this, girl, is how ye clean. Didn't yer mam teach you this?"

First with the calling on gods I knew didn't exist like I was still a small child, now not being able to school my eyes, let alone my face? This was a bad day.

"Ah, dear heart I am so sorry, but ye gotta understand ye speak much too well to be mistaken for one of the streets."

"I worked hard to talk properly. Better chance of not getting hit." Forget schooling my face, my mouth had up and run away too. What the hell was wrong with me? Did sex leave me stupid?

A soft chuckle came from her lips. "Girl, yer face says more than ye intend. Tell me, is he cute?"

I felt myself blossom crimson. "Just some guy," I mumbled. Instinctively, I clutched at the coins still in the pouch. She looked at me, then to the purse. Who the hell was this woman that she could read me so easily? I braced myself as recognition dawned on her face. So much for getting clean, I would be out in a moment, ducking and dodging blows. To the hells with that. I started to move and was turning towards the door before my butt left the chair.

Her hand caught me before I could do more than stand. "Calm down girl, I ain't gonna fuss at ye. Only the gods know what ye been through that made that option look good, but I got two things I will say on it for ye."

I stopped and looked at her with suspicion. She sat me on her kitchen table and arranged my legs with each foot on a different chair, legs agape much as they had been earlier, with him.

"First off, life makes all women whores." Of all the things she could have said, this is not what I was prepared for. "We all spread for men because of money. Be it because they love us, or our fathers sold us to them," she looked me in the face, "What ye be thinkin' a dowry is, girl? We all want to be taken care of, for some man to change our life, and for that we spread our legs. Only difference is a street girl does it for many men, where a wife does it for only one. And you know why we get told it's better that way?"

I shook my head. I had never had anyone talk to me this way before in my entire life. No one I knew had ever dared say such things, let alone say them so bluntly. It was kind of chilling.

"So that when something mewling drops out of our bellies some man can claim a boy for his heir, or a girl as a commodity to marry off. Can't do that if ye don't be knowing who put the little leech inside of ye."

I don't know what the look on my face was, but I do know if felt kind of scrunched up. "You don't like kids?"

"Oh, I love children! I love my own mightily. Hells, my sister had a girl who I guess would have been about your age, and I would have loved her just as much if I had ever met her."

"What happened to her?"

A soft smile spread across her face. "They died in the plague a few years back. More'n a few years at this point. My dad sold me off to my husband 'fore my sister was of age. She met a man of the church and fell in love. They moved to this city, so I got my husband to move here so I could be seeing her and my little niece. But, by the time I got my boys wrangled and my husband got his business moved, she'd passed on. The girl was dead too. I been to both their graves." She chuckled then. "Hells, even her husband had died a hero off in some war or other the year before, so no family here for me after all."

I nodded. A lot of the orphans at the home when I was there were in for the same reason. If her niece had lived, she probably would have been in the orphanage with me. That turned me sour. "Be glad she died. Orphans aren't treated well around here."

To my surprise she didn't yell at me for my attitude. "Ain't that just the truth, now? Don't get me wrong, I'd have taken her in, but that would have been months after they had already shuffled the poor girl off." She looked me in the eye. "There be no way to warn you of this proper. It will burn." With that said, she put the opening of the skin up to me, slipping it in. Then she released all the demons of hell on my insides.

"Bloody shit! What in the hells are you doin'?" It took everything I had to stay as still as I did. Even then, my ass was off the wood. My feet were still on the chairs and my arms were braced on the table, but the pain had me tensed and arched backwards.

As the vile fire filled me, I could hear the splash of the liquid hitting the floor. I didn't care. Tears welled in my eyes while whimpers escaped my lips. This hurt more than what that beast of a man had done to me. Was she punishing me for my impurity?

No that didn't feel right.

"It be kitchen vinegar with a little mulled wine, cut about half with water. It be stronger than it needs, but this way we can be sure the bastard gave you nothing. Neither crotch-spawn, nor crotch-rot." With that I felt the last of it run out of me. The fire died, but not all the way. I sat there and whimpered. "Now, when ye do this again, and don't be doing it with the vinegar more than about once a moon, usually after you stop the bleedin', make it four waters to only the one vinegar."

I nodded. I wasn't going to be taking her treacherous advice, but hey, I could at least pretend I was. "Thank you." It was the only thing I could think to say. The burning was still there, more like a dull ache now, and sadly this latest violation didn't leave me feeling dirty. Not like the first had.

"Now, to the other thing I was gonna be telling ye," She began as she bent down with cloth and bucket to clean the mess off the floor. "What ye did today is the start of a hard road, girl. Some can do it, some even like it, if ye believe the words they say, but it be hard. My husband's a tailor, an' some of his stuff be on the backs of women walking for their meals. We help 'em when we can, but it is hard on a girl. Takes a toll. Your first year of it you'll age ten." The water sloshed in the bucket as she rinsed the cloth for another go at the floor, "If you make it. After that it kinda peters out to about two years for every year on your back or knees, but by thirty summers ye'll be old. Old in body and old in heart. If yer lucky some man will want to make you honest before that, but as soon as ye drop no man will be takin' ye. Oh, they'll still buy an hour of yer time, but not buy ye for life. If ye be doin' this, then so be it. If ye got other options, I say do that. Though, if ye be doin' this, find a house not an alley. Houses at least have a Mum to looks after ye. Ye don't keep all the coin, but tis safer."

She stood up. "Now ye welcome to stay for a meal, I even got some basic work for ye if'n ye up to it."

"I wish I could." I was surprised to find I meant it. "But I gotta be getting back to my friend. She be needin' the coin for the healer so they can work on her." Damn, my accent was coming back listening to this woman.

She noticed my dismay. "Now there be a rat after my own heart, and a fine thing it is, too. Go on an' take care of your friend."

As I slid off the table, she moved fast and surprised me, grabbing hold of my shoulders and kissing me on my forehead.

"I'd a been blessed if'n my niece had half such a heart. May the Gods bless you and may the one that can call your heart find you soon." It was a blessing the likes of which I had never heard before, and for once being blessed didn't irritate me. This mad old bird could keep her imaginary friends. From me, today, she had earned the right to be delusional. As I headed through the door, I heard her call out to me once more, "If you be needing help again, my house will be here for you."

On the way back to my side of town I thought about it. Let's face it, she had sons older than me. She might try to marry me off to one, to make me an honest whore instead of a dishonest one. If today's events had taught me anything it was that I was a much better thief than I was a whore.

I was going to have to find and trust a new crew. It could be done.

12 Jax

Blodeuo 9th 396 AFU

Things were bad, really bad. Piper wasn't doing well and spent most of her time babbling at me about things I had no clue what they were. Her hand, or rather, the stump, was fevered hotter than she was, and she was hot enough for worry. She tried to hide it from me, hide the red lines and swelling creeping up her arm, because we didn't really have the money to get her to a proper healer. The barber had already come and gone, doing his worst. It just wasn't enough. Given that she was an Orc, she still had a decent chance of survival on her own. They were a hardy bunch and bounced back from sickness that put humans in the dirt, but decent was not good enough.

She'd pushed me out of the way, shoved me and let herself be caught by the Guard. I got her caught. In other words, she saved my life, possibly at the cost of her own.

So, I hooked up with a group of young-bloods. I was the senior, so it was my plan, my call, my hit. I had a Slight for the window and a Second-Story Man for the rope work, but the traps and alarms were my problem. The house was one of the only three-story ones with the jewel stand on the top floor. I had cased the place many times as a maid when they needed extra help for parties. There were lots of locks and lots of traps, and all of them were hidden well. A third-floor entrance had the least problems. It was a set of maid quarters that was largely unused for anything but extra storage for her 'Ladyship's' outrageous dress collection. Honestly, if I thought I could move the crap she called fashion I would. It might be worth more than the jewels, but clothing like that would never fence - it was too recognizable.

This was one of the other houses I had planned to hit, before everything happened... before Piper sacrificed herself for me. Now I was going to make good on it. Piper was supposed to be the strong man on this, and I couldn't stand the thought of replacing her. On top of that, who the hell did I trust who qualified as a strong man?

This was a good crew, and we were looking at forty small crowns for the pickup. My cut would cover rent and fixing Piper up, no problem. Our Slight was eleven winters old and called Re'll. The Second Story kid was a guy about my age called Bear, whose family fell on hard time later in life than most of us.

His dad had been a sweep and taught him harness and climbing work for when he took over the job. Unfortunately, his dad ran afoul of some high ranking Noble, someone that all the rumors just called 'Grace'. They had bought their way into the Houses, and nobody on the streets was sure if they were a Lord, Lady, or just rumor. They were a kind of boglin to blame misfortune on. I had worked with Bear before, and he was a nice guy. Piper and I had both considered asking him to join up with us.

The job itself went extremely well. Bear got us up to the right window, and I cut the wire and jimmied the lock slide as well as the bar. Re'll slipped in and out just as fast as you could want. Nothing went wrong. We were in and out in less than a quarter mark.

The problem didn't hit until we got almost to the way point to split up, so we could meet back at the fence. I stopped just beforehand, sensing something amiss. I had the bag and let the others go in before me.

Two Brass, the lowest level of guard, jumped them as they rounded the corner. I watch Bear take a sap to the head, and the other just picked up Re'll. Re'll didn't fight, he just let himself be pulled out of the way. I could have waded in, it might have bought enough time for Bear to get out.

Instead, I booked.

I had found our snitch. Someone had to tell the others, the locals, and the Guild about Re'll. I didn't owe Bear anything. He was a good kid, and I hated seeing him pinched, but it was a first roll. He would be bumped and bruised, but nothing more. Tomorrow would see him on a wash gang or street sweep.

I ran as fast as I could, but Re'll must have finally got through to them that there was another one of us, as I soon heard feet pounding behind me.

As I hit a proper street, the bricks underfoot gave my custom shoes more to grip than mud, letting me put a little more ass behind my sprint. I didn't look back, and these guys didn't use the whistle. That was odd, since it meant no back up. This stunk. Something was going on, and that something was bad.

I did a couple of loops through back alleys and got far enough ahead to duck. I sat and watched them look for me, as I pretended to be just another beggar boy. Short hair has its benefits. A quick donning of an old dirty cap, sit down, control your breathing, take the corner boys spot and his cart and no one even looks at you. Why look at a cripple, even if it is a kid?

When they moved on to look elsewhere, I slipped away. Jax's place had changed since the day he shorted us so long ago. He had moved to a more respectable part of town and was head of the Guild. He looked up as I slipped in.

See, Jax always does his own receiving. Much less theft that way, he says. He smiled at me as I closed the door. "Chloe my girl, on time as always. You keep this up you'll be sitting where I am one day," the cheer in his voice said more than the smile, but then his face fell. "How's Piper?" His concern was not for her health, not really, but a concern for one of his kids, his many hands. Being one handed might end her lift and lay days, but she was still good as a tough if she survived.

I had shut the door behind me and put the bar back down as he spoke. Jax raised an eyebrow at me but waited. As a gentleman, you covered the niceties first. I smiled at him, "Still fevered," then I looked him in the eye to add, "Fire the last guy you had bleed her. He said he didn't work on filthy Orcs. I had to persuade him."

Jax frowned at that. "Can't have racism in this Guild, it's bad for business. Poor doesn't know blood, nor does it know talent. I will see to him."

"That's not all," I took a deep breath, "Re'll is a snitch, Bear got the club. They were waiting on us at the split up."

Jax's frown turned to a dangerous scowl. He had, after all, been the one to recommend Re'll. "Careful love, for all you know he is my nephew, and did you go back for Bear?"

"No, and I don't care if he is your son, he's playing you." I was furious! Jax may be an ass, but he was a fair ass, and this wasn't fair.

"Good girl," he grinned at me, leaning back into his leather chair, "That is what I like to see. You did well, and Bear can handle a pinch. You also did right to stand up to me. If you ain't still keeping with that plan of letting out and hitting the roads for gold and adventure, I want you by my side. If you are, then when you get tired, you come see me. You've always got a job anywhere I am. As for Re'll, I'll handle him." With that he took the bag and handed me a sack of coin.

I was getting ready to leave when the door flung itself open without the permission of the occupants, the hinges, or the bar I'd put across it. I heard a mailed foot hit the floor.

Jax had long ago set up the door so if it was kicked in, doing so would give cover, at least for a second or two. A cloud of chalk dust obscured all vision in the room. I had been about to leave, so I was close enough to the door that it glanced off my shoulder, saving me from being completely coated in chalk, flour, or whatever it was. It also spun me to the bolt hole, though the shock of it numbed my hand enough to set the coin purse loose from my grasp.

The dust was already settling. The guards had simply come through with crossbows ready and pointed at Jax' desk. I had a choice, money or freedom. Then Jax did something I would never have guessed of him. He drew all attention to himself so I could get away.

With his hands held high he said in a loud voice "Oy, you sodden wankers! That door was bloody hard to make! Do you have any idea who all, in this tired, podunk town, owes me?" He was stabbing his finger into his chest and kicking his desk to make even more noise to cover my escape.

It was the last I saw of him, or the forty small.

I had escaped with my neck, but it was clear that 'house work' was too hot. When I got home, I was getting Piper and getting the Hells out of here. I was careful all the way home. Even then, it took me doing my best not to jump at every sound. At one point I hopped into a rain barrel to get the last of the dust off me.

As I entered the single room I had shared with my friend for over a year, my friend who I had been with since I was little, I found it empty.

In her normal place was a note. It simply said 'God wants me to move on, wants you to move on too. Got plans for you, he does. You be a good girl, and know you are loved. But me, my hand hurts, even though it isn't there. Goodbye Chloe Thunderhammer. Yes, I know, and have always known. Be safe.'

I broke down crying. I had never managed to convince her, to show her that Church was like any other con; like any long game she and I had pulled ourselves. Now, an imaginary man in the sky had come and taken away the last good thing I had. Rent was due in another two days, it would take the very last of my money. My last hope was the Fair.

If I could make it to Fair, I would be fine.

I would be fine.

I would be fine...

13 The Death of Reason

Aros 26th 397 AFU

I learned a great many things on the streets. I learned everyone is out for themselves and everyone uses everyone else. The man who gave you food and walked off? He was trying to make himself feel better or buy his way into Heaven. The Noble making a fuss about crime? More often than not, it's because he owns something down here and is trying to get heat off of himself.

People praying to a god? They're trying to curry favor.

Everyone has a price, and everyone wants to get paid. The greatest among us, our great and good leaders? I have seen nearly every one of them down by the docks, all of them doing what they condemn others for, and worse. Oh, good people do exist, but they are good because it makes them feel good. That's what a conscience is after all, your internal accuser.

I do good when I can. Mostly so I know I am not like them; like the ones that walk by starving children on the street and ask why the Guard doesn't lock them up where they will at least get fed. I lived my life like that. Trying desperately to not be 'one of those people.'

Too late, I realized the truth.

If I had spent more time looking after me, I would still have money. Still have a home. My stomach hurts. No, actually, that is a lie. I think it should hurt. It doesn't, not really. It just feels hollow. My chest is what hurts; my ribs, my muscles, hell even the skin feels cracked. The cold is both torture and relief.

The cold and wind beat at me. The snow and ice don't even crunch under my feet, since I don't weigh enough to break the surface. I can't remember the last time I ate anything, and the only sound I hear over the wind is the clicking-popping-rattle thing that happens when I breathe. I am glad that my nose doesn't work anymore, though I can still kind of smell the filth of the street. Of course, maybe that's just me I smell.

No one cares. The sick houses have turned me away so many times that they said if they saw me again, they would call the Guard. I stumble around, asking for farthings, anything. Anything at all. Maybe if I had money, they would let me in. I've been at it for hours now.

It's no use. They won, I lost.

They understood that if you aren't the user, then you are the used. Now I guess I am used up.

It's over. If I live through this, I will stop giving a shit about others and take care of me, and only me.

No, that's another lie. I can't do it. I would rather die than become like them. Even if no one but me ever honestly tries to help, at least I will know I did, and I don't care who knows and who doesn't.

I will know.

I see an alley, and it looks to be out of the wind. It's kind of dark, but maybe if I'm quiet I can get some rest next to one of the chimneys. A little warmth is better than none.

As I huddle next to the warmest spot of brick something occurs to me. How many are like that because they gave up? How many hungry nights until they became something they once reviled? How many good deeds turned against them before they started giving up? How many times did the world slap them before they figured out that the world wasn't fair and joined the ranks of the people doing the slapping? I could remember being younger, thinking that the world should be fair.

I knew what the problem was. It was money. If everyone got rid of money, then we could all live in good houses. People didn't need big fancy houses. That was just greedy. Everyone should be made to do what was right.

The more I thought of it, the more I wondered... but who's right? Maybe we could all agree on what was right? I chased the thought around for a long time, thinking how people could be made to be good, and exactly what good meant. That was when I ran into the ultimate problem, and with that thought I understood why religion was invented and how truly wrong it was.

Religion was exactly what I thought it was. A system of making people behave by giving them rules to live by, all of it enacted through fear, obligation, and guilt. People were punished when they worked against religion.

The fever was obviously worse than I thought. In my mind, I had almost endorsed the thing used to crush us all.

Maybe instead we could all just look after each other? Give away the food until all had enough to eat. Tear down all the fancy houses and give proper homes to all. Make sure everyone was treated with the basic dignity everyone is owed.

Of course, the problem with that became almost immediately apparent. Someone would have to be in control of it, and if they were in control then sooner or later, they would stop being fair. As far as the thought of keeping people armed to prevent that, how is armed better? As soon as someone wanted what someone weaker than them had, they would take it because they would be armed too.

No, sad as it was to say, we had the best system I could think of. The Lords may be greedy, but sooner or later you could shame them into doing the right thing. Hells, if you could complain loud enough and get people on your side you might even affect real change.

Coughing, I decided that was what I was going to do as soon as I could. Complain until I got enough people to give weight to my voice and change something.

The cold had other ideas. Slowly my aching limbs stopped aching. Cold became comfort and slowly I began to feel sort of warm. That was when I knew I was never going to get up again. I had heard this story too many times.

I was dead.

Well, one thing was for sure. Now I'd find out if I was right. Soon I would indeed know the answer, were there really gods, or not? If there were, I was so going to give him or them a piece of my mind.

Then I heard the wings, and I knew I was wrong. I looked up, sad to have been wrong, strange as that sounds. I was going to ask for an accounting of all the suffering I had to endure, mine and everyone else. I guess they knew that, since it wasn't an angel that came for me...

Author's Note 8

Beta readers are a good way to tell if you're on the right track, one of mine is a man named Moose. Moose is one of my dear friends and loved the short stories and novel, but had one burning question, "So, what happened with Piper?"

Piper, it seemed had become his favorite character in the stories. This next bit is dedicated to Moose. Here you go my friend.

Piper 1

The pain was intense. I had thought I had experienced the worst pain of my life the day they cut off my hand, but it was nothing compared to the weeks of recovery from the fever that had set into the stump. Chloe had done her best, but I knew she was getting desperate. She had spent a week talking herself into going out and being an Alley Girl to make enough silver to get me a decent healer. So, I left her a note while she was out one day, no idea what she was doing, but I wasn't worth her selling herself.

I snuck away and joined the miners at the quarry. Yeah, I know, it was for the Bishop's new Cathedral. At that point it was the only way I could see anyone fixing me up so the fever in my hand didn't take me. I had intended to use the time to gather more evidence for Jax to use against the Bishop.

They fixed me up all right, even set me up with a basic hook. I'm just glad the Guard didn't realize I was off handed. Losing my writing hand would have been a bit more than I could take.

As it was, the quarry foreman saw even a one-handed Orc as nothing more than a strong back. Despite everything I knew about the Bishop's double dealing and such, the work camp actually ran honestly. Within a week I was better and being worked hard, both pulling carts of stone, and helping to move the larger blocks. The place ran so well and so much on the up and up, I didn't notice the missing workers. After all, people 'drug up' and went off to other work all the time. It never occurred to me anything was going on, until one night I was the one 'drug up'.

Something must have been in my drink, because I didn't do more than roll over when they came in, two big guys, humans I think, and took me out to a covered wagon. It was a drunk wagon... the irony didn't escape me.

I came to, the next day in a different camp with shackles on my wrist and around the latch of my hook, which was now bolted into place. The chains were even around my ankles. I had been sold, it seemed, to a mine further north. See, slavery is illegal, except for chain gangs made out of low lives. That's perfectly legal, and with me missing a hand I was just another criminal sold to do work too dangerous for good, honest people.

I have no idea how long I was in that pit, but thankfully for me, they didn't realize a big dumb Orc could be a pickpocket. Someone hadn't scouted their target very well. I took my time and got the bolt's weld loosened, then off. Once free I made as much of a nuisance of myself as I could. No, I didn't tear anything up or make a sound, I released my fellow captives. While the blaggards took care of our employers, I snuck out of the compound and headed south.

Word to the wise, don't head south in winter. I was soon surrounded by more snow and ice than I had ever really had to deal with. I am a city girl after all.

So, we are clear here, I had my hand cut off, then the stump got infected, spent weeks in my best friend's care with no idea what was going on, and now I consider the pain I am currently in worse than both of those.

Ice, hobbled feet, and an unseen rock conspired to make me twist my leg.

A twisted ankle doesn't sound like much, and in truth when it happened, I would have agreed with you. I got off my ass thinking the only thing I had done was bruise my butt and worse, my pride, but like I said, I didn't grow up like this, in the snow and ice.

Snow and ice for me was a rare chance to play. Begging don't bring much when the high and mighty are sheltered in their warm homes or hurrying to one. They don't give a lot of coin then.

So, I had no idea walking on a sprain was stupid, nor did I know that much snow meant I didn't feel the injury as well as I should. The next morning it hurt, but I just grabbed a stick and moved on, the day after that it was worse, but by now I was getting close to South Point, close to home and my sister.

Chloe isn't exactly my sister, but she is damn close. She is this short little red headed human girl. Not at all like my over six-foot-tall self. With my olive-green skin and limp black hair, I look like my wild cousins, Orc Full Bloods, but I got human in me, even if the only thing it really gives me is a more human smile.

Whatever. Chloe has never treated me as anything other than a person. For that, I would brave any cold and a little hurt foot.

We Orcs are stocky, and by human standard naturally muscled. We're big, and strong. I think that is why humans always think we are so dumb.

When I woke this morning, I would have to agree with them. My leg had cramped up in the night. Calf, thigh, the whole thing, one giant cramp. What's worse is I think it pulled the bones out of the ankle socket.

In my dream, I felt the pain building, and for a moment I thought that I was still back in our little crap hole apartment waiting for Chloe to get back with medicine. It made me smile for a brief moment, till I realized it wasn't my arm hurting.

Nothing is like waking up to pain. A good morning wake up is this realization that you lived, and you can see the real world again. Chloe always woke like she was still among the lands of the dead, at least till we got something in her, usually chickaree when we could afford it.

This was like slowly being prodded, as your own body stands off to the side screaming something was wrong, but your instincts want you to stay asleep, so you don't feel it. All this while your survival will is joining your body telling you to run. As you wake you slowly become aware of your heart, only it isn't beating in your chest. Oh no, it is beating in the ankle making the pain worse with every pump of your heart, a pounding which is getting faster as you wake.

The fire was nearly out, and I had only gathered enough wood for the night last night. There was no way I was going to be moving today, but at least I had found a decent shelter in this little cave. It was a rock crag cut out of the side of one of the Great Smoking Mountains. They get the name from the ever-present mist that never seems to burn off. From a distance it looks like someone's campfire had burned low, and that mist was ever present, no matter which way you look.

The cave entrance was a little on the short side, I had to duck to get in, even limping like I was last night. It opened a few feet in and went back a good forty lengths. Nice and wide with an uneven floor as well as a few depressions for things like a fire pit. Someone had used this place for quite a while. Nothing was in here now, however. Be it ever so crumbled, it looked as if this might be home for a while. At least until I could get this traitorous leg to behave.

Wood was needed first, if it got any colder in here, I wouldn't live through the night, but walking was out of the question.

So, I crawled out into the snow.

Crawling in snow isn't fun, and here I was crawling with one hand, dragging my twisted leg behind me. I was gritting my teeth so hard I kept hearing these little pops as they ground against each other. I managed to get about two body lengths out before the pain exhausted me.

As I lay here in the snow, I can feel myself, sobbing.

"Damn it, damn it, Damn it!" It can't end this way, I will not die less than a day from home, less than a day from my sister. "You stupid, selfish cow. Too damn proud to let her help you, too damn proud." My eyes were wet, but they stung like they were dry as the cold wind whipped past my face.

"Admit it," I heard Chloe's voice as clearly as if she was standing right behind me. "You thought my virtue, and me not dying in hell, was worth more than your life. Completely forgetting that sacrifice is part of the bullshit they pour down your throat every Firstday."

I choked at the memory. She had never said any such thing, but she knew the word as well as every priest I had ever met. "No, I knew that it would break something in you to be a whore."

"Why? Because you couldn't do it? Look, I may have hated it, but I don't believe whores are bad. It's your bullshit gods that would rather people starve in the streets than get fucked for a little coin so they can feed their kids." Her words were so clear in my mind, I shook my head. I sat up and looked around for her. Who knows, maybe she really was standing right behind me.

As I searched the white landscape, I didn't see her. So, I answered her anyway. "I wasn't going to ask you to do something I wouldn't do. I would never ask that of you."

"You didn't ask me. Hell, one good shag and I could have gotten you the medicine and a healer and we could have coasted until I finished putting the crew together to do the job you and I already had planned." A soft chuckle echoed through the wood. "But no, just like the rest of your church, I can't make my own mistakes, you got to take it out of my hands."

"I couldn't let you do it." I found my strength again and stood up.

"Why not? For all you know I got fucked days before you left and that's how I got you the medicine that got you well enough to leave me." The voice was matter of fact. "Did you object because my father wouldn't approve? Because the Thunderhammer name means something?"

"Yes." I spun around looking for her. She was here damn it. I could hear her, hear the footsteps as she moved just out of my sight. "Yes, you're a noble. Hell, you're royalty."

From behind me again, "Is that why you were friends with me? Because I was a royal?"

Something in me snapped. I stood straight up, I felt it as the muscle in my leg tore, but I also felt the bone pop back into place. It was a kind of nice pain in a way. "No, I did it because it was right. I didn't put it together for a while. Jax kept me looking out for a red head, but that wasn't until we started working with him. I didn't trust him not to betray you. He had me go look at your grave, even dig it up. When he saw the body, his questions were answered. Mine just began. It took me a while, but I figured it out."

Close enough to touch, right at my ear. "And what would you have done with this information?"

Tears rolled down my cheeks, my sister thought I was after her for… I didn't even have words for it. "Nothing, it didn't matter to me. I love you. I've loved you for years."

"Call out to your gods, you always cared more for them than me."

Her words cut deep. Then I realized, this wasn't Chloe. Some snow daemon or something, but not my Chloe. "Be gone daemon, be gone from me. In the name of Ca'talls, be gone from me."

Spinning around like that on a leg already hurt is about as smart as people always treat me. As I hit the ground all I could think was that maybe I am as dumb as they say. After all, I am going to die out here.

Falling from your height doesn't hurt, falling on that leg did. Traitorous limb.

I screamed. I screamed a lot. I cussed too. Every word I have ever heard Chloe use crawled out of my mouth.

She would have been proud, really.

When the pain would let my brain work, I looked around. You have to understand, cutting through the forest helps if you are trying to make up for time. When gathering food and firewood, in the woods is better than on the road. Snow tends to obscure things, the white blanket tends to cover branches. In this case it served me well. My fall and tantrum had uncovered an old rotten log. As cold as it was, I wouldn't have to worry about bugs or snakes, even if they were under it. I wouldn't be their problem.

I dragged me and it back into my cave, with a few more trips out for some of the greener stuff I could keep the fire going for at least tonight. Tomorrow might be a problem, but you take problems as they come, not borrow them from the future.

As the fire caught the smoke bellowed out of the cave opening, I laid down to keep my head as close to the floor as possible, the litter I had collected made a decent bed.

As long as it didn't catch, I would be fine.

Great, now I was in pain, freezing, and now worried I would catch my bed on fire. Growing up on the streets taught me that leaves and stuff make good bedding and keep the ground from eating your warmth. As I lay here, however, I began to realize just how lucky I was to have made it this far with no wood's knowledge.

"Hello?" A voice drifted in. "Is there anyone in there?" Someone was outside the entrance of my impromptu little home.

I sat up as quietly as I could, no need to give myself completely away.

No, the smoke did that, and it did it again as I inhaled a lung full of the stuff. A face full of smoke and the resulting coughing fit gave me away just as well as if I had started screaming here I am. The difference being that if I had screamed out my location I could have still acted. You try doing anything but coughing when your lungs are full of smoke.

"I hear ya, I'm coming. Let's get you out of there before you kill yourself." Her voice was deep and husky, and still sweet and soft somehow. As if she had spent her life growling orders and ruined what was once the whisky voice of a bard.

Through the haze I saw a human woman dressed in simple leather britches and tunic. She belonged in these woods. Taking hold of me, she helped me back out into the cold. The woman must have been in her late thirties, her black hair was streaked with gray, and she had a very prominent white witch's streak at one temple. Her arms were strong, her face held lines but still somewhat youthful, and her eyes were the blue gray of low storm clouds. She was short, even for a human. Most people are short to me, but she was strong enough to all but lift me up and out of my homemade 'Piper Smoker'.

I chuckled at the thought. Smoked Orc. Bet it wouldn't taste good.

She kicked a discarded cloak around to cover the snow better and sat me down on it. "Ya trying to make jerky out of yourself girl?"

It hit me right, her making the same joke out loud that I had made in my head, my leg, the absurdity of it all. Everything came crashing down. I dissolved into a fit a laughter that doubled me over.

I could hear humor in her voice as she spoke again, "That's right, a good chuckle will help clear your lungs, but you'll choke soon enough." She sat something beside me. "Let's see if I can undo the damage you did to that fire."

2

Soon this human had me back out of the cold and onto some soft furs from her pack. "I'm not sure you'd make it to morning with the set up you had. Between the smoke and the way you had this place set up, not to mention burning stuff still so green." She shook her head. "What's a city girl like you doing out in the woods, and why are you shackled?"

I'd never felt so foolish in my life. Most people see me do something dumb, they shake it off as I'm 'just an Orc.' This woman saw a city girl, someone soft who didn't belong here. I took a deep breath to answer, wincing a little as I did so. I had no idea breathing was connected to your ankle. "Trying to get back home. I escaped a slave labor camp. I shouldn't have been there, I paid for my crimes."

"The ones you got caught for anyway." Her voice was teasing, but I still flinched. Guilty of one crime and caught for it always meant to people that you were guilty of far more. It was right in my case, but not everyone's. She looked at me. "Don't be like that girl, not every rogue is out to line their pockets and I know it. Most are just good people trying to get by, and some are even trying to help others. Like that Chloe girl who stole all those orphans a while back."

I'm glad I wasn't drinking anything, I would have spit it out. "Do what?"

I watched as a predatory smile spread across her face. "I thought it might be you. Chloe worked with an Orc girl who would be about your age, and last I heard she lost her hand. Can't be too many one-handed girls like you around."

I had taken the woman for a simple Warden, but no, she was a Ranger, a full bounty hunter, and I was in no position to do anything about it. I tensed and looked for an advantage, any advantage. "No one is supposed to know she did it, supposed to know we did it. Did the Bishop send you to finish me off? I don't know where Chloe is, so torture will get you nowhere."

She chuckled, it was cold and sent a chill running through me, and I had heard laughs like that all my life. "Relax girl, the Dwarves know you two did it, and they have no more love for the Bishop than I do," She shook her head and looked at me, "...or you do for that matter. Let's just say it's my business to know who certain people are, and what they do." She leaned in close to me. "I even help certain people get the information they need at the right times."

I could feel every muscle in my body relax at the same time. This woman may be a stone-cold killer, but I placed where I had seen her before. "Jax. You work with Jax."

She smiled, "We've crossed paths." She settled back against the cave wall, "Call me Sara."

I shook my head, I should have known she wouldn't just confirm it, any more than I thought 'Sara' was her real name. "So, if you aren't out looking for me, what are you doing out here other than saving my life?"

Her words chilled me, not with her inflection, that was perfectly normal, but with their content. "I was out here looking for you. Kind of a last-ditch effort before heading on. Jax is gone, and I can't locate Chloe, Bear or anyone else." She shrugged as she tossed more good wood on the fire. "I knew you had disagreed before Jax got taken down. No one knew who Chloe was really, so I'm pretty sure the girl taken south was her, and Bear got hanged." She looked at me, "Thieving now carries a death sentence."

I searched through what she had said. Chloe wasn't at South Point anymore, nor was Jax, and Bear was gone. I had no reason to go home now. In fact, it might be more dangerous for me to do so. "What do you mean no one knew who Chloe was, so she was taken south?" South Point was the furthest 'south' the Kingdoms went.

"I tried tracking her down first. Like I said, I knew you had gone to the work camps." She shrugged and stood up, pacing as she talked. "Took me a week of asking around, you two did a bang-up job of not being noticed." She sighed. "Finally, I manage to come across rumors of a beggar girl going from one sick house to the next. Eventually, I tracked that down to a starving waif with red hair and a cough." She leaned against the far wall of the cave. "She was last seen ducking into an alley presumably to get warm. Only no red headed girl ever came back out." She shook her head and started moving again. I watched her feet walk out the same pattern over and over again, nine steps one way, turn, nine steps the other. "Given what I was hearing I would have guessed she died, only no one moved a body out of that alley, and no indigent corpse with bright red hair had shown up." She turned and looked at me. "Then I overheard some of the wall Guard talking. It seems about the same time she turned down that alley, someone saw a small group of LeatherWing flying out of the city. One of them had something wrapped up in a bundle."

"So, she could still be alive?" Suspicion and hope fought for my voice. A lot of people think the Southern Demons are just that, but we Orcs owed them our lives, and our freedom. Of course, legends were one thing, but this might be something else. "What will they do to her? Will they help her?"

"If they got to her in time, sure. For all their well-deserved fierce reputation, LeatherWings are a bunch of do-gooders. They will give you their last bite to eat, the clothing off their back, will suffer almost any insult, though they do have their breaking points, and they will never harm someone weaker than they are. If they hear about it, someone doing so, they will most likely kill for it." She sighed," So yeah, if it is her, and she is still alive, Chloe might be the best off of all of us at the moment."

I leaned towards her, she knew them. "You've seen them, been with them?"

She chuckled and her cheeks turned slightly red. "Yeah, in more ways than one. I've fought with them. We've got some stuff in common, neither of us like when children suffer."

"Are you scouting for them now?" Given everything going on around here and in my home kingdom, children suffering was a reality.

My hope died when she shook her head no, "Can't, this is something they need to figure out for themselves. See, they are rather... insular, currently. Outside of their lands they will help when they can, but they prefer to be a 'safe place' to run too. I could yell at them till I was blue in the face, it wouldn't matter. They will need something bigger than me to get them moving."

"Can you find out if she had been taken by them?"

A nod and a quick smile were my replies. "Right now, we have to get that leg set. You've pulled a few muscles and that ankle is completely out of place. It looks like you and I will be bedding down here for the winter. I can send word back and forth. We'll find out what happened to your friend."

As grateful as I was for this, I had to wonder about my luck finding this woman. Then again, part of me didn't think it was luck.

3

I scooted over to throw more wood on the fire, thankfully my little cave had enough wood in it to keep me a few days, considering the snow had drifted up to completely obscure the opening. I also had food enough for now. Water was easy, she had left me an iron pot to melt snow in and to soften the beef rations.

I hadn't left this place in over three weeks, turns out not only had I popped things out of sockets, but I had also cracked one of the two bones in the leg. She had set it, wrapped it with leather and had sticks woven in with the leather to help keep it steady.

She had looked after me since then and had gone back and forth between here and South Point and Light only knows what other places. If she wasn't such good company, I would be getting paranoid. The one time I tested the 'don't stand on your leg' order, I paid for it.

It had already been several days since I last saw her, and the hole she dug for necessity was ripe. I was a prisoner again, not of chains, but of weather and my own leg. Sadly, my jailer was an absentee landlord, not that I wasn't used to that. Thankfully she had managed to get the tools to get the real chains off me.

Firelight, an air channel, a shit pit, as well as dried meat, cheese and these biscuit-like things that I could have used as a sap back a few months ago. I felt like I wanted to see if I could dig my fingers into the cracks of the natural rocks and see if I could drag myself up by the walls themselves. At times like this 'she' was always there.

"How's the broken leg there, friend?" Always her voice, sometimes her words, sometimes they were just my own thoughts fed through her mouth. "Done anything else stupid today?"

"You're not her." The sound of my own voice echoing off the walls caused me to jump. I hadn't meant to speak. "Shits."

"Ha, I knew it! You can't ignore me forever Piper, I'm haunting you."

I felt the sigh escape me, long, slow, and deliberate. I was surrendering to this. It was that or go mad. "You aren't dead Chloe." I shook my head. I had thought of a plan for the next time 'she' showed up. I already tested her against the Lords of Light, and she didn't flee, so despite my first guess she wasn't a daemon. So, I tried testing her knowledge, but of course she knew everything I knew so that didn't work. Then I tried just ignoring her. After she sang old bawdy songs for hours last time before giving up, I decided a new approach was in order. Unless of course, I wanted to hear about where the good king and his rod is again that is.

So instead, I was going to ask her things I did not know, things like what her dad was like, but right now, that was furthest from my mind for some reason. "So how are you doing, wherever you are?"

There wasn't an immediate answer. Maybe I had stumbled upon how to get her to leave me alone after all. It would figure, it would be my luck after all.

The voice was sad when it came. "I don't know."

I relaxed a little bit. "What do you know?"

"That I am still mad with you, but that you need me right now." Her voice was as sweet as ever.

"Why do you think I need you?" I asked.

"Hello?" She said in her smartass smarmy way. "You're shit on your own. Too pig headed to ask for help, too stupid to admit you're smart, and too proud to admit when you're wrong. Of course you need my help."

I looked around my current 'home', and it was hard to argue with her. "I should have just let you do it, you were trying to help. It's just, that is so much dirtier than our normal stuff."

"We once hid silver in chamber pots to sneak it out of one of those fop's houses. Silver, in shit. Do you remember?"

I remembered all too well, we had to sift through every last bit of it to get some of the smaller stuff out. We didn't use that trick again, if I had my way we never would. Human shit is disgusting. "So? Still doesn't smell as bad as the back alleys after a good night. They smell of the docks at high noon when the guts go bad."

"Washing helps, and you're exaggerating. Your stupid church teaches you that it is better to dig in shit than to upturn your ass." I snorted. It was true enough. Waste workers were everywhere, and work with everything including cleaning up refuse like that, and to most people they were still cleaner than whores.

I sighed again. "Fine, whatever. I still didn't want you going through that, not for me." I felt the tears start to hit my cheeks.

"Your mother went through it for you. How can I call myself family and not?"

I flew hot. Looking around I tried to discern where the voice was coming from, it always felt like it was coming from just outside my field of vision. Now I was sure something was there, Chloe would never call my mom a whore. "What did you just say?"

"The truth, but you're too stubborn to think. You're taught to think only one way." I could hear mirth in her voice. "Now you can't just end the conversation, so you will listen." It was coming from my other side now. I twisted too fast, I heard my back make the same popping sound knuckles sometimes make, only louder. "You mom was no whore, but she did fuck. That's how babies are made. Or do you still believe that lie that baby Orcs are picked from vines?"

I felt a growl building in my throat. "You know damn well I don't."

"Then accept that your mother fucked."

My mom. Chloe had no idea, but she knew my mom. She may not be old enough to remember, but I was. I remember the strange white thing in the wooden cage, almost the same color as the sheets my mom bleached, but the little creature has hair the color of coppers set loose into the air to catch the sun. Chloe thinks I am just a year or two older than her, but I was nearly four winters when the white creature came into mine and my mother's home. Mamma called it a baby, and said its name was Chloe. I don't know why mamma left that job, I don't know why mamma left, but I knew that fire headed creature when I saw it again. If we counted right, I was only three actual years older than her, but it's the principle of the thing.

"I know where babies come from." My voice was low, but I wanted to know where this was going.

"No, say it."

I gritted my teeth. Then I started getting her point. Why was it so hard for me to say that my mother, at least once, had screwed someone? I felt conflicted, like I knew she had, but part of me was actively hoping she didn't enjoy it, actively hoping... what? That she had been raped? That she had been innocent of conceiving me out of wedlock?

I felt myself jerk back painfully into the wall behind me at the thought. I just wished my mother had been raped rather than... what? Enjoy a good screw?

Apparently, this is what her voice was waiting on. "Sucks, don't it? I don't know what worm just crawled through your head, but that is what it is like, those teachings. Worms, fat and ugly, crawling through and saying things to you that you know you should never say."

I felt sick to my stomach. Thoughts of worms were not helping that at all. "What do you want me to do Chloe, admit that my mom was wrong to have me? Damnit, I know that." I felt tears stream down my face, I knew I was a mistake and an ugly one at that.

Her voice was soft, as it would often be when she scored one of her points home like this, "You're not a mistake, and your mother didn't do anything wrong."

"I'm a bastard." My voice was quiet, and I could feel myself sobbing. Chloe was always going on about how you should never let the other guy see you bleed, or in this case cry. She always tried to be so hard, but I just wasn't.

"Why? Because some man decided you were? Because some church said you were. Either you believe in these all powerful wise and knowing gods or you don't. If they are what you think they are, do you think you were made just to punish your mom for enjoying a good fuck?"

Wait, what? Chloe always argued on the side that I had been lied to, why the sudden change? "I thought you always said the gods were lies to keep us in line?"

I could hear the chuckle in her voice. "Well yeah, and you've spent your life making up for being a mistake, a mistake you didn't make, and a sin you didn't do. How can you expect yourself to pay for not only your sin, but the sin of someone else? Someone who, you told me, while she was alive that she took great joy in you, helped you, and you loved her. I want you to look me in the eye and tell me what she did that was so wrong, how you are so wrong."

I was crying so hard that when the snow hit my leg I jumped.

4

I scrambled to get away from the sudden cold that had invaded my personal world. I also might have made a noise or some such. Sara rushed over to see if I was all right, concern showing in her voice. "Did you hurt yourself?" The smell must have hit her then, because the face she made was comical. "Possibly escaping for fresh air?"

I shook my head, "Smells bad, but I've been in worse." What a sad statement from my young life that that was the truth. "Tried talking to her."

Sara nodded, but the frown on her face told me what she thought of that. "I still don't think that it's your friend." She took a deep breath; the regret was instant. She looked around for a moment and started figuring out what she was going to do first. "Before you ask, yes, I made the rounds, and yes, some Leather-Wing did indeed take someone from South Point. Turns out it is a young woman, but that is about it, for new information."

Sara told me she had hit every contact she had when she went out. This was the most news we had ever gotten. "Any way we can find out if it's her?"

She frowned harder. "Not really, not right now anyway." She shook her head and looked at me, "What am I supposed to do?

Just come out and ask them 'Hey, did any of you kidnap Chloe Blackthorn? Her friends miss her and kind of want her back.'" She shook her head again and looked down at her feet. "They might be a very understanding people, but to them, they haven't harmed whatever girl they took. Hells, they've saved her if the rumors are true." She took a collapsible bucket out of her bag and went for my 'hole' to clean it out. "Just because they are a different culture doesn't make them bad."

The effluvia started to reek worse with it being moved around, so I scooted closer to the reopened entrance. "I know that. My mom told me stories that her mom and so on told her. The LeatherWing freed us from slavery. I just can't believe they now practice it."

She sat the ash bucket down next to the hole and took the full bucket of ick outside. Mercifully, when she came back in a few moments later, she left the befouled thing out there.

"They don't. Not like you and I understand it. It's kind of hard to explain, they understand that there will always be a need for servants, so they invented, or reinvented a set of rules that keeps the servants from being misused and gives them the ability to leave when they wish... sort of."

I hoped my doubt showed on my face. "Sort of?"

Wood ash made the smell better, so she was sprinkling it in the scooped-out pit, so she could finish cleaning it. She stopped ashing the hole and straightened up to look at me. "I wish I could explain it better, but trust me, if that is Chloe sitting up there in Vela's lands, she is as safe as a gold piece in a miser's pocket."

I had a name; Vela. "You know this woman?"

Sadly, she shook her head and got back to her work. "No, I just know of her. We've never met." The fresh air started clearing my head.

"What can you tell me about her?"

She sat the ash bucket down and tossed another log onto the fire. When she was satisfied with that, she sat down across from me and spoke. "She's hard, but not in the way you think of it. She doesn't have to pretend or shut off her emotions. If she believes something is right, it doesn't matter how much it hurts her personally, she will do it, even while tears stream down her cheeks."

Taking out her water skin, she put it to her lips and pulled on it. I didn't understand how it had thawed so fast, surely the cold had long seeped into it, and as of yet she had not been out of that cold for long. She handed it over to me, with the first pull I understood.

"Whiskey." I choked out between sputters. Chloe might love that stuff, but it wasn't to my taste. The burn felt good though, and it wasn't more water. I found myself welcoming the flavor because of that.

She nodded, then continued, "She has a few small campaigns under her belt, has earned the title of 'Vela of the Spear', and she's been the reigning Queen of the Bone for most of her life. After she took the throne one of the southern border marches tried to take some of her land. It's where she got the title 'of the Spear'."

It felt like the wind had escaped me, but I couldn't tell you from where. "So, if it is her, she's in the lands of a War Queen?"

She shrugged, "Pretty much."

Leaning back, I thought about it for a moment, "Can we rescue her?"

Sara nodded, "It's possible," her face showed the likelihood of that working without her saying another word. "But first we would need to get you better, and you're still having hallucinations."

I felt myself slump. "Any ideas on that, oh wise one?"

"Sure, but you won't like them."

I gritted my teeth and felt my jaw pop. "Go ahead."

She stood up and went to the fire. "Let's get some food in you first, as well as the willow bark."

She spent the next mark or so fixing me a tea of the bark, as well as some other 'things' she said that would help me with the blood fever. The stew she fixed isn't what I would call good, but it was better than some of the stuff I had paid for at the inns Chloe and I visited.

She began without preamble. "Your fever is responsible for what you've been hearing, at a good guess, fueled by the guilt you feel for running off, and made worse from the crap they feed the slaves to keep them docile."

I glanced down at the wooden bowl, I had figured some of that out. "Maybe, but some of it doesn't make sense. Chloe was always against me being a believer, this one is not." I shoveled a bit more of the mush into my mouth. "She's pissed with me for what I have done, but it's like she is tearing down the teachings, not the faith. Chloe always thought it was dumb to have faith without proof."

She shrugged. "She has a point."

Another one, great. What do I do to attract them? "Not you too."

She turned to me, a look of surprise on her face, the witches' streak falling over her eye. "What? A non-believer? Gods no child. I am very much a believer. I just refuse to follow the blind."

I blinked. "The blind?"

"Your priests." She sat down and started her own stew.

"The priests are called to service."

Her smile was sweet, but also kind of sad. "Who told you that?"

The priests, they had told me that. It hit me so hard that the words never left my mouth. Sheepishly I looked back down at my bowl. "Some of them are good."

She nodded. "Yes, some of them are. But trust me on this, they all go to class to learn what to say and how to say it. Some believe, but to some it's just a vocation, like blacksmithing, and to some it's a path to power and wealth."

With all I had seen the Bishop do, that last one I had no answer for. I was sure Michael was the first type, but I also knew Mattathias, to him I could see it was just a job. I hadn't bothered looking at it until now, but she was right. "Why doesn't Father" that was as far as I got.

"Just make them behave?" She took another bite and seemed to be thinking as she chewed. "What does a child learn if Father always makes the choices for them? Can you truly call a person good if a Guard follows them around and makes sure they always do the right thing?" She looked at me. "What Chloe saw as proof of an uncaring god at best and no god at worst is simply a parent letting a child learn. We were given the rules, told what we should do, and yet we always worry about what we can get away with" she chuckled, "just like a spoiled lordling."

I thought about it but did not see what she was getting at.

With a sigh she asked. "What are the tenants of faith for Ca'talls?"

I knew my lessons well. "Men are to be good and just, women are to be loving and kind, and children should obey their parents." She nodded, so I continued. "Steal neither from your neighbor nor borrow from one without cause. Ca'talls is King of the gods and your king as well; you would do well to remember this. Respect what has been joined in Ca'talls' name, be it contract or wedding vows, and do not defile them. Do not be proud of false things and do not boast of things you have not done. Do not indulge in strong drink to excess, or in flesh to excess, nor eat to excess, nor anything of the glutton. Keep your mind pure and your body will follow. Keep the word of the brethren for they are my voice on this world. Kill those you see doing evil, when you know they aren't repentant." I took a breath and continued. "Do not collect wealth to excess, for to store treasure on this world is to place it where it rots and thieves take it but give instead to the temple so that they might do my work." It all came so easily, and simply saying those words gave me a bit of peace.

A peace that shattered with but a simple question. "And?"

I blinked at her. "And what?"

"I heard a lot of don't do this or that in there. About how to be a man and woman and how if you are not, then you're bad. Don't steal or borrow, don't disrespect the king of gods, don't break contracts or deals made in said kings name, but if it isn't in his name, go for it. Don't be cock of the walk, and don't party too hard. Oh, keep the mind on pure things, don't worry about the rest. Obey the church and give to the church because the church can be rich, but you shouldn't be. Last but not least, kill anyone who disagrees with you." She leaned back. "That's how not to be 'bad' in your church, so how do you be good?"

I was floored to say the least. "Now see here, you twisted what the commandments are." Again, she interrupted.

"No, I just said them in a different way. Now again that is what not to do. Anyone can 'not do bad'. Not doing bad doesn't make you good."

"Yes, it does."

She raised her eyebrow, and with such a simple gesture I felt as if I was before a king who I had displeased.

Her words justified my feelings. "Really now? Tell me how good the people doing no bad to you, but not helping you and your fellow rats really are. The ones that walk by, shake their heads, reported you to the Guard for no more wrong than you sitting on a corner begging for food. Chased you out of warm spots because you smelled bad to them?" Her words burned with the challenge of it. "Tell me of the goodness of these not bad people." The venom in her words, her manner of speech, and the scorn she showed. I saw, and I was frightened.

She screwed her eyes shut and held out both hands to her side's palms down. I watched her rebuild her composure. I had seen many people do such to calm themselves. She had lost her temper, but I had seen. This woman before me was a mother or had been at one point. Her fervor brought on by the suffering of children had made the reflected light of the fire turn her eyes the color of wisteria.

She was so much more than the simple woods woman she pretended, so much more than the simple killer I took her for. That barring only comes with power. "Who are you?"

She shook her head. "Just a person, a woman trying to do good in the world, not merely doing no harm."

I had to push, I had heard such evasions all my life. "You've killed people?"

Her eyes were still closed. "Oh yes."

"You were a mother?"

A sad smile spread across her face. The kind that is both pain and joy. "Yes, a long time ago."

"Have you taken me as one of your children?"

She opened her brown eyes and looked dead at me. "If you wish, but I am a hard mother to follow, and I expect people to learn, not just memorize."

I snorted. "Now you sound like Michael, he has a problem with people just saying words and not doing deeds."

"I'm no priest." Her words were soft but seemed almost a challenge. As if she wanted me to understand something she could not say, but also did not.

This was the most I had ever got her talking about herself, I wanted, no, needed to know more. "You're a Noble, no, a Royal, aren't you?"

She shook her head, "Once, now others rule in my stead." She let out a sigh.

"That's how you know about the LeatherWing, you've dealt with them."

She nodded. "Yes, I have."

"Do you really work for Jax, or does he work for you?"

"Neither we'd worked together in the past. I do odd jobs and the like for him."

I had to know. "Does he know who you really are? Is Sara your real name?"

She chuckled. "I'm sure he has his own ideas, but no, I don't think he does, and yes Sara is my real name. I've been nothing but honest with you."

"You're a Queen," I began. Then I realized how right that felt. "Shit! You are a Queen!" I just cussed in front of a queen. I had been letting a queen tend me, carry my shit out in a bucket. She had been waiting on me, hand and foot. I tried to get up, to show her the respect long overdue, to apologize, to do something, anything.

She laid a hand on my shoulder and pushed me back to sitting. "I haven't been a Queen for a long time Piper. I chose this. I felt it was the best way to help people. Not just mine but everyone. Please," her words were soft, "I'm just Sara."

"So, what happened?"

"Another time perhaps." Her smile said she knew I would not let this go. I wonder what else I could get out of this woman. "Right now, we are dealing with the fact that you keep seeing your friend."

5

She was right, I was using this to avoid talking about it. "She's pointing out where" I swallowed hard. "She's pointing out where I was a fool to leave. Where I did it so that she wouldn't be condemned to The Hells for prostitution."

She nodded and leaned back, with an even tone she asked, "Do you think that whores are going to Hell?"

"As good as most of the ones I know are?" I shook my head. "Yes." It hurt to say so, but the tenets are very clear cut. Sexual immorality is something that will see you burn.

She simply nodded again. "Do you think that is fair?"

I felt the tears in my eyes. The truth was, I left that day. I left because Chloe was gone for a nice long while. I couldn't face her if she had done it. It would be painful. "No, I don't think it's fair. It's just the way things are."

"So, you follow a god you don't believe in."

I was taken aback. "Of course, I believe in him. He's real." The words were almost a plea as they left my mouth.

She gave me a look reserved for small children. "And the last time I looked the Bishop was real, that doesn't mean I would follow him or believe in his message."

"But he's just a man. He isn't a god." How could she not see the difference?

"You follow a being, that you think is doing something you don't think of as right. You don't believe in his message." She looked at me and the look she gave me was of pity.

That got my iron up. "We aren't gods, and we don't get to decide what is right."

She nodded, and seemed again to be thinking, "Wrong. No, we aren't gods, but we do get to decide what is right for us. Do you not believe that the All Father wrote the law upon our hearts?"

I shook my head, she didn't get it. "Yes, but the devil and all her tricks twist it, she makes good feel wrong and wrong feel good. Getting drunk and overeating are pleasurable, they feel good."

"Yet when you see a child with nothing and you know you ate more than needed, how do you feel?" How could she still be talking so calmly?

I snapped at her. "If you are good, then you feel like crap, if you are evil you don't care."

"And yet the people rewarded with more through their works are the ones who walk by you while you starve, by the laws of your god they aren't doing bad things, and yet you just called them evil." Her cool voice burned into my brain, stoking a rage deep within me.

I felt the words burn my mouth as I spat out my response. "Because they are selfish. Selfish and petty and only do enough so that they can fool themselves and others into thinking they are good. They give enough so they can be seen as being right and just, but really a blackness is in them." How could she miss that they were just playing the part?

With a voice switched from honey to cold steel she replied. "Yet your friend would have turned her first trick to see to your need and to take care of you. She would have done this, and she would not be worrying whether others thought it right or clean, and you fled from her in shame." She leaned forward and looked at me. "Your friend sacrificed to do right by you, but men who look down on you for being less, being poor, told you her kindness made her filthy, so you fled."

It hurt. It felt as if my heart seized up. I couldn't breathe, worse, I had no air in me. The blackness that should come when breath leaves you didn't, and I was left with the pain. I couldn't speak.

She twisted that knife. "You chose the church, your church, over her. You chose people that hate you for being a half breed monster over the one person who loved you for you." She calmed herself and settled back. "A church you had worked against, stolen children from, saw how wrong it was, and still you were taught never to question it, never to disobey, even when you felt it was wrong, that is the god you claim. Not Ca'talls, that church, that man. It's not Ca'talls or any god you follow, but men."

She was right, and I knew it. I knew it because the one thing that had burned itself into my mind as soon as I could realize what I had done, was that I had to get back, had to apologize, had to make it right.

Sara nodded at me as she took out a pipe and began to pack it. "And that is why she comes to you. She isn't here. Your mind is torturing you with the guilt that you know you did something wrong." I watched as she lit it and smelled the aromatic smoke of brown weed. "It has nothing to do with gods or devils, and everything to do with you and her."

"Is there hope for my soul?"

She shook her head. "No. Because you worry more about your soul than doing what needs to be done, more about your soul than helping others."

Numb, I asked. "What do I do?"

"Find a god that speaks to your heart, no matter how hard the road of their faith and walk is, look for one that speaks to you. Forget about 'saving your soul.' There is nothing you can do for that. Concentrate instead on living a good life, a life of purpose and servitude to those lesser than yourself, those without power. Do these, and you will find it is a good life." She drew forth a long pull and let loose with the breath of a dragon, filling the space between us.

Her words were tempting, but so were the words of the devil, and the devil was a woman after all. "Like before, like when we were running cons?"

She looked at me. "It wasn't the cons. It was the helping the poor no matter who they were. When you were doing that, even as bad as you felt for the thefts, you still had your way, your faith. Where is that faith since then?"

She was right. When we started out it was just us for us, and I felt rotten. We stole just enough to get by. Then Chloe had her plan, and it seemed...right somehow. I confessed to the Father, to Michael, every Firstday but he had even said I was doing the work of the Gods. I knew it to be true with every smile, every begrudging rule break, and every waif we brought in. Where had I lost that?

My hand. I had been working against the Bishop, I had been doing good. Why had I lost my hand? Why had it cost me so much? Why had god punished me?

My voice was slow and steady when I asked, "It's never easy, is it?"

"What dear?"

"Doing the right thing?"

"And they will hate you in my name, they will hate you because of me." She spoke as if quoting something. "This doesn't mean that they will hate you because you are better or see yourself as better, they hate you because you helped. They hate you because you broke the rules." She had a faraway look in her eyes. "You didn't let the poor suffer, die, you stopped being in it for yourself, or to escape the hells, or go to one of the heavens. They hate you because you did what they will not." She sighed. "They hate you because they can't control you. For you have another master." From her tone I think this was an old argument, an old explanation. "I don't care what god you follow, or don't follow for that matter. I don't care what you smoke, drink, or how much. To me? It only matters that you honestly believe that helping others is the right thing, and it doesn't matter who those others are."

She and Chloe agreed. Chloe would have liked this woman. I looked at her, and I asked, "Are you, are you one of the Sacred Light? Are you a god? An angel?" My thoughts turned dark again. "Or are you the Devil?"

She slumped as if something had been taken out of her. "I am not a God of the Sacred Light, nor am I an angel. And while yes, I have been called a devil, I am not 'her'. I'm just a girl who got tired of seeing people suffer, who got tired of the lies we all tell ourselves and others so we can feel like we are better than the other guy. I found my faith, and I started just trying to help people."

"Are you lying?"

"If I were, would I tell you?" She chuckled at her own joke. "But no, I am sure that the girl in Vela's camp is Chloe. We'll set off for there as soon as you're better. Well, that, and as soon as winter loosens its grip on our necks."

6

A few months later, when the snow had cleared and Sara had gone out and back again, both hunting and keeping tabs on her contacts she came into the cave grinning. I hadn't heard from Chloe since that day, nor had I really learned that much more about my 'special friend', but today that didn't matter.

"There's been a sighting of a girl with short red hair, looking gaunt on the roads headed east towards the setting sun. There are only two things out that way, Cliffport, and Five Rivers." Her joy was almost as large as my own, this was the most news we had had all winter. It made my heart ache with the need to see her.

"When can we leave?" I stood up fast enough to twinge my leg. It was healed but still some mornings it was stiff and slow to move. "What do I need to pack? Is anyone with her? Do you think she will go all the way to Five Rivers? She always wanted to go there." I had only meant to ask the first one, maybe the second, but questions kept pouring out of me, I couldn't stop them.

Sara slapped her hand over my mouth. We had become quite close. "One at a time. The girl is the right age and I believe she is Chloe. As it is the best lead we have, we leave as soon as possible. I'll take care of the packing, and she isn't alone if it is her. She has a group of people with her, at least two of them are LeatherWing. As for her headed all the way to Five Rivers, it doesn't matter. She will have to stop in Cliffport so that is where you'll be heading."

My face fell. She was with people, a group. That was our plan and I told her to do it without me, but still. We were going to be adventurers, me and her. I shook my head. I had run off, she probably still hadn't forgiven me for that. "Are you sure they are going to Cliffport?"

"Absolutely, it is the only thing on the road they were on. A Trade caravan saw a sickly red headed girl walking that direction." She was beaming, and now that the shock of not being part of the group already had worn off, I could feel myself brightening again.

"Wait, you can't go all that way. Jax has you working around here."

"Sweetie, Jax was caught shortly after you left."

"I know that, you told me, but that leaves you here being the only one to help Michael with the Bishop."

She nodded.

"Gods, what am I going to do?"

She looked at me like I had lost my mind. "What do you mean what will you do? Go, find her. Apologize. She is going to need you."

"How? I don't have any money."

She handed me a pouch, "I got the money for you, and what's more I have people waiting on you in Cliffport. Now my information is well over a month old, but if you hurry, you might catch her before she leaves there."

With that it was settled, I was going to catch up with her, apologize to her. With any luck, I might even get the courage to tell her; tell her how I feel.

I was still standing there in a bit of shock. I was going to see her again. Then a creeping dread began to fill me. I could follow the road, I might, might, be able to get there on my own. But given what I had learned, and what had gotten me trapped in this cave for so long, I needed help.

"I can't. I want to but I can't." A chill that had nothing to do with the retreating cold filled me.

She turned to me, confusion showing on her face. "Why not hun?"

I shook my head. "I'll get myself killed on my own in the woods."

A rich chuckle escaped her lips. "Well then, it is a good thing I've got you a traveling partner then." She kept packing my bag for me. "Well, at least I will. She's been waiting on you a couple of days out of town. Turns out she's a wanted woman and as such doesn't want to get this close to town." She stood up and smiled at me. "Till then, you're stuck with me."

7

Life is never quite what you make of it. I never thought of my right hand as being particularly useful. Sure, I held stuff with it, if I didn't need to do anything with it but hold it. Yes, I propped myself up with it, picked stuff up with it, scratched with it, pushed things. Look, what I'm trying to say is this. Your off hand, your dumb hand? Yeah, not so dumb. I never fully appreciated how much I use my right hand until we hit the road. Sure, I ran into problems at the labor camp, and at the slave camp as well, but when the majority of what you are doing is pulling things hooked to a harness you don't use your hands that much. Yes, when I was gathering wood by myself and alone in the cave I ran into problems as well, but nothing like actually trying to live with it.

Walking through the wood, drinking water out of a skin while still moving. Lots of little frustrations that seem to go on and on, that only now that we were on the move and my head was clear, seemed to irritate me. Sara was no help. No, she didn't expect me to do it all, but she had no sympathy for me either.

One of her many words of wisdom on the subject was. "Complaining won't bring it back, nor make it easier. You have a new limitation, and you will have to learn to get used to it as well as find ways around it."

After that particular gem, I snapped. "What the hell would you know about it?"

A smile crept across her face. "Who, me? You'd be surprised. I know you're frustrated, annoyed and embarrassed. I know it makes you feel powerless and useless. I know it hurts even though it isn't there, and I know you're more mad with what you think I am thinking than at anything I have actually said or done."

Her voice was so smug, and I was already angry. "Oh? And what do I think you're thinking of, oh great mind reader?"

There is a mode of speech, a way of making sounds not come out of a mouth, but simply fall from it like ice spikes during thaw. It makes the spoken word both chilled and completely disinterested. A kind of offhand comment as if you are explaining to a person complaining about itching that they are sitting in the ant bed that you had warned them about only to be ignored. A way of talking to a person, not as if they were stupid, but rather silly and what you were saying was simply not worth their time. In other words, condescending as hell.

That was her tone. "That you are a burden, that you are useless, that I am having to do all the work, that you should be grateful that I am taking any time with you at all." She took a deep breath and continued. "That I am wasting my time, that you're too dumb to learn," She stopped and looked up at the sky, the kind of thing someone does to see what else is in their head. "And finally, that you earned this and have no right to complain." She turned and looked towards me. "Did I get it right?"

I stood there blinking. Everything she said rang true, as if, even though I hadn't thought it myself, that somehow, I had felt it, knew it, lived it. To have someone give voice to your private insecurities is unnerving.

She sighed. "Piper, you've been through a lot. You've had the foundation of your life shaken, you lost some of your ability, and for a while your mobility. The infirmity you suffered was extended by whatever they feed you at the slave camp to keep you out of it, then you made yourself sick all over again with your flight back home. Only to find out you were wasting your own time."

As she continued, she walked over to me. "It's all very natural for you to feel that way, because that is what everyone has told you for your entire life. If everyone has treated you this way, how could I not be thinking those things? Am I not normal? Am I not only a thinking person, but a royal at that? Of course, I am thinking those thoughts, so of course every sigh, every look, everything I do and say to you is actually a show of my frustration with you."

I took a step back. "Well, yeah." I knew she was patient with me, but I also knew that was exactly what she was thinking. How could she not be thinking that? It was what I was thinking. "Are you going to stand there and tell me that you're not?"

Her answer was not what I expected. "I grew up, as you would see it, the daughter of a merchant. I was a brat and had something of a temper. My father, he saw something in me that made him very afraid. He believed I needed discipline, so he sent me to a school billed as a place to learn discipline. He didn't check too much into it, and due to his ignorance of languages not his own, he took the word for silent killer to mean the same thing as a group of bards. He may have realized his mistake if my mother and her lover had not had him slaughtered." She looked directly into my eyes. "I tell you this because I was born no better than you. Since the day you found out I was a queen you have treated me as if I was somehow better than you. I am not."

I blinked, confused. "What does that have to do with all of this?"

That smile crept back to her lips, the one I had realized was her 'patient smile', her court face. "It has everything to do with this. I'm better than you so I am taking time out of my better life to help a stupid crippled Orc thief. One who is, at best, a minor burden and at worst a waste of my precious time, time I could be spending taking down the Bishop."

Again, she was saying what I knew to be true. I felt my face burn. My skin has a green tint to it, we aren't like in the tales the bards sing of, all green like a plant. It's more like a greenish glow to our skin. Granted, when we are dusty it makes the green the primary thing people notice, and my wild cousins aren't known for bathing, so I don't get too mad with the bards. Blushing doesn't so much turn us red as darken our faces. If you see an Orc's face darken it's probably a blush, or a rage. People do get all red in the face when that mad. So, a dark faced orc is either embarrassed or upset. Just like most humans we tend to want to hit what has made us feel that way, so caution is the order of the day when you see that happen to one of us.

Me? I hung my head. I have more control of myself than that. "Yes. You could be. I'm taking you away from something much more important."

My face, or more my cheek and jaw blossomed with pain, the noise of it hit my ear with the sound of flesh hitting flesh with force. Not the thunk of fist on face, but hand on cheek. I'd been slapped! I didn't even see her move. I tried to register where she was when it hit me. I was still in motion. She had slapped me off my feet. I was over a foot taller, and the Lords of Light only knew how much heavier, and she had knocked me, not on my ass, but completely off my feet with a simple slap.

I landed hard on my right side. She was standing facing me, her right hand still in front of her at its completed arc. She hadn't slapped my face; she had slapped through my face pushing me with it as she turned.

Pain welled up, as I felt the bruise form on my cheek, and I tasted blood in my mouth. I spat it out. Red started creeping into my vision. "What the hell was that for?" My voice surprise me, as mad as I was, I expected it to sound, gruff... instead all it sounded was scared. As my brain caught up with me, I understood why. I hadn't seen her move. Something in me remembered she was a killer, even if my rage didn't care at this moment.

As she stood over me, she began to speak very slowly. "One, no one is better than you, not by birth. Two, a person is only better at something than you are. If you wish to become better at whatever it is they are doing you follow their lead. Three, never assume someone is wasting their time with you. It is their time not yours. If you think you are wasting your time with them, then move on. You don't get to make that call for other people. Four, anything else is arrogance and stupidity at best, evil at worst and you are damn sure better than that."

I couldn't stop my mouth, as the words flowed forth as water from a burst dam, I knew with all certainty, that at a bare minimum I was getting hit again. "Thought you just said no one was better than anyone else."

She offered me a hand up instead. "I said no one is better than you by birth. The decision to treat people as lesser lowers the worth of the individual doing it. When you treat someone as less than a person, you yourself become less because you cut off some of the connection you have to other people."

As I was on my feet once more, I angled my head down to meet her gaze. "So, you don't see me being crippled as making me lesser?"

She spat on the ground. "Crippled, Orc, Thief, none of it makes you less than me. You're a person. It took me years to learn that lesson, tens of them."

"Back when you were a queen?" She had opened up, so I was prying.

She nodded. "Trust me, I made up for it. I've spent my life undoing the damage I did when I thought that way." Her word and tone held the sorrow you here when someone thinks of themselves as a monster.

I pushed. "What happened?"

I watched as she deflated a little with a sigh. "I watched people who thought that, tear their homes, their very lands apart. It got so bad I even tried to do the same to myself, to tear myself into pieces until nothing was left but what was wanted. Then, when that didn't work, I tore into myself." She smiled weakly.

I nodded, not because I understood, when you see your world fall apart, sometimes it feels like there is nothing left. "Well, you didn't."

She turned and looked at me, going unnaturally still. "Maybe I did? Maybe I'm a ghost and I'm haunting you." I watched as her left arm dropped and became loose by her side. Her body stiffened in places that shouldn't and went limp in places that should remain rigid. Her back seemed to spasm as she talked. "Maybe I was just waiting for the right time to strike?" Her head slowly seemed to cock to one side as one of her eyes became off centered while the other looked at me still. "Maybe it's time you know who I really am!" With that she lurched towards me.

I stuck out an arm and pushed her back. "Please." I snorted. "Chloe does shambling undead so much better."

She staggered back from the shove, laughing as she did. "A Guard talked me out of it. All the while calling me a simpleton and chastising me for how selfish it was just to give up once I began to understand what was wrong."

I nodded, that I understood. Chloe was big about helping when you saw something you felt was unfair. "And you were a queen, so people had to follow you."

"Actually, my first kingdom fell completely apart. It was more like a town that I took over. They were happy to see the back of me. When I stopped playing by the rules, they stopped caring what I thought." She started walking again and I followed.

We went on in silence for a bit, then, "The second time, I found myself Queen because I was the one who got the area running again. A disaster had befallen the place and I knew what to do. Before I knew it, bam, I was a Queen, and this time, I kind of earned it."

"So why leave?" As we talked, I looked around at the returning greenery. It was a new start, a new year. The forest was becoming alive again.

"Because it was time." She too was looking around "I'm a great doer, not so good at the day to day. So, I set up an advisor with the titles, lands and so on, and as long as the few rules I set out aren't violated things should run fine." She stopped and spread her hands in gesture to all that was going on around us. So, I looked.

I could see everywhere that spring had come. Trees were putting on leaves, grasses were shooting forth from the snow not yet melted, impatient to see the sun again. I watched a wood monk, with its brown fur and black squiggles, run about looking for what food it could find. The world was alive once more.

She started moving again as she spoke, her tone was more than a little wistful. "My season was over, and spring had come to my people. I was made a queen by them, in 'winter' a time of desperation and turmoil, and as a winter queen I thrive. Spring, however, is meant for those other than me."

I snorted. "In other words, you got bored and went out looking for the next problem to fix."

She smirked. "That too."

8

We talked, walked, and camped for the night. I learned that she was basically going from place to place, trying to help people. She saw it as penance to her god, and to people, for her sins. "Not that any good deed washes away any of my sins mind you, nor do they earn me a place in the heavens."

I shook my head, I didn't get that. "Wait, you don't believe in the balance, that it's our job to do good and outweigh the bad?"

"It's not a score card Piper. Thinking of it that way is to miss the point. Each of us does things we know we aren't supposed to do, either things our gods tell us don't do, or that our hearts tell us is wrong." She shrugged. "But we do it anyway, sometimes because it's easier, sometimes because it feels better, sometimes because we just don't care."

I found myself nodding. "I know this stuff."

"Then what you have missed is this. Every time you sin, you make a mistake, and every mistake is an opportunity to learn. At bare minimum, it is to learn what not to do." She smiled at me. "That's why you can't get rid of nor erase sin. When my god freed me from the burden of it, it was more freeing me from the overwhelming guilt. The crippling aspect that tells me I will never be good enough."

This confused me. "Then where is the threat of punishment?" How could you make people behave if you didn't punish them?

She shrugged and got up to head for the tents she had taught me how to pitch. "How good is a man that only does good because he fears the pain if he does bad? That's not good, that's fear. My god wants people to *be* good, not *do* good." With that she left me to think.

***

When morning came, I woke to the sound of someone, something moving outside. I knew from months of being with Sara that it wasn't her. Yesterday on the road I had to wake her, just like I had to for every day she had slept in the cave. She was never awake on her own before noon.

I was very used to that, thanks to Chloe's sleep headed nature, just not quite to this extent.

That meant that whoever, whatever, was moving around outside was not my current partner. Yelling might alert Sara, it might not. She was hard to wake. I had often wondered if she had died in the night. Thankfully not.

As quietly as I could I looked out of the tent to see who, or what, was outside. My heart stopped beating in my chest with what I saw.

The familiar red leathers of a South Point Guard greeted me as the person wearing said armor was inspecting our camp... mercifully their back was to me.

I crept out of the tent, small clothes being my only armor. As I looked around, I realized no other guard was with this person. A lone patrol, way outside of town. Probably on the way home and checking on our camp to see if they could find any mischief.

They never turned as I got close. As soon as I could, counting my good fortune that they seemed to be in another world, a world of their own thoughts, I lunged and grabbed him from behind. I wrapped my arms around his... her chest, using my left hand to grab my hook and squeezed. If you squeeze hard enough a person becomes disoriented, possibly even passing out. I didn't want to kill her after all, just knock them out until Sara and I could get away. I felt her back pop as I squeezed the air out of her.

The Guard flung her head back, but only hit my chest, you've got to know how to do this. If she had hit my nose, I would have had to let go.

I saw her face, and immediately dropped her. "Hanna?!?"

"Good to see you too, Pip." She sputtered out that greeting to me as she crouched on her knees where she had fallen. One hand on the ground, one on her chest. "Glad you're up and about. Who the hell did you think I was?"

Stunned to find her out this far. "A Guard."

She chuckled. "Not anymore, but the armor fits." She made an offhand gesture as she fought to get her breath back. I offered her a hand up.

Sara's grumpy morning voice carried over to me. "I see your traveling partner made it." I heard her flap hit the ground as she went back inside, undoubtedly to go back to sleep.

Hanna, our Hanna, looked at me and smiled. "Come on, let's go find Chloe."

Author's notes 9

You ever start something that seemed like a good idea at the time?

After Chloe's Collar was done and at the editors, I got sick. I was halfway through Chloe's Fathers when a Chronic Migraine changed my life. By this point in time, it was April of 2016. I had a good job that was paying for my editing, I was just about to start HRT, and Father's was all but finished. Then, with a quick pop... all of that ended. Over the next two years we tried to figure out the cause of the headache that would not go away. It robbed me of speech, movement, even thought itself at times. It was an Intractable Chronic Migraine with Hemiplegic episodes. Two years of relearning how to walk and talk despite the pain. We lost everything because I lost my job. My sub at the time thought I was faking, and if it weren't for my husband things could have been so much worse. We sold off what we could, packed the rest up and left our home to find help, only to wind up homeless in Ohio. Things... happened. Thankfully August Gate's is a good friend and gave us a place and help getting our lives back.

Part of that was me trying to write again despite the pain.

I picked up a thread from the short story Jax, namely his capture. People liked him, so I figured, why not. The second novel had long been finished by this point, and I needed a way back into my own world. How would wily Jax escape this trap... especially since, well spoilers.

So, I wrote a short story. Once it was done, I really liked it, and had everything but a name for it. Due to things that happened in that story, I named it the Hanged Man. I then did a cover for the story with all intentions of it being a one and done. Only as I looked at the cover, I realized I had my 'in', I had a theme. So, I began writing The Arcana, a Jax serial story. What follows is the first half of that serial.

00 The Fool 1

<u>Cryf 12th 381 AFU</u>

When your best mate asks you to do something, no matter how dumb it is, you usually do it. So, I found myself back on the road to the one place I never wanted to be again: home.

Marky boy and I grew up in the same town, a real shithole named South Point. He was the oldest son of important dead parents, and me? Well, let's just say we met when I failed an attempt to relieve him of his purse.

I could spin you the tale of being the son of a whore, or the bastard of some noble, hidden away and kept secret, but the truth is Rycard Jackson Wills was the son of a tailor.

Dad didn't drink too much, he didn't gamble, didn't do any of the bad things people like to blame being poor on. He worked hard, knew all the right people, and still failed miserably. His fashions just never caught on. He was one of those good men who just couldn't take handouts, had to earn it all the right way you see. In the end, that was what took his life. When one of his many loans came due, and he couldn't pay? Well, that as they say was that.

No, no one roughed him up. He just didn't have the money. Since his life was built around the idea of being a 'real man'? He stepped off a chair one day and his feet never made it to the floor.

The note, such as it was, said that if he died our family wouldn't have to pay back the money, a hardship clause it's called. The creditors didn't see it that way and mum and me, we got sent to one of the many workhouses. She worked hard, and both of us tried to pay off his many debts. A real uphill battle that, so I got another job working nights.

If the law wasn't going to protect us, then to hell with it.

Inside a year with the help of my second job I had paid off her debt and my own. She found out how I pulled off that little trick and kicked me out over it. Didn't stop her from being debt free. Last I heard she'd married some bloke in another town.

Such a good church woman, my mum.

Needless to say, I was expecting quite a wallop when the meat-hooks of a noble closed round my wrist. What I took to be a grown man was a boy my age, think 13 summers if you're interested, the blighter had filled out early is all. He was a good church boy too, but he took that to mean, that if a piker was fleecing you, he must need it more than you do. Bloody fool gave me the contents of his pouch, then asked me what was around here to do for fun.

We was thick as thieves after that. He taught me how to be a noble, and I taught him to loosen up.

When he took up the cloth, I knew I was gonna get the boot, but by the gods he was going to do it to my face. We'd heard the chimes at midnight as the old saying goes, and if I was to get the brush off, I was going to make him do it as a man. Only he didn't. The bloody fool took me on his mad, meteoric rise to power, with him.

Together we fought monsters, devils, demons, heretics, and worst of all as far as I was concerned, hypocrites. We met a girl, both fell in love with her, but she picked him over me and yet somehow, we all remained friends afterwards. Take that every bad play I ever got dragged to.

When the babe was born Nyssa opted to stay home despite being a damn good sword in her own right, and so Marcus, me, and the gang used that entire bloody compound as a base. Rutting thing was certainly large enough even for a place inside the walls of the city. It was temporary, we all knew it. Marcus was one of the most important Holy Champions his church had, and no way they were going to let him go to waste in a backwater like South Point.

South Point isn't exactly unimportant mind you. It's a Border March, the southern-most March in the loose affiliation of fiefdoms that pretentiously calls itself a kingdom. The only real power in these parts is the church telling us we're all one people. The local common language is colloquially called Northern, it was about the only thing we really had in common, and frankly it's because the church taught Northern as the preferred tongue. Trade speak on the other hand is just about what everyone lowborn speaks.

Don't get me wrong, the church might be the only real power in the area, but it is far from a single force. You got Ca'talls, Ba'teece, Protista, Meth'adilis, Pentagla, Sou, Prestira, Lut'har, and a handful of local gods all calling themselves the Sacred Light under the All Father, and all claiming to be the one true inheritor to Heaven. So, they spend as much time fighting with each other as doing any good.

Personally, I pay a bit a service to Sou. She's the Goddess of Wrath and frankly I think she likes me.

Guess I'll find out when I die.

Which, come to think of it, might be on this trip.

It took years, but while we were off doing yet another set of 'good deeds' for the church, we got the news that we were headed to Five Rivers. The way of it was a prophecy from one in our group, our seer. Frankly it sounded like a con to me but, hey, that's pretty much all church is, so there you go.

Then we got the news. Nyssa and Chloe, Marcus's wife and little girl, were dead.

I was devastated, but Marcus didn't believe it. Our seer had a hand in that, telling him his daughter was gonna come back and save us all from the devils or some such. I like the old bat, but she and her Goddess are both nutters.

Still, he must have been paying attention to me at some point, because he was convinced, they were either killed or something, something, conspiracy. As his spy master, I got to leave my very cushy new position in the world's largest city to go back to a town I hated, to see if the woman both of us loved was really dead.

So, here I was, new haircut, cut close, I'd let it grow out over time, my beard gone, and I was in the clothes of a well to do merchant to go with my new name. Names are like clothing, change them to fit the mood I say.

When I hit town no one knew me, it let me slide in and about without questions. My boy had himself a brand-new statue in town, the inscription said it was for all the work he did for the church, the people thought it was because he was dead. No one that I knew of, had said that, but people seemed to just know it. Marcus was very much alive, at least he was when I left him. On his own, well, I trusted the others to look after him if I wasn't there. Everyone in town knew Marky boy was worm food, but no matter how hard I tried, I couldn't find who started that particular rumor going.

His house was now part of church property, forfeited for back taxes on paper. I was beginning to agree with him on the conspiracy thing. Bad for business when the paladin is more paranoid than the thief.

Only one small plot of land still had his name on it as owner; the graves of his wife and child.

You know, sometimes the gods are nice, they provide rain at just the right time.

2

Took near a month to set everything up, I joined the local guild, something I had avoided for the last 15 years of my life, I firmly believe in that don't shit where you eat thing, so no one knew me. I hadn't gone by anything but Rycard in town since I met Marcus way back when anyway, and well, Jax suited me just fine. Keeping your aliases with a theme might get you caught, but it helps you to remember who you are supposed to be.

Got myself set up as a money changer and lender, one who did a bit of quiet laundry out the back for the good people in need, read nobles and merchants. It was a long con, but I got the feeling I was going to be here a while.

One, the tax thing I knew was bollocks, Marcus was as straight as an arrow, besides I'm the one that made sure of his math, two was the whole he was dead thing. Some official documents had 'Markus Thunderhammer' as dead, while others had 'Marcius Thunderhammer' in debt with his positions sold off, while finally 'Marcus Thunderhammer' was a town hero who served the church valiantly.

Somehow Marcus's house and all his property were in Marcius's name. These weren't forgeries either, they were original church documents. Nyssa had been married to the same guy but had also been married to Marcus which explains how she is buried in the only land he still owned. Then I found out she was also married to Markus... and had been told her husband was dead just months before her own passing.

Everything I was looking at was church record, all of it accessible by any scribe of the church. It was also bloody impossible. They had to be forgeries, but if they were, they were from when the documents were originally filed and some of those had been as much as ten years ago. Looks like Merra might not have been as daft as I thought.

Digging up the graves was the final straw. Nyssa was snuggled nice and safe right where she should be, though her 'sickness' was suspect as she seemed to have been one of the only plague victims at the time. Chloe's plot was almost unbearable for me to dig up, it was a child's grave after all.

The child in the box wasn't the right size. Chloe had been larger than that the last time I saw the little carpet rat. Yes, the hair was red, but this babe was small, two or three years, a toddler. So, if she wasn't dead, where was she?

3

Note, when the town hero has a kid, every babe after that will be named for them for a time. Chloe was the most popular name in town for little girls all under five. Worse, the last skirmish with the neighboring lands had left quite a few of them orphaned. Seems their moms had all had taken to prostitution and other things, a lot of them got sick, some just went missing. While we had been off grave robbing and cult bashing, orphans became a big problem for a while, that is it was, until the new orphanage was set up just outside of town.

Took some doing and a year of work, but I managed to gather enough clout to check there for the girl, even managed to get them all in one spot, but not a red head among them.

The streets were a different story, they were crowded with kids misplaced by the war, by debt, and well, by life itself, and quite a few of them had red hair. Lots of peasants got red hair. Red hair and fair skin just ain't common among the nobles. So, I got an idea, I was going to start turning these little light fingers into a real working sub guild, all working for me of course, and all working on finding out what the hell is going on in this damn town.

Time to get started.

01 The Magician

<u>Heliwr 23rd 381 AFU</u>

Once, on these very streets, I was a halfway respectable young man. Hard to think about I know, but still, there it is. Now? Now I am known as the miracle worker, the wizard, and the mage. You come to me, and I make your problems disappear. It's a useful reputation to have. Of course, very few know that the man with a very posh shop is quickly becoming the go to for the nobles to clean up messes.

Trust me, it's useful. It gets me into places to 'fix' documentation I might not otherwise see. Not everything is kept in the church, and there isn't exactly a central anything in a town like this.

Besides, I got kicked out of the church. Seems that someone noticed I was looking into papers of the orphans. Of course, that would be because the orphans are sewing clothing and such. They call it Angel Made if you can believe that. Dodgy shit, wonder how much Marcus's old church is making off of child labor?

I still went to service regularly. Needed to keep an eye on things and seeing as how most of the new gold relics and such, were things I myself had liberated, with Marcus's help of course, church was obviously the place to be. Some were family heirlooms passed down through generations of Thunderhammer's. From what little Marcus knew of his own family history, he could trace his line back to one of the few minor royals that had survived the LeatherWing purge. Though how his ancestor pulled that trick off was anyone's guess. Other items that suddenly found themselves church property and proudly on display were wedding gifts to the happy couple. I had bought that holy cross myself.

The thing is the more I dug in, the more I saw the same ear marks. This wasn't so much some vast conspiracy as it was one man who had means, ability, and motive, not that I could guess what that motive was. Marcus and Nyssa weren't exactly targets, more like casualties. Almost every prominent family had similar paperwork, not just in the churches, but in the noble's records as well. All of the recent deaths of prominent landowners, most in the war two years ago, had seen their debt paid off by the church and their lands legally forfeited. That in and of itself wasn't unusual but surviving family members all seemed surprised to find out they were in debt at all.

The paperwork didn't lie, and the church was all too willing to 'help out' for the standard donation of any lands not utilized in seven seasons. It was all very tidy, all neat, and all shit.

I might be pure magic at fixing things like this, but my opponent was a miracle worker.

Of course, that's when I first heard a name to go with my new-found nemesis.

"His Holiness is on the move again." I looked over at the drunk who had rooted himself next to me, a man named Paslle.

A distasteful man whose work was to shake whores for a cut. His black hair and blue eyes always looked dull to me. The problem was I helped him out with The Guard once and now the blighter thinks we are friends.

"Excuse me?" I turned to look at the slob. "Who?"

"That's right, you new here ain't ya. Been in town less than a year." He punctuated his keen observation by trying to clap my back and spill my drink. It had worked the first time, but I had long since realized any time he thought himself a wit the blow was shortly to come. My drink was well on the counter.

"That's right mate, a year." Nearly two now, but he didn't need to know that.

He looked at me, wheels turning in that bloody thick head of his, no doubt the bone getting in the way of the smooth function of cogs. Finally, miracle of miracles, his eyes sharpened, "How you make Lieutenant in less than a year?"

I nodded to the keep to 'top up' that swill he loved so much. "Because I anticipate what's needed, that, and my warm smile and personable attitude." As his mug filled, I watched as his eyes disengaged from thoughts that were harder than the feeding of his addiction. "Now who's on the move?" I asked.

"His Holiness, he's kind of a local legend, a real boogey man type deal who's supposed to be responsible for all kinds of stuff. Like, ain't you ever wondered why the church always seems to be in everyone's will, or why some laws are just suddenly on the books, but no one can remember the edict."

I smile. "As a matter of fact, I had. I thought it was just something local. Like a shit Duke or something."

Watching a brain-dead drunk try to swill his booze and shake his head at the same time is enough for you to question the existence of any kind of creator, benevolent or otherwise. Such a feat defies logic and decorum both, yet here it was on display before me.

"Naw man, local Duke is tight, or used to be. Suddenly a few years ago this stuff starts happening, like deep work stuff, and all of it gifts ta the church." He looked at me with eyes that make that of a pig's seem intelligent. "At's why they Call him His Holiness." Then he leans in to whisper close enough I'm going to have to polish everything I own due to his breath. Hells, I might even take a second bath this week. "Only thing is," He slurred, "I don't know no one that will admit to have'n ever met the guy in person." Suddenly he was making a wild gesture over at another man, one of my fellow Lieutenants. Such a thing gets some people's attention, but most are used to ignoring him when he was this far gone. "Mal says that the whole things smoke to keep the guild together, you know a boggle to give us something to fear, seeing how all them new laws all seem to be about keep'n people like us off the streets."

I thought about that for a moment. Sussing it out myself would be far less painful than trying to mine any more from the 'reputable-man-about-town' who was already cross eyed, head back, looking at the bottom of his mug, as its semi-liquid contents slid down what passed for his neck.

It seemed I had quarry after all, and I bet he was quite real. Worse he, or she, was actually known. That bothered me. Rumor was a powerful tool, and this one apparently liked to pretend he was on the side of the gods. What's more a drunk spilling his guts in a bar only a few of us knew about meant that the information might be something of a fever, spreading like a fire through the whole of the village. Given what I had already found, I feared I would need to pull out all the stops.

First, I upped my recruitment of young toughs, the squirrelier the better. Red heads of course caught my eye first and foremost. I set them all with similar tasks, promised all of them a fat pay, then stiffed them the full amount while giving them a knock on the head. I needed to know who was going to stick to it, and who would bow out. Chloe, the right one, if that was what she was even calling herself anymore, had always been a fire brand. She wouldn't quit because someone got the better of her. Hells it meant I would never get rid of the brat.

After six months I had 9 teams all of whom were rip raring and ready to go. Six of them had Chloes, all about the right age, and all of them were, shall we say, the spit in your eye type. Nyssa, gods above, she had been a beauty, but how do you tell one peach skin red head from the next. Red hair was a throwback, even from the families with darker skin, get a red head and bam, you got that peach like complexion even on a darker tone.

Sadly, the kid still had blue eyes last I saw her, but kids grow out of that, so no help there. I tried to look for hints of Marcus's little angel, the girl who worshipped the ground her daddy walked on, but none of them really had that. One was fervently religious, most were a bit more passive about it, lip service and all. One was not only an ardent anti-theist, but she kept getting into fights with others who disagreed with her. Funny thing was, her best friend was an Orc girl who was as devout as a church mouse. Same Orc I had paid to help me dig that night so long ago.

I saw Nyssa in all of them, Marcus in a few, and none of the girl who I once knew. I hadn't seen her a lot, Marcus usually had me out and about, but Chloe wanted to know everything. If she was in these girls, the streets had already killed the girl who thought stars were the diamonds of the gods.

Together my little knot of a network was called The Cards, real original I know, but the kids loved it. I had each, based on how much of my trust they earned, doing more than lifting. Churches, convents, merchant houses, more, any place records could be stored. I had the quick ones trained to fake and copy anything they saw, not to replace mind you, I want them to bring me the forgeries. No sense tipping my hand too soon with someone noticing their fakes being replaced with more fakes.

No, this was the long haul, and I needed more than anything else, to be the Mountebank. Have each and every group in town all watching the wrong thing. It's easy enough when you do exactly what's expected of you. Like with any new job, do what they expect you to, let them see you doing it, smile and nod when needed.

Do all that? Well then you can get away with whatever, whenever, and as often as you like. Whatever you need to get the job done.

02 The High Priestess

<u>Ymuno 26th 384 AFU</u>

When looking for someone, you start out by finding out who else they've pissed off. As near as I can tell His Holiness has been a busy boy. He'd pissed off the Sisters of the Sacred Light. Those girls, they don't just worship a god, not Ca'talls, not Lut'har, but the whole sacred order, thank you very much.

Good bunch of girls, right nice, good company.

No not like that, but if you ever want to waste an afternoon discussing the finer things in life, from wine, to philosophy, to history, they are the lasses to go and see. It's the history I was most interested in, for that, nothing beat Essa Amore.

Essa was a pip even when Marcus and I were kids. Back then she was just a Mother, now she was Reverend Mother. The years hadn't dimmed her smile, and while time had laid a few fingers on her ebon face, it hadn't dampened the light in her eyes. Her hair was grey, and she was a bit more bent than I remembered.

Problem was, she remembered me.

Why shouldn't she, she was Marcus's tutor way back when, and as such mine. Most people might not remember the little tag along kid, but I gave her enough hell she'd never forget me, and she gave it right back. Not by relying on her position, or my low station, but by being smarter than me at every turn.

God, I love that woman.

Thankfully she agreed to meet me out by the old ruins. She couldn't risk going to my shop, and she wouldn't out me by talking to me at the Church. To be honest, the bone crushing hug was a welcome feeling I didn't know I needed.

"Rye boy, you in neck deep and don't even know it." She gave me a look, the same one that usually meant she knew the toad was in her desk. "A lot of people have raised the questions you have, you're not the first, and I doubt you'll be the last." The look she gave me, I knew things weren't right.

"All dead I take it?"

With an expression I was all too familiar with, one that said the answer was a bit 'thick' she continued. "Hardly. That many dead would raise eyebrows. No, some suddenly came into money or prestige. Some died, some got caught trafficking in goods best not talked about." She turned and fixed me with a stare that brought back all my school days. "Only the ones that get noticed, mind you."

"Anyone notice me?" I had to ask.

"Oh, lots. Everyone has noticed the new fence in town looking into anything and everything to get dirt on the right people." Her face warmed. "You finally learned to cover your tracks boy."

"High praise coming from you."

"Rye, you always had something to prove, never realizing you didn't have to prove it to me. I knew how smart you were, also knew one day you'd relax into it."

The smile that jumped to my face, and the way I could feel it lighting up were in sharp contrast to my ingrained senses of 'don't show emotions you don't have to.' The inner conflict resolved itself with my shyly lowered head and me scuffing a foot like I was still in school.

"Ahem." Shaking myself out of being a teen once more, I looked at her, then stopped myself from one of my normal cutting remarks. She hadn't earned one. "So, anyone looking that isn't an idiot?"

She smiled at me, "One, a warden who comes into town from time to time, really quiet, doesn't talk much, always has something else they are looking for when they have to hit the records, always seems to find herself looking into the same things you are."

"What do they look like, I've worked with a few Wardens, maybe I know them."

"A woman, short, black hair with tight curls with a witches streak, and light skinned, the kind that doesn't tan well."

Searching my brain, I could think of a few who matched that description. "Anything else?"

A warm smile greeted me, "She's from south of The Bone."

Barbarian territory. The Bone, a strip of land to the south, the isthmus between the Fresh Water Sea and the greater waters of the Lantix. It was the gateway to the frozen south, and the home of the tribes of LeatherWing and all their ilk. Civilization wasn't a thing you thought of when you picture it in your mind, despite the fact that trade caravans made good money down there from time to time. They rarely brought things down to sell, mostly jewelry, some goods, electrum, even some mythrum. The hardest part was mythrum ore, while uncommon, it did exist up hear in the north, but it tended to make furnaces explode. The Elves could work it, but so could whoever was down in those frozen wastes. It lent a lot of credence to a huge elven population down in those wilds, possibly even an Unseelie strong hold.

Unseelie meant Sith, and Sith always meant trouble.

Worse, the Bone itself was controlled by a tribe of Leather-Wing, a warrior woman named Vela. She was known for her brutality when dealing with anyone she considered to be an invader.

"What brings her so far north?"

"I'm not sure. But she's asked to meet with you?"

A knot formed in my stomach. "Me? Why?"

Essa looked at me with a smile I was all too familiar with, the minx was setting me up. "She said she needed to move some things, things best left unseen and asked me if I knew anyone."

"She asked a Nun to help her move illicit goods?" Not a smart move that.

"She figured out I wasn't happy with the way things are and wondered if I knew others equally unhappy. I told her of you, Jax that is. An upstart fence who worked with kids. While not the most honest sort, I told her I believed your heart was in the right place."

"Still taking me to task." The chuckle left me with no great reluctance, it was just as sign that no matter what, I would always have more to learn.

She fixed me with a stare that was well and truly earned. "Boy, the Sisterhood started as a way to help those seeking to escape the persecution that happened before the unification of the light, back when the gods, or at least their priests, were actively at war with each other."

"I'd always thought you were an axillary of the church, a way to help the priesthood."

"Before Unstoma? No Boy. Each Church was a separate thing, each with its own petty concerns. They told their followers that the gods were at war to see who got to rule the heavens. The Empire brought us together and the Sisters were seen as instrumental in that." She shrugged. "After that we just became tradition. Each and every church has Sisters, but most just ignore us. We find it works in our favor."

"Every one of you?"

"No, you have to prove yourself before you know what the sisters are actually about."

The Sisters were a mystery cult, who knew? "So, I take it I have you're support?"

She shook her head. "Rye, we help who we can, where we can, and when we can, but we won't risk detection. You will support us, not the other way around."

I thought for a moment, then nodded. "Yes ma'am. I know how games like this work. You use me, and I will reap the rewards for my own benefit."

She came over, wrapped her arms around me and whispered, "Good lad."

"Now when do I meet this woman?"

03 The Empress

<u>Aros 11th 386 AFU</u>

A good con takes months, sometimes years. I knew I was going to be here for the long haul. What I didn't count on was the patience of my newest partner. Only thing was, she wasn't ready to be partners yet.

She had been pointed my way by an old teacher of mine, a teacher who warned me she was coming. Sara was her name, and she was, at least according to my teacher, someone who knew things and got things done. A traveler and Warden, she patrolled most of the wild southern lands as well as the roads and woods around South Point.

Sara of course, only knew me as a fence. So far, I had moved some basic adventurers' fair for her, a few odds and ends that came out of a tomb or two, some substances best left unmentioned, a piece or two that I was sure came off the back of some wagons, you know the usual fair.

Today was quite different.

Oh sure, the song and dance were the same, a huge pile of stuff, ranging from arms and armor that had survived their former owners' demise, to a few gems and letters of bounty. Those didn't concern me; she could unload those at the Guild

Hall. No, it was a deed to a keep, one of Marcus's ancestral family keeps that brought me up.

"What the fuck is this?" no need to keep things civil when you're working out your back door.

With a shrug she said, "Something that fell through the cracks."

I looked it over for a moment, it was real, old, and an original. I'd seen the updated copies, again, ones with the wrong name on it. This one was pristine, old but it had the correct names on it, right down to its current owner, one Marcus Thunderhammer.

When the church updates documents, originals are vetted by comparing them to the copy at the nearest monastery, the one at the largest temple in the area, and the one in the records in the town where the land was located. The three should match of course, if they didn't there would be an investigation.

The copy I was holding wasn't old, it was ancient. You could see the subtle differences in the inks as each new name was added to the list. It wasn't just an original, it might very well be *the* original.

"Hold on a minute love, I think you might have something here."

She smiled at me, her eyes dancing in the dim light of the lamp. "Take your time." She watched me, a look of amusement played across her features, as did a look I didn't much like.

She was pushing me, time to push back. "You know." I opened the hood of the lantern. "Fakes are an easy thing to come by, little work here, a few chemicals there and voila." I completely unfolded the paper and moved it towards the lamp. "Only thing is, you got to be really careful. An exposed flame is what you need to activate some of the things alchemists sell that will make something look old but get them too hot." I left the statement hanging.

She didn't budge. "Get them too hot and they burst into flame of course, but originals? They're a different matter. The church treats them with an ink that flashes blue and then glows, showing the rune mark of the priest that penned the document."

I smirked. "Or gold, if it's from the old empire."

We both waited to see what would happen, or rather I waited, while she grinned. Slowly the paper warmed, and the silver started to show. I know a real document when I see one, but you don't leave such things to chance.

To be honest? I wasn't sure what I was expecting. I knew it was old, I knew it was probably an original, but when the gold showed up on the deed itself, I nearly dropped the paper.

Moving it quickly away from the flame I let it cool, and the magic that proved what it was worth, faded with the heat.

I smiled up at her with the sweetest smile I could muster and pulled the crossbow from under my desk. What? I deal with thieves all day, every day.

Her smile never wavered.

"Oh" I said. "You're good, and you're cold." She hadn't moved. "Let me guess, death curse? I take you out and it activates? Because no way you're dumb enough to walk in here with that and expect to walk back out alive without insurance. It's too much of exactly what I've been looking for to be a coincidence, and you certainly weren't surprised by the 'revelation' it's an actual Imperial deed."

She gave me a slow blink. "I'm not worried, I've got all the cards."

"Do you now?" I raised my eyebrow. "I kill you and I've got the deed, I can take it to a guy and then, well. I'm a rich man. You've read it, you know what's on it. So, you're baiting me with it, and you're no fool."

"Precisely." She said each syllable as if she were feeling each individually as they left her mouth, caressing them as if they were a hated lover. It didn't help that somehow there was suddenly a pronounced hiss in the way she spoke.

I watched this woman, every instinct I had suddenly on razors edge. No, this wasn't the first time we'd done business, but all of that, everything before was a con. My old teacher had said she was a ranger, a woodsman, and one that she had known for years. I'd asked around about the woman and no matter where I turned, I had gotten the same thing, a loner who would breeze into town from time to time with either information to sell or trinkets she had found in some dark hole. Everyone knew she would gather information, and everyone knew with absolute certainty it was simply to sell to someone else at a later date. Only a few of the people I talked to even had the barest clue that she was gathering certain information in favor of, other, often more profitable, material. From the threads I could pick up, I knew she worked for someone who was on the same scent I was.

Or so I had thought.

"How long have you been playing the simple woodsmen?"

"Long enough to track anything I wish."

"Who are you?"

"Sara will do." She leaned forwards, her smile completely predatory. "But to put your mind at ease, I do work on behalf of someone extremely interested in the same goal you have. They're quite aware of a stirring in certain political circles and wish them stopped. The pay's not much, but it suits my interests."

"And those interests are?"

She looked at me, as if considering lying for a moment. Would even I be able to tell if she did?

"I have a problem with abuse, of any kind."

"We have that in common."

"That would be why I took something from my personal stock. I had to be sure."

"And are you?"

"That you're the break for the Storm Crows?" She leaned back and smiled once more. Earlier I had thought of her smile as predatory, but that would involve the concept of chase and the possibility of escape. Neither her smile nor her eyes, offered either of those sweet lies. "Oh, I think so. Now, are you going to trigger that, or can you put it away like a good boy."

Setting the crossbow on my desk, I folded my hands and leaned forward. It wasn't going to be doing me any good at the moment, I couldn't shoot her, and she knew it.

"Ok love, so let's start over." I put on my best noonday at solstice smile and began. "Hi, I'm Jax, and you're Sara. Pleasure to make your acquaintance. We have a mutual enemy, and that's nice and all, but it doesn't make us friends, allies at best." I leaned back. "You have, as you said, got all the cards, so show me your hand." I looked her dead in those doe brown eyes, "Blow up my skirt." It was a challenge, and I hoped she was holding the flush she thought she was.

She nodded, "Alright, lets save ourselves some time." She took a deep breath. "Sara really is my name, but it's not what I'm known by, and no you don't get to know. My current, and primary employer is in New Caledonia, they have a vested trade interest in keeping things quiet in this region. Dig enough and you could have confirmed it on your own, and I expect you still will, but this saves you from having to look for the threads."

I'd been to New Cali once, years ago, strange place. "Ok, let's say I buy that, for the moment I don't have reason not to." She had me off balance, she knew more than I did. Never let a power structure like that last unless you know damn sure you can trust the one holding the rope your collar is tied too. I needed more information, but I had to be careful. How best to get her to slip up?

"That's your primary, and you want me to believe it's one of the merchant houses." Starting with intelligence, impressing her with what I knew wasn't much of a gamble, after all she knew who I was, who I really was. She had me pegged already, or so she thought. Let's see if I can shake that. "Of course, the only merchants from that far north that come this far are the gnomish spice traders, and I doubt they care very much what the politics of the human kingdoms here abouts are, since they skirt around most of the kingdoms, going instead up the Mistress to Cliffport. Then coming through Mist Song pass to here, then down the Bone."

She watched me, her eyes dancing with mirth, I was amusing her.

Perfect time to press my luck. "Which leaves one of the Seven Knights of the Eight, or the Queen herself." I nodded. "You're well connected."

She smiled at me, it was a softer thing than before, almost warm. "Go on."

Good news, she was willing to play, bad news... I only had a few of the gamesmen. At least I finally knew what game board I was on. Let's see now, she obviously thought she had given me enough to work with, doubtless I could ask questions, but she'd be tight lipped.

Why?

Why indeed?

This wasn't something you used on a subordinate, this was what you used when you were in deep and need an ally. She wasn't scared of the crossbow because, whatever she was in, was far worse than a quick death in a back alley. She was in deep and needed help, but she needed to know the person she was asking for help could handle it. That really turned things around.

Of course, if I just came out and said it, I blew the whole deal, I needed to prove it. If I failed, she'd spin some bullshit and move on to the next likely person to be of help.

The worst part? No matter how this ended, I wouldn't be completely sure of which it was.

Damn, I was getting turned on.

"Ok, so, you." I stopped to gather my thoughts. The revelation of what game we were playing and my excitement over it had derailed me. "Doesn't matter if it's the Knights or the Queen, not really. All that means is how much money you got immediately behind you; the knights are damn loyal."

"But given a lot of leeway."

"True, but in this case it hardly matters."

Her face was impassive, I'd asked her to blow my skirt up, and the tables had gotten flipped so quickly I hadn't realized it. At the moment, I wasn't enough of a breeze to do more than stir the hem at her ankles.

Time to blow hard, take some risks. "Back stories like ours are at best part truth, so you really do go down south as well. And if you're headed all the way north? That's a large territory." It was, well over three months from here to there even if you could somehow just zip through with no interruptions. "Means you don't patrol the entire thing by yourself."

Her eyes narrowed slightly, just enough to catch in the flickering light.

Gotcha. "My, my, The Blade in the Hills." I leaned back and crossed my arms, "You're a bleeding legend you are." She was also supposed to be a half elf. "Righter of wrongs, freer of peoples, protector of the ways." With each word I could read the irritation on her, it was like a scent in the air. "You don't work for her, you are her."

The woman had everything, hell we even did a job for her once, though I'd never met her in person, not before today. "What in the nine hells do I have that's so valuable as to make you tip your hand to me?"

I watched her think, it was almost as if the gears were turning right above her head. A war of sorts was playing out before me, shown only in minor twitches on her face. She had come in, backed me into a corner and had tried to set it up so I worked for her. She had wanted and prepared to have the upper hand, but my wild guess, and make no mistake that's exactly what it was, had paid off. It had knocked her off her game, albeit only momentarily. We all slip up, and she was good enough to know that.

The problem was, she needed me as much, if not more, than I needed her. Otherwise, why give me something from her private collection? This woman, or her predecessor given the length of time the organization had been in operations, ran the largest single group of rangers and wardens in the land. To call them information brokers would be like calling me a thief, true, but it just didn't cover it.

They freed slaves, waylaid bandits, stole crops to give it to hungry families, kept the Elven Road a secret, and much, much, more. That last one even I hadn't been able to find, and not for a lack of trying. No, she needed me. Now she was trying to decide how much to tell me.

She nodded coming to her decision. "I'm the inheritor of a very old operation. Yes, I am The Blade, but the person you see before you isn't the first and may not be the last, that solely depends on if I'm successful this time around."

"This time?"

"Each Blade has one job, and one job only, to end an organized threat to all the peoples of the land." She leaned forward. "I'm not talking some petty cult or dark cabal, nor am I speaking of one of the many brotherhoods that silently puppet entire fiefdoms, no I'm talking about what put those people in place."

I blinked at her.

First off, that meant she thought there was, what? A grand unifying conspiracy? Second? I mean come on. If there were, I mean... it was ridiculous.

"So, you honestly think there is, what a cult or something working to what?"

She closed her eyes and let out a sigh. "Look, Jax? Right? Look, Jax, let me ask you a few questions, the same ones once asked of me. Ok?" She looked at me and as she did, I saw it, she dropped all the pretense, all the bullshit. "If, when I'm done, you don't want to work together, you can keep that, and, well, anything else I find." She leaned back. "But if you believe me, or hell even if you just think I'm not completely bats, we work together."

With her defenses down, I saw a much different person. She was hard as any nail, probably twice as tough, and she carried a lot of blood on her hands, undoubtedly, enough to drown in. She firmly believed everything she was about to tell me, and I was betting they were Hill secrets, secrets these people both killed for, and died to protect. Yet, she wasn't a fanatic. She knew how mad she sounded and was willing to share. and even let me live once I knew.

That's a lot of trust, for both me and her, her to trust I wouldn't disagree and keep her secrets. Me to trust if I did disagree, I wouldn't be just one more pint of blood on this woman's hands.

"Answer me this first. If I said, right now, that I would help you, no questions asked, do what I could to further your goals, mostly because they seem to align with mine, else you wouldn't be here... Would you still want to ask me these questions?"

"I'm lonely Jax, and I'm scared." She let loose a breath that had been held in the tomb of her resolve for far too long. "If I'm right? We're on the verge of something so big it will change the face of every map we have. You're working on it from one end, that's what brought me here." She leaned in and looked at me, the fire light danced in her eyes. "If I fail? It won't be years until we can try this again, it won't be generations, it will be centuries. The Hills exists because the founder knew it couldn't be done alone, and yeah, we bring in people who can help. But you're the first person I've met, who can make the leaps of logic and reason necessary, and is willing to be wrong, in an attempt to be right." She smiled. "I need a partner."

Like I said, a lot of trust. "Go for it."

"What things do every one of these groups have in common, slash off the dark god of the week, or the money, and everything else, what is it?"

That *was* the question wasn't it. All of them seemed to be evil, well most of them. I had run into one or two in my time that were convinced they were good, even tried to do the good things, but that always struck me as window dressing. Besides evil didn't exactly fit either. I'd seen evil. Creatures who looked human but delighted in causing suffering and doing the worst things imaginable; rape, murder, worse. The mind can get dulled seeing too much of that. You just stop feeling after a while.

I'd say killing, but, I had more than my share of blood on my hands. Granted I made an effort not to go slaughtering, and well, I can't say there wasn't any innocent blood, but I didn't realize it when I did it. Not that that makes it any better.

Yet she was convinced every one of them had something in common. "I suppose, if I had to guess, they all seem to love to tell others what they should and shouldn't be doing. But then, that's any fanatic." Churches seemed to love to do that too. "But most of the gods love telling us how to live our lives."

"You're on the right path, keep going."

Everyone loved to tell others what to do when it came to it. We all had our own codes after all; me, her, the guy down the lane, the butcher, the baker, and so on. We thought of other people as bad, as wrong, whenever they did something we didn't agree with. Stealing always seemed to be a big one, but to me what does it matter if I steal from the lord when he steals from the peasant? I watch people starve daily. I do what I can to help, organize them, get them in the guild, make sure jobs are aimed at people who can afford to get hit. Most of my guild then takes and makes sure everyone else has food. Not all guilds are run that way, but that's the rub, isn't it? Like I said we judge good, and evil based on our own code.

That was just life. People like me knew good and evil were subjective. I did the best I could, but I got no qualms about what people think of me. People were the problem after all. If they gave a damn, I wouldn't have a single rat to go fleece anyone. See people you got to work around. Move some to help you, go around others. If you really wanted to do good in this world you had to break or at least bend the rules. People in power love their rules.

Well, at least when it came to making the rabble fall into line. Those same rules never seem to apply to them.

"Had a Lord the other day all but run down a child. There's a law about horses on the streets you see. You're not supposed to be mounted. Of course, nothing was done to him. He said he thought that they were trying to steal his purse, so he jumped up to get away. Knocked the kid down, the beast's hooves clipped him good. He's in a cell right now." Kid gets ran over, he's the one in the clink. Fucking bastards. At least they got a healer into him. I had the bribe for the guard to get him out ready. That would be happening later tonight. "But the Lord, he paid a few gold to pay for the healer, and he is still sitting pretty."

That was another part of it wasn't it? Every single one of those cults, their rabble lived by the rules, but the leaders? More often than not they broke them. All with good reason according to them mind you, but they broke them.

"All of them, every single one of them, they control by fear. They make the people afraid of something; being tossed into one of the hells, displeasing the elders, not being good enough, some outside influence is going to come in and take over."

That last one I had seen all too often. Best way to notice a cult in town was how they treated someone from outside. Ran into one group that was all too happy to put outsiders up for the night, take care of them, fatten them up for the god they were sacrificing them too. Even then? Ask a question and you started pissing people off.

"They hate to be questioned, and who can blame them. I can walk into the church right now and sit down with Father Long, ask anything I want. Hell, I regularly do. We have fun even though he knows I'm going to pick him apart. Those guys though? They say they like questions, well some of them. But if you disagree with them in any way, you're the bad guy."

That was true. Setting yourself up as an alternative authority was also a good way. Marcus had done that a time or two. They always questioned his Champion status when he did.

"So, let's see, they use fear, hate outsiders, can't be questioned, must be obeyed." Sadly, that was most towns too, so I wasn't sure where she was going with this. Maybe it was where *I* was going that was bothering me.

She nodded, "Yes, that's a common way of doing business, most leaders do things like that in one way or another, but come on, what's the one standout trait?"

It hit me. "They're all 'right', no matter which thing they're peddling, they're all 'right'. Not just that, they are so 'right' anyone who disagrees with them isn't just wrong, they're evil." That was it, I mean I hit on it earlier to a degree, but no this wasn't me thinking the local Lord was a dick, he was, and an evil bastard to boot, but. "Anyone not them is the enemy."

She smiled, but it was kind of sad. "All of that, you're right, it is all of that, but those are just symptoms."

"So, if those are the symptoms, what's the illness?"

"Are you familiar with the barbarians to the south?"

"The tribes? Yeah, I know of them. Never met one." Anyone in South Point that knew its history knew why we were a border march. Just past The Bone were the LeatherWing. Barbarian was a good way to describe them. Most of their cities from what I could tell were little more than huts on mountain sides. The human settlements under their protection were proper towns but were few and far between. They seemed to be content to mind their own business.

"What about them?"

"They have a belief, one I first heard way back when I was a child who thought themselves and adult, and no I didn't hear it from them, rather a priestess. She told me this, the lie that lets evil take hold is simple, 'I am the best there is, no one is better than me and I deserved and earned everything I have. All are beneath me. Any who do not do what should be done, do not behave in the proper way, do so because they think they are better than me, better than the rules. They wish to take what I have earned. These people must be stopped at all costs.' This is their deepest commitment. Its why they enforce rules they do not obey." She smiled at me. "Or as the LeatherWing put it, the first lie, I'm better than you, I'm scared you think you're better than me."

I thought about it. "That's too simplistic."

"Is it now?"

I blinked at her. Life, and peoples were a complicated thing. Good, bad, everyone, "Yeah, everyone lives their life as if they're right, if they don't, they'd go mad. Even the greediest person you know knows that how they live their lives is the only way."

"Yes, and the most pious does the same."

"Exactly."

"But the greedy person thinks everyone would do the same if given half the chance, the pious? Does Marcus think that way?"

With a snort, "Marcus would give you the last pence out of his pocket if he thought for a second you needed it, and he's well aware most wouldn't."

"Does he think they're bad for not doing this."

"Mark? Gods no." I let myself relax a bit. "He thinks people are people, and that most would help anyone they could, if they weren't terrified of being taken advantage of."

"Exactly."

"Look, I agree with him, most folks just want a fair world, someplace where everyone can get a bite to eat, be taken care of, you know how it is." The bloody problem was the ones who didn't want to do any work.

"It's the lazy that are the problem." She said.

"Damn right."

"But you, people like you, every day you take from others to live."

"Well, it's not fair, is it? We got people starving out there."

"So, you don't want a fair world, a world with rules that everyone lives by, but a just one, a world you have to make every single day because there is no justice except what we make."

"The rules are stacked, they benefit the people who already have everything. Guys like me at least give them what for."

"The rules are made by the people in power, and they protect that power with the rules."

I nodded. This was an old argument I'd long since worn thin with the big guy. Rules, laws, they protected people, but only by accident, not design. "I keep telling him, when men are good, laws are unnecessary, when men are evil laws are broken."

"You've been a rule breaker for a long time, why?"

I thought back to my dad, always painful that was. He obeyed the rules and died for it. "I got tired of the rules killing good people."

"All of these cults, even the most evil and loathsome believe in a set of rules that are completely unquestionable, all of them. And they are going to make the rest of us live by those rules. Why? They know better than we do how the world works and if they could just get more people to follow those rules…?"

"Then everything would be right in the world." That's what her saying boiled down to. These people broke those rules because those rules didn't apply to them. They were already good, no not good, they were already right. If they could make everyone else realize how right they were? "They want everything to be 'right'." I took a deep breath. She had a point. "So, someone is making sure, like you, all of these people come to what? The same conclusion? How do we stop them?"

"A lie travels to the next three towns before the truth ever manages to grab its cloak. That's the grand conspiracy, there is no grand conspiracy."

"But you said?"

"I said we have a chance to stop it and if we miss that chance, it will be centuries before we, before I can try again. The threat will never end. Right now, a leader, a few of them, actually, have let this worm into their ear, they rule by it. This is sadly par for the course. But someone who knows how to turn this to their advantage exists. A small group of people have, for generations, been prepping the kingdoms for such a great man to come up and save them, to make everyone behave… just like the old days."

A pit formed in my stomach and swallowed the knot that had been building up. "Unstoma, someone really is trying to bring it back."

"In reality? No. Unstoma is dead, but the idea of it? Ideas are blade proof, to the good and to the ill. Evil ideas need a face, something pleasant to look at, and more importantly, something to fear. Every time anyone longs for the good old days, someone is there to capitalize on it. The brush is currently just right to spark a blaze."

I nodded. "So how do we stop it?"

She shrugged. "We don't. Such things can't be stopped, not unless you want to go force everyone to do what you think is right."

I could see her point. "Options?"

"Set things up, find people, make safe havens, educate people. Teach people to read, how to fight, build strong communities. Make sure they can survive the fire. If we do, we limit the damage."

Now it all made sense. "You're setting people up like me all over, aren't you?"

"That's the plan."

"Any others here in town?"

"Don't worry about it. I don't want you all knowing who each other are, it's safer that way."

"How will I know who to help?" Or who to work against for that matter.

"Don't go by the look of the cup, watch for what pours out. See if I told you look for this, or look for that?"

"And the other side found out, or even a neutral party, they could pretend to be one of your groups."

"Exactly. The world's turned upside down, girl like me needs help, but everyone who helps will put themselves at risk. So, I look for what pours out of the cup, that lets me know who to talk to."

I looked at the deed. "This proves Marcus is the rightful owner, and yeah that will help, a lot."

"But it won't tell you who's doing it, and no, I don't know who it is either." She leaned back, and I was relieved to see the predator had come back. "I'm hoping you can find out."

"I'll do my best."

04 The Emperor

<u>Ymuno 2nd 391AFU</u>

Life, as they say, is a funny old thing, I'd come back to the town of my birth to help out the only real friend I ever had. I set myself up as a virtual nobody and over a scant few years, I had amassed enough power behind me to be quite the comfortable little lieutenant to a decent, if somewhat thick Master of Thieves.

He wasn't a bad guy; he just wasn't a particularly good Master of Thieves.

I say was because sadly his feet aren't touching the ground.

None of the leadership was there, hell no guildsmen were, we'll have our own wake for the poor sod later. Right now, we're dealing with a crisis, namely who is to be the next Master of Thieves. Any of us, his lieutenants, can be.

The top running is Brant the Bold. He's one of the biggest toughs in the guild, a real well to do bully boy. He's cracked more skulls than anyone else here, including me, well including Jax. My real resume isn't exactly well known around here for obvious reasons.

Like most guilds, our leadership is a democracy, also like most guilds our politics can be extremely back stabby, unlike them, with us it's literal. Right now, I was feeling a bit of the blade twist despite my back being firmly against the wall. Brant was living up to his name and being excessively bold.

"Look around you," he bellowed. "We're being picked off one by one. Our last road man was picked up when? A fortnight ago? How many of our lites are right now, as we speak, cooling heels in a cell? And who do we even have left to fill the spot with Anden gone?" He asked. "Huh?" He turned and looked at the gathered crowd. "Me? Jax?" With a chuckle he turned his gaze to me. "Jax the sitter, Jax the cleaner, Jax the laundryman?" He looked around. "He doesn't even get his hands dirty. He's not one of us. He's not at risk." He wheeled back to me, stalked over and got right up in my face. "He's a glorified merchant."

Stale garlic and rancid onions would have been a finer smell in my opinion. In pure self-defense, I waved my hand in front of my nose. The condescension was merely a happy by product, honest.

"Look at the fop, he thinks he's too good for us." He dismissed me with a snort and prowled back to the center of the gathering, leaving me propping up the wall. "He runs kiddy cons, hits churches, and what has it got us? Day in, and day out, patrols up and down the street, that's what."

Brant knew his audience; he was getting cheers and 'hear hears' from every man, woman, and child who made up our little family.

"Now don't get me wrong, panty pinches like Jax be useful, lot of coin to be had in nicked nickers. But we're at war. How long before they be knocking at our door?" I watched as the ripple of fear gripped every loin, short and curly or not. "We got to take it to the guard, got to strong arm them, got to remind the top who it be who really rules these streets." He nodded to himself. "Not to speak ill of a man who no doubt still be swinging, but this lay low policy didn't do much for him now did it?"

He drew himself up to his rather impressive height. He was orc tall, with his blonde hair greasier than a cook's pot, his teeth showed the numerous fights he'd been the last one standing in, and his skin showed he spent much of his time these days underground. He commanded the room with such ease that I'd be worried, if, that is, there had been a brain between his ears.

Each of us got to have a say, and each of us knew better than to interrupt the speaker. As such, I didn't let his baits get to me. Not that they were much of a bait mind you.

"We got to get tough, show them faint hearts who's boss. It's us, and them, and I know where I stand. What more I know you lot stand with me, I'm saying what every bastard son of you been thinking. We can't let them push us round no more." More cheers rose, that may have been worrisome if I didn't know how free he'd been with coin beforehand.

He bowed, ceding the floor to me, that simple gesture of graciousness, earned him another round of applause. Hell, I joined in.

Me joining in ended all further sound in the room. I even kept clapping as I strode towards him, adding a trumpet whistle on his behalf. Brant just stood there looking dumb founded.

Time to show these people what it really took to make oneself the Master of Thieves.

"Give it up." I kept clapping as I strode closer to the man. "Let's hear it for Brant everyone." As I drew in, I put my hand on his shoulder and spun him to face the crowd not me. "Give the Bold another round will you, you lot, come now, don't be shy, he paid good for it. Let's hear it for Brant the man who made you all a bit richer if even for today."

He closed the distance between us by facing me and leaned in close. "What you playing at Jax."

"This." I said with a smile. With a movement practiced from years on the road, I pushed my dagger straight into his black heart. As his eyes grew wide, I pushed him off my blade and showed it to the assembly hoard.

"Lesson one kiddies, if I kill you, it will be face to face." I looked around. "No quiet coup, no we'll get rid of him in his bed in the dark." I looked over at a few of my guild brothers. "Yes, I know all about the plan." Didn't matter if I did or not, no one would ever believe them. It was true incidentally. "Brant had planned to eliminate every single one of us, and pick his own toadies to surround himself with, so to my fellow lieutenants?" I paused for effect, "You're Welcome." Step one, build loyalty.

"Now, by guild charter, I've not done anything untoward, though usually no one is bold enough to do it so blatantly and out in the open." I chuckled at my joke, thankfully I wasn't the only one. Got to love black humor. "So, let's not go crying foul. But face it, despite what Brant said, the ability to get your hands dirty doesn't a leader make. Though I hope this is a lesson to you all, that people you think won't, can indeed, and often do." Address what was seen to be, or at least said to be, a short coming. No one could say I wouldn't get my hands dirty now, not when I stood before them quite literally red handed.

Every eye in the room was on me. I say room because that's what it was, an actual room in someone's home. One of many bad ideas I was going to have to fix.

"Good to know I have your attention. Now, when I'm done speaking, if any of you would like to show me the door, say by pointing at it with a dagger through my own chest, feel free. At which point, much like Brant, I will leave this little gather feet first. Before that, you will let me finish talking!" Once you have their attention, take command, own up to what you did, who you are, and make your peace with it, or apologize.

"Now then, where to start. I'll start by saying that Brant wasn't entirely off base, the leadership of this guild has been somewhat lacking of late. We've gotten used to lax security and lax practices." I looked around the room. "Which is why *I* took the liberty of ensuring that tonight, we actually would be secure." A nock at the door made everyone jump, they positively cringed when a guardsman just walked in. "Hello Hanna love." Demonstrate power.

Hanna looked around the room, then to me. "The area is secure Jax, though it took some doing. Seems there was a guard patrol that was supposed to come this way, but I got them handling a fight down at the docks." With that she just nodded and left.

"My, my." I looked around. "I wonder what they could have been coming all the way out here to these quiet little homes for?" Hanna was a real find. She was as straight as Marcus was, and only worked with the likes of me, in hopes of catching real problems, problems like His Holiness. One of my little squads did good to find her. I was going to have to give Piper and Chloe a raise.

"I'm sure all of your paid off guard, warned you about that, right? No? I wonder." Everyone here had at least one guard on the take, but that was the problem, a bought guard could be bought off you, if they were paid more money by someone else. Loyalty bought with coin goes to the highest bidder.

"Look around you, all of you. We're soft, stupid and weak. Go to war with the Guard? Are you daft? Did you forget this is a Boarder March? Why do you think the Duke always comes here to the Margrave to get his troops?" Point out holes in the grand plans that fear made. It helps when you've already removed their strong man.

"What are you, thick?" No eye was on me, every single one was on the floor. "Anyone notice I didn't pack this place with my supporters? Huh? Did you miss that?" I watched as more feet shuffled. "No, my lot's out right now working. I didn't bring them here to pad the vote. But I'll tell you what, every single one of your territories is taking a beating tonight as mine clean up." That got some grumbles, it always does when you point out that not just britches, but knickers were on the floor.

"You want to know how to weather this? Better yet how to turn this into a gold mine? I do. I want to know how to be what we are, thieves, opportunists, the people who have the jobs we have because we fell through the cracks." I looked at my gathered ne'er-do-wells. "Cracks that this crackdown has only widened. That's right boys and girls, things are bad, we're definitely feeling the pinch, but so are a lot of other people." Here's one for you, people like us don't do well in places that are freer, but let there be a crackdown? Oh, then people like us pop out of the woodwork. "Every town, every village, every land, we all know what happens. The law cracks down on something, who provides it?"

"We do!" Came the chorus.

"Damn right we do. Right now, how many of the demihumans pay higher taxes for moving goods? Huh? That's a smugglers paradise right there. How many shops got to pay extra for spices? How many?" I could already see them start to get it. "How many nobles are going to honestly be going without fire powder? Without coffee itself due to these new 'laws' on trade? How many of The Guard do you think would look the other way if instead of handing them gold you slipped them a few grounds? How about the crack down on Dwarven Ale? Or Elven Whiskey?" I looked around. "Not your cup of tea that? How about tea then? The Duke just upped the tax on all trade routes." Whet their appetites, get them asking you the questions.

"But we got no highwaymen?"

"Who's faults that? The Guard? No, it was our own stupidity." I looked at each of them. "We started waylaying everyone didn't we. Why? Cuz numbers were down?" Time to start getting into what I wanted. "What did we do with that money? Huh? What? To pay our bribes? No that got foisted out on us, to save money they said. How about to pay our sick?" I looked around. "No, what do the old timers have to teach us but their secret routes, or to show our young'uns how to lift or lay better? They're just a drain on us. We lost old Fred last season to the cough. The bloody cough." I threw up my hands. Fred had been my first night job, he taught me the art. "No, where did all that extra money go from stepping up? It went to the fine clothing the uppers wore."

I stomped over to the corner and grabbed a chest. Taking it to the center I up ended it and let the silver and gold spill out. "Where do you think Brant got the extra money to bribe you?"

"You got nice clothes." Someone grumbled.

"That I do." I fingered my shirt. "Stollen right off the dress makers dummy for the Duke himself. Only cost me a shilling, and a promise that I gave the seamstress first pick of the silk I nicked at a good price."

Time for the final lesson. "Now, you show me the door, and you can keep all that." I gestured at the fallen money. "Or you can get nice shirts like this for yourself."

"We're listening." I looked up at the speaker. It was my old bar mate Paslle. Damn providence, you never know when a good deed's going to pay off. I felt my face split into a grin with a brightness to damn the sun itself. If his thick head got it, none of them could miss it.

"Simple, old chum, we build a community. What keep is going to turn us in, if we're pinching for them, rather than pinching them?" I looked around at the surrounded mass of unwashed, and slightly washed flesh. Time to open up. "South Point is small, ish anyway. We all know each other more or less, but we got well over two thousand souls that call it home. The rabble don't like us cuz we feed off them. But if we turned our attention elsewhere, started feeding them? Well, no son of a whore in this town would turn us in."

"But where the money going to come from?"

"Good question, it's almost like we live in a trade hub. Why do you think everyone pays the Margrave? Hum? Because we get all the goods from the Bone, all the goods from the river, the dwarves, the elves, we get all the goods from the sea." I looked around, "It all flows right through here. Only, thing is, the people don't see the money from it, now do they? The merchants do, the nobility does, the lords stick their dick in it, but us?" I made a rude gesture. "Not a drop."

I gazed at all of them. "We're sitting on the largest smuggling operation we could ever want, we'd have to work hard, be lean sometimes, spread the wealth, but we could do it, and well?" I fingered the collar of my shirt. "All of us could stand to dress a bit better. Makes it harder to paint us as thieves and low lives. Might even be able to get some of us in The Guard."

I looked around and watched as the rats running those little wheels in their heads furiously worked their little legs.

Time to leave. I turned my head slightly raising my chin, gave a slight nod, then bowed deeply, and walked out.

No one tried to point the door out with their knife. Never leave them with what can't be done, always leave them with what can.

05 The Hierophant

<u>Ymuno 21st 391AFU</u>

Life is its own punch line.

I sit here, drinking strong elven whiskey, I prefer it to the dwarven stuff, well, most of the dwarven whiskeys at any rate. Best stuff I ever had was made high in the mountains by a clan with a name I can't even pronounce. It tastes the same way a razed village smells. This is almost as good. A little less smoke, a little more peat.

Oh well.

What the hell am I going to do?

I came back looking for Marcus's daughter, a daughter he had with the love of my life, a woman of pure fire named Nyssa. On their wedding night I looked for comfort elsewhere and Cynthia was there for me. A few weeks ago, I met her son.

He's the right age, he's as small as I was, hell besides being red, he's got my eyes.

Call's himself Cyn. Not sure if it was meant as a lark, or a shortening of Cynthia's kid or what, but damn. He's got demon blood in him. Makes me wonder about what my mum said when she found out I'd turned to the life.

"That devil blood of your Da's done turned up, and look at you, a no-good thief." Good church woman my mum...

I wonder if that was what she meant?

Looked into the kid after he burst through my shop door, a wild elf on his ass. Fool elf came along and ran face first into the door, just as I got this ash skinned, red headed, horned, and tailed thing, under my display table. Slowed the beast down enough to make sure the boy was well hid. I do mean beast, this elf was sniffing for him and looking around as if he were a hound, I half expected him to hike his leg at any moment.

Two As'True Dwarves slid in after him, a pair of lovers. Good lads by the look of them. I figured I'd spin 'em a yarn, send them on their way, rattle the whelp's bones for him for coming into my shop by the front, and that would be that.

Then that elf mentioned Unstoma.

I heard his tale, and I had heard words like that before. Got to stop Unstoma from rising, and now the shit was in my shop. I got the trio out of there as fast as I could, I can't have them scaring legit clientele after all, but I knew I could use them to my advantage being as we were on the same path.

Found out the boy had pinched the elf's purse. Gods this one was thick. Then he comes running in here to hide, gods only knew why. Told him what I told them, come back at dusk, and for god's sake, come around back.

A face like Cyn's is hard to miss, I'd seen it before, he'd been there when I so graciously took the mantle of King of Thieves. But running into my shop with his marks pursuing him? I needed to know more. Was he just stupid, or was he a plant to try to dethrone me?

That's when I found out who his mum was.

God rest Cynthia's soul. A late-night job with a noble went tits up and she didn't make it. That noble died the next night.

Exactly as I'd have done, good Lad.

It was the first hint of fatherly pride I had for the boy.

I know I got a soft spot, hell, Piper and Chloe, their crew, Bear, Dwalt, Ella, Chloe and Elon, all of them. They're my kids. Every damn one of them has made me proud in one way or the other. Hells when I'm gone from here Chloe Blackthorn is going to be King of Thieves, if she survives that long that is. She's certainly smart enough. Pip's going to make a great lieutenant for her, hell they already do the job on the small scale.

That night I sat Cyn and his new friends down and gave them the bare bones. They were interested. One of them, a cleric named Tarn, called me on claiming the boy was my nephew... so I told him the truth out of reflex. See tell the truth first, you can always lie later.

Sent them off on a basic 'shop run'; undead, a curse, secret rooms. Same thing a hundred of us had been on for well over four hundred years, cuz no one could figure out how to break the damn curse.

But Cyn did.

Gods damn me, I have a son.

Tonight, he slides in with a local legend. A scrap of a map with squiggles on it that tell its tale. Marky boy and I had searched this entire town looking for that scrap, us and a hundred others. He found it. Well, his pet dog, the wild elf, did anyway.

It's a map to a location of some ruins, hidden way up in the mountains somewhere. The group that made that map, disappeared. They swore to the heavens that there was more under the ruins and that worse it was the center of an Unstoman cult to the God Emperor. It's the kind of place people like us go and die.

God help me, my solution to that problem is almost as bad. I sent him to deliver it to Marcus. Hell, I even gave the boy a family name. Of course, I told him I was Willum Jackson Taylor... if his lips loosen around the wrong people no one will notice. Mark will. Mark knows my full name, my real name. Maybe he'll tell my bastard.

Honestly, this is harder on me than I thought it would be. I mean, I thought about it, I'm not exactly a chaste man. The idea that somewhere out there I'd given rise to a crotch goblyn hadn't exactly escaped my mind. I would like to say I mostly stuck with whores, who of course know ways of mitigating the risk. No, in my twenty years of being out and about, I rarely had a cold bed, if I even had one at all that is. Never bedded anyone in group, wasn't even tempted till Nyssa, didn't want to complicate things, but once I was in town? A wench here, a tart there, a working girl if need, a farmer's daughter.

I swear that bottle had more in it. Oh well, need another one. Good thing I'm stocked.

Town's on lock down, got two armies just outside and the local lord holed up within our walls. I'd say the Margrave would be by soon to deal, but my boy already saw her, and if she has plans to intervene in this dispute, she didn't tell him. That bitch is tough as nails though, if these fops annoy her enough, she'll send both armies back with their tails between their legs.

Gods, how am I going to get my boy out? Do I want him out?

Not really. But as long as he's got that map, he's a target, and I love the boy... Gods help me, oh god I actually do.

I need another drink.

That map, could it be a key to something about what's going on? Doubtful. More like it's a matter of the same thing the Crows were doing back in the day. Getting crap out of the hands of imbeciles who would use it for nefarious purposes and putting said items in the hands of *our* imbeciles, who would use it for our nefarious purposes. Sorry, I just don't trust anyone with a sword that can suck the soul right out of your body... We destroyed that one.

This gets worse every day, small things really. New laws, again small ones, codifying things people just take for granted. Today's was a doozy and I doubt even my boy noticed it. It didn't affect him, hell it doesn't affect most people. All merchants must pay a tax, seems reasonable. The thing is, if you're local that tax is one thing and if you're not that tax is another. How do they tell if you're local? A brand-new stamp of course. One based on your trade house. If you have a human trade house stamp, you're fine, if it's the trade house for another race? Well then, you pay more taxes of course. Seems simple right? Most everyone in town is human. The merchants were all for this. The local house, and I use that loosely, is centered in a town three months travel from here to the north, right in the heart of human land. The Dwarven guild? It's centered two days away. Care to guess who most of our merchants deal with and how often? True the Dwarves only make low end stuff, the kind of stuff everyone needs. It's only a few farthings more, not bad right?

It adds up. Our merchants, the low-end ones, are going to wind up paying through the teeth, especially the few non-human ones we have. The other house? Well, they do silks and the like, all high-end stuff. Lower taxes for the rich, higher taxes for the poor. That is what it is. Except for of course the Gnome stuff, that's taxed to hell and back. It is also mostly spices, and other things, from up where it's warm year-round. People who could barely afford spices now, just can't after this.

But humans first? Am I right?

Meanwhile outside our walls right now is an army wanting their tax money. Money that was paid, but hey it makes a good cover to raise taxes on the poor and have you thank them for it.

It's tradition after all.

Tradition. Bah...

What the hell am I leaving my boy tradition wise? A life that could easily see him taking a step that never sees his feet hit the ground again?

Yeah, they just changed the rules for that too. First offense? 30 lashes. Second? Lose a hand. Third? Third, you take that step. Got the news day before yesterday. It is not announced yet of course, but it's already drafted. You'd be amazed at how quickly the higher ups come to me to clean their dirty clothing just before one of these things hit. I get all the best gossip.

Cyn is just too noticeable. Boy already can't go to most places without being run off, every guard knows him on sight... it's good he's gone. Saved his life, I did. Saved it by sending him out into the world as someone who is likely to get his fool self killed trying to pry a bobble out of the hands of the dead.

He's an adventurer, a mercenary, and gods help me it's his best chance to stay alive.

Best not to think about it. I got nothing else to give the boy. Some father I am.

When did this bottle get empty? Did I spill it? Gods, I hope not, be a hell of a mess to clean up.

Doesn't look like it.

Think I'm gonna take a nap... yeah, a nap. That'll help. Just need a few minutes. Got to figure out if there is anything I can do for the boy. Marky boy will help. Yeah Marcus... he's a good guy. He'll help.

Hope Cyn makes it. Kid deserves better than me, but we're both kind of stuck.

Gods look after the boy... please...

06 Lovers

<u>Blodeuo 19th 392 AFU</u>

Over the years, I've seen a lot of faces first thing in the morning. Humans, Elves, and an Orc or two. What can I say? I'm a guy who likes personality. I usually prefer women who I know can kick my ass. Which might explain why I just woke up next to Sara.

Last night was... what the hell happened last night?

Looking around we were definitely not in town. Furs, leather of a tent, barely any light was coming in at all. The only light sources were a glowing stone set in a larger stone bowl and an oil lamp. She was asleep, and I was, less than clothed.

Think damn it. Did I get plastered last night? Worse did I hit on and then bed a woman who, who what? Lifting the covering furs slightly I took a look to see if my state of undress was mutual.

The swell of her hip, the curve of her back, the smoothness of her skin... the complete lack of scars.

That was disturbing.

Rule one kids, look for what doesn't make sense. I was naked, with a naked woman who I barely knew, and while I did have a thing for her type, neither of us had even talked about anything like this. In the grand scheme of things, maybe not a problem. Now add in we weren't in town, and this beautiful swordswoman, from what I could tell, didn't have a single scar. At least not on her back.

Not a succubus, I was still alive. While not as evil as some believed, and certainly not a demon or daemon, they were still a powerful Fae that lived on the energies of sex. The Last Kiss was supposed to be where they got the best of you, something men didn't tend to survive. Me being alive ruled that one out, not to mention their favorite prey were adulterers and rapists. While I was a first-class bastard, I was neither of those things.

There are other shapeshifters of course, people who take strange forms, all of them were dangerous, and I might be, currently, in bed with one. One that was already someone I knew to be capable of violence all on her own.

I moved slowly and got the lamp, making as little noise as possible, holding it close I examined the skin on her back a bit more thoroughly. As the light came in I began to make out faint lines, slight imperfections in the skin. With the added light, I could see she was scarred. I felt myself relax a little, even as I became fascinated with the map that was her survival of past battles. The telltale lines of a dagger cut, the longer stroke of a sword slice, the ragged wounds of claws. The girl had seen her fair share of her own blood spilled.

"Enjoying yourself?" The words were soft, the rebuke less so.

"Admiring the scenery." What else was there to say, my hand was definitely on the purse. "Can't blame a guy for wanting to know who exactly he's in bed with." She rolled over and looked at me. "Quick question though, and I mean no disrespect, why am I naked in what I can only assume is your boudoir?"

"Boudoir? Old Unstoman? Really? That's a big word." She sat up and pulled the furs tight.

"What can I say, I'm a man of many talents."

"What do you remember from last night?"

I opened my mouth to quip about drink and too much of it, then I stopped. I had been asking myself the same thing before I got paranoid about shape shifters.

Not to let that bother me, "Not much." What was the last thing I remembered? "I was at my shop, being all respectable like because…" I'm only all respectable when dealing with nobles. I don't bother with airs for the common folk, they prefer a down home approach. "I think the Margrave was in my shop." That didn't seem right. Margrave Halonis was a no-nonsense woman who wore a LeatherWing skull pauldron, a real family heirloom from the war. My silks usually held no interest for her.

"Halonis was there, ok. Why?"

Thinking made my head hurt. "Something about, something…" What was it? "A chest, a chest had been found at her old family keep, out on the island."

"Ok, a chest at Blood Keep. Then what?"

I was being pumped for information and didn't know why. Time to buy myself some time. "Where are my clothes?" She was covered up, I suddenly had a great need to be.

"Behind you, on the left."

Reaching over I grabbed my jerkin, my travel jerkin. It was stiff to the touch, dried after being soaked. The breeches under it were also the same. I had been traveling and got wet, soaked to the bone in fact. My knives, small sword, bracers and small clothes also showed the same thing, and all were there. Well, all but my boots.

"I went in the water." I pulled the shirt to my nose. "Fresh water from the smell." It might have been spring, but the melt was just starting to speed up. That meant the water in a river. "You saved my life."

She smiled. "You'd have done the same for me."

"Why all the questions? What happened?"

"We were conscripted by my cousin for a little errand. Some old documents and a chest found at the keep still fell under family business, an old tithe to be paid off, of all things."

"She wanted us, you and me, to go down to the LeatherWing lands and deliver..." I could almost see it. "Something." I took a deep breath. "You because you've dealt with them, me because she trusts me."

"Yep, if I delivered it, it wouldn't count as from her, but with you as emissary."

"Everything was fine, until we started back down." I stopped putting my clothing on. "We were attacked."

"Do you remember by what?"

"Surely not the LeatherWing?" Barbaric as they could be the blighters were honorable to a fault. "No, something small, a lot of them. They cornered us on the bridge." Cornered us, more like herded us. All we had was the torch light and they were always maddeningly out of sight, at least until the end. "Goblyns."

The foul things faces swam into my memory just like they did into the firelight. The size of children of about eight, their faces were a mass of scars both ritual and incidental, ears large and pointed and too big for their heads, teeth crooked and sharp, skin the grayish white of rotten flesh, and hands with three fingers and a thumb on either side.

"They got us on the bridge and kept coming, eventually pushing me off." I looked at my weapons, two daggers, small sword, but not my arming sword. The bridge in question was over the river true, but the water was well below, the snow melt had made, what was probably a calm waterfall, a raging shower that left the wood of the bridge slick. "How did you, how did you make it out?"

Asking how she saved me was important, but honestly with that many of the filthy beast on us I was more interested in how she was alive. Any fall like that was bound to have rocks under it, that explained my head. It's simply that I had the sense knocked out of me.

She let lose a sigh, "After you went over, I had them on both sides. Better part of valor I'm afraid. I jumped." She looked at me. "Besides, if you died..."

She jumped, of course she did. If she hadn't, no telling how I would have ended up. Jumping she was prepared for the water, me in a fall? Not so much.

"So, where are we? Where are the beasts?"

"By the time I got you out of the river, we were close to one of my holes. I stashed us there, well here. As for our pursuers? No clue. Didn't see them, and we were more than a mark's walk down river."

Love and light, that water must have been moving. There is a saying about gift horses that I think applies here. "Well at this point I'm just glad to have my skin." Fastening up my belt,

I took a better look around. "A heat stone? Rare thing that." Most items that keep magic were rare after all but making them was easy. Any charlatan could make something that lasted long enough to get the marks coin.

A smile was the only answer I was getting.

"So, what now?"

"Now we go warn South Point."

Good point.

07 The Chariot

<u>Cryfder 11th 392 AFU</u>

Of all the things I've learned in this life, nothing will surpass this, it doesn't matter how many times you get knocked down, it only matters how many times you get back up. Dean was about to learn that the hard way.

"As you can see, old man, I've got all the cards." His smirk was insufferable. "I've got the Guard in my pocket, the Lord Mayor where I want him, and a patron."

I looked over the writs, the marks, and most importantly the goons the little shit had brought with him. "I take it, this patron goes by the name His Holiness?" That wanker had been a pain in my side since before I took power.

"I don't know who that is." His grin belayed his lie. "Besides, isn't he a myth?"

I nodded. "That he is mate, that he is."

Dean was an up and comer in the guild, a real go getter. Problem was he was more ambitious than he was intelligent.

"I've got you Jax." He said with all the glee of a child who just caught a wild cat. "I got you." He was about to find out how big my claws were.

Time to change tactics. "So you do. What do you want?"

He blinked at me. "The guild, I want the guild. Did you think I did all this to curry favor with you?"

No, I knew what he wanted, or rather, what his patron wanted. "That would have been the smarter move."

I watched him blink, one of the slow ones, the kind that says he didn't comprehend.

I stood, stood up so fast his bully boys had their crossbows pointed at me. Time to teach these children how the world works. I turned my back on them and reached for the bottle. "Dwarven scotch." I turned back to him with it, as well as two carved tumblers. "Finest in the land." Sitting back down I put both glasses in front of myself. "Let's drink to your success." I pulled the cork and poured us both enough to get the point across. "Then I'll tell you what you should have done."

He looked at me, at the four large men with their deadly bolts pointed at me, then to the glasses. "All right old man." He took the glass that had been slightly closer to me. "I'll give you one last drink; let you preen a bit. But you're not leaving this office alive."

I watched as he put the glass to his lips and drank, not a savor, not a pull, he tried to pour it down his gullet like it was common grot. That was his second mistake. He wasn't used to good scotch. As I took my sip, savored the smoky and smooth taste on my tongue, felt the burn of it, he sputtered like a gnomish wood chopper.

"Dean, I like you, I really do. I'm sorry it's come to this." The worst part was, I really was. He was a good lad all things considered.

"I..." That was as far as he got. His breath escaped him all at once and he had to fight to get it back. "I'm sure you do. You should have respected me, shown me my due." The coughing and sputtering were, in a word, pathetic. This was going to be a sad end to a sad man.

"How old are you Dean?"

"24 winters."

I nodded, "That's right 24 winters. You've done good work in such a short time." I sipped more, and this time so did he. Lesson learned. "Why did you take the one closer to me?"

"Never take the cup first offered." He snorted. "Every thief learns that right quick."

I nodded. "Yes, every thief does. They learn it or they don't live long enough to make it to 24."

"Damn straight."

"So why did you take the cup closest to me?"

A confused look crossed his face. "I just told you, every thief..." He trailed off. Color drained from his face as realization took over. His eyes slowly made their way down to his cup.

"Don't worry boy, I didn't poison you." Relief washed over his features. "Before you go to barking orders at the men you brought with you; Hiram, Stan, Paul, and Elon, you should know something."

"What?" His voice was sullen like a child's. I had already out maneuvered him, and he knew it. Oh yes, this could work. "Let me guess?" He locked eyes with me, regaining his footing. "They all secretly work for you, and you've had me pegged from day one?" His voice shook a little at the end. Self-control wasn't something he had learned yet, and his men had already seen him falter once. "They are some of the oldest members of the guild, you should have paid better attention to them. Bribing them was easy."

He missed the fact I knew all their names. "Oh no doubt, and no, they don't secretly work for me. They openly work for me, as every member of the guild does. But here's the thing Dean. Me? I'll be gone one day, so will you, just like the last guild master, and so will the guild master after us, and the one after that. But Hiram, Stan, Paul, and Elon will still be here when people like you and I are farts in the wind. They aren't loyal to me, they're loyal to the guild."

I locked eyes with him. "See, you managed to do something behind my back. That's a feat and something to brag about. These boys? They saw it. So, the question is, is old Jax slipping?" I leaned back and picked up the bottle and poured more for myself and offered him some. "So, they let you bribe them, come down here and they let us dance." It was complete bullshit. They had been bought and paid for fairly, but the lie made them sound noble. Even thieves like to think themselves the heroes of their own story. "So now they will wait and see." I nodded, he wasn't there yet, but I hoped he, and they, would be soon. "They wait to see which of us is the true King of Thieves."

"I could order them to kill you now."

I let a grin split my face. "No doubt. Hells, they might even do it. But they would just be on the lookout for your replacement because you turned down my challenge."

Here it was, any misstep, any deviation, any screw up, and I wasn't walking out of here. What I said was true. These men had no loyalty to me, had been bought and paid for, and if

Dean wanted, he could end it right now, or hell at any time in our little game. Dean thought my opponent was him, it wasn't, it was time. If he didn't get me, one day someone would. His Holiness had managed to get one of my men to turn on me. The game as they say, was already up. Dean didn't know it, but his game was up too. Right now, because I had already stalled long enough, there were doubtless men, my men, waiting to come in at my signal.

Two reasons not to do it. The first, well, they could still take their shot and I would still be dead. I didn't like that outcome. The second, the big one, was these four men, they needed to leave here under their own power, they needed to tell everyone how when faced down, I stood tall. No groveling, no better offers, no backing down. I needed these four men to live and see I had beat His Holiness, or the next idiot to take the offer the man gave wouldn't be as stupid as Dean. I had to prove I was King of Thieves.

My life hung in the balance of my bullshit.

I liked those odds.

Well, my bullshit and my self-control. Because to tell you the truth? One wrong word and I knew I wouldn't be safe, even if I walked out of here tonight.

Some of the real undercurrent of the situation seemed to finally make its way into Dean's thick skull. He looked back at his 'men' all of whom still had a bead on yours truly. He didn't catch them eyeing each other, but I did.

Treason is punishable by death, they knew walking in tonight, it was kill me, or they would die. I just gave them an out, and they knew it.

Good.

"All right, let's dance." He slowly sipped more of the scotch. "I've beat you. What's more is I've been doing it for months. This took me near a year to set up, and you suspected nothing. What with your running off for gods only knows where and coming back when you feel like it. The guild is tired of it. It needs strong leadership."

"No." One word. It was all I needed. I said it calmly and dismissively.

His drink stopped before reaching his mouth. "No?"

"No." I took another swallow.

"I most certainly did. I went out, did the leg work, got the evidence for leverage," He would have continued but I interrupted him.

"No." I repeated it as if talking to a very small, very dull, child.

"Damn it, No what?"

"The guild doesn't need strong leadership. It doesn't need someone over seeing every little thing, forcing their will on it. It needs smart leadership."

"Yeah, well. I'm smarter than you."

A smile tried to pull at my lips. "No."

"Gods damn you, what do you mean no?"

"You're trying to curry favor. Trying to impress. Oh, to be sure, you did things without me seeing." I looked at them, the writs, the blackmail, the letters of note and mark, getting the mayor was a nice touch. "But so does every slip, snip, pick pocket, bully boy, and madam in this town."

"Exactly. You don't know what's going on in your own house."

This time I didn't stop the grin, instead I turned it into a knife to wield. "Exactly." It was so gratifying to see the confusion on his face. "You don't get it do you?" It was like watching a donkey try to work out math, he didn't even see the problem. I twisted the knife. "First and foremost, if no one shits till I tell them, everyone gets constipated real quick." All five of them were looking at me as if I had sprouted wings. "Second, if I know everything everyone is doing at all times, I know everything everyone is doing at all times."

"Yeah, it's called control."

"Yeah, it's called everyone gets caught if I get pinched." I looked at him, and I mean really looked at him. He was young, but his face already bore its share of marks from life. Small scars above the eye, a few on the upper lip. The face of a scrapper, boy had probably seen more fist fights than a man twice his age. His short hair was a mess, neat in a way, but the kind of neat that came from being short and board straight. Real 'run your fingers through it and go' hair. Still, it was tousled, probably trying to go for a tougher look than the 'innocent boy' the natural flat hair normally gave him. "See, if we centralize, if someone gets pinched, then they have all of us now don't they. If I don't know everything everyone's up to in detail, then I can't sing, now can I?"

"I wouldn't sing."

"Dean, you've already proven you would."

A snort was my response. "Yeah? How."

"Who contacted whom?" I leaned back once more, played with the cracked and chipped paint of the whitewash on the wall, flicking a piece off with my nail. Time to get someone in here to fix that. "Did his Holiness contact you or did you contact him?"

With a smirk, "His Holiness? Man, that's just a legend, he ain't real."

"You and I know better."

"Fine, so what if he is?"

"Who contacted whom first?"

"All right, I'll play. Let's say I contacted him."

"Good trick, how?"

He raised a single eyebrow at me. "How?"

"Yes, how?" I leaned forward again, hands out of sight. The little shit didn't even flinch. I took my chance. "Hello, your Holiness, I work for the Thieves guild in South Point. I'd like a job."

He shifted uncomfortably. "No man, nothing like that. I put feelers out. Guy has his thumb in everything. I knew it was just a matter of time…"

I cut him off, "Before he contacted you."

"Well, yeah."

I leaned back, a quick move. It made the crossbows jump a bit, but thankfully nothing fatal.

"So, he contacted you."

"Once I signaled I was ready." He didn't just try, he sounded confidant, as if he just knew things were on his terms.

"Too sure. Ready to sell out the guild to an outsider."

"No man." He waved a hand playing it off. "Ready to make my move, to take over."

"You know, we have rules for that, you could have, should have, called a vote."

"And let you talk your way out of this?" He pulled out his own small crossbow. I had been so busy making sure these next steps were right, I hadn't seen his hand go down. Must have been just after he played off the treason. Wicked little thing it was. The tip of the bolt looked wet.

With a smile he explained. "A little shit, some piss, makes it nice and septic. It'll take a few days, but it will be worth it. Shouldn't have taken your eyes off my hands, you've gotten slow."

Kid was right. Problem was, he had one plan, I had three. "Fair point." I reached out and took his glass, refilled it without looking at him by using my finger to gauge when it was at the right depth, then did the same to my own.

Dean grinned again, he wasn't counting on the bully boys to kill me, he knew at this point they may not. So, he was going to do me slow, but he was going to explain it first. Bloody amateur.

"See, I know how this is played. You're trying to talk your way out of this, right now. Trying to get these fine men to side with you, let you walk out of here." He shrugged. "It's a fair game. All I have to do is out maneuver you."

"Too true, but let's get back to how you've already sold them out."

"See, you say that?" He picked up his glass, then sat it down. "But you can't back it up, cause it ain't true. I won't break." He leaned forward and made his case. "And I won't sell out these men."

"And I said you already have."

"Prove it." He threw the scotch back, the whole tumbler at once, this time he didn't get vapor lock. "Cause the way I see it, I'm quick, and I adapt fast. I learn."

"All right, my final move, two really. Once I've made them, the gentleman can remove the body, I won't even make a fuss."

"Go for it."

I watched him; he was sweating a little. Good. Part of him already understood the game was over.

"One, his Holiness isn't guild. Oh, he can join same as anyone else, no one is stopping him. But he hasn't. He doesn't have the guild in his heart. You? You went to him with guild business. If you did it once, to get power in the guild, power you should have earned, then you'll do it again." The four men looked at him, then me. Each of them took a step back away from Dean. "Oh dear, already all out of friends."

Dean for his part suddenly looked pale, coughed a little bit. "I'm going to double cross him, you got to know that."

"I do, so does he. You still brought in and outsider."

Hiram looked at me, crossbow still pointed in my direction, but no longer at my head. "What's the second move?"

"Crushed and rendered apple seed." I watched as Dean's eyes grew large, he finally got it. "I said I didn't poison the first glass." I watched as he struggled to breathe, face already turning blue. "I did miss you and your back-room dealings and like you, I forgot to keep my eye on the hands. The difference is, I don't give warnings. I do what's necessary. I don't gloat until after its all over and no one can do a damn thing to stop me. I don't want to be recognized for the cleverness of my master plan; I don't need a pat on the head." I stood up and straightened my collar. "I'm not interested in glory. A Thieves Guild runs on money, on keeping things smooth. Oh, you got some dirt. Me? I got the mayor's entire staff, I also have connections with the Gnomes and Dwarves to move the goods, I know the Elves."

I walked around and picked his drooping face up and looked him in the eye. "You played a child's game against a master. You nearly won; I congratulate you. You could have been someone. Now? You're just dog food."

I turned and looked at the four bullies. "Get him out of my sight." Turning my back on them I calmly walked back around my desk to sit down. Any one of them could have ended me then and there. I knew it, they knew it, but I needed them to know it, I was Jax, master of thieves, King of Thieves.

That is, after all, how these games are played. "And boys? Good work."

08 Strength

<u>Aros 14th 392 AFU</u>

Life, as they say, isn't fair.

No shit.

Fair is for games of chance, it's for games of skill, not life.

Trust me on this, you don't want life to be fair. You want life to be just. See fair says if someone doesn't, or can't work, then they don't deserve to live. Fair is everyone pays to play. Just is everybody, and I do mean everybody, deserves a shot. It's why I'm a thief, or more specifically the kind of thief that I am. It's how I run my guild, it's how I run my life. Justice trumps fairness every time.

I'm no saint mind you, a little murder, some mayhem, that's just business. I do my best to instill this kind of thought in my crews. I keep an eye on my ranks and promote due to ability, intelligence, and merit. I also keep an eye out for my godchild. Merra, ding bat that she is, says she's still alive. The girl is a little touched, but she's rarely wrong.

Chloe Thunderhammer, she insists, is alive.

Well, she might be, but I don't think she's in South Point anymore. If she is, however, she might be the Slip I have in front of me.

I looked across at the two of them, an odd team to be sure, but one of my best when it came to basic entry, and the small stuff. Not to mention the smaller of the two had the quickest fingers I had ever seen. She could work a crowd like no one's business. What's more is they both had scruples. I was quite proud of the two of them.

Piper was an Orc girl, still young but already into her growth, she was taller than me with broader shoulders and would keep growing. Once she filled out, she would be a right fright. Today however, she still had a way to go, this made her look gangly, like a teenage farm hand. Anyone who thought her stupid never bothered looking into her eyes. She was sharper than a barber's razor, head strong, and most of all, she was kind. That's good for this business. Bully Boys are a dime a dozen. Enforcers need something more. I had plans for Piper. Oh yes. She'd make a hell of an enforcer. Yet as I watched the two of them, both looking at me a little worried as I had called them to the carpet, so to speak, I realized something. Piper could be so much more. She could be a real spy. I'd have to court her slowly, convince her to work for me without letting slip who I worked for... but yes. She would do nicely.

The shorter of the two was a different matter entirely. Blackthorn was the name she called herself, and spy? Most certainly not. She was brash, outspoken, and well, a loudmouth, but if Piper was sharp as a razor? Well Chloe Blackthorn was in a league all her own. She was a little mastermind in waiting, a leader, a thinker. She was the next guild master of this place. Well maybe not the next, but I, and anyone else who came after me, was just keeping her seat warm, and I think she knew it.

Piper studied me; Blackthorn studied the room. They were a crew of two, yet often worked with others, and both had, well, let's call them side projects. They were solid. That was the cover I was using to get this face to face with them. I needed to know.

I hadn't seen my godchild in years, not since she was four in fact. Back then she was a chubby little cookie snitch. She had a light in her eyes, a bounce in her step and any food you left vulnerable was quickly in her mouth. She rarely cried and had a habit of sneaking everywhere she went by virtue of just being quiet of foot. No malice in her heart, and quick to try to help anyone, or anything. She had thought that stars were crushed glass glittering on the fabric of the night sky, and she had loved both my long hair and beard. Her hair was the color of polished copper, and her eyes were the grey blue of a cloudy day.

She looked a lot like her mother to be honest. Except the eyes, she got Marky boy's eyes.

Chloe Blackthorn had red hair and grey eyes. Her hair was cut shorn to her scalp, and her eyes were guarded, full of storms. If this child, this girl of nearly 14 had ever been chubby there was no trace of it now. Her features were hard and angular, the face of too few meals that came far too irregularly. She was hard as well. I had heard stories, rumors mostly, of things she had done, beatdowns given for slights. If true she never bragged about them. She was armed, even here. A small knife she didn't turn over at the door laid up her arm under the sleeve.

Ten years is a lot of time, maybe enough to do this type of damage. Hells, I knew it was enough to physically turn the chubby little carpet rat into this. I was running out of candidates fast, and I needed to know. Her father needed to know.

"So, no doubt you're both wondering why you're here."

Both shifted in their seats, Piper spoke first. "Well, yeah. We were about to lift a full load from the Miller."

I raised an eyebrow. Wasn't a lot of trade in bread. Well, there was, but it wasn't normal fair. It would be hard to move. "I'm assuming you mean grain."

"Flour," was Blackthorns sullen response. "Fuck face is mixing stone dust in."

Ah, now it made sense. "Doing charity work again?" She gave a dismissive shrug. "As long as your tithe is met." I knew they would, no worry there. I might have to look at the miller myself. Stealing the prebaked flour was an interesting move, but it would be effective, if they could pull it off. "I take it you're going to float the flower, wait for the stone dust to settle out?" They both nodded. "Then what?"

Piper grinned. "We got a person to show it to as we do it, then we just hand it all over to them. They get to show their higher ups and make good, and the Miller gets what's coming."

Hanna, had to be. "Smart girls." I watched them both soak up the praise in their own way. Piper grinned; Blackthorn became slightly less sullen with her eyes softening. "But no, I wanted your input on something. Your thoughts as it were."

Chloe raised an eyebrow. "Why? We're nobodies."

"You are nobodies of the right age." That had their attention. Like I said, neither was dull. "What do you two know about Marcus Thunderhammer?" Now the game begins.

Piper was taken aback by the question, Chloe surprised me with her answer. "You mean the jerk who is the reason I, and half the girls my age, are named Chloe?"

"So, you're familiar with him I take it?"

"Who isn't." Piper asked. "He's a legend. A paladin of the highest order, son of a noble that supposably outranks everyone around here, and he was raised right here in South Point." Her voice all but glowed as she spoke. Seems Mark has a fan.

Given her ties to the church, that tracks.

Chloe's reaction? Not so much. Given her outspoken views on the church, mainly that all religion is a con, her distain was spot on to be sure. Her knowing about the name Chloe coming from Marcus is new. Kids her age didn't normally wonder where they got their names. "How did you know about the name thing?"

She looked at me and blinked, "You're serious?" She took a deep breath and let out a sigh, before her face completely changed and became happy, friendly, animated, "Oh, hi I'm Chloe, what's your name?" She said with a chipper singsong voice. "Me oh I'm Chloe too". Then she giggled. It was a little girls giggle, and completely appropriate for her age... and it sent chills down my spine. It was humorless, thoughtless, and utterly soulless. I had heard rumors of her pulling cons as one of the soulless, the broken. Now I believed it. She fixed me with a stare that had no warmth in it whatsoever. "Jax, it takes less than a drip to ask one of the older women why everyone is named Chloe. Then you get to hear all about the sweet little angel the great and powerful Thunderhammer had, and what a tragedy it was she died, poor lost soul." She made a retching noise.

Hatred? That I might could have delt with. Anger? Anger I could get behind. This was cold apathy. Someone who was soul sick of the whole thing.

A quick glance at Piper said there was so much more here.

So, I pushed. "That's a little cold."

"Look, I feel bad for the girl, I really do. But she's dead. Not an angel, not a poor dear. We got kids freezing in the street and people are still worried about the welfare of a girl who died years ago."

Ah, now it made sense. Blackthorn had a side hustle where she pretended to charge street kids for a nice dry place to stay. Oh, she did charge them, that way she could brag about it, but I'd long looked into it. If the kid brought in so much as a farthing, they were in. Made her look like a hard ass for ripping off kids. It helped her rep and got a bunch of kid's warm meals and a dry bed. Despite her awful and hard exterior, she was a bleeding heart.

It's why I was holding out hope.

"Fair enough." Time to twist things a bit. "Only thing is, some people think she ain't dead."

Both of them stiffened, and neither of them saw the other one do it. Piper spoke first.

"So, she's where?"

"No one knows." Bait was laid, now to sweeten the trail. "According to my sources, she was smuggled into an orphanage after her mom died, whether to hide her from someone, or to hide her away and forget about her is anyone's guess." I of course had no such source, but Chloe Blackthorn had escaped the local orphanage, and she was far from the only one her age to have done so, security was tightened after that.

Piper's mind was racing, she was thinking hard.

Chloe was first off the mark this time. "So, are we looking for her to protect her, or ransom her?"

Good girl, look for the angles. "Not sure yet, like I said I want suggestions."

"Well," she began after giving it a moment's thought. "If were looking to protect her, her being on the street would probably be best. Ditch the Chloe name all together, lay low. If she's smart? She's already doing that, and no way she's still alive now and not smart. So, look for people even less visible than us. Muck raker?" She considered it for a moment before continuing. "Possibly, under all that filth, who would suspect a little Miss Princess?"

A muck raker? I hadn't thought of that. Might be worth a check. "And if we were going ransom?"

"Eh," she said with a dismissive shrug. "Toss me at 'em."

"Do what?" Piper said in disbelief, turning and looking at her friend as if she'd never seen her before.

"Pip, I'm serious. I mean, think about it. I'm one of the older Chloe's we've ran into, so I got to be about the right age. It's been years so the stars alone know what the brat looks like. I've pulled long cons before; my rooks are second to none in our league. If they want her for good reason, great. I get to meet some long-lost Aunt or something that probably never even laid eyes on the girl. If they are her enemies and mean to do her harm? I'm no push over and the guild's got my back. It's better than giving them the real thing."

There it was, my heart broke a little.

God why couldn't it have been you? Sharp as a whip, strong in mind, and quick on your feet. Marcus would be proud to call you his kid.

I know I am.

Time to make it official.

I stood up. "Far as we know, as far as anyone knows, the daughter of Thunderhammer is dead and died with her mum. I just needed to see how you two reacted to an impossible scenario, see if you guys could think around corners." I offered out my hand to the two of them, Blackthorn first. "You two are both Toughs now. Congratulations." Walking them both to the door I continued. "This means more base resources available to you for jobs. Now go get that grain."

I watched them both go... Chloe might not have been Marcus's daughter, but I was damn glad she was mine.

09 The Hermit

<u>Cariad 13th 393 AFU</u>

"Where's the money Jax? Where's the protection?" The voice was loud, clear and to the point. We were in a barn, one of many safe houses where the guild could meet just outside the city. The meeting was called as an emergency.

Too bad, I wasn't there.

Oh, I was, physically.

In reality, I was standing in the sun, in the market square, looking at a pair of feet wrapped in loose rags that would never finish the fall the body had started a heartbeat before.

Her name was Chloe Smith. A cute girl, dark curly hair, familiar blue eyes, and a fair complexion. An orphan who had been adopted by a local Smith named Grazer. Old man Grazer had fallen on hard times just last year, and his daughter had been caught stealing bread to feed him.

Three years ago, she would have been in a pillory, not hanging by the neck.

She was a kind girl, the right age, and no one knew who she had been before becoming a Smith's daughter. She was the fifth hanging this week.

"Are you even listening?" The voice demanded.

"To what Kith? Your bitching about things beyond my control? Or the fact that you've squandered the money you've made on booze and whores?"

Kith pushed his way to the front, shuffling straw ahead of him as he shuffled his feet. He stopped right next to Ayn's ass. I thought that fitting considering how much he was braying. "We're getting slaughtered out there."

"No." I said from my customary throne, in this case a milking stool. Why does this blasted thing only have three legs? I feel like I'm going to fall over. Granted that's because I'm trying to look bored.

"Excuse me?"

"No, 'WE' are not." I stood up, screw that stool. "Thieves are hanging, but how many of them are us, are guild?"

A woman, Re'ah, that's her name, spoke up. "Wait, are you doing this?"

I looked over at her, "I'm hurt you would ask, let alone think so." I looked around at our numbers, at my guild. Of course, only the lieutenants and up were here, the official meeting wasn't for weeks yet. "Let me be clear, they are targeting 'thieves' but we're not being hit, and it's because of the rules I sat in place when I took over."

"So, we're just supposed to overlook this?" She asked.

Years ago, when I came here, it was to do a job. These people, all of them, thought I was an outsider, something I would never quite be forgiven for. If they only knew. The truth was, these were my people, and this was my guild.

The question was, what was I going to do?

I paused for a moment. What *was* I going to do?

I looked around at the gathered masses, some of them undoubtedly worked for His Holiness by this point. Bastard was closing a noose around my neck with each passing day. But right now? Right now, they needed me to lead. To do that, I need to show my hand, not the whole thing, just a few of my cards.

"Anyone notice anything odd about the hangings?"

That got a few murmurs... it was impossible not to notice.

"Kids, not young kids, mostly those just old enough to be charged as adults." Came one voice.

"Lotta girls too." Came another.

"No bruisers or bully boys." Kith finished.

"Exactly." I looked around at my people. "And why do you think that is? Dead young girls will cause a hell of an outcry. Not to mention, where are all the toughs?"

A murmur broke out amongst the gathering. A real chorus of "He's right", "What now?", "Why", and "What do we do?" The interjections spread throughout the crowded barn, even the donkey got in on the action with his own brayed thoughts.

"Wait," finally came a voice, it was Re'ah's again. "It will cause an outcry, so why do it?"

I looked at her. I could have played it a lot of ways, called her thick for not seeing it, played dumb and lead them to it, but no. "Isn't it obvious? You can't send girls to the front lines, nor can you send them to the mines, it's seen as cruel." And slavery" I waved a hand, sure it was illegal, but since when has that ever stopped a high and mighty lord. "But if the people cry out, get upset that the law is being applied like it is, well then, a stent digging dirt is seen as so much better than a short drop, now isn't it?"

"All the while," Kith added, "The strong ones are being sent there anyway because no one cares."

"Bingo."

"So, what do we do?"

What do we do indeed?

"These laws," I said mostly to myself, "They're seen as gods sent." I stopped moving. Marcus won't be happy with this plan. "We got to change that."

"What?"

Louder, to everyone, to the stars themselves, "I said these laws, they're seen as god sent, on high from the church these people think the laws are the will of the gods." I looked around. "The people support these laws because they think their lives are made all the worse because people like us exist. The Lord Mayor, the Duke, they get to claim they are helping protect the people..." I turned to look at everyone, to make eye contact with everyone. "They support these laws because our betters have got the people convinced that our hand is in their pocket." I turned to Re'ah, "What did you do before you took up this life?"

"I was a milk maid." She sniffed, "Good life too until the church seized Markle's farm."

"Kith, you were a guard, right?"

"Well," He looked uncomfortable. Guard, ex or not, were not amongst the most liked people here. "But I had debts, one thing led to another..." He trailed off. Debts, legal debts. It was an all-too-common problem, many a head was nodding with him. "This pays better," he added, "And we look after each other."

I nodded. "That we do." I clapped him on the back as I moved through the crowd, through my right hands. "We know that fake laws, and fake security only benefits those who have the gold, the name's, the title, or the position already," I looked at each of them slowly, "But those that don't?" I nodded. Every man and woman here, well man, woman, and other, already knew that the guild was the only place that would take them. "So? We show them."

"How?" Someone asked.

"We do the thing most of you have been quietly moaning about Blackthorn doing." That got some grumbles. "I know, she's been cutting into some of your profits, but look at it this way... how many of her little strumpets would turn her in?"

That quieted them down. "It's simple, the Lords and Ladies have The Guard, the armies, and the churches, all telling the good folk of South Point that we, you and I are the bad guys, all while they hang 14-year-old girls until their feet stop twitching." My voice raised, far more than I meant it to. To hell with it, I was pissed, and them hearing it might do them some damn good. "They have people cheering for it, lining up to see the next set of little legs dancing their last jig."

I let that sink in while I got control of myself.

"Fuck 'em." I took a deep breath and started my hometown on a journey I wasn't sure it would recover from. "We're making South Point a Thieves City." Mark was going to kill me.

Everyone looked at me dumbstruck. It's not that something like this hadn't been done by other guilds, or in other cities, or even cities this large before, it's that all of us knew, if we did this, and the guild got a bad head, that they would be condemning their friends and family, their children, to things...

"Jax, I mean..." Kith looked around. "Don't get me wrong, but you're talking overthrowing the Lords."

"If we overthrow them, and the city... what happens if we wind up with a bastard in charge?" The fear was real.

I could see their concerns written on their faces as if a scribe had come in and inked them all.

"Things like what? Our kids being strung up?" I offered. "Forced into lives of crime?" I gestured, "Maybe being forced into slavery?" The point wasn't lost on any of them. "So, we don't do it the old way, like I said, we take a page from Blackthorn's book. We start out by making things safer on the streets for the average person."

"How?" Re'ah asked.

"No more protection money to start with. Oh, we still offer the protection, but we don't charge. We stop hitting any and all low-level targets. We start offering help." I took a deep breath. "I've been taking ten percent of your earnings, buying things to sell in our inns, booze mostly." I spread my hands. "Now we use it to buy food, medicine, we start helping out anyone and everyone the Guard is stepping on."

There was a snort. "We ain't the church, we a business."

"Oh, we step up hurting the rich."

"That will just make them come after us all the harder."

"Yeah, it will." I agreed. "But with us feeding everyone? Who do you think they will side with?"

Muttering was the order of the moment, at least till someone dropped a fat, vile, turd right into the conversation. "What about His Holiness?" There was an intake of breath. By this point, everyone knew he was real, but invoking him was like invoking the devil herself. It was seen as bad luck. "We set this up and he takes over? Then it's just handing him the rest of the town then ain't it?"

"So, we decentralize. We make supply lines that run parallel, we take and make power structures in the guild so that if I get caught, if you get caught, if we all get caught..." I looked at them all again... "Things keep running. Because here's the rub." I paused, I needed all of their attention. "If we keep going the way we are, he wins anyway." I nodded to myself, "Make no mistake, we all know he's behind this, and we know, he'll win eventually. We know some of our own, maybe even some of the people in this barn tonight, work for him. He's already made one play for us. So, let's make it so he can't get it. Let's fuck the bastard and send him and his pet nobles a great big heaping handful of not a damn thing they can use."

Kith looked at me, then at Re'ah and then to the others. "Where do we start?"

10 Wheel of Fortune

<u>Cariad 19th 395 AFU</u>

I stood at the edge of the copse of trees just outside the fields of South Point. Hanna was to my left, and Sara to my right, as we watched 600 odd souls don armor and practice with weapons unfamiliar to them, pole arms mostly. The camp had been hastily set up last night, and on the wind, the barked orders of the Sergeant of Arms could be heard trying to whip them into some form of shape.

"What is it this time?" I asked.

Hannah let out a sigh, "Officially? The Baron's cows, some 20 in all, got loose and wound up in one of the Count's farms. The beasts took out three fields of new corn and wheat before they were discovered." She shook her head. "So, he ordered the lot rounded up and put them in with his cows." She turned and looked at me. "The Baron of course is claiming theft, the Count is saying he can either forfeit them, or pay double the value of the fields."

Sara rubbed the back of her neck. "Unofficially?"

Hannah gave a shrug. "The Baron caught the Count cheating at cards."

I growled. "And at least half of them won't make it home without new scars." Looking out over this crop, it was probably more than half. These were just the first recruits. South Point was about 12,000 souls all told, 600 doesn't seem like a lot, but it was one out of every 20 abled bodied man. In theory. In practice? The Guard themselves were about 300 people. Add in this had been going on for the last decade? The war wounded were starting to pile up. What's more is last year he had called for additional forces. That got his army up to nearly 900.

The gamble paid off, the Baron took one look at the stronger force and gave up the field.

"If he thinks 600 will do it this year, he's sadly mistaken." Both I and Hannah looked at her, waiting. "The Baron's been gearing up for this all winter."

I could feel my guts dropping. "Any Winter Born?"

Hannah piped up, "I've never understood that." We both turned to look at her. She had the good grace to look embarrassed, I don't think she realized she said that out loud. "I mean... sorry."

"What's to understand?" I shrugged, "The Count is playing into the Baron's hands, and he's been building up all winter. If he's actually got some Winter Born, well it's likely that his men will be much better trained and much more ready."

"No, that I get."

"Then what are you missing?"

Finally, she asked "Why does when a soldier is born matter to how good they are?" She gave a shrug "I mean, I've heard it all my adult life. Don't face a winter born if you can help it, face a summer soldier."

Sara answered. "As a friend of mine says, it has nothing to do with *when* you crowned, but everything to do with *when and why you were* crowned." She pointed at the field. "Those, those are summer soldiers. They plant crops in spring, go and fight all summer, and then come harvest they are hopefully back home."

I stepped in, "Winter's Soldier, or the Winter Born, are like the Margraves men." Taking a deep breath, I continued. "They hold the line all winter. Their life is bad food, worse beds, and training. When the summer's done, they don't go home, because they're already there."

"So, professional soldiers."

I shook my head. "A professional soldier is good, but they fight for money. It's in the name, it's their profession. A Winter Born will hold the last outpost in the dead of winter because it's his or her outpost to hold. Every Winter Born I ever met has fought for something deeper, not money. While some can get rich off what they do, being given lands and titles and such, they all are in the fight for an idea."

Sara sighed, "And that makes them damn hard bastards to kill."

"If they're principled, why would they work for the Baron?"

I looked over at Hanna in disbelief. "How long would it take you, telling the god's honest truth, to convince someone that the Count and his wife were absolute wanks who didn't have the sense to pour piss out of a boot with pictographic directions printed on the heel?"

She frowned. "He's an idiot to be sure, but... I mean he's not that bad."

"Not that bad?" Sara asked. "600 men, right now are preparing to fight, maybe die, for what?"

The answer was as simple as it was disgusting. "Bruised egos, that's what." I ground out. Looking out over the poor sods, those who were about to die, I felt bile building in me. "How's he picking them?"

Hannah hung her head. "Lot. He calls it fairer that way."

"A fucking lottery?" Sara growled in surprise. "Are you kidding me?"

"Easy love." I looked at Hannah. "So how do we mess this up?"

Sadly, Hannah shook her head. "Even if you steal the cows and give them back, he will just blame it on the Baron, and it will be an even bigger mess."

I thought about it for a moment, "Sara? Any idea what the Baron actually has?"

She nodded grimly. "Manpower wise, he's still short. I think he's managed to get three maybe four hundred people. The problem is, I know he managed to smuggle in an elven archer about mid-winter."

Archers, damn. Most years the two idiots were just pushing back and forth with pikemen, once they traded some cavalry, but horses were damned expensive. So were good bows. "Anyone we know?"

"Thankfully no, none of the big names anyway. From what I hear it's one of the ones on their Wee, so the training isn't going well."

"Where's he getting the bows?"

"Right now, they are using hunting bows to train with, easy enough to come by, but he's got a shipment of war bows coming in from the north."

"Any idea of the arrival date?" Hannah asked.

"Six days from now."

I thought for a moment, then grinned so large I felt it. "Plenty of time."

Both women looked at me. "What are you thinking."

"I've got a in at the camp, being the good upstanding citizen I am, I'm going to donate all new tunics, livery, and tabards to our newly minted fighting boys."

With a single eyebrow raise Hannah asked, "And you just happen to have all of that laying around?"

I grinned. "Of course. How do you think I smuggle things in and out of Eastend and Westend?" It was a bit of a stretch, none of our counterfeit uniforms would pass close inspection. "Besides the Guild will be all too happy to help, it means our fakes become the new real."

Sara looked at me. "How's that help us?"

"The big problem with things like uniforms is it makes people stop thinking. They see the tabard, and they assume you are what the tabard says you are. With our Army getting new gear, the old gears got to go somewhere."

"Ok, and?"

"Well, if it's coming from the north road, and the warehouse the old gear gets stored in is burgled, and then brigands with that gear steal the bows." The face Hannah gave me could have curdled milk. "You could work at a cheesery with a look like that love."

"Jax, that will just make things worse. He'll still blame the count."

"Of course, he will. Right up until he sees the new duds and hears people bragging about the civic pride of the towns people. Bragging which will start as soon as tomorrow."

"And?" Hanna asked?

Sara looked at her. "And, if the Count is bragging about new uniforms, and the thieves have old uniforms, it means either he believes the story about the old ones being stolen or he believes that somehow the Count has out maneuvered him again."

"I'm betting on the latter."

"But everyone knows Dawnken is a moron."

I nodded. "Exactly, Dawnken is a pompous ass who will brag about new clothing, and yet somehow not use the new bows he just stole? Not bloody likely."

Sara's grin finally matched my own. "So, either he is a moron, or he's not, and since everyone knows he is, how did he pull it off? He must have his own Winter Born planning things, a Winter Born who now has war bows, bows that no one can find on the battlefield."

Hannah finally got it "And if no one can find the bows, they must be well hidden because no one would go to all that trouble and not use them. They must be on the field somewhere."

"And with that we just turned this season's war into a lot of posturing as both sides try to figure out who has the bows."

Hannah shook her head, laughing. "You do, you have them"

"No" I said as I turned and started walking away. "I got someplace else that needs them."

11 Justice

<u>Gwynt 19th 396 AFU</u>

"There are four, FOUR! Different temples in the stupid town," I turned on Wilhelm and really let my ire out. "Ca'talls, Ba'teece, and his wife Suo, and Lut'har. Not to mention every Podunk soothsayer, plant speaker, bone rattler, and ghost whisper a city this size should have, and you're telling me none of them will perform even a simple healing on one of our own?"

"Yes sir, I know sir." Wilhelm mewed, "It's just..."

"Just what?" I snapped.

"She got caught robbing the Bishop's home." Gary said.

Everyone shifted uncomfortably. I looked around at my lieutenants, hard men and women right down to the last. Yet all of them were shaken to their core.

"Bishop Torn is not him, he's not His Holiness." How I wished he were, it would make things so much easier, but no, Torn was just a lacky.

"Maybe." Wilhelm said. "But he's made a big deal of it. The Count has declared no one from any church is to help her since she went against the will of the gods."

A bottle of 20-year-old brandy paid the price for his words as I threw it against the far wall. Never let your anger lash out at your people, and never break their stuff, only your own. "Are you telling me we have no one that can help her out?" I looked at them all. "They cut off her hand." I looked around at them, each cringed as my gaze touched them. "She's the fifth one this year, we got healers for all of them, right?" We had, every single one of them had had a healer see to them as soon as we got the poor sods back from the town's twisted idea of justice.

Beth, gods love her, was the one who stepped forward. "None of them robbed a holy man. Jax, we all know what Piper means to you, what they both do. But no one will touch this. If she's seen healed up and ready to go…" her words trailed off.

"It blows the cover of any priest willing to work with us still." Gary finished.

"What about surgeons?"

Wilhelm looked at the floor. "All gone, all off at the field hospitals."

The damn war.

"They're not even doing anything, too damn scared of phantom archers." I took a deep breath. "Have we got anyone worth a damn?"

Gary leaned forward. "I got a barber, fixes my men up sometimes. He knows herbs, swears by this fungus he found, says it makes the wounds glow blue."

That was a new one. "You trust him?"

"One of my guys still has an eye we thought was gone."

"Send him. Tell him to charge the girls half, Chloe won't take a handout. We'll take care of the rest, hell I'll pay him double if Piper is on her feet quick enough."

He nodded, "Done."

I looked at my four remaining seconds, really looked at the four of them. Wilhelm was a mousy little man, he ran numbers and games of chance down by the docks. His job was making odds and beating them. Beth and Annas both worked what was left of the "off load". Outwardly they were two respectable teamsters and stable masters. Nothing, legal or otherwise moved in South Point without them knowing. Gary used to run protection for the brothels, back when there was such a thing. Now he just ran muscle. All of them were smart and knew they needed the guild.

Nevertheless, the guild wasn't what it once was. Decentralizing and setting up different power structures had bought us time, but that time was running out. Sure, things were in place for what was to come, but damn it.

"There was a time," I said softly, "Not that long ago, when this just didn't happen."

Annas looked at me, "In the last year, we've lost the docks due to fire, thank the gods that little traitor was caught, all of the whore houses, and all but three of the money lenders."

Beth jumped in, "All of the higher ups have either jumped ship, been arrested, or are dead."

"Not all," Wilhelm said with a sniff. "Two found religion."

"Funny that, they find God and our business goes to pot."

"Nothing funny about it, we all know who it is," Gary began. "We're just too scared to say it out loud."

"His Holiness." I looked around at them all. "That specter has been a thorn in our side since before I came here."

"What are we going to do? At this rate the guild is all but dead." Wilhelm's voice was sad, distracted.

"Do you lot want to know how every guild like this gets started?" I looked around. "Hmm? Should I tell you?" I looked up from my desk. "It's because the great and powerful make people like us unavoidable. No one sane wants our jobs. Greedy? Who do you know greedier than the people who legally do what we do? Hmmm?" I looked at them each in turn. "The farriers guild sees six times our revenue in a week. The coopers? How about the Masons? That's not even getting into the trade houses. All legal." I spread my hands. "And all owned by people born to it."

"You lot?" I shook my head. "You've got as much to lose as I do." I stared at all of them. "Not to mention I know each and every one of you run as much aid to the districts as you can without being noticed." They all shifted uncomfortably. Charity work was regarded as a liability in most guilds, it was a way too be leveraged. My new edict was to do this very thing, but everyone hid what it was they did, hid it well too. "Should I tell your secrets? Did you think I somehow missed you were all bleeding hearts?"

"Now, inevitably someone rises up through our ranks and wants more power. They forget why we started. After all, we all know, it's every man for themselves, so you take care of you and yours and I'll take care of mine. Suddenly people are getting hurt, people from the bottom, our people." I spread my hands. "Someone like me steps in and quietly weeds out the rot, it takes years." I held my breath for a moment, to give them time to think, to process what I was saying. "So, my most trusted people make sure the bars stay free of the worse stuff, there are two sets of prices for grain, one for the rich one for the poor, and a man who keeps his thumb on the scale so that people can suddenly and miraculously pay their back taxes." I looked at the four before me. "Thought I wouldn't notice?"

All of them looked down at the floor.

"That's why you lot are all still here." Since I made my declarations to make this a thief's city, I had been watching who did what. Some of the dead? My work. It was the best way to ferret out the traitors, or just the bastards. I took a deep breath. "They will come for me soon, I know that. But I've made sure you lot are out of it. Upstanding businessmen and women, the lot of you."

"Why?" Came Beth. "If you know they're coming, why stay?"

"Because if I don't, they will go looking for you. If I'm taken down, public like, they stop."

"What," Gary asked, "Going to be a martyr and rot in jail for us, or worse hang?"

"Don't be daft." I smiled. "I got it covered."

"So, what's the plan?" Annas chimed in.

"The plan? I keep running the guild to the last, I get taken, reports of my death will of course come out, and you lot? You keep doing what you're doing and wait."

"Wait?" Four voices in course, is quite loud in a small room.

"Yes, you wait." I sighed. "You are needed. The guild dies on paper, but people like Chloe and Piper have basically made their own, and they aren't the only ones. On top of that, while His Holiness has been working with, and playing, the Count and Baron off each other to get more power, I've been working with the Margrave and a group of Wardens." I looked at them all seriously. "So, you, wait."

Annas leaned back and sighed, "In the meantime, our people suffer."

"That's where you lot come in. You're going to do everything you can." I felt the years wash over me. "Justice won't come from sitting on our asses, but you lot being hung certainly won't help it. Do what you can, where you can. Support the shadow guilds I encouraged to pop up outside of standard hierarchy."

They all nodded.

Wilhelm said. "So, that's it. The guild is dead."

I got up from behind my desk and put my hand on his shoulder. "No. You can't kill ideas mate; you can't kill community. We're not dead, just changing."

After that, they gathered up their things and left my office... I hoped I was right. If they knew half of what I did they would be scared shitless. Secret cells, people disappearing, and worse.

Time would tell.

12 The Hanged Man

<u>Blodeuo 9th AFU</u>

Iron shackles really bite into your wrists, especially when your toes only touch the ground because you have big feet. Sure, it hurts, the weight of my body dragging me down puts a killer pressure on my shoulders, and since they arrested me this morning, I've been just kind of hanging out. My hands are numb, shoulders too, it's uncomfortable sure, and a little inhuman, but not nearly as bad as the smell.

Now that is the real offence. Old moldy hay laid out, nice and neat in the corner, and it has sat there for the gods only knew how long. The reek of stale piss permeated every last nook and cranny of this hole as it was the lowest cell in the place. The pipes drained the awful stuff from the drunk tanks and cleaner cells above. Those pipes ran right along the celling of my new home and over towards a collection of them along the wall, that woefully went to that pile of putrid straw.

The only light in the place came from the cracks around the door, as well as the small, barred window, that was at eye level in the thing. There was no outside air, no access to the outside and no one to hear me scream or yell or anything else, save the Guardsmen standing just on the other side of that door.

Before you get too many ideas that door is solid oak planks held together not with nails but with iron bands. The only reason the guard could hear me is that window. All in all, this little cell, this four-foot by six-foot hell, was no place for any naked man to be, little less the man that until the predawn hours of this very morning was one of the most powerful men in this city.

My name, as far as these pillocks are concerned is Jax, and I aim to keep it that way. Jax strolled into town more than a decade ago with a list of names and an array of secrets that took me from being just another nobody, to the head of the Thieves' Guild in less than three years. Everything about Jax is me, but with a little polish in some places, and some roughness in others. My black hair is close cropped, and I only shave about every two days. I'm overdue for that, but it gives me a scruffy, worn look.

As Jax I had my hand in every dealing, black or otherwise, that happened in this town in the last decade. Black deals like this very cell. It's meant for people best forgotten, people that you need out of the way, or just want to put a little pressure on. Officially it doesn't exist, which means with me in here, I no longer existed. Good trick considering half the nobles in this town owe me more than a few coins, and more than a few favors.

How someone like me end up in here you ask? Simple, I pissed off His Holiness. No one else has the balls. His Holiness, as far as I know, isn't actually affiliated with any church. I know, I've looked. He, or hells, it maybe she, gods know I've found more than a few birds who climbed to the top of some pretty nasty piles. They are a shadow figure pulling the strings of the church, as well as the Lords, to build a power base. He's been at it for over twenty years.

This whole Jax thing was a favor to a friend, Marcus Thunderhammer. As I hung by my arms, I thought about the last decade, what led up to it, and Nyssa.

Mark and I were, ironically, thick as thieves, never disagreed until Nyssa. We both courted her, and he won. I was so angry with the both of them until their wedding. I had agreed to be Mark's Arms Man and as such had his sword as well as my own. That put me into the position most people like me would dream of in this situation. I had come up with this daft plan of betrayal and intrigue to get what I wanted, what I felt I deserved and had been robbed of. That was until I saw how sickeningly happy they were together.

I never felt like retching and hugging someone at the same time before, but there you are. See, men like me, all men really, just want two things, control and family. We'd been denied both our whole lives, and here, on that day I gave up my control to get my family. Got drunk that night, wound up with a kid. Wonder what Cyn's going to do when he finds out ol' Jax is dead.

Besides, I could have never brought myself to cheat on Nyssa, and with my eye and appetites, I would have been in torment.

For all this time I had two jobs; one, confirm Chloe being alive and two, find His Holiness and any evidence I could to root him out.

Fifteen years is a long time to be on the job, one job. It's the longest con of my life, to date at least. Sad to see it all go downhill. Did find a couple of possibilities for the girl. Sadly however, when a local hero has a kid a lot of other babies born around that time wind up with the same name. Chloe is the most popular name in this town for girls who would be about the right age.

I have nine of them working for me or did. One of them was even there when the guard came for me. She got out, at least I hope she did. She had been one of my favorite picks for Nyssa's daughter. Had the hair, and the fire, but red hair while a little uncommon for the nobility, is quite common in the lower ranks. On top of that, some babes grow out of fiery red hair. Besides she had neither Nyssa's build nor Mark's. She did have grey eyes. No, this girl was slight as a wisp. Nyssa had been larger, and Mark is huge.

Besides I had found another girl, right age, black hair, right name, Mark's chin, Mark's demeanor. A local merchant's daughter, only thing is the man sewed seed everywhere and no other field bore fruit. Not to mention the girl looks nothing like him or her mother. She was my bet, but always keep your options open.

On the way down here to my new little kingdom of shit, one of the guards let slip that things weren't going to be so easy for thieves like me anymore. A new law had been passed after the Bishop's house had been broken into. Anyone stealing from Clergy or Lords would now be hung, no first or second warnings.

I asked him where I would be going, he sneered at me and told me "The Tomb M'Lord. Tis the only hope for a future ya got."

As I waited, all I could think was 'good man'. Lenrick had done his job well, even managed to get me some info too. I would have to make a few marks, leave a few signs, let the locals know not to dally around anymore. Let's hope the masons I bribed when this place was being built were worth their gold.

So, I hung in my cell, like so much meat on the hook. I waited for a bit longer till the changing of the Guard let a familiar face peak in at me. Lenrick with his crooked nose peered through the bars on the door. "He eaten yet?" As he spoke, he turned his head toward the right, showing me his ear. No earring. Everything is set up.

A voice of the unseen guard, one off to the right, "No, but I think we are supposed to take him down now."

"God's why?" Lenrick's voice showed distain. "We'd have to touch him for that, not to mention go in there. I thought the plan was to forget about this one till 'e added to the smell?" Good man, cover your ass. You did your part.

"Your shift, you want to leave him there do it."

The half elf shook his head. "This is stupid. He's chained, ain't like he can go nowhere. Let's hit a tavern and get a drink. With any luck, maybe the squad will come for him. I know I don't want to be here when they do."

Surprise came out of the voice of the other man, "His Holiness actually do that? Send people to make someone disappear?"

A sharp intake of breath through the nose, one to clear the sinuses and make a kind of snort was the answer, "Seen 'em once. Was asked not to say anything. Now picken' up this guy? He was at one of the fancy parties I had to stand post at. He's gone for mornin' or I owe you a month's pay."

God, I knew I picked right when I found this guy. He was covered and so was the other guard. With this rumor planted, only his Holiness would know for sure what actually happened, would know I had slipped through his fingers. Anything else and he would actually lose ground. He had taken on Jax, and it looked like he won, why admit he lost? It's how these things worked.

I watched the light go with the reseeding voices and once it and the sound were gone, I got to work.

First things first, out of these shackles.

The chain of them was hung on a fixed hook and I was already on tip toes. I had kept my hands clenched most of the day, one of the guards thought it was because I had something in my fist and had forced my hands open. I made sure I spread my fingers wide when this happened, otherwise the game may have been up. One of the men who arrested me had slapped me in chains a little too big, not much, only slightly. I've got big wrists, and a wide set of fingers when they are outstretched, but my hands are actually kind of narrow. I unclenched my hands and relaxed them slowly lowering my feet to the ground as I did so.

Steal scraping against skin hurts, but those leaking pipes aren't a flawed product, they are designed that way. The fetid piss that had been dripping on me this entire time made for a decent lubricant to slide the shackles off my hands. This whole place was like that. Sure, it was meant to be something to torture people without leaving a mark on them, but when I had learned this place was being designed, I made a few special modifications to the plans. That way if I ever found myself being on the wrong side of that door, well I had a way out. A substantial bribe to the workers, who were already being bribed to do this anyway, and no one was the wiser.

Once I got my hands free of the irons it was time to grope around in the dark. Thankfully both cuffs finally gave way at the same time, otherwise I might have made noise or worse wacked myself with the one I had just freed myself of. I felt along the wall behind me and followed it to the corner and from there to the pipes. Sure, I could have just turned and bumped into them, but a naked, piss and slime covered man, huddling in the dark, has got to have some dignity.

The problem with a set up like this, is that you have to make sure no one else finds it. That means you got to make it hard to spot and harder to get to. The stone floor of this place was slightly tilted towards the pipes that led to the sewers. This is because at the very bottom is the grate. A small, thumb tall, two-foot-wide, opening that adds to the decor of smell as it lets the ever-dripping liquid drain into the small underground tunnel that fed the city waste out into Devil's Pass, our local river. That hole was my way out.

Once I found the pipes, I began to unscrew them. Each pipe was done with a set of threads that made sure they all turned the same way. They were short threaded, that meant they leaked, and that leak was one more way to harm the occupants of this cell. For me however it meant they would turn freely and would move easily out of the way.

As they say, best laid plans and all.

Four years of runoff water had snarled my well thought out plan. None of the blasted pipes wanted to move, and my slick hands couldn't get a grip on the bloody things. The pipes, four of them, were about as big around as a woman's arm. I could easily wrap my hands around them but couldn't get any damn purchase.

Naked, cold, stinking, and with my plan falling apart, while on a timetable that needed to be stuck to, I found myself not even able to get to shit creek, let alone bitching about whether or not I had a paddle.

"You know what would be great right now? Tools, something to work with." I chuckled at myself, "Talking out loud, are we? Yeah, right, that'll work. Real big help that is."

If dawn came and I was still here, I might as well just keel over and save the hangman the trouble.

Panicking accomplishes nothing. Sure, it will make you run, and if you got a place to run too that's great, but even then, you are liable to run into a new danger and never realize it.

"Now what do you suppose I've got to fix this problem with?" Bad habit that is, talking to yourself. Great way for your plans to be overheard. "Not like there's anyone to hear me down here."

Rotten straw was what was at hand. I did a quick feel through to see if anyone left me any little gifts, unsurprisingly no. I felt around the floor, at the door, around the walls until I came back to where I started. "Nothing. What a gormless job you did of planning this out old son."

I stood up and straightened myself, standing might help me think. As I did my head ran right into the irons still hanging from their hook.

Rubbing the new duck egg my head had just been gifted with, I realized I was free, I could feel my grin widening. Reaching up I grabbed onto the things and gave the chain a flip. Of course, it came down straight onto my stupid nose, but I didn't care.

I made my way back over to my egress, and holding both cuffs in one hand, I threaded the chain around the pipe. Once I had the loop through, I widened it, slipping the cuffs through the loop. Now I had something to bite into the damn things with. Pulling it tight I used the chain to turn the pipe. Oh, sure it was hard work, cut into my hands something awful, and it didn't make the best lever, but it gripped well enough and got the job done.

Once all the pipes were off, I reached down and felt the lip of the wall, that little intake, that drain. It was too heavy to trigger by hand, but by laying down one pipe and using another to get the lip of the stone, I pushed up and heard the stone make a metallic click. Grinning, I pushed the wall in, and opened a small door to the sewers of South Point. It took a moment, but I got the chain back over its hook. Once on the other side of the pipes, I found screwing them back in to be much easier. With that, Jax was dead and disappeared, never to be seen again. Leaving the chain would raise questions, but fuck it, His Holiness could choke on it.

I shut the stonework door and heard the spring catch again. A little late, but still out and gone. As long as I was out of the city proper by dawn, it would be a clean get away.

***

"You're late." Her voice was impatient, but never had I heard so much relief in it before.

"Problem with the plumbing" I snarked, "it got backed up." I had taken a quick dip in the river to wash a lot of the stench off me, at least that was the hope. "Get everything?"

She nodded. "All of your files, all the 'proof' you had manage to collect." She turned her eyes on me, even in the dark I fancied that I could see the flash of them. "It's not enough," she declared.

Looking at her cloaked form, this woman who had been my agent, friend, and in some ways, my employer over these last few years, I realized how little I knew about her. She had shown up out of nowhere after all, and she knew who I was, and what I was doing, but an ally is an ally.

"There's more, there always is. South Point isn't the only place to feel His Holiness's hand. What of Chloe?"

She snorted, "Your little adopted daughter is fine." Letting out a sigh she rubbed her face. "The heat is off her and Piper, at least for now. Piper is in more trouble than your kid."

"Do what you can for them." It was closer to a request than an order. I trusted this woman, but I had been buried in this town, I couldn't give her orders anymore.

I watched as she nodded. "As soon as I get back. I have to meet with one of my contacts." She turned a warm smile on me, a lock of her hair fell from under her hood. The brown of it seemed to shine in the faint moon light. "They will both live, and I will get them out of here, my life on it." With that she spun her horse and had it trot off deeper into the wood. She was headed south.

"So long Sara, I hope you have better luck than I did." Shaking my head, I took the beast she had left for me and headed off to the east, off to Mark. Can't wait to tell him how much I screwed this one up.

Author's Notes 10

All caught up. Good. Now, if you have read the first novel, I hope you enjoyed it. This next part happens after the end of that story. In other words, beyond this point are spoilers for the first novel. Please, stop reading here if you haven't read Chloe's Collar.

Still here?

Good.

This next short story wasn't supposed to be one. It was supposed to be part of the second novel. It covered an important plot point, showed the aftermath, and was an integral part of the story.

It also didn't fit.

I blame it on the migraine, but when this went from first draft to second, it got squeezed out of the story all together. Other parts served the narrative much better than this did as the starting point. So, Bitter Sweet became its own standalone thing. I hope you enjoy it as much as I enjoyed writing it.

Bitter Sweet

Blodeuo 16th 397 AFU

"Chloe, honey? The frostcream is ready, it has both Heartberries and Black Bloods, just like you asked." The concern in Alabaster's voice was palpable.

Jerking as my mind snapped back to the here and now, I looked up at him. His smile was warm, and as always, he was trying to keep things light.

I hadn't heard him come up, and to be honest, that terrified me more than the mild start. It wasn't so long ago not being aware of my surroundings would have cost me my life. It didn't matter what I was thinking, or who I was with, the cost of such a mistake was death.

We had hit Dragon's Rest around noon. Noonish? Is noonish a word? It is now.

The people of this town were wonderful to us, certainly better than other villages we had been in. They welcomed us in, seemed genuinely happy to see strangers, and were open, warm, and caring. Most places, even along the trade route we were traveling, were ok, they just weren't welcoming to outsiders. Here on the other hand, people were hospitable to a fault.

Dragon's Rest consisted of an inn, two houses, a tannery, and a town square all within a wall that was mostly decoration. It didn't even have gates, just arches for the roads with its west side open to the fields that waited to greet the morning sun. The square of course, is where the local farmers brought their wares. In a town this size I was willing to bet barter was the preferred coin.

The big draw for this place was a family tradition going back well over two hundred years, it currently rests in the hands of one Mary of Cream. No one in the Cream family ever worked, not at any traditional job, and they never held any position or title most would recognize. What they did was let people make and store huge blocks of ice in their under-basement. That way, all throughout spring, summer, and fall, the Creams could provide the locals with the gift of their name, Frostcream.

This frozen delight was made from cream donated by all the local farmers to the family every morning. Others would supply her with honey and all manner of fruits they had collected and dried over the seasons. If you were a local, Frostcream didn't cost you anything, but travelers could expect to lose a few silver for this wonderful treat. All that money went to buying things from traveling traders and other towns and paying their taxes to the local Lords.

I had been looking forward to it, as Sliverleaf had been going on about this place for days, until Mary asked about Ba'call.

Now here I was, playing out that mew, Ba'call's last sound, over and over again in my head. The mew that had paid the coin for the last time I had got distracted. That sound, and the last words she ever spoke, endlessly marched through my mind, my promise to her was burned into every thought.

It had been over a month, and still I woke some nights screaming out that promise, begging her not to die. I would do anything if she just wouldn't die.

Now?

Now I sat looking at golden goo that had a riot of red and black streaks in it from the berries, and all I could think about was her. I remember her telling me about this place. Telling me all about how it got its name for a dragon that had been out adventuring and stopped here to sleep for three days on a stone in one of the fields. Saying how, before that, the town had been known as Triumph because they had finally rid themselves of a cult of Waban that had been here for longer than memory.

That rock was now a bit of local history and color. The town's kids continued to scour the dirt around it looking for dragon scales. A lot of them claimed to have found one over the years, and a small shrine of dubious chips of things that look like rocks, sat next to the town well. I guess their guest had a shedding problem.

As I sat there with the wooden bowl on the table before me, watching the sticky mess slowly melt, seeing the colors bleeding into each other, the red, the black, the same colors as the wound, I realized Alabaster had been speaking to me the whole time.

"I'm sorry Al. I don't know where my head is."

He smiled as he reached out and petted me. I had eventually gotten use to such intimate contact from him and his sister. They really didn't think anything about touch, and I've come to find it quite relaxing. Leaning into his hand I accepted the moment of comfort.

"I know exactly where your mind is, and so is Sliv's. We all are there with the two of you, but come, you know what she would say if she were here."

I chuckled. She would be trying to shove the spoon in my mouth all the while squawking about how the bird needed to hide in the cave because a dragon had once been here, or some such nonsense. "Yeah, but if she were here, she wouldn't have to. We would all be watching her make a mess of herself with the stuff." With that, I shoved a little bit of the melting goop into my mouth.

For a moment, all thoughts of Ba'call were banished from my mind. The cold of it was a shock, but the sweet combined with the tartness of the berries locked my jaw. It hurt, but the taste was incredible. Every bit of it was like a color going off in my mouth, colors I had no name for. There were bursts of sweet and sour that made my tongue contract and my jaws lock up, only to slowly release as I adjusted to the tart and rode the sweet into the world of the blessed silence of distraction. I had had honeyed nuts and glazed sweet bits before, but somehow this was sweeter than pure honey. I found myself enjoying it and making sounds usually reserved for my favorite savory dishes.

I looked up in time to see Sliverleaf coming over with her own bowl. She was wearing a self-satisfied smile on her smug looking face, "Wonderful, isn't it?

Sometimes I could really punch that girl. Or hug her. Yes, definitely hug her. "Sit down string bean." I sighed as she took a seat. "It just got to me. I can't help but blame myself every time I think about it. She called out a warning, and I stood there like a moon mesmerized calf."

"She died protecting a friend. For her, there could be no greater honor and few better deaths. As for you being rooted from fear? I didn't see it. Neither did anyone else. It was simply faster than you." Her words were soft, but a hint of iron underneath said even she was getting tired of my self-flagellation.

"I just wish I could have done more."

Alabaster took my hand and spoke. "Soon you will. We are on our way to see what else, if anything, can be done. You will get to fulfill your promise to her. That is how you honor her."

He's right, and while I wouldn't call what I was feeling silly or a waste, it was preventing me from being in the here and now. So, I sat and enjoyed what I could; the sweet concoction, the people around me, and the ambiance of the town. The cheer was a little forced, but it was real. Somber, I think it's called.

Once the bowl was finished, and the place started picking up a bit, I decided I needed air. Don't get me wrong. I was still completely wrapped in my own head space, but I wanted, no not just wanted, needed to see more of this little place. Small towns and villages don't look like much if you're just passing through, but each and every one of them has something uniquely their own. This one knew Ba'call, and I wanted to see if I could see what she did.

We had arrived in town at high sun, so it was the first time in a while that we weren't racing dusk to get camp set up. It's nice to sit and watch a sunset sometimes, and today I was going to. Since the death of Ba'call, I had been trying to do more things like that.

It amazes me how much this has affected me. I had lost people before and knew I would again. Some of them I had lost to disease and some to violence. I'd watched people die all my life, but no one before Ba'call had died as a result of pushing me out of the way of my fate. Yes, Piper lost her hand doing much the same, but she was still alive, at least as far as I knew.

It should have been me, but it wasn't. So here I was, sitting on Dragon's Rock, staring at a bright orb of flame as it made its final descent into the east and the other side of the world.

As I sat there watching the sun paint the clouds a beautiful dark purple, I felt someone coming up behind me. Looking over my shoulder, my breath caught.

Arwen, out of armor and clean, was something to behold. Long, lean muscled, glistening with sweat from the heat of the day, his skin ruddy with sun, his dark hair loose with the curl of it bouncing with each step he took towards me. He was a sight. He certainly got more of a tan than I ever would, I burned and freckled to the point covering up was the only option. That half smile he always seemed to wear when looking at me complemented the eye patch he had made of some discarded bits of turtle shell we had found by the road. The red and black pattern was striking; it brought out the color of his skin, hair, and remaining eye. The green that I first thought of as chipped emeralds peered into me. His shirt was not laced up, giving me a good view of that chest of his.

I shook my head to clear it. He wasn't walking up to me like some god of lust; he was just strolling up, but those soft looking pink lips were moving ever so slightly, but what my eyes saw my brain didn't hear.

"What?"

"I asked if you wanted to be alone." His smile seemed to brighten the darkening sky.

Okay, something was definitely affecting my mind. I mean, Arwen was kind of cute with his chest and all, but come on. I saw the guy every day. The only thing different was the frosted cream stuff. Maybe it had an intoxicating effect, scrambling my mind like a mild alcohol.

Is frostcream an aphrodisiac of some sort? I had heard of such things, and hell, some were sold on the streets of South Point. Not that anyone there ever seemed to need them.

"Are you blushing Chloe?"

I felt my face flame.

Well, I am now, thank you very much jerk.

Instead, I said, "Sort of, I seem to be…" Shaking my head to clear it didn't help in the least. Arwen was interested in me, so was Alabaster. Neither of them had made a big deal about it, nor had I, but there was no sense in giving him the wrong idea. It would…complicate things.

"I think I'm a little drunk. My mind was wandering, then of course when you asked me if I was blushing, and that made me think about it, so…"

That had started off so much better in my head.

He looked at me, nodded to what I was saying, then asked, "Mind if I sit?"

I shook my head no, scooting over to make room for him, an empty gesture at best, as this rock was huge. Still a nice thing to do for someone who was polite enough to ask. It also, as far as I was concerned, showed that I wanted the company. If I had merely gestured at the huge stone as to say there is plenty of free space, it would have been like saying 'Sure, I can't stop you, but I don't necessarily want you here or even care'.

As he was sitting down close to me, I realized something, I cared... I cared a lot.

Don't get me wrong, Arwen had more than earned my respect. He had also more than returned my friendship without pressuring me. We had laughed and joked together and now, here I was sitting suddenly wondering if I had messed up my hair the last time I had taken my dagger to it. Just thinking about it made me embarrassed that it was cut so short.

"So." He looked out to the eastern horizon where the sun was slowly disappearing. "Nice to see a sunset when you can actually enjoy it. Isn't it?"

My mouth kept moving, words kept spilling out, but my brain wanted nothing to do with any of it. "Yes, I suppose it is." I turned and stared out at the setting sun; the tops of the clouds were a brilliant orange while down lower they bled to a purplish color. 'Purple' simply didn't do that shade justice. As I watched, crimson streaks burst through the clouds and the fingers of color started to interlace.

His hand came to a rest on top of mine.

My mind went blank, either that, or it ran for the hills. I'm not sure which. All I knew is it had nothing to say at that moment. My heart was pounding as hard as if I was suddenly in mortal danger.

I've trained for most of my life not to freeze up when that happened. You see, the mind has a habit of locking up, so you must train your body to respond without it.

Of all the defensive things I could think to do, simply snatching my hand away was by far the best option.

Instead, it turned over to grip his.

I looked up to explain that I was getting a little nervous, that I didn't really know what was happening.

I mean, I knew what was happening.

I was squeezing his hand as he was squeezing mine. None of this was making any sense. So? Why was I doing it? It didn't help that my heart was pounding so loud I could hear and feel it, as if it was in my skull. It was crowding the spot where my mind once was, making it even harder to think.

His eye met mine, and as it did, air rushed into me painfully going past a catch in my throat. Lips tingling, I looked at him, and he, at me. Something soft brushed against my lips, there was a spark, a tingle like you get from a shock on a cold morning. I could remember chasing Piper around, popping her with those little zaps. That is what it felt like when he brushed against me, one of those little zaps on my lips.

All at once, I was pressing my face into his, and an ache I didn't know existed was being soothed, a hole being filled.

My lips against his.

Tears stung my eyes, then rolled down my cheeks, all from the pain and pleasure of this kiss. No, this wasn't something so simple as a kiss, we tried to lick, nibble, bite, and pull ourselves into each other. It was a hard and hungry kind of thing.

It scared me.

That fear was all it took to get my brain to come back from its trip to the woods to take a shit or whatever it was doing while it left my body and me on a kind of demented automatic.

It took one look at the situation, then flashed Alabaster at me.

I pulled away, and he looked at me with his remaining eye. "What's wrong?" His hand petted the side of my face wiping tears away. With a soft voice filled with honest concern, he asked "Are you ok?"

I had to close my eyes; there was no way I could speak if I kept looking at him.

"Alabaster." It was meant to be a word, but it came out more of a breath. That breath had an immediate reaction as Arwen stiffened.

"And Rowan." His response was just as breathy, then with more force behind it, "Lady of Joy help me; I have no idea what we are even supposed to do in a situation like this. It's never come up."

He thought I meant us being owned by the two of them. I was speaking about being in love with him and Alabaster at the same time, and not knowing which was real.

Like I said, things were complicated.

Author's Notes 11

Alright, this next part isn't so much a spoiler, it is however something that happens after the end of the short stories, during the events in the second half of Chloe's Collar.

I was at this point still trying to find a regular buyer for my work. I was frustrated with self-publishing and wanted to see my stuff on the page. I came upon a request for submissions by trans authors, the catch, it had to be all new work. While the Arcana qualified, it was much too large, and they didn't want a serial. They wanted something that could stand on its own.

So, I went back to the mines and looked for an important character I hadn't used before, someone who was hinted at, but not fleshed out. I knew who it had to be, the Margrave. She was a background thread in several stories, but not one who had been met or really even fleshed out on page. I of course already had her family history, what she looked like, how she acted, what her motivations and temperaments are... have I mentioned I might be a little too into world building?

At any rate, for the last offering of this collection I give you The Eve of War.

The Eve of War

I can think of dozens of places for a clandestine meeting, the Hog's Tooth wasn't one of them. Given what was going on, maybe that was the point. Twenty years ago, an Inn like this would have been inside South Point, but while the Lord Mayor hadn't been able to shut down the Adventurer's Guild Hall, he had been able to run their inns out of town with new laws. More than a day outside of town to the north and off the main road, it still had a roaring business. This far south, right at the edge of civilized land there was always a need for mercenaries. I had hired a few myself after all.

I had never been to The Tooth, never met my contact except through intermediaries, and due to my station didn't often go without escort, back up, and guards. I have to say, it's somehow not what I expected, and exactly what I should have.

The outside was a large two-story whitewashed building, wooden cross beams, and a thatched roof. The wooden shutters were the color of the place, though they seemed to neglect to pick one. Some were brown, some orange, most were red. The blue door was a bit of a shock, even I couldn't afford to waste blue paint on a door. Inside was a riot of sound as a minstrel strummed in the corner and patrons sung along with his bawdy lyrics. It was just past mid-day and the fact that this place was so crowded set my teeth on edge. There was work to be done and here...

I took a breath, here were the damned. Not in some religious sense. No these were cut throats, swords for hire, bully boys, wizards, wayfarers, priests, pathfinders, wardens. All of the faces were young, full of life, drinking while they could, for tomorrow they all died. No, not all of their faces, a few bore lines, some even had grey, but such people were left be, off in their own dark corners. As soon as I entered and the door closed, everything stopped, and all eyes were on me.

I've spent my life training in war, as did my father and mother, and their father and mother and so on for nearly 20 generations, I knew I was being sized up. So, I gave as good as I got. Dwarves, Liberi, Elves, Orcs, and somehow the bulk still seemed to be human. Male to female was about an even split. I became acutely aware of the sword at my hip and my well-worn brigandine. The pauldron, my family crest of sorts, was left back at the keep. A LeatherWing skull would be a giveaway.

The lamps were fish oil but high quality, the bar and hearth were an island at the center of the side wall, and the walls were more or less white, showing they had been washed recently, probably regularly. The place, such as it was, was clean. Smell wise, mutton and potatoes were roasting, bread was baking, and the beer smell wasn't stale. All in all, not a low-quality inn. The biggest thing was that mere moments after I entered, the whole place collectively lost interest in me. Looks like my contact picked the right place after all.

Speaking of which, how was I going to spot a woman I had never met in person? All I had been told was look for the witch.

Half the people in this place qualified as witches or what not in someone's eyes.

I made my way to the bar, looking into the dimmer parts of the place as I went, back to those 'old timers' who were keeping to themselves. After all, she would be one of them.

"Wat'cha drink?" Came the voice of the mountain behind the bar. An older woman, she was big, big bones, big muscled, big chested, hair the color of old steel with curls brought in tight to her head, locks twisted down either side of her temples. The style was old, the woman looked older. Still if a fight broke out in here, I wouldn't bet on the brawlers.

"Dwarven, hard if you got it."

She eyed me for a moment. "Dwarven's been outlawed in South Point."

I didn't break eye contact "This ain't South Point."

She snorted, got a bottle and I pulled out my mug. "Na, it ain't. That don't stop the local Guard from coming out once in a wind to cause a ruckus and try us." She generously poured the golden-brown liquid into my simple wooden tankard.

"I'm not guard."

"Smell like it."

"Smell again."

She looked me up and down, then into my eyes. "Soldier then." I gave a slight nod. "Looking for work, slumming with us? Or looking to post?"

The look I gave her wasn't friendly, but I knew it wouldn't shake her. "Personal."

She shrugged. "I'm here if ya need." With that she walked down to the next person seeking her wares. I got to looking for my witch.

The brief conversation had let my eyes finish adjusting to the gloom, natural light wasn't a big part of this place. The windows were bullseye glass and more glowed than illuminated. In the deeper recesses I saw a mage at their book. A girl who could have been 20, or 200, who can tell with elves, sitting with a little winged cat-like thing with a bald head and a scorpion tail. The beast was nuzzling her hand affectionately as she fed it bits of peach. A woman who looked like she came from a wood carving of a witch right down to the hat. I almost started towards her until I spotted a woman in the far back with dark hair, pale skin, leathers, and a hood pulled far enough up as to show only part of her face. A Warden, a real one. I would have overlooked her except she had a white streak of hair that was pulled forward out from her cloak.

A Witch's Streak. That's when it hit me. Damn the woman.

I took my mug and walked to the back table and asked "Sara?"

The woman with dark brown eyes looked up at me, "Margrave."

'Sara' was my own dear cousin. Here she was playing games and I was in need. Granted, Sara had renounced all claims years before I was born, but still.

I sat down at the table; 'this woman' had the information I needed. Wardens were a notoriously independent lot, but this was a bit much. They 'guarded' the ways between, as such, if there was a threat to the lands under my protection, she would know. Her leather armor was worn, well maintained, as was the blade by her side. She, like myself, didn't go for the vanity dip between her breasts, but went with something that allowed for extra protection without the flash of 'boob plate'.

She waited for me to settle. "Thank you, for the in person meet."

"When they took Jax the Tailor, I thought all was lost."

"Jax lives. I got him out of South Point myself."

That took me aback. "I couldn't find out anything."

"With respect 'my lady', you're the person they are hiding things from."

"Indeed." I thought about it, if only for a moment, "How bad is it?"

She reached down beside herself until she brought up a folio and map case. "Bad. The person Jax was only able to identify as 'His Holiness' is part of The Old Inquisition."

"The Inquisition was disbanded." I knew I was frowning as she handed me the documents. "They were the enforcement arm for the old empire, ensuring the God King's orders were obeyed." They were technically part of the Church of the Sacred Light, but after the fall the Churches of Ca'talls, Suo, Ba'teece, Pentagla, Protista and Lut'har had purged their ranks of those fanatics. "I thought the only inquisition left was the ones meant to keep the Church pure of such influence."

"Some people want a return to the old ways, to become great and powerful again."

Sadly, I knew that call all too well. I looked over what she gave me. "This..." I stared in disbelief. "This can't be right. A build up this large?"

"300 from this town, 400 from that, so on and so forth, all up and down the coast. Most pulled from skirmishes like that your Count and Baron have been up to for the last few years."

"Few years? They've been at it for nearly 15. Ever since…" I trailed off.

"Exactly, ever since the Thunderhammer."

"Damned old fool. If I'd have known he'd be this much trouble, I would have fought beside him myself and kept him alive."

With that she smiled at me. "Yes, well. As you can see, they have four armies ready to move, each with more than 3000 people, all training for years." She sighed. "And those are just the ones I've been able to confirm with my own eyes. According to some of my scouts?" She let out a sigh that had traveled every road, "There could be hundreds of these camps all up and down the coast."

"12,000 soldiers." At full readiness, I could call in almost 4000. "I can't stand against this." For years I had been asking the north for help, for more men, for more authority. It had gotten me nowhere. "I see now why they weren't worried about the South." The Kingdoms of the Light weren't really much more than a bunch of fiefdoms with a mutual support pact. We were all that was left of the old Empire. We had a shared language, even if someone from the extreme north probably couldn't understand someone from down here, and I knew from experience that speaking to someone from the East was difficult till you got used to it.

Still, my family had guarded the border from the horrors of the frozen south since the fall nearly 500 years ago. This felt like a betrayal.

I wiped my face with my hands and looked at her. "Any idea what they are planning?"

"Given what they have been up to behind the curtain for the last two decades?"

An increase in taxes, an increase in the number of purity laws, an increase in severity of punishments, and increase in laws to push out the other races... all true to form. My family still had records of the old inquisition. "Blood will run in the streets." My options were limited, none of them good. "I need to speak with the bitch. Can you arrange it?"

Sara blinked at me for a moment. "Am I supposed to know who that is?"

"I know damn well you go to the south, down through The Bone. Can you get me in contact with that Empress of theirs?" I watched, with some amusement I might add, as this woman, this warden, a hardened warrior just gawked at me.

"I, well, no."

"Why not?"

She seemed to be at a loss for words. "Other than I haven't been that far south in an extremely long time?" She took a deep breath. "The last I heard she never went back to their capital. She's not there."

That was disturbing news all on its own. "If she's not there, if she still walks the world, and the Empire comes back?" That daemon and her ilk slaughtered everyone who resisted last time they invaded. Still in their own way they were honorable. You can't fight an enemy for generations with-out learning about them. "Even more reason to contact her. Broker a peace and hold back The Inquisition."

She seemed to give it a moment's thought. "If you do this, you will be choosing sides and declaring war on, well, the kingdoms you're sworn to protect."

"No, I and our family, for generations have sworn to keep the people of these lands free." I turned the idea over in my head myself. I didn't like it. "Those people include more than just the humans that live in these lands, and I know what will become of those people if the inquisition is back... not to mention the long list of what the inquisition considers to be heretical, including a woman holding power." I swallowed hard. "The LeatherWing have been my enemy all my life. But to be honest? They have been far less trouble than my allies." Not to mention, that though I couldn't prove it, I suspected a few of the mysterious grain finds over the last few years were their doing. "I know of their laws, and I don't find them odious. It's merely their hedonism and lack of decorum that irks me." Drunkards and letches the lot of them. "They are... different, savage even, but they are preferable to what is to come."

She nodded. "Well, there might be a way." She thought for a moment. "No guarantees mind you. The magic will work, but you aren't likely to get the Empress, but you will get someone who can help you."

"I'll take the chance."

"Are you familiar with their law of the stone?"

I was. "An odd form of justice, one that might see you dead."

"To the south of your keep, not the family keep, yours, in the forest right up next to the sea, you will find a circle of their stones. Do you know what to do from there?"

"A circle of five stones, within this circle is a sixth stone at its center. At any time, anyone that has any grievance, they may place their hand on the sixth stone and call for a hearing." It was said if someone put their hand on that center stone, no harm could come to them. "And they will come?"

"That's my understanding."

I nodded. "Any words of wisdom? You've dealt with these people."

Her first response was quick and sure, "Be honest, they don't like liars." Her second less so. "Be yourself. Jax liked you, they liked him" She took a deep breath "Halonis, these are honorable people. Treat them as you would an honored warrior and you should be fine."

"Even if the daemon herself shows up?"

"Honestly? I don't think she's a daemon, nor demon for that matter. Just someone who was cursed."

"Eternal life, hell of a curse."

"Yes, it is." For a moment her tone set me on edge. Sara was family, but she was an adult when I was a child. I'm pretty sure she's half elven. It would explain her wanderlust. In that moment? Had you told me she was somehow full elf, I would believe it. That many years were in her voice.

"Go to the stones Halonis. Call for a hearing. They will come."

"Who will? Who will come Sara?"

She shrugged, "Whoever is needed. The stones know, or so they say."

2

Two days later, or I should say nights. Full armor on, skull pauldron, fur lined cloak and all, I stood in the light of twin full moons and placed my hand on the rock. Behind me were my two most trusted captains. They knew why we were here.

"I can't believe I'm doing this."

"Something we can help with Margrave?" Came one of their voices.

"No Tim, you and Alden stay back, cover me."

I looked around into the night. I honestly didn't know what to expect. The wood was deep, all ancient oaks, white pines and maple trees. The stones were well worn, and if you didn't know what they were they looked like the stone circles druids set up to sit on. One central stone, with five sitting stones around it, all evenly spaced and far enough away so that you couldn't just reach out to touch the person sitting in the middle.

Honestly, I've seen lesson circles set up like this.

Reaching down again I sat my hand on the top of the center stone, "I call for judgment."

Nothing. No lights, no sound of thunder, no feeling of peace. Sometimes I really hate magic, so often you don't see what it does. I turned back and looked at my men.

"Anything?"

"No." Came Tim.

"Something." Came Alden.

"Talk to me old man, what you got?"

"A pressure, in my head... not a headache, nor brainstorm. More like," His voice trailed off. He looked around for a moment, up to the moons, then over to one of the stones. "A call."

"Anything like trying to explain basic foot-work to me when I was young?"

He laughed, a deep sound. It was good to hear that laugh, it meant he was still himself. "Hardly, that did cause brainstorms." He walked closer, looked at one of the five stones. "I think it wants me to touch it." Looking at me he raised an eyebrow. "Do you think it's wise?"

Tim came forward. "These waters are so deep, that it's pick a direction and swim, hope for land, or go ahead and drown."

With a nod from me, Alden touched the stone.

"Anything?"

"Just that I no longer feel the pressure." He sat down on the rock. "And this is the most comfortable stone I've ever sat on."

Tim looked at him. "You must be mad. It's freezing out here."

I thought about it for a moment. "No, he's right. I'm not cold either." I nodded. "We knew, in basics, how this worked. One from each of their five races called to judge. Alden must be the human one."

"What do we do now?"

"We wait." I too sat on my stone. "Build a fire Tim, take care of yourself. The two of us should be fine."

So, we waited.

Dawn came, no one showed. To be honest? I was almost relieved.

"Well, this is a bust." Standing up should have hurt, I had been sitting in the same position all night. It was a reminder that the magic was working.

"You still need more patience." Came an old familiar chide from Alden. "Neither of us ache, nor hunger. We are far from their land. Perhaps it just takes a while."

I kept up my stretches, it was something to do. I could wait, I just needed something to do while I did. Apparently, patience wasn't my ability to wait, but the grace with which I did so. "A heavy rider could have made it here by now." I looked around, feeling uneasy. "I wonder what they are waiting for?"

A flutter of wings came from behind me, "To figgguer out," said a strange voice, "what the Margrrrrave callsss upon usss for judgment for." Looking back, I saw one of the raptors. The bird was truly massive, standing up to my navel, but with its wings still outstretched, tip to tip was easily three if not four times that. It folded those wings and got comfortable on its own stone. Its talons were as long as barn nails and its beak looked sword sharp. Two small arms were crossed in front of its chest, each peeking out from under its wings. Like the LeatherWing, this was a six-limb creature.

Next came the cat, GrassLords they call themselves, hunting cats one and all, and all as fierce as their wild kin. This one was female, a sight that let me know rumors were true, they did indeed have four teats. This one was white with black spots covering her fur, she had twin curved swords on her hips.

The sound of crunching brush turned my attention back to the other side, and my heart froze. I had seen a few in my youth, tall, proud, powerful, this one was a doe, but she wore a crown fashioned from woven vines upon her head.

"Devil Deer." The words were a breath, a sound, something whispered not spoken. I knew they were one of the five, I had told myself I was ready for this. I wasn't. LeatherWing? They were an enemy, I knew them. The cats, these GrassLords? From time to time, you heard tales of them, maybe even saw one, though this was my first time seeing a female. The Raptors, the self-styled SkyLords? For all their size they were hunting birds. Devil Dear on the other hand were truly mystic creatures. Both good luck and ill omen, they knew no border.

Her front hoof struck the stone. "We prefer The Heard." Her words weren't in trade, nor my own Northern tongue, but I understood them, just as I understood she wasn't speaking of a herd.

"Why do you call yourself that?" I asked.

"Because when they speak, we listen, they will be Heard." From out of the woods, the final judge stepped forward. In hand she held a shaft of a spear, long, proud with a head that was more short sword than spear head. An iron cross guard like those for boar hunting sat back a hands width from the last of the blade. The woman who carried it was LeatherWing, a dragon like human, wings on her back, clawed hands and feet meant to snatch, her skin was purple, wisteria blossoms in spring, her hair a dark violet, her face almost angelic in its beauty if not for the nine small, curved horns, three over each eye, and three up the middle.

Vela of the Long Spear, Queen of The Bone had arrived.

She and the others sat on the rocks surrounding me, with Alden taking up the fifth. Three obvious predators, one prey, and a man.

Time to cut to the chase. "Shall we begin?"

Vela regarded me. "Before we do, outlander, have you questions? We will not have this done in ignorance."

I did actually. "You call yourselves inclusive, the Empire of the Five. Yet, you forget all the other races, elves, dwarves..." That was as far as I got, the four of them were laughing too hard to hear the rest.

It was the Heard who spoke up. "We do not forget them, you do. They are man, only humans are so arrogant as to think man means only them."

"But they are all different?"

"Aaare they?" Came the voice of the bird man. "I am Bird, sshe is deer, sshe is cat, sshe is LeatherWing, what makes Dwarf sso different?"

"Well, dwarves are, well they are miners and farmers..." How did I explain this? "They're just different."

Vela shook her head. "They are different in culture. You can still breed with a dwarf, yes? They still have a head, two hands, two feet? Yes? While you can breed with me, if I am the mother you will get a LeatherWing, if you are the mother, you will get a man. For as different as you think the other 'races' are, you are not that different. Culture is the key. All man has a perspective that can be good here." She shrugged. "If long sight is needed, an elf. If perseverance, a Dwarf, and so on." She cocked her head to the side. "Do you understand?"

It was hard to argue, at least I couldn't think of a good one. "One last question, I take it the magic of the stones is how I can understand all of you?"

"Yes." Came the reply from the cat, "and we you. Now dear Margrave, what is this about?"

I took a deep breath. "It's simple. I have word that the Old Inquisition is alive, well, and mobilizing. I've suspected something going on behind the scenes with the local nobles for years. We all know what will happen if Unstoma rises again." I looked around to gage their faces, anger and shock was my best guess, but how does one read the truly unfamiliar? I decided to push on. "They are coming with an army, 12,000 by count."

The cat was the first to speak. "I'm sorry Margrave, but are you not sworn to protect these lands from us?"

I knew this was coming. Oaths were of great importance to me. By legend they were of greater importance to these people.

"My oaths are not to land, nor noble, but to the people, all the peoples of this land. As of late the nobles have been playing a game, deciding by law and creed who counts as people. To me that is a betrayal of the trust placed in us by the people. I owe no loyalty to oath breakers." I swallowed hard, hoping to conquer the lump in my throat. It didn't help. I talked past it, pride be damned. "I formally request..." The words stuck. Taking a deep breath, I tried once more. "I formally request to bring my lands into the protection of the Empire of Five, to help uphold her laws, such as they are, and only request that we can keep our ways."

For her part, Vela merely nodded. "The five of us will speak on this as equals. Please petitioner, give us time."

"Does it matter that one of my own men is amongst you?"

The LeatherWing turned back to me, "Should it? Would you not vouch for this man's integrity?"

"Alden is my oldest friend, and the man who trained me as my weapon master. His integrity is beyond reproach in my eyes."

"The stones picked him, that is good enough for us."

Tim came forward, "Yes, but why did the stones pick him?"

The Doe spoke, "Your Lady seeks to change allegiances, who better to judge her motives than her teacher?"

That shook me to my core. At least, now I was starting to grasp the reason the deer took the name they did.

The five wandered off, speaking in hushed terms, deliberating not only my fate, but the fate of my people.

Tim came up to me, even in the light I could tell he was still cold from being out here all night. "How do you think it will go?"

I took a breath. "The LeatherWing will get involved, if not now, then later. I hope now, it will mean less death."

"Then why the deliberation?"

I shook my head. "Tim, I called judgment, they have to make a decision."

"But you just said, they will get involved one way or the other, you're offering them your army to stand by them."

"Exactly." I shuddered. "I just called judgment on myself. They, right now, are deciding my fate, whether I live or die."

"How? Why?" He looked shaken, and I couldn't blame him. Break the law of these people and it was a death sentence. It's why they had so few laws. "You came for help?"

"Yes, but did I come to them to help my people, to save my own skin given what the Inquisition will do to me, or to gain power because we both know, as do they, my army couldn't stop them if they attacked again?" I looked back, "They are discussing my motives. That's why the stones chose Alden."

"Alden will side with you, you know that right?"

Tim would, in a heartbeat. He wouldn't hesitate. Alden would be honorable, speak to what he knew. "Tim, in a real sense, if I get what I am asking, I will become the most powerful human in this land. I'll go from being Margrave to Queen. If they are going to give me this, they will want to know they aren't giving it to a monster."

He stood tall. "We'll see about this, I'll set them straight."

"What can you say that Alden isn't already?" That brought him up. "We know the honor of these people. They help any, they take in any, they look after all. I trust them."

"So?"

"So, we wait?" I may learn patience after all.

Sunset came before we had our answer. Alden walked up to me slowly, to his left was the GrassLord and the SkyLord, to his right Vela and the Heard.

"This, is not easy." His voice shook. "But they have agreed, you are acting with honor." He took a deep breath. "However," he looked over towards the lavender colored LeatherWing, "Vela wishes to add some stipulations."

I nodded, "Very well, what are they?"

"I will extend my land to include everything that was once yours. You will lose title, land, and authority, the authority you had anyway." Her face softened slightly. "My lady" she paused

"Halonis, as Margrave you did what you could, but in truth, you could have stopped this at any time. I understand your oaths and honor stayed your hand; the same honor now brings you to us. Had you come sooner? Well things would have been different. If we leave you as Margrave, your people will see you betraying them. But I have a better way. At least I hope it's better. Your family has old ties, become my liege lord under my banner with the understanding you are doing so to save your people from our onslaught. It will be seen as a compromise, and one where you are giving up what you had."

It was possible, it might work. The gods only knew if it would. "I can keep our laws, our ways?"

"You will rule as you see fit. We have no interest in telling any how to do so, so long as your people, my people are seen to. There will still be those who think you have betrayed them, but with having less power than you had before, no army to command, it may make a difference."

A smile crept up my face. "That might just work."

PEOPLES OF M'DIRO

This section is a description of the various peoples who call M'Diro home. In each book when a new race is brought up for the first time they are described. This is meant as a handy reference to them if needed.

Humans:
The range in adult height from 4 to 7.5 foot (1.22 to 2.13 meters) with most being 5-6 foot (1.5 to 1.8 meters). Human hair and skin tone vary from light to dark with Blonde and red being the least common and shades of brown to black being most common, skin tone goes from pale to dark as well with most being a deep tan. Eye color runs the gambit from green and blue to grey to black and various shades of brown. Men tend to be larger than women.

Orcs:
Larger and stockier, Orcs are two different groups, one being True Orcs the other being a hybrid of Orc and human often just referred to as Orcs because they are the ones most humans interact with. Orcs as a whole are 5 foot to 8.5 foot (1.5 to 2.6 meters) with 6 to 7 foot (1.8 to 2.13 meters) being the norm, True Orcs are larger still. The differences between the two is slight, with

True Orcs being somewhat bigger overall, and having slightly flatter faces. Skin color is slightly darker with a green tent. The only purely human trait that Orc's got from the mixing is having curly hair.

Liberi:
With one exception they look completely human, hair color, eye color body proportions and everything else. That exception is height. Ranging from 2.5 to 3.5 foot (.7 to 1.06 meters) they often pass themselves off as children if they can get away with it in the lands of the "big".

Dwarves: The average Dwarven height is 4 to 5.5 feet (1.22 to 1.37 meters). They are a stocky lot, often seeming as wide as they are tall. Most are a deep brown color in hair, face, and eyes. Blonde and black do exist, black is more common in the mountains, blonde more so down on the plains. Red hair is all but unheard of but given all known dwarven cultures have a red headed god, being born with your hair already soaked in blood is seen as the sign of a strong warrior. Both men and women can grow thick beards and often do as a sign of age and pride.

Gnomes:
These people are a hardy group that prefers to live in wetlands. Ranging from 3.5 to 4.5 foot (1.06 to 1.3 meters) with the women being taller, these grey skinned people claim to have rocks in their bones, and they aren't wrong. Far denser for their size than they should be, only their wide feet keep them from sinking into their home terrain. Hair is usually brown, deep

brown, light brown, or some such with eyes that are bright but also brown.

Elves:
The people known as Elves, much like the Liberi have another name for themselves, The People. At 4.5 to 6.5 foot (1.3 to 1.98 meters) the most striking features of these people is their hair and eyes. They always match, and they are always the color of gems. They do have pointed ears, but they aren't much longer than the human ear. The second thing you will notice is that all of them have what humans would call the secondary sex characteristics of women. All have breasts and wider hips.

LeatherWing:
Overall the morphology is simple; 9 small horns on their head, 3 over each eye and 3 down the middle of the forehead, clawed hands and feet, wings that are over 3 times their height if not more, and a tail that can be flattened out in flight that when they are firmly on the ground and relaxed looks much like a penis. There are 8 different skin colors: Red, Orange, White, Green, Blue, Yellow, Purple and Black. In each color they can go from lighter to darker, so a green can be something like lime, or something like olive. Colors seem to be sex based with Red, White, Blue, and Purple being sex specific to the female form, and Orange, Green, Yellow, and Black being male form. Reds and Oranges tend to be larger and stronger, Whites and Greens tend to have better memories, Blues and Yellows tend to be better with logistics, and Purple and Blacks tend to just be more powerful. Height wise they run the gamut from 5 foot

(1.5 meters, usually a purple) to 9 foot (2.75 meters, usually a black) and everything in between. Hair color normally matches their skin to a degree, but eye color can be disturbingly human to utterly outlandish. They can fly, for between 10 minutes for a poor flyer and 30 minutes for a strong flyer. They are capable of running on all fours or two legs.

GrassLords:
These cat-like people are 4.5 to 6.5 foot (1.3 to 1.98 meters) tall but depending on the age could be much lighter than they look or much, much heavier. Any large cat coloration is normal for them except the mane of a lion. Eyes are blue to orange to green to grey. The most notable feature is, as felines, they do not have a single set of mammaries, but instead have 2, giving them 4 breasts. They are capable of moving, walking or even jogging (but not well) on two legs, but can't run like that forcing them to all fours to do so.

SkyLords:
An avian species of raptors. They stand 2.5 to 3.5 foot (.7 to 1.06 meters) on average. They are both hawks and eagles and tend to decorate their feathers. They have 6 limbs, two wings, two arms which are under their wings, and two legs.

The Heard: Also known as Devil Deer they are almost indistinguishable from normal deer in every way. Normal deer don't wear jewelry, nor the trophies of the hunters who failed.

About the Author

R. F. DeAngelis is Trans Woman and activist with a chronic pain condition and dyslexia. She honestly believes that the story will set us free and refuses to give up despite the curve balls life throws at all of us. She has been in a committed relationship for 20 years and is a practice of BDSM as a top with a wonderful family and support structure she loves very much.

CPSIA information can be obtained
at www.ICGtesting.com
Printed in the USA
LVHW010613180322
713722LV00009B/892